Water gurgled. The bag moved. I reached out a hand to stop it drifting away down the tide. Then I stopped, frozen, hand out. And I shouted, a big, horrible shout.

I was looking into a face.

It was greyish-white. It had lank, colourless hair plastered over a round forehead. The eyes were open, dull lumps of wet glass. They were looking at me, and the slot of sky with the heads silhouetted, and the rigging latticed above. But they were not seeing any of it, because they were dead as mud.

SAM LLEWELLYN

BLOOD KNOT

A SIGNET BOOK

SIGNET

Published by the Penguin Group
Penguin Books Ltd, 27 Wrights Lane, London W8 5TZ, England
Penguin Books USA Inc., 375 Hudson Street, New York, New York 10014, USA
Penguin Books Australia Ltd, Ringwood, Victoria, Australia
Penguin Books Canada Ltd, 10 Alcorn Avenue, Toronto, Ontario,
Canada M4V 3B2
Penguin Books (NZ) Ltd, 182–190 Wairau Road, Auckland 10, New Zealand

Penguin Books Ltd, Registered Offices: Harmondsworth, Middlesex, England

First published by Michael Joseph 1991
Published in Signet 1992
3 5 7 9 10 8 6 4 2

Copyright © Sam Llewellyn, 1991
All rights reserved

The moral right of the author has been asserted

Printed in England by Clays Ltd, St Ives plc

For
Fred, Helen
&
Patna

1

I was in my usual place, hanging on to the backstay, bending my knees against the plunge and slide of the big boat's career through the short Thames Estuary seas. From up here I could look over the helmsman's shoulder at the green corpse-light of the steering compass, swinging on SSW. Dean, the helmsman, had dyed black hair bound into a pony-tail with a Turk's head, and a salt-black silver earring in his right ear. He had been coming to sea enough so he no longer needed watching. I watched anyway, out of habit.

Watching was one of the penalties of running an old boat: a constant slide of the eyes over fifty-five feet of wet teak deck, forward to the bowsprit, and the three foresails set above it; up the seventy-five feet of mast, down the taut belly of double-reefed mainsail, shrouds and runners, into the scuppers, where the evil-smelling grey waves sluiced away the little shreds of sick the crew had left there during the past thirty-six hours.

Above the roar and bubble of the boat's wooden belly came the knock of the pumps. We had had big winds and short seas ever since *Vixen* had stuck her bowsprit out of IJmuiden harbour. When an old boat bounces her planks twist, wringing in water.

The rig was sound. The pumps were working. Frowning against the ache of too little sleep, I peered ahead.

Far out there in the dead grey, the needle-sharp blink of the

Longsand Head buoy pricked the murk. *Vixen* heeled to a gust. Dean eased the brass-bound spokes against the tug of the weather helm as *Vixen*'s long nose pulled for the eye of the wind. We were moving into the shelter of the sandbanks that run fanwise from the mouth of the Thames. We knew exactly where we were. That was a relief.

Night was falling.

The wind was blowing hard from the west, where bloated clouds hid the Essex coast. It was a dirty dusk, and a dirty sea, mixed with London's sewage, thrashed by the wind into streaks of yellowish foam. But the wind had come down from force eight, gusting nine. That was a relief, too.

Vixen's crew consisted of eight seventeen-year-olds who had been sent along by their probation officers to get their minds broadened. Whether or not anything had happened to their minds, together we had hauled *Vixen*'s ancient bones through twenty-four hours of blue murder, and we were still in one piece. Now we were within spitting distance of a landfall, it was possible to feel relieved.

Not too relieved, though.

The eyes did not stop their slither. The dirty mainsail towered into the stinking wind. Normally, masts are held up by wire guyropes called shrouds. The capshrouds go to the top of the mast, to keep it upright. The lowers go to the middle, to keep it stiff. This evening, one of *Vixen*'s lowers was made not of wire, but of a length of her anchor chain. This was because it had gone bang sixty miles west of IJ-muiden, causing the mast to whip about like a fishing rod. So I and Pete the mate and four seasick kids had got there with the chain, and the chain was holding.

The reason we had not put back into IJmuiden was that this evening Chatham was full of Tall Ships, relics of the Age of Sail, crewed by kids of six nations, getting their characters improved. We were supposed to be there by now. The parties had started without us.

The crew were looking forward to the parties. They had a right to. Two weeks ago, when we had sailed from St Katharine's Dock at the beginning of the cruise, they had been white, frightened brats with eyes that scuttled away from yours. Now, their faces were scorched with sun and wind, and they looked straight at you when you talked to them, because if they did not, they might miss something.

Vixen's sharp nose dug up a clod of water and shovelled it aft down the deck and into my face. It tasted flat and dirty as it ran down the neck of my oilskin. Dean swore and shook himself hard enough to clatter his earrings.

I laughed. Things were going so well, I actually laughed.

Vixen blazed an arrowhead of foam between the sandbanks on either side of Black Deep. I ticked off the ruby and emerald flick of the buoys on the much-corrected chart in the doghouse, the little hut that protected the front end of the cockpit. It started to rain; the wind moderated. The watch on deck stumbled into the thick night to shake out the reefs and change headsails. At 0100 *Vixen* slid past the coal-black slate of the Cant, in the funnel-shaped throat of the Thames, and picked up the winking red procession of the Medway channel buoys. Too late for the parties; but there was always tomorrow.

We were all on deck by then. I had the wheel, and there was Pete the mate, and the huddle of kids. The kids were telling each other that they had made it, in voices hoarse with cigarettes and seasickness. We slid past the high-piled lights of the Olau Line ferry, towards the dotted tower of red on the chimney of the Isle of Grain power station. The tide was high, coming up for slack water. The rain had stopped. The Medway is a filthy river, floored with black ooze, its air soured by power stations and refineries. But tonight, it was a rink of black glass down which *Vixen* glided like a skater.

''Ere,' said a dark figure at my elbow.

It was Dean. Dean was a furtive Londoner of about twenty, with a penchant for the low life which had brought him much trouble from the Law. This was his third trip on *Vixen;* he had turned into a watch leader, and a good helmsman. Now, he was holding out a fist, fingers thick with tarnished silver rings. Clasped in the fingers was a bottle.

There was rum in the bottle. There was no drinking for *Vixen*'s crew. Normally, I would have been angry. But we had come across a vicious North Sea, and there was not much that could go wrong in the Medway. Or so I thought, at the time.

3

So I just tipped what was left overboard and handed the bottle back to Dean.

Dean's arm rose. The bottle arched into the water. Dean was not the kind of kid to be impressed by the idea that littering at sea was illegal. I said, 'No more bottles.'

One of the girls said, 'Yes, boss.' There were giggles. Two weeks ago, there had been a lot of silence, and no giggles.

The anchor party went forward. Chain clattered as they flaked it on the deck, ready to let go. There was more giggling. Ahead and to port, the flick of the buoys was fading against the dirty red glow of Chatham. There were other shapes down there, huge and spidery against the lights: the masts and spars of full-rigged ships. There were *Kruzhenstern* and *Soyuz*, the Russians; and Finns and Swedes and French and Spaniards and Norwegians and even a Chilean, all manned by kids in their late teens, getting a taste of seasickness and boat handling for the good of their souls.

Vixen's wheel was smooth and polished in my hands. Water gurgled under her dolphin-striker as we crept across the glassy black river towards the anchored fleet. The only sound was the distant howl of late cars from the shore, and a low, bee-like buzz of singing. There was always singing, on the ships. A lot of the kids came from backgrounds where there was very little to sing about. The sea was the best thing they had ever seen.

'There's *Wilma*,' said Dean.

I eased the wheel. We were passing under the stern of a topsail schooner. She was tied up to a huge barrel-shaped mooring buoy. The anchor-light at her forestay cast a yellow glow on the yards of her square sails. *Wilma* was one of the other two ships that belonged to the Youth Venture Trust, the charitable organization that was chartering *Vixen* this season.

Someone on her stern yelled, 'Better later than never!' Suddenly everyone on *Vixen* was intensely interested in the process of anchoring. I moved her up until she was in the thick of the fleet, parallel with *Wilma* and fifty yards away. Gently, she eased round, head to wind, sails flapping, losing way. I drew breath.

I said, 'Let go!' in the conversational tone in which all orders were issued on *Vixen*.

I had done it hundreds of times. Next came the roar of the chain, the clank of the links passing round the capstan's drum, the groan of seventy-year-old timbers as *Vixen* settled back on the chain and drove the anchor's ploughshare blade into the mud.

This time, it was different.

In the split-second pause after the order, there was a sound that should not have been there: a small sound, a little *clunk*. The anchor splashed, and the chain roared. We fell back. I said, 'What the hell was that?'

'Was what?' said Dean.

'Get me Marie,' I said, and went for the side.

It was dark over there. the tide was ebbing now, flowing past slow and smooth. There were bubbles from the anchor chain. And something else, thumping gently under the curved white wall of *Vixen*'s side.

''S a boat,' said Marie.

I looked round at her, sharply. Marie had been the lookout. She was a tall girl with square, narrow shoulders outlined against the sky. Her voice was slurred. She had been very quiet since Amsterdam. Her breath smelt like petrol. She had had more than a lot of rum.

'Where's the bottle?' I said.

''S empty,' she said. The fumes were coming out of her mouth like steam from a boiling kettle. But until six months ago, Marie's real enthusiasm had been heroin. Keep calm, I told myself. No shouting. *Vixen*'s motto, when under charter to Youth Venture: *Do as you would be done by*.

'What's that boat doing there?' I said.

Dean was already grappling with a boathook. 'Dunno,' she said. She was hanging on to a shroud with one hand, to stay upright. Her eyesockets were deeply shaded in the glimmer of the shore lights.

'We ran it down,' I said. 'You're the lookout.'

She mumbled, 'It was drifting. All sunk down.'

There was no time to worry about drifting dinghies. *Vixen* had fallen back on the tide; the anchor chain was taut. I squinted across at a couple of streetlights that lined up. If they stayed in line, the anchor was holding.

They slid out of line.

'Dragging, Bill,' said a boy at my side.

The closer of the lights crept rapidly forward. The wind was the merest breath on my cheek. The sails flapped and bellied. We would have trouble sailing out of this against the tide. Astern, a group of lights on some sort of quay was coming towards us.

Unless the anchor held, we were going to find out exactly what sort of quay it was, under the eyes of anyone who was still awake in the biggest Tall Ships fleet since the movement began in the 1950s.

My palms were suddenly slippery with sweat. I bent down, turned the ignition switch in the cockpit bulkhead. The light glowed cherry red. I hit the starter button.

The engine said *thunk*, and stopped. I hit the button again. Nothing.

'Loose connection,' said Dean.

I shook my head, swallowing nothing. *Vixen* has no gearbox. The variable-pitch propeller is driven directly by the engine. I had heard that *thunk* before. The last time had been when we had wrapped a lobster pot's tailrope round the shaft off St Malo. 'Propellor's foul,' I said. 'Foresail, please,'

I kept my voice quiet, the way you do when you have got eight kids on board, and they are tired, and so are you. The lights of the shore were still sliding. We had no motive power. There was a time when I would have done some shouting. The echo-sounder said two metres, which is what *Vixen* draws. We were going on the stones. Soon.

'Anchor in,' I said.

Forward, the windlass started to clack. I turned the wheel, gently, so the dark finger of the bowsprit pointed up at *Wilma*'s long white hull. The mainsail bellied, filled.

'Anchor aweigh,' called a voice from forward.

The smooth glass of the water was marred by a slight frosting. Breeze tickled the sails. Something was wrong with the steering. It had stiffened, as if whatever was wrapped around the propellor was interfering with the rudder as well.

6

The sweat was all over me now, a nasty, clammy sweat. I shoved the wheel again. It was getting stiffer. Effectively, it was stuck. I began to have ideas.

Vixen had belonged to me since I was seventeen, so I knew her well. She was big, and old, and unforgiving. What she would do now was sail on until she hit *Wilma* with a big bang. We had lost too much ground to try anchoring again. The sails bellied, hung limp; the wind died. No wind, no rudder. Hard to manoeuvre. My mouth was dry. Someone with no taste offered to get out and push.

A puff of wind batted my cheek. Suddenly, my lungs began to pick up oxygen.

Pete was standing by me. The horizontal jut of his beard was silhouetted against the lights. He was giving off waves of anxiety strong enough to curdle milk. I said, 'We're going alongside *Wilma.*'

He said, 'What if she drags too?'

'She's on a buoy,' I said.

'I've got that dinghy alongside,' said Dean. 'Nice one.'

This was no time for admiring dinghies. Pete shuffled up the deck, arranging warps and fenders. *Vixen* hung in the black Medway, sails filling and emptying with the dull rattle of old, stretched Dacron. Ashore, the lights had steadied. The feel of the deck under my feet told me that we were sailing; sailing at perhaps one knot, crabbing across the muscular black tide that was trying to sweep us up back into the street lamps.

Ahead, *Wilma* lay low and sleek on the water, her two masts towering into the dark. *Vixen*'s bowsprit was aiming at the root of her mainmast, slipping gently aft as the tide took us sideways. Jamming the wheel with my knee, I hauled in the mainsheet. A puff of wind filled the mainsail. The wake chuckled as she heeled, the bowsprit pointing up, towards *Wilma*'s bow, forty yards away now.

'Stand by to let go headsail sheets,' I said. 'We're going alongside.'

Nobody had explained anything. But two weeks of applied democracy on *Vixen* breeds a team spirit that sometimes comes close to telepathy. The sheet hands crouched by their cleats. Bow and stern warps were ready in the fairleads. Apart from the gurgle of the Medway, there was no sound.

'Let go,' I said quietly.

Then there was sound.

The three big foresails, unsheeted, roared like thunder in the sudden gust. The mainsail took her on. Relieved of the foresails, her bowsprit swung to port, looking for the wind. I let the mainsheet fly. *Vixen* glided alongside *Wilma*. Her fenders kissed the hull, bounced, and would have shoved her back into the tide, except that by that time the girl with the bow line was on to *Wilma*'s deck and we were tied up, fore and aft, alongside.

I leaned against the doghouse and watched the sails whizz down, trying to look as if I was doing it for relaxation, and not because my knees were made of jelly.

By the time the crew were flaking the mainsail along the boom, there were people on *Wilma*'s decks. One of them was tall and broad-shouldered, clean-shaven, dressed in an old blue Guernsey with an old-fashioned yachting cap pulled square over his eyes. There was another man beside him, small, in a grey suit with black shoes. 'What's the big idea?' he said.

I told him.

'Dear me,' he said, mildly. The mildness was deceptive. Otto Campbell had done time in the SAS. When he was not captain of *Wilma*, he was running an adventure school for tired businessmen halfway up Cader Idris. He was tough and sharp as a rhino hide whip; a good man to work with. 'You'll be all right. We're tied on to a buoy.'

'I noticed,' I said.

He grinned at me. He said, 'Hi, Marie.' They had met in Amsterdam.

Marie said, 'Hello.' The word came out on a cloud of rum. Otto wrinkled his nose. 'Been having a party?' he said.

'A tot.'

Otto nodded. The man with black shoes did not smile. 'Oh,' said Otto. 'This is Superintendent Robertson, Medway Constabulary. We've got the Minister aboard.'

'The Minister?' I was acutely aware of Marie, hanging from the shroud beside me, belching.

'Neville Glazebrook is paying an official visit to the organization.' There was irony in his voice. Youth Venture was a charity dependent on goodwill and influence for its funds. But those of us who merely drove the boats had enough on our hands without fawning on big shots. 'Your brother was here earlier. Waited for you. Had to leave. Constituency business, he said.'

Neville Glazebrook was Minister of Transport. Once, he had been Minister of Defence. He had strong Naval leanings, and liked to sail fast yachts. He was stout, and jovial, and his daughter was married to my younger brother Christopher, co-owner of *Vixen*, of whom I saw as little as possible.

I said, 'I might pop over tomorrow,' trying to inject a little finality into the conversation.

He grunted, and said, 'I'd better get back.'

I was tired, not in the mood for politicians. There was a lot of clearing up to do. I said, 'Goodnight.'

Beside me, Marie made a disgusting sound. Then she was sick, on the deck and between the two boats. Suddenly the night smelt like a distillery.

I saw Otto's long chin in profile as he looked away, pretending not to notice. The policeman watched, cold-eyed in the decklights. He said nothing.

Two of the crew carried her below to her bunk. The rest worked in apprehensive silence, looking at me out of the corners of their eyes. I kept quiet. Pete yapped away at their heels, driving them on. I coiled down lines with a hollow under my breastbone. When one of the crew throws up a pint of rum on the shoes of a police superintendent who is looking after a Minister of the Crown, the captain has grounds for worry, even if the captain is a relation by marriage of the Minister.

Meanwhile, there was the routine of care for *Vixen*, companion of my youth, love of my life, and bane of my existence.

By the time we had put on springs and trussed the sails neatly, the fleet had gone to bed. The kids staggered to their bunks, and I went home.

Home consisted of the two aftermost cabins. There was the saloon, with a self-righting table and French polished panelling; and a cabin aft, with a big single bunk, installed by *Vixen*'s first owner, who had caused her to be built in 1922 with the

9

fortune he had made supplying margarine to the British army at the time of the Somme. The galley was on the way forward to the two bunk-tiered cabins where the crew slept, girls aft, boys forward. I heard Pete grunt as he crawled into his sleeping bag on the buttoned-leather settee in the saloon.

Pete came from Pulteney. He was a grouch with a heart of solid oak, and one of the last time-served wooden shipwrights in England. He loved *Vixen* better than he loved his wife. *Vixen*, in her turn, depended on him for the care and refashioning of her old oak bones.

I laid myself on the berth, all six foot four of me, shut my eyes. For a couple of minutes, I felt bad about getting the crew in too late for their party, and dragging the anchor, and putting up a black with the Medway police.

Next thing I knew, grey light was leaking through the deck prism above my head. I stumbled forward into the galley.

There was a tin pot of coffee on the domestic-sized Calor stove. I felt my way to a cup. My eyes opened, and I became able to take things in.

A red sun was clambering through the tangle of masts and spars beyond the granite quay of Chatham docks. The big ships, brigs and barquentines, were all inside. Only us little fellows, less than a hundred feet long, were anchored in the river. In the dawn calm the water was smooth as oil, shot with puddles of blood where it caught the sun.

I took a suck of coffee, gave the cup to a member of the early watch and made my deck rounds. Then I shoved my hands into the fur-lined pockets of my waterproof coat and went aft, past the shallow cockpit, to lean on the backstay.

The dinghy we had run down streamed down the tide from the counter. It was painted white. There was a name stencilled in black paint on the inside of the transom. The letters looked wrong. My head was so numb that for a moment I could not work out why. Then I knew. They were in Cyrillic script. What they were trying to say was *Soyuz*.

'Nice little boat,' said Pete. His eyes were bleary over his heavy red beard. As usual, he was wearing a T-shirt, jeans and no shoes. It was five a.m., and cold, but twenty years of cajoling wet timber in February gales had vaccinated him against cold.

'Marie can take it back after breakfast,' I said. *Soyuz* was a Russian barque, crewed by Naval cadets, currently moored in the dock basin. She had friends on board, who would be pleased to see her. Also, the job would make her feel useful.

For the moment, she was hanging around the rail. She was a pretty girl, tall and lanky, with black hair and Irish blue eyes that jumped at you out of a face that three weeks ago had been dead white. Now it was a rosy tan, except for the hungover shadows under her eyes. Her nails were badly bitten, and she kept looking at the dinghy.

Most boats carry their propellor in front of the rudder. It was one of *Vixen*'s quirks that she has a quarter screw, which means she carried hers to starboard of the rudder, where it would pick up any garbage that was going.

I did not fancy a dip in the Medway. The conventional first line of defence against a foul propellor is a breadknife lashed to a boathook. So I made the lashing, with the fluency of long practice. Then I thrust the breadknife like a harpoon into the gap between *Vixen* and *Wilma*, following the curve of the hull. Some of *Wilma*'s crew gathered at her rail, gawping. One of them made an intelligent remark about shark fishing.

Vixen's propellor has picked up a fair bit of rope in its time, and I was a connoisseur. Your average buoy-rope feels hard as wood on the knife. This did not feel right; hard, but a little yielding. The growing light had turned the water mud-grey, impenetrable. I prodded violently with the boathook, sawed up and down a couple of times. The breadknife snagged.

'Caught one?' said a wit on *Wilma*.

I tugged again. The knife came up with a jerk. Strands of wet blue thread were caught in the teeth.

'Got 'is trousers,' said the wit, a thin, blond youth with a sharp face.

The nasty hollow was back where my stomach should have been. I wished he would shut up and go away.

There was a rope ladder in the lazarette. We hung it over the side. I stripped to my boxer shorts and went across the guardrail, fast, without giving myself time to think, the way I

11

had done things before I stopped being a journalist and started being I full-time yacht owner.

It was late July, but the Medway is always cold. The water stank. The gap between the boats' sides was a smooth-walled crevasse noisy with the gurgle of the tide. I let myself hang in the icy water at the bottom of the ladder, and felt for the propellor with my feet.

I knew *Vixen*'s hull as well as I knew my own body. My foot found the propellor first time. And something else. A cloth sack of something hard but yielding, jammed against the hull by the blade of the propellor.

Above me, there were heads, including Pete's, bearded, silhouetted against the light. I said quietly, 'Get rid of these people and take off the decompressors.'

The decompressors remove the pressure from the cylinders of the engine, allowing the propellor to freewheel. I heard Pete's hoarse shouting. The heads vanished. I stamped hard on the sack of stuff. The propellor blade trapping it moved perhaps two inches. I felt the sack sink away, then rise sluggishly, bumping along my leg. It broke surface.

It was not a sack. It was a bag of navy-blue cotton, sodden with water.

The people on deck were already back. One of them said something about a sack of potatoes. Then he stopped talking, in the middle of his sentence.

Because the thing had rolled heavily, and I could see a line of silver discs running down the bag. Buttons.

Water gurgled. The bag moved. I reached out a hand to stop it drifting away down the tide. Then I stopped, frozen, hand out. And I shouted, a big, horrible shout.

I was looking into a face.

It was greyish-white. It had lank, colourless hair plastered over a round forehead. The eyes were open, dull lumps of wet glass. They were looking at me, and the slot of sky with the heads silhouetted, and the rigging latticed above. But they were not seeing any of it, because they were dead as mud.

2

Next thing I knew I was on deck, and the faces were all turned towards me, white, mouths open, as if they wanted to say things, but could not find any words. My heart was trying to batter its way out of my ribcage, and I was shivering, not with the cold, but with the hard, spastic vibration of dynamited nerves.

Seeing the faces helped. They made me realize that there were people I was responsible for beside myself. I could hear my voice, giving orders. Pete was hanging on to the body's tunic with a boathook, and I was down the ladder again, in the cold wash of the tide, tying a strop under the arms. We pulled it up on the mainsheet, using the boom as a derrick. It lay on the deck, and streamed water, and stared sightlessly at the sky. Dean brought a blanket, and we covered it up.

The engine started easily this time. We cast off from *Wilma* and motored for the quay. I pulled the mobile telephone from its locker and rang the police. There were other calls to make, but the shaking started again, and I could not manage the buttons.

I had seen bodies before; too many bodies, in Beirut and Cambodia and all the other hell-holes where they had sent me to ask the questions and write the stories. Getting mixed up in the stories was out, they told you. Tyrrell the journalist was there to record and report. This one was different. This time, there was nothing to record and nobody to report to.

This was just someone dead in dirty old England, and I was mixed up in it, and everything was much more complicated.

I set the crew to refurling the sails, to keep their minds off things. *Wilma*'s tender arrived alongside, and Otto Campbell heaved himself over the rail. His long, hard face looked shocked and pale.

He said. 'What the hell happened?'

I shrugged. He was not asking how a body came to be wound around the propellor. He was asking how Bill Tyrrell had made a big, stinking mess of things right under the nose of some very important people.

I did not answer. Just for the moment, important people did not seem all that important. The red blanket over the boy glowed like fire in the early sun. I was thinking about what lay underneath it, touched by the cold, random finger of death. And I was thinking about Marie, drunk on watch. *It was drifting*, she had said. *All sunk down.* If she was telling the truth, it had already been awash. The body could have been inside it.

A lot of people were going to want to know if she was telling the truth.

Otto bent, lifted the blanket, looked at the uniform. He said, 'He's a Russian.'

That kind of information was Otto's speciality. Just then, I did not care if he was a Martian. That came later.

The sun slid behind a mat of lead-coloured cloud. Cold rain hissed on the grey water. Two police cars wailed on to the quay, their blue lights scything the rain. Superintendent Robertson came aboard.

His face was cold and grey, to match his eyes. His staff bustled around taking photographs. An ambulance swished away into the rain with the body, raising fans of water with its tyres. The cold of the river would not leave me, and my stomach was queasy with exhaustion and nerves.

I went through it all for their benefit, from the dragging anchor to the discovery of the body. When I had finished, he said, 'How many of you had been drinking?'

I said, 'What do you mean?'

Nasty things were happening at the corners of his thin policeman's mouth.

14

'That girl. She was sick. Stank of drink. How old is she?'

'Seventeen.'

'Do seventeen-year-olds do a lot of drinking on your boat?'

'They smuggle it aboard, when they can.'

His eyes swivelled towards Marie. She had not taken the dinghy back to *Soyuz*, because the dinghy was evidence. She was crouching on a hatch cover, face the colour of flour, knees under her chin. His top lip did its best not to curl. 'I wouldn't let a kid of mine on this boat.' He paused, glaring at the sliding black water. 'Don't go anywhere. Some officers will be down to take statements.'

I watched him heave his thick, fawn-mackintoshed body up the rungs of the quay ladder, and felt as cold and dismal as the sky. There would be more inquests than he knew about.

Both watches began to scrub. It was not a popular job; normally, there would have been moaning. Today, they worked in tight silence, under the lash of the rain.

Some of the Tall Ships' crews were made up of Naval cadets, and some of sea cadets, and some of kids who had paid to go along for the ride. Youth Venture specialised in naughty kids. The idea was that you whipped them off the streets, and got them cold and wet, and worked them hard, until they recognized the existence of other people. It worked. *Vixen*'s crew had become a team. But it was a team that had come out of youth custody and drug rehabilitation hostels and community service orders. It was a team that knew trouble when it saw it.

Ten minutes after Robertson had left, more trouble arrived. It was as dapper as a bantam cock, wearing a navy-blue pea-jacket with gleaming gold buttons. It had knife-creased blue trousers, crisp black hair with iron-grey temples, and a close, meticulous shave. Its chin stuck out like the ram of a battle-ship, and it stood on the quay for a moment, raking *Vixen* from stem to stern with eyes the colour and hardness of sapphires. It said in a brown, mellifluous voice, 'Bill. Let's pop below a minute.' Then it skipped down the iron rungs like a monkey.

Youth Venture had two ships of its own, *Wilma* and *Xerxes*. *Vixen* belonged to me, and Youth Venture had been chartering

15

her for the past three years. Rear-Admiral Dickie Wilson, R.N. (Ret'd) was the President of Youth Venture. He liked *Vixen* because he liked things that were old, and elegant, and aristocratic. He disliked me for the same reasons.

He led me down the companionway of my own boat. 'Sit,' he said, and pointed at my own settee.

We sat. He glared at me from under his eyebrows. He said, 'Do you know who you ran over?'

I said, 'A Russian.'

'Off *Soyuz*,' said Dickie. His voice was jovial. His eyes were not. 'I've just been with the captain. Apparently this chap was out for a row. For the good of his health.' He paused, to let it sink in.

It sank. I said, 'My lookout assures me that the dinghy was awash when we hit it.'

'Who was your lookout?'

'Marie Clarke.'

He made a note in a small book, his face long and impassive. He said, 'It was Marie who was sick on a policeman. Drunk, I hear.' His eyes were narrow and dangerous. He said, 'I won't ask you how she managed to be drunk. I'll just ask you to consider what you say very carefully.'

What he was saying was that there was going to be mud slung, and that none of it was to be allowed to stick to Ministers, or organizations, or any other source of influence that might put Youth Venture in the way of a donation or Dickie in the way of a knighthood.

I said, 'Marie says the dinghy was awash. I believe her. I'll write you a report.'

He said, 'So this Russian chap just happened to be swilling about in the river, and landed up in your propellor.'

'That's right.'

He opened his mouth to say something. But I chartered *Vixen* to Youth Venture at highly advantageous rates, and *Vixen* was a good advertisement for Youth Venture, except when she was mowing down *matrossi*. So he shut it again and said, 'I'll read it with interest.' Then he trotted up the companionway.

The crew were assembled on deck. He clasped his hands

behind his back, and swept them with his hard little eyes. The rain made round dark spots on the immaculate pea-jacket. Finally, he said, 'Which one of you's Marie?'

I saw her white face look up at him. He pointed to the companionway and said, 'Come down here.' Oh, no, you don't, I thought, and started to follow. But Johnny Rowse planted himself in front of me. He was a nervous, mouse-like boy, with an enthusiasm for driving cars that did not belong to him.

'It's Dean,' said Johnny.

I said, 'No time.' I could already hear Dickie's voice through the skylight.

'He's done a runner.'

I stared at Johnny's blue-and-pink eyes. Dean's pony-tail and skull rings daunted the faint of heart. But he had evolved from a technicolour wideboy into a reliable watch leader, give or take a slip or two. More than that, he was smart, and wily, and dishonest only with people he thought deserved it. Over three trips in *Vixen*, he had become something approaching a friend.

'WHY?' roared Dickie's voice from the skylight.

I ran below.

Marie was sitting on the buttoned leather settee with her stringy black hair falling over her face. Her hands were dirty, and over her ears. Dickie was standing with his fists on the table and his face red as a cock's wattles.

Vixen's saloon is six feet three inches high, lofty by modern standards, but I have to stoop to get under its deckhead. I knew I was towering over him, and I could smell his resentment. 'Get along, Marie,' I said quietly. 'I'll see you later.' She scuttled away forward, through the galley.

Dickie took a deep breath that swelled his chest like a robin's, and looked at me with eyes hostile enough to fell trees. He said, 'Press conference scheduled for now. Both of us go. Get smartened up. Let us pray that the press is asleep.'

I shut myself in the head.

Dean did not like policemen any more than policemen liked him. What had driven him away were the good old reflexes of the jungle. I had hoped that they might be giving way to something a bit more civilized.

I sighed, and scraped the black stubble off my jaw. It is a big jaw. I have got a big face, to go with the rest of me. It has been bashed about a bit, in the violent places where I did my work. There is a scar on the forehead from a flying bottle on the Gaza Strip, and my nose was not improved by contact with a brick wall during a police search in Khartoum. Shaving was about as useful as putting powdered sugar on a hand grenade.

I combed the lumps of black hair behind my ears. It could have done with a wash; but *Vixen* with a full crew is not an easy place if you are keen on your grooming, which I am not. I put on a tie, and inspected the blazer for gravy stains. The crew had been throwing mashed potato in Amsterdam, so the blazer needed cleaning. I pulled on a black leather jacket instead, and tucked my jeans into the leather fisherman's seaboots I wore to keep my footing on *Vixen*'s deck.

Outside, Dickie looked me up and down like a regimental sergeant-major, but prevented himself from saying anything. We went up the wet iron rungs and splashed through the puddles on the quay to a low clapboard building by the dock basin. There was a room with perhaps forty chairs facing a dais. Behind the dais was the Youth Venture battle flag, a square of blue bunting with the device of a galleon rocking across squiggles of waves. The air was sour with the smell of wet clothes and cigarette smoke from the twenty-odd ladies and gentlemen of the press sitting on the chairs.

My mouth was dry as dust. My Rolex said nine o'clock. Most of my life I had been one of the people down there among the chairs, clutching the tape recorder and the note-book. It was possible that none of them would have heard about dead Russians, yet. They would just eat up dead Russians. I knew how Dean must have felt. Calm down, Tyrrell, I told myself. Dickie would give them the flannel, and we would get away on the tide, out of reach of the kind of questions that would wreck lives and sell an extra ten thousand newspapers.

Dickie led the way to the plastic chair behind the baize-draped table on the dais. I felt a moment of deep nostalgia for the dubious warmth of the rat pack, and the stories that came and went and did not touch you at all. Then it was too late for nostalgia, because we were sitting down, and Dickie was talking in his warm, brown voice.

'Every year Youth Venture takes seventy-five young people who are in trouble, and shows them the sea at close quarters. *Very* close quarters.' He smiled, the kind of smile Francis Drake might have used to melt Elizabeth I's knee joints. 'Our young people learn to sail: to hand, reef and steer, as they said in the old days. They learn to rely on others, and be reliable themselves. It is a source of great pride to us that after we have finished with them, ninety-eight per cent of them stay out of trouble for good.' Again the smile, and a glance across at me with his stony little eyes. 'So here we are at the end of our second cruise of the summer. Next stop the Baltic, roughly four weeks from now. Meanwhile, please write about us, because we need the publicity, because the publicity brings in the money.' Some of the hacks even laughed. Dickie had not reached his present eminence by being tongue-tied in front of crowds. 'So,' he said, with a philanthropic beam. 'Any questions?'

It was muggy and damp in the room. I found I was holding my breath. Dickie had rushed them, without any of them realizing it. But if anyone had a tame policeman in Chatham, the hard questions would start now. There was a short, encouraging moment of silence. 'Well, then,' said Dickie, too quickly. 'If –'

'Snape, *Mirror*,' said a familiar voice. 'Where exactly does the money come from?'

Dickie liked money questions. He did not know what I knew about Mike Snape, which was that no question Mike Snape asked was ever going to be straightforward. 'Charities,' he said. 'Patrons. We have various . . . anonymous benefactors, who contribute to funds administered by our Trustees.'

'What about government money?' said Snape.

'Very little of it, I'm afraid,' said Dickie, with a smile warm enough to toast bread at.

Snape had a baggy, unresponsive face with a sharp nose. 'So that wasn't why Neville Glazebrook was on board *Wilma* last night.'

19

Dickie smiled. 'Mr Glazebrook is an old friend of Youth Venture,' he said. My palms were sweating.

In the back of the hall, a mobile telephone chirruped. My heart began whacking at my ribs. A freelance interrupted Snape, asked the usual anodyne questions: why had I given up journalism for sailing old boats? I suppose I must have given him the usual stuff, about peace and quiet, and prying into other people's lives stopping you doing anything with your own. But I was watching the girl with the mobile phone. She was talking in a low voice. Her eyes were wide open, staring at me as if she wanted to use them to nail me to the Youth Venture flag.

Dickie had seen her, too. He was stroking his upper lip with his finger. I stopped talking. He said hurriedly, 'Well, mustn't keep you.'

But more telephones were ringing now, and it was too late. Editors were telling their people that they were in a press conference with a charity that spent its leisure moments mowing down Russian sail trainees. The rain-sodden air began to brood with an electricity I remembered well. Sweat was running inside my T-shirt. The girl with the mobile phone looked quickly around, decided she had no chance of an exclusive, and said, 'Can you give me any details of the death of a Russian Naval cadet this morning?'

I kept my face still, the way I had seen people on platforms keep them still all the way from Peking to Valdez. No comment, was what you said.

Dickie, Mr Public Relations, did it better. He said, 'It was an immensely regrettable incident. There will be an inquest. Until that time I'm afraid it will be inappropriate to make any further comment.'

There was a babble of questions. Dickie shrugged, looking grave and diplomatic. 'Out,' he hissed, without moving his lips. We stood up. The babel moderated. Snape's nasal voice cut through the din. 'What is Neville Glazebrook going to think of being mixed up in the killing of a Russian cadet?' he said.

I said, 'He was not mixed up in it.'

'He was there,' said Snape.

'Then you'd better find out from him,' said Dickie. The anger was coming off him in waves.

'Sorry, I'm sure,' said Snape, with heavy irony.

I knew Dickie's anger was directed not at Snape, for asking the question Dickie had wanted to avoid. It was directed at anyone who was coming between him, and his knighthood, and the pursuit of money and influence via the good offices of Cabinet Ministers. Like dead cadets, and lookouts who had drunk rum. And Bill Tyrrell. Especially Bill Tyrrell, because Bill Tyrrell was big enough to show the marks.

The rain was warm and wet. Dickie walked beside me through the puddles, while the pack trailed crabwise after us, shoving tape recorders in our faces and yelling questions. 'Get out on the tide,' he muttered. 'Go home. Don't talk to anyone.' He sounded quiet and reasonable, but the schemes would be running round his head like hamsters on a wheel. Put Tyrrell out on the sea. Get room to manoeuvre.

It was his nature to manoeuvre. Mine was to ask questions. I said, 'I'm going over to *Soyuz.*'

He glanced at me with his bright blue eyes, made a calculation. Then he shrugged. 'If you feel you must,' he said.

Pete was already winding up the fat bottle-screw at the bottom end of *Vixen*'s new shroud. I went below.

The fo'c'sle was dingy, the glass prisms obscured by a paste of water and scouring sand. Marie was crouching on the starboard bottom bunk, stuffing tightly-rolled clothes into a kitbag. I said, 'Where are you going?'

'Away,' she said. Her face was a white glimmer behind the curtain of her hair.

Marie's parents inhabited a leaking flat in Liverpool. Her father beat up her mother, and she did not like their company. By the time she was fourteen, she had moved out with some school friends. They stopped going to school, at first because they were bored, and later because snuffing up smack had suddenly become a full-time job. Marie's teachers had been of the mind that Marie should have been at university. Instead, she had arrived in Birkenhead Juvenile Court for soliciting and mugging a sailor, and had asked for twenty-three other offences to be taken into consideration. She had come aboard

Vixen last year, angry and sullen-eyed. Three trips later she had a place at teacher training college, and a watch leader's berth on *Vixen* any time she wanted one. She and Dean had been *Vixen*'s success stories. Until last night.

I said, 'Where's away?'

She hooked a strand of black hair behind her ear, shook her head. 'Dunno,' she said.

I said, 'We need your help. We're going down to Fleet.'

She looked me in the eye, which was something she would never have done when I had first met her. It was the look you get from the Arab kids in the Gaza Strip, that says I hate you not because of who you are but what you are, on the side of the ones who hit you until you agree or you die.

So I said, 'Last night was bad luck. We'll get fixed up.'

She smiled, a proper smile. She said, 'You're nice, Bill.' She squeezed my hand. Hers was cold as ice.

I left her unpacking, and went back to my cabin. It was half past ten, and my stomach was howling for breakfast. I ate four fried eggs and half a loaf of bread. When there was one egg to go, Otto Campbell came down the companionway.

He was wearing a blue blazer and a white shirt, very Naval. Nobody seeing us for the first time would have worked out that I had been a foreign correspondent for a broadsheet newspaper, or that Otto Campbell spent most of his time persuading tired businessmen to play muddy games in the name of Leadership. 'Coming ashore?' he said.

'Dickie says not,' I said.

Otto's past had brought him into contact with a lot of important people, and he had been known to pass on their views discreetly, to friends.

'What would you do, if you were me?'

He pulled down the corners of his mouth. 'Get out,' he said. 'Sail round the world. Leave Dickie to sort himself out. He'll manage.'

I said, 'There'll be the inquest.'

He said, 'It was bad luck, was all.'

That was true. 'How was Mr Glazebrook?'

'None too pleased,' he said. 'Heads are bouncing around on the floor in the Cabinet. Being around dead bodies can tend to draw attention to a chap.' There was a pause. 'Did you know that Russian bloke had been on *Wilma*?'

I stared at him.

'Seeing some mates,' he said. 'Singing. Poor bastard.'

I said, 'What time did he leave?'

'Came aboard at ten-ish,' he said. 'Left at eleven-fifteen. Check with the crew.'

Vixen had come up to her anchor at eleven-thirty. 'Are you sure?' I said.

'That's what they say. I must be off. Mayor's giving a reception, bless his heart.'

So *Vixen* and the Russian had been in the same water within ten minutes of each other. Assume that Marie had been lying. The dolphin-striker under *Vixen*'s bowsprit could have rolled a dinghy under, and nobody any the wiser. The tide would have swept the body back down the hull into the propellor, rearranged him so he jammed the rudder, held him there. And that would have been that.

I rowed out to *Wilma*. She was a fat schooner. The crew were in the fo'c'sle, playing cards. 'Yeah,' said a watch leader. 'Eleven-fifteen, he left. Slightly pissed. Said he was going to look for the moon in the water, and wait for his beloved.'

'Beloved?'

'That's what he said.'

I rowed ashore, climbed on to the quay and splashed through the puddles and up the white-and-mahogany gangway of *Soyuz*, the Russian barque. Cadets in navy-blue uniforms saluted sharply. It was the same uniform that had been on the body in *Vixen*'s propellor.

I had met Captain Petrov in Amsterdam. He was standing in a day cabin lined with heavy mahogany panelling, staring out of the window at the rain. He turned when I came in. He had a face like weathered stone, slashed with a loose, gloomy mouth. A *papirossi* cigarette smouldered pungently in an ash-tray.

'*Kofe*,' he said, without looking at the cadet who escorted me. 'Sit down, Mr Tyrrell.'

I sat on a green leather chair. He sat behind a desk. *Soyuz*

23

had a Naval feeling, quite unlike the Boy-Scouts-on-the-water of the British boats. I said, 'I have come to express my deep regret at the death of your cadet.'

'Rebane,' said the captain. In their slits above the grey cheeks, the eyes were surprisingly warm. 'A most terrible accident.'

I said, 'We were anchoring in the dark.'

He shrugged. He was a seaman. He knew the problems.

I said, 'My lookout told me Rebane's boat was awash.'

'Awash?'

'Full of water.'

He nodded. His face was worried, his hands grey and blunt below the braid of the sleeves, stained with nicotine between the second and third fingers of the left. He would be staring at mountains of forms to fill in, interviews with people who had no understanding of the difficulties of looking after two hundred cadets in a strange country. He did not much care whether the boat had been awash or not. It was enough that one of his cadets had gone missing, and he had not known until the body was brought back.

'Rebane took the little boat before, without authorization, to go somewhere, a pub drinking place maybe; he liked to go to drinking places. Of course, we could not follow him. We have as you say neither the time, or any more the wish.' He jabbed out his cigarette, lit another and coughed smoke at his cup. 'He was a fool to go out into the night in the boat. But he was a fool. Eighteen years old, one of those crazy Estonians. He make, hmm, much noise about politic. A wild kid. And he is dead, and we are in trouble.'

Cups clattered as a cadet steward elbowed the door open. We drank the coffee and stared out of the porthole across the grey water at the jumble of masts and rigging. There was very little to say. After perhaps two minutes, I got up. 'Please convey my condolences to his parents,' I said.

'I think you are going to get a big problem,' said Petrov, bleakly. We shook hands. I left.

At the bottom of the gangplank, the press was a huddle of pastel anoraks. I put my head down and shouldered through. Pete had moved *Vixen* off the quay on to a buoy. It would be quiet out there, in the gurgle of the tide. I waved for the tender. The anoraks jostled me, yapping questions. I hardly heard them.

There were two oarsmen in the tender. The mouse-like Johnny Rowse was rowing stroke. He looked sly, and cocky, and excited. 'What's wrong with you?' I said.

'Back and forf, back and forf. Filf, you name it.'

'Filth?'

'Police,' he said, and put on an Inspector Knacker accent. 'Taking statements.'

'It's normal,' I said.

'Yeah,' he said. 'Don't worry, nobody told them nothing.' He winked. 'Marie was scared shitless. So we brought the filth out, and while they was talking to Pete, we brought Marie ashore.'

'Brought her?'

'Bag and all,' said Johnny, with relish. 'Reckoned she didn't want to talk to no busies.'

I stared at him.

'Lost her bottle,' said Johnny, smugly, leaning on his oar. The tender came alongside without a bump. Two weeks ago, Johnny and the bow oar had not even known how to row.

Vixen's cabin smelt of the usual smells: wood and leather, lamp oil and bilge. I picked up the portable phone and called the police. Superintendent Robertson wished to speak to me.

His voice was dry as dead leaves. 'Ah,' he said. 'Mr Tyrrell. Perhaps you can help me.'

I told him I would if I could.

'We've taken statements from your crew.'

I told him I knew.

'One of them,' said the Superintendent. 'Marie Clarke. We . . . couldn't find her.'

I said, 'She's left.' You bloody fool, Marie, I thought.

'We have reason to believe that she can assist us in our en-quiries.'

'In what way?'

'She was the lookout, wasn't she?' The voice let me know

25

exactly what policemen thought of ex-junkies who were drunk on watch. 'Any idea where she might have gone?'

I said, 'No,' without thinking.

'Ah,' said Robertson. 'Any inspirations, give us a ring, would you? Oh, and we'll need a statement from you.'

'Now?'

'We'll send someone to Devon,' he said. 'It's not a nice business. That Russian was drunk, you know. Best to get you out of the way of the press.' Lines by Superintendent Robertson. Script by Dickie Wilson. 'So don't go off anywhere, will you? And let us know if you find Miss Clarke. We'd like you both at the inquest.'

I said I would be there.

We hung up. I stared at the French polish on the saloon panelling, and told my head to stop aching.

It paid no attention. It kept telling me that what I had to do was find Marie before the police made mincemeat of her.

I picked up the telephone again, called the railway station. Nobody had noticed her. If I went there in person, or to the bus station, I would be trailing journalists like a bull trails flies. Besides, Marie was expert at disappearing. There was no future in hanging around Chatham.

I went on deck. The rain had stopped. The wind had gone southerly, and the sun was out. There were a lot of sightseers on the quay, and nearly as many journalists.

Pete was levering the new bottle-screw with an oversized screwdriver, his beard fluttering in the breeze. In an ideal world he would have rebuilt *Vixen* from top to bottom once a year.

I said, 'Let's get out of this. Everyone aboard?'

'Course they are,' said Pete, sniffing.

The tide was ebbing. *Vixen* had swung so her bowsprit was aimed at the dirty heart of Kent. 'Five minutes,' I said.

Pete wired the bottle-screw. The sails went up and rattled. The windlass clacked. The anchor broke out and the nose swung, sails filling, until we were pointed north for the river's mouth.

By six o'clock we were moving along the north coast of

Kent. I was in my usual place, hanging on to the backstay, keeping an eye on the helmsman. The air was flat and evil-smelling. It would be good to get into the clean green water of the Western Channel.

But I knew that it would take more than clean green water to clear up the mess we were in.

3

We fetched the flash of Start Point bang on the nose at midnight two days after we had sailed from Chatham. At first light, our grey bow-wave was crunching at the mudbanks of the River Poult, and the Basin was a copse of masts against the pinkish-grey sky beyond the lock.

The air was cold, with the peculiar chill of five a.m. It smelt of salt and rot, low tide. Oyster-catchers were whistling on the mud, and the wind lisped in the reeds. The watch on deck had pulled off the foresails and lashed the main along the boom. They were excited, chattering as hard as the marshbirds.

The lock gates opened silently. *Vixen*'s great hull slid between the walls. Water churned under the counter as I pumped her propellor into reverse. Eric the lock keeper grunted as he took the lines. The brickwork of the lock was black. It streamed like the walls of a grave. We rose into the daylight, resurrected into an older world.

Fleet Basin is all that remains of the Fleet Canal, down which in the Napoleonic Wars horses dragged barges laden with beef and grain for the victualling of King George's Navy. The canal fell into disuse at about the same time as the wooden walls of England. All that remained of it was a reedy ditch, much frequented by duck and wading birds.

The Basin had fared better. It was a granite-coped hole in the marsh some hundred yards square, and had once served as a wharf for the victualling of ships. As a result, there were the remains of some sheds and a mill, where beef had once been salted and hard tack biscuit baked; and a whitewashed brick pub, the Lord Rodney, known for no identifiable reason as the Hole.

In the twenties, a grain elevator had been built beside the basin. In the late thirties, the road that ran five miles across the marshes to Pulteney had been lined with a series of low-rise asbestos-roofed factories. Nowadays, the factories were workshops, in which men in filthy overalls did slow, unreliable work on yacht engines and farm machinery.

Since the Second World War, and the introduction of bulk freight, the Basin had gone steeply downhill. An occasional coaster still struggled across the shoals of the Poult to load coal or aggregate from the piles behind the East Quay. But the Basin's chief merit was as a harbour for yachts. They were not the kind of smart plastic machines you found in Neville Spearman's marina, whose well-dredged entrance gaped downstream. Fleet Basin boats tended to be old, and have seen better days. Some of them, like *Vixen*, had had glorious pasts, racing in front of the crowned heads of Europe. Others were plain derelict.

We moved slowly alongside the quay. The crew hung fenders over the sides. Dim shapes materialized out of the half-light. One of them was wearing striped pyjama trousers under a blue jersey, and there was a heavy-breasted woman in a lace nightdress and thick-soled leather seaboots. They took the lines, and made them fast to the rings sunk in the stone. Then they drifted aboard, down into the saloon, where the smells of bilge and polish were now mingled with coffee from the galley.

We all had coffee, the Basin people and the crew. The crew were quiet now, tired. They were leaving in an hour, going back to real life in a minibus.

Ed the milkman had saved the day before yesterday's newspapers. 'You're in there,' he said, with pride.

'Blimey,' said Pete, who had dived in the *Sun*. 'WILD BILL RAMS RED KID.'

I poured milk into the coffee, and grinned. I did not feel at all like grinning. Snape in the *Mirror* had the angle. He

29

pointed out that on a recent trip across the Atlantic, *Vixen* had been towed in by the Falmouth lifeboat, steering gone. He also said that while our Tall Ships' skippers tended to be professionals, I was an amateur who had come late to the game. By the end of the piece, there was very little doubt in the reader's mind that Bill Tyrrell was a semi-competent who should not be allowed anywhere near the lives of others. The source was not named. But I recognized the scuffle of feet as they ran for cover. The feet belonged to Dickie Wilson.

The heavies gave me a good going-over on page two. There were expressions of horror at the shockingness of the accident. There was a brief résumé of my career, in which the words *enfant terrible* were used twice. And it was pointed out that the whole business had taken place twenty-five yards away from Neville Glazebrook, the Minister to whose daughter my brother was married, and to whom my brother was Parliamentary Private Secretary.

The only consolation was that there was no mention of drunken teenagers. That would come later, no doubt.

The coffee drinkers left. The crew ate their last breakfast at the long table in the men's bunkroom forward. Then they cleaned ship, and packed. The minibus came to take them back to London. They said goodbye, and thanked me as if they meant it. They looked brown and happy as they climbed in. I watched them go. Dean and Marie should have been with them, singing on the motorway. I wondered with a familiar mixture of gloom and exasperation where they were, and what they were doing.

Pete shouldered his bag, unchained his bicycle from the bollard against which it had been leaning for the past two weeks. I watched him push it across the lock gate and disappear round the corner of the grain elevator.

A couple of reporters climbed out of a Ford Fiesta and started shouting questions at me. I told them everything was *sub judice*, posed for a photograph. Then I slid down the companionway, pulled the portable telephone out of the locker and switched it on.

The crew had cleaned up everything but the coffee cups. It took ten strokes of the handpump to fill the sink. It was only half full when the telephone rang.

The voice was thin and level and careful. 'Bill, old boy,' it said.

'Christopher,' I said. Not Chris; my younger brother was a man who liked things done properly and given their full weight.

'Why don't you come and have a drink?' he said.

I said, 'That's very kind,' to fill time while I thought of an excuse for not going.

'I very much want to discuss *Vixen*,' he said. 'Tonight.'

One of the reasons I had stopped being a journalist was in order not to have to deal with people like Christopher. But under the terms of our father's will, he was my co-Trustee in the *Vixen* Trust.

'I've been at sea for ten days,' I said.

'How relaxing for you,' he said. There was a petulant edge to his voice. I was getting a tan while he stared his responsibilities unflinchingly in the eye. 'I am at Lydiats with Mummy, and I have contrived a free day. I am sure that you will find it *advantageous* if we meet.' The petulance had turned sly, which meant he was talking turkey. 'Drinks at six?' The telephone went down.

I pulled out a grease gun and a toolbox and started on the steering gear. The noises of the Basin were the clock of water against hulls, the whine of power saws over in the sheds, the scream of gulls in the big blue Atlantic sky. Nobody cared about the cadet Rebane. Dickie was worried about Youth Venture and his knighthood. Christopher was worried about what Neville Glazebrook would think. And Neville Glazebrook was worried about his stout pink image being smirched by proximity to corpses. They would all be looking for scapegoats.

Marie was good scapegoat material, and so, by extension, was I.

I had run into a lot of objects in *Vixen*, in my time. When you hit something like a dinghy, it makes a good bang. Also, whoever is rowing it can be expected to shout.

I had said, *Let go!* And in the split second of silence after the order, the *clunk*. A sound as if we had hit a floating log. Or a dinghy awash. But the dinghy had just left *Wilma*, so

31

how could it have been awash? And if it had been awash, how come the cadet Rebane had been inside it?

I badly wanted to talk to Marie. She and Dean were good friends. He would know where she had gone. But now he had vanished there was no way of finding her.

Slowly and carefully, I jammed grease into the steering gear, and wound the wheel to work it in. The sun was out. It was hot now, the way July is meant to be. I sat back against the coaming, feet stretched along the seat. I was tired, with a dull, aching tiredness that furred up the conduits of the mind.

It was three and half years since I had driven up to Wales to pick Otto Campbell's brains about some grubby work with a contract to supply helicopters to Iraq. Otto liked to keep his hand in with what he liked to call the Intelligence community. As usual, we had sat in his office and drunk a bit too much whisky, and he had dished the dirt on the Iraqi deal. At the end of the evening, he had said, 'Why don't you do something useful with that boat of yours?'

The idea of doing something useful is extremely attractive to journalists. I had landed up taking boatloads of Youth Venture people on *Vixen* whenever I could wheedle some time out of my editors.

I liked it; the kids were a rackety bunch, but enthusiastic and fresh and quick to learn. Coming off a story and taking them sailing was like climbing out of a sewer and jumping into a rock-pool. In fact, I liked it so much that three months ago I had written to Martin Carr at the *Tribune* and told him that I was accepting the long sabbatical he was offering me, because the more stories I wrote, the less sense anything made. During those three months, everything had gone at tide speed and wind speed; a honeymoon. I could see black water in front of the bow. As the stem cut it the water peeled away, not in a wave, but in pieces of a jigsaw, clattering –

I woke and sat up quickly. My head felt worse than when I had dozed off. The clattering was the rattle of shrouds. A voice said, 'Ahoy there.'

It was a woman's voice, sarcastic. The light caught her butter-coloured hair. My mouth was full of glue. I said, 'Claudia.'

'The creature from the Black Lagoon,' she said. 'What are you doing back?'

I did not feel up to explaining. I stumbled below and put the coffee pot on the stove. Claudia worked for Age of Sail, a Gosport rare boat broker. Her own vintage eight-metre racing yacht was moored two down in the Basin. She had bought it as an investment. Investment was a powerful force in Claudia's life. I had met her two months ago in the Hole, arguing with the man who was doing the dirty work on her boat and drinking the only bottle of Bollinger in the cellar. Our friendship had ripened rapidly. Within a week, she was sharing *Vixen*'s big bunk with me. Within a fortnight, I was wondering whether this was due to affection for my person, or the fact that the shipwrights had torn the internal fittings out of the eight-metre for rebuilding, rendering it uninhabitable at weekends. She was tough, closed, and harder to read than a burnt book.

The problem was that she had clear grey eyes, dancer's legs, and a tongue like a switchblade. When I took the mugs on deck she was sitting against the skylight, her hands locked behind her blonde head. A labourer on the gravel-pile at the far side of the basin was shovelling air as his eyes tried to prise their way into the shadows of her navy-blue Saint Laurent shorts.

She drew the legs up defensively under her chin and sipped her coffee. She said, 'What the hell's got into you, Tyrrell?'

The tiredness returned, heavy as concrete behind the eyes. I said, 'What do you mean?' I knew damned well what she meant.

She said, 'The Pulitzer jury think you are an award-winning journalist. The Admiral's Cup people think you're one of the best helmsmen in the country. But you've ballsed up this Youth Venture business. And here you are in a dead-and-alive hole, living like a boat bum. You've got no job, no house. I guess you haven't got much money.'

I said, 'You're here too.'

'Weekends,' she said.

'I'm fine,' I said.

She said, 'You can do better than sailing round Europe

with a bunch of juvenile delinquents. If you must sail, why not sail for someone good?'

What she said about the Pulitzer jury was right. My career had kept me spinning round the world for ten years, collecting stories, filing them, and getting sent off to the next hell-hole. I had won some prizes in the process. But winning prizes did not eventually matter a hell of a lot. What mattered more and more was that the events I had covered were things that happened to people.

There had been heat, and clouds of flies, and a ramshackle collection of flat-roofed houses scattered on the lower slopes of the dusty mountains. The kids had been throwing stones at the Israeli patrol for an hour. The Israelis were sweating, fingering their guns. The officer was young and inexperienced. He did not like standing still with the sun beating on his helmet. But I was there with Jack and his cameras, and the officer knew the world had its eye on him.

I said, 'What are you going to do?'

The officer looked down at the bullet-smashed fig tree where the children were standing, head-dresses wrapped round their faces, waiting. He shrugged.

One of the kids threw a stone. I had been talking to him the night before. His name was Hassan, and he had no house, because the Israeli army had pulled it down in a reprisal raid. Hassan lived in a tent in the ruins, with his family. Throwing rocks at Israeli patrols was the only method he had of taking responsibility for his own life. He reminded me of Dean.

The reason I was there, on the back of this lorry, in the swell of fear-sweat and the stones rattling on the roof, was nothing to do with any story. It was because while Jackie was there with his cameras and I was there taking notes, nothing was going to happen. The pin was out of the grenade, but we were sitting on the firing-lever.

I looked at my watch. Two hours to filing time. A couple of thousand miles away, the *Tribune*'s subs were waiting to shovel the words into the belly of the beast. Nothing written yet.

I said to the officer, 'You leaving, then?'

'Sure,' he said. 'You follow us.'

I started to sweat, then; a cold sweat, of relief. The officer turned away. I raised a hand to Hassan. He waved back. There was a last flurry of stones, and the boys trotted back from the fig tree into the village.

I followed the lorry's drab green tailgate in the hire car. The dust gritted between the teeth.

'Got rid of them,' said Jack.

I nodded. For once, I thought. When we got on to the made-up road, the lorry peeled off, and we headed for Jerusalem. I filed.

Next morning, the telephone woke me. The voice on the other end was high and breathless. Hassan's voice. 'They came back,' he said. 'They burned the village. My brother has a bullet in his head.'

I started to say something.

'Pigs,' he said. 'You look, but you do not see.' The telephone went down.

I cooled my feet on the tile floor, nauseous with rage and guilt. The officer had known his hack. He knew that anything that happened after six o'clock was not news. He had led me to where I had wanted to be led. It was nobody's fault but my own.

The telephone rang again. Martin Carr was on the line. 'Bloody marvellous piece,' he said.

I hung up on him. All over Great Britain, the middle classes were chewing toast and marmalade and clicking their tongues about Hassan. To facilitate this righteous indignation, I had allowed myself to be persuaded to leave early, and Hassan's brother had a lump of lead in his skull.

I did not want to get angry with Claudia. But she knew the soft spots, and I was too tired to be able to stop. 'If boat bums are so lousy, how come you're one?'

'Weekends,' she said again. 'I do up the boat, I sell her. And I am gone.' She turned. Her eyes were grey as cold water.

'Just like that?' I said.

'Just like that,' she said.

There was a long, nasty silence. Businesslike was the adjective for Claudia.

'You probably need a drink,' she said briskly.

I was too dozy to argue. Besides, she was right.

We went to the Hole, where Cyril the landlord was addressing his Parkinson's headwag at a clientele consisting of a birdwatcher and a tramp. Then we returned to *Vixen* and made love. Making love to Claudia had given me an insight into the thought processes of an item of gymnasium machinery. She demanded one hundred per cent efficiency, fulfilled the requirements of the machine, exhausted herself and lit a cigarette. I watched her profile for perhaps five seconds. It was hard and efficient and beautiful. Claudia liked power. Tyrrell had stepped off the power ladder, so Tyrrell was just for fun.

Since the Gaza Strip, Tyrrell was like a man in a daze; emotionally numb, one of the walking wounded. Claudia and I were a community of emotional invalids. On the whole, it worked quite well.

I went to sleep. When I woke up, she was gone. I got on the telephone. Marie's probation officer did not know where she was, and her parents did not care. The Medway police did care, but they had not found her. There was no answer from any of the numbers Dean had given me. At five o'clock, I gave up, shaved for the first time since the press conference in Chatham and pumped cold water on to my head from the brass rose of the shower. Then I arrayed myself in a cream shirt and the dark-blue linen suit in which I had conducted the last interview of my career, with ex-General Noriega of Panama. I took the van keys off their brass hook on the bookshelf above my bunk, slid my bare feet into a newish pair of Timberland deck shoes, and climbed ashore.

The van was in the car park. The starter motor whinnied for a long time. It was an old Transit, with patches of red primer where I had ground off the rust. I had sold my BMW to buy it at the beginning of my sabbatical; there is a limit to the amount of oak planking and anchor chain that you can cram into a BMW. The engine caught, emitting a cloud of half-digested diesel. I hauled the bonnet on to the marsh road, and trod on the throttle.

4

Pulteney used to be a small, cute fishing village of the kind
loved by tourist boards and inhabited by rheumatics. Fifteen
years ago, property artists had realized the cash value of a
horseshoe harbour, a lifeboat station, and steep tiers of granite
cottages. Nowadays, the houses changed hands for more
money than the fishermen had earned in a lifetime, and the
few fishing boats remaining in the harbour rubbed sides with
expensive plastic fun palaces. There were tubs of geraniums
all the way up Quay Street, and several yacht chandleries
selling pastel-coloured oilskins. There were also two deli-
catessens, an interior decorator's shop and a gift emporium.
The last grocer's shop had recently closed down, because of
the supermarket that had opened on the main road inland of
the town. All in all, it was pretty much your average British
fishing village.

Lydiats Manor was a few miles inland. It had been a private
house until a couple of years previously, when its owner had
abandoned the struggle with dry rot and sheepmeat prices
and moved to Scotland, where he was now a pillar of the
Clyde Cruising Club. It was large, elegant and Jacobean, built
of fudge-coloured stone, standing at the side of a knot of
barns in a green and otherwise empty valley. The barns were
now fourteen houses, and the Manor had been sliced up into
lumps. My mother and her husband lived in what had been
the West Wing, and was now known as the Lawn House.

I was a quarter of an hour late. They were standing on the terrace outside the French windows, arranged like the principals in a drawing-room comedy. There was Christopher, the director of the comedy, in sharply creased burgundy linen slacks and shiny brown veldschoen. Next to him was his wife Ruth, Neville Glazebrook's daughter, in a Breton striped shirt, cotton dirndl skirt, Capri-brown legs and low-heeled patent leather shoes. She had a pretty, sharp-boned face with a surprisingly full mouth. Her mouse-coloured hair was pulled back from her forehead, anchored by a big velvet bow. She was looking sideways at Christopher with what might have been dislike. My mother was short and square, a little glassy-eyed, with her usual surprised expression and her usual anaesthetizing dry martini. Georgie, my stepfather, was fussing over a trolley-like gadget loaded with bottles. He was always fussing over something; it was his substitute for thinking. They all posed in front of the smart stone mullions and tried to look pleased to see me.

I found I was thinking of my father as I had last seen him; hands in pockets, chin stuck on the chest of his blue serge suit, patriarchal black beard fluttering in the breeze, standing by the taxi that had come to take him off to the station and out of our lives. My father had always given the impression that he was looking at things nobody else could see. This made most people uneasy. Not me; I had always suspected that those invisible things were the only things worth seeing. But I had never found out what they were, because when I had known him, I had not been of an age to ask.

I kissed my mother and Ruth, and grinned at Georgie, who bristled his toothbrush moustache at me. We talked awkwardly about the garden. Then Christopher edged up, and cut me out of the crowd with the smoothness of a dog singling a sheep from the flock.

We came to a halt in front of a bed of pink phlox and late delphiniums. He said, 'I'm worried.' He did not look worried. The woman who had interviewed us for the Big Brothers series in the *Tribune* Sunday magazine had claimed that his face was a rationalized version of mine. It was several sizes smaller, hair a neat pepper-and-salt instead of an Ethiopian mop, nose and chin straight and tidy instead of big and fleshy and aggressive. His eyes were bland. They met mine without fear or meaning.

I kept quiet. Journalists and helmsmen both know that you stay alert, and let the other guy show his hand.

'About *Vixen*,' he said. He waited. I let him. 'I'm very perturbed by what happened in Chatham. There's been a lot of press.'

I nodded, brightly. He was beginning to get the slightly sulky look of someone used to adulation and not getting it.

'Actually,' he said, 'it's this whole *Vixen* business. I don't think it's doing you any good, or those delinquents you take with you.'

'Oh?'

He was a politician. Politicians love to fill silences. 'There are stories of drunkenness. Talk gets round. Gets to the press. It reflects badly. I have duties, as a Trustee.'

I looked around at the over-restored barns, the silver estate cars lying like fish on the bright yellow gravel. Christopher stood there in his beautiful burgundy trousers, smirking.

Christopher and I had lived in a state of armed truce for the first seventeen years of our lives. Then *Vixen* had arrived on the scene, and with *Vixen* the *Vixen* Trust.

The basic purpose of the Trust was to stop me selling her and spending the money on motorbikes. It gave me a forty-eight sixty-fourths' share of *Vixen*; Christopher held the other sixteen. Christopher was at liberty to dispose of his shares without my consent, whereas I was not at liberty to dispose of mine without his. This arrangement was designed to make it easy for me to buy him out. Unfortunately, it was based on *Vixen*'s value some twenty years ago. Then, she had been a pretty boat of an unfashionable type. Nowadays she was a classic, worth the best part of half a million pounds. My father had been obsessed by the sea, to the exclusion of most other things, including the psychology of the individual. He had been aware that other people did not share his obsession. What he had left out of account in founding the Trust was that I would not have got rid of any relic of him while there was life in my body. Christopher, on the other hand, had ignored the boat, but revelled in the Trust as a system of levers he could use to frustrate his brother. Every time he made himself awkward, he was exacting a small revenge on me for having known our father better than he had.

'So what are you proposing?'

'I propose that *Vixen* be sold,' he said. 'Unless you want to buy me out.' He smirked. He knew how many articles you had to write to buy a quarter of a boat like *Vixen*.

'Really?' My mouth had suddenly dried out, and my heart was beating much too hard.

'I honestly think it is time that as a family we asserted our, er, mutual independence,' he said.

Ruth was pecking her sharp nose at Georgie, who was laughing into his white toothbrush moustache. In Georgie's book, the best thing about being married to my mother was the opportunity to fawn on the daughter of a real Cabinet Minister.

I felt immensely weary. I said, 'If I have to sell her to pay you off, she'll go to some rich idiot, end up chartering in the West Indies, and the kids I take out will be in jail. If Ruth wants money, why don't you go get a few more directorships?'

I knew it was a mistake as soon as I said it.

'I think that is a disgraceful imputation,' he said. 'You are behaving in an impulsive and immature fashion. As usual.'

I said, 'If you go against the intentions of the Trust, there are going to be lawyers and press everywhere. Are you ready for that?'

'There are lawyers and press everywhere already.'

I said, 'Whose idea is this?'

'What do you mean?'

'You didn't think it up by yourself?'

His eyes shifted. Got you, I thought. Rankle as it might, the *Vixen* Trust was one of the Tyrrell family's household gods.

But Christopher was Christopher, as well as a Tyrrell. He said, 'As Parliamentary Private Secretary to a Minister of the Crown, it is my duty to preserve impeccable standards in both public and private life.' Then he looked smug, as if it had been a great line.

'So you're bailing out.'

He smiled, and sipped his sherry. It was the expression he had used when he had been six, and had swiped the last biscuit. I knew that if I wanted the facts, I would have to go digging.

So the Tyrrell brothers walked back across the lawn.

I had been a race-winning helmsman, when I had been a helmsman. When you are a helmsman, you learn to keep your emotions out of the way, and concentrate on winning the race. It was a habit of mine that had kept me calm while I was interviewing some of the nastiest people on the planet. It was going to be useful now.

Ruth was wearing a smile with about a pint of lemon juice in it. It was directed as much at Christopher as at me. My mother said, 'Everything all right?' and looked across nervously at Georgie.

'Course it is,' said Georgie. They had been married fifteen years, during which time he had taken her over, mind and body. 'Well, m'boy. We don't see you nearly enough.'

I grinned at him. He thought I was a dangerous subversive, and would cheerfully have danced on my grave. 'Busy life,' I said.

'Has been lately,' he said. 'Saw in the *Telegraph*. Heard, too. Dead Russians, eh? Shocking bad timing. Happening just then, I mean. Glazebrook there, and so on.' He rolled the name round his tongue, the howling old snob.

I nodded at him, and turned to my mother. The skin round her eyes was creased with worry; she knew Georgie hated my guts. 'Could you stay to dinner?' she said.

I said, 'I've got to interview someone,' and watched her face fall.

She said, 'Georgie's off golfing at Brancaster in a month. Come and keep me company.'

'I'd love to,' I said. Decencies observed, she looked relieved. So did Georgie. So, I suspect, did I. We all made small talk about summer holidays. After half an hour, I kissed those who needed kissing, and started to leave.

Christopher came after me. I said, 'Where do you want to go from here?'

He said, 'I'll get a survey done.'

41

I said, 'Is this Ruth's idea?'

He flushed. Ruth had ambitions like jet engines have thrust. 'Don't be childish,' he said.

I said, 'A couple of newspaper stories about an accident. You and Glazebrook happen to be close to the scene. So what's all the fuss?'

He said, 'You've upset some very important people. Work it out for yourself.'

I looked at his small, priggish face. I know things you don't know, it said. And I'm not telling. The anger droned in my head. Calm down, I thought. None of the Wild Bill stuff.

I turned, walked away through the ankle-deep gravel, past the black cypress screens behind which the inhabitants of Lydiats hid their private lives, back to the van. What important people?

I drove to the Mermaid on Pulteney quay. It had a sawdust floor, scarred wooden tables, and Adnam's beer, trucked in from faraway Suffolk. It attracted customers who had lived in Pulteney all their lives, or who could not stand the clubby gentility that hung like the smell of aftershave round the new Pulteney Sailing Club at the far end of the quay. Charlie Agutter was at the end of the bar, looking for omens in a large glass of Famous Grouse.

Charlie was a yacht designer whose forebears had run the local shipping line. He had beaten me into the team for the 1984 Olympics, but only just. I ordered a pint of Adnam's. We talked boat, for long enough for me to forget that I was on the point of losing mine.

'So you're not a reporter any more,' he said. 'Thank God for that. Come back to racing.'

'Too busy.'

'Got just the boat,' he said. 'Fifty-footer. Delivering it to Neville Glazebrook. Cabinet Minister bloke.'

'He wouldn't have me aboard,' I said. I had introduced Charlie to Glazebrook.

'He would,' said Charlie. The whisky was making him uncharacteristically enthusiastic. 'Because it's dead right for you. Lovely boat upwind. You'd beat the arses off 'em.'

'I wouldn't even bother to ask,' I said.

He shrugged. 'You'd win for him,' he said. 'Don't think you'll get away with this.'

I laughed. One of Charlie's missions in life was to make people feel better. Then I went back to the Basin.

It must have been eleven-thirty when I arrived. The van's suspension clattered as the tyres hit the brick hardcore in the car park. Someone had propped a motorbike beside the derelict paraffin tank truck at the far end. The Basin lay black and glass-still, the boats two deep alongside, *Vixen*'s mast towering above the rest. It was the sort of night that made you feel like the only person on the planet.

Vixen had been with me a long time, and I had come to take her for granted. She was not just a boat. She was part of my family. Shut up, Tyrrell, I thought. It's the beer talking. I hunched into my suit jacket, marched round the quay, and stepped over the lifelines.

Vixen's deck was a giant spearhead of weathered teak. The Youth Venture kids had given it a fierce scrubbing before they had left, and it gleamed pale silver under the moon.

I stood for a moment and ran a sentimental eye down the sweet curve of the planking. Then I bent forward, frowning.

There was a spot of black beside my foot. There was another in front of it, and another, leading in a dotted line to the hatch. When I had left, it had been clean as a whistle.

The hatch cover was open. Whoever was in there would have felt the slight roll of the boat, heard the stumble of feet on the deck. I put my head to the black square of the hatch. I said, 'Who's there?'

Silence. The yellow windows of the Hole wavered in the black water. Then a sound. It was a low, nasty sound. Down in the saloon, someone was crying.

I went down the companionway fast. My fingers met wet, sticky patches. I put my hand out to the shelf by the barometer, found the box of matches and lit the lamp.

The yellow glow spread over the red-brown Honduras mahogany panelling, and the worn tan leather of the settees, and the clutter of rolled charts under the chart table. There was bright blood on the deck. There was more on the thing sprawled on the settee.

It was human, the thing, but only just. Its clothes were ripped and tattered. The worst part was the face. What I could see through the spider's web of blood was swollen and black. There were cuts. More blood had run in a muddy river down the upper lip.

The thing on the settee was Dean. Cool Dean, slick Dean, who had worked his way up from general purpose delinquent to Youth Venture watch leader.

'Bastards,' said Dean.

Between the first-aid kit and a couple of kettles of water, I managed to get the blood off the face and out of the matted black hair. It must have been a painful operation, but Dean kept quiet. He was your authentic twenty-year-old hard nut, not about to spill his guts in the presence of the Skipper.

'All right,' I said, when I had thrown the third bowl of bloody water to the Basin's shrimps. 'What do you want?'

He said, 'Nothing.'

I said, 'You ran for your life as soon as we got into the Medway. Now you bike a hundred and fifty miles just to bleed on my clean deck. Come off the grass, Dean.'

He squinted at me from puffed-up eyes. He shook his head.

I got up, opened the locker, gave him a glass of Bell's, and took one for myself. His nose was bleeding again. 'So,' I said.

'That bloke,' he said. 'That Russky.'

'What Russky?'

'The one that got drowned.'

'What about him?'

'Terrible.' His eyes shifted sideways.

'Yes,' I said. If you pressed people like Dean, they skidded away like a cake of wet soap.

'They was looking for Marie,' he said.

'Who was?' I sipped the whisky. Dean was not used to telling people things. It spilled out in no particular order. You just had to wait, and piece it together as best you could.

'I was in this squat,' he said. 'There was these blokes. The door come down. They wanted to know where Marie was, they said. I told them I didn't know. They started kicking.'

The police were looking for Marie. I was looking for Marie. I said, 'Who were these blokes?'

'Security blokes,' said Dean. 'You always get security blokes round the squats.'

'What did they want with Marie?'

'Dunno.'

I said, 'So why did you come here?'

He stared at me blankly. 'Those security geezers,' he said. 'They're a new firm. Well 'ard. They said they'd keep after me. I thought maybe you might need some help on the boat.'

This was as close as Dean would get to a scream for rescue. I shrugged. 'Why not?' I said.

He nodded, swigged his whisky like a duke. He was doing me a favour, now. Dean was on top again.

'What are security men doing in the squats?' I said.

'Coppers have to wait for lawyers. These geezers had pick handles, and blue hats.' He took more whisky, without being asked. He was warming up, now. 'They come in to chase everyone out. Normally it's all peaceful. Not this lot. But I got stuck in a corner, and one of them stood on my leg and the other one hit me. They was shouting: mind your own business, keep your sodding nose out. But I said, piss off, and I went out the window, down the fire escape. The fire escape's not that safe, like.'

I said, 'You were telling me about the Russian.'

'Oh,' said Dean. 'Yeah. He was a fan of yours, was all.'

'What do you mean?'

'I went drinking with him and Marie in Amsterdam. He was asking a lot of questions about you. He said he wanted to meet you. He told Marie he was going to come over and see you.'

'He told Marie?'

'She fancied him. He told her a lot of stuff. Reckoned he was a big fan of yours. Seen you on telly.' The words were barely recognizable, distorted by the whisky and the bruised lips. 'He said he'd row over and see you when we got in. Maybe he was on his way when we hit him.'

'Maybe,' I said. His eyes were glassy and opaque in their puffed-up sockets. I called him back from whisky land. 'Why did you and Marie run away in Chatham?'

'Do me a favour,' he said. 'There was going to be Law

everywhere.' The eyes were not merely wandering. They were avoiding mine. One of Youth Venture's big virtues was that it gave people like Dean the idea that there was such a thing as letting people down.

I said, 'I've got to go to the inquest.'

He sat up very straight. His mouth hung ajar. 'Inquest?' he said.

'A lot of questions,' I said. 'About how it happened. I'm in dead trouble.'

'Yeah,' he said. 'I seen in the papers.' He did not sound convinced. He had slid part of the way back into his old world, where the only trouble Dean recognized was trouble Dean was in.

I said, 'I have to find Marie.'

He said, 'I ain't seen her,' and wiped the blood from under his nose.

'Can you find out?'

He did not meet my eye. He said, 'Maybe.' He leaned back on the buttoned leather. His head lolled sideways. He was asleep.

I put a blanket over him, and went next door to my bunk.

Security guards, I thought. Why would security guards want to know Marie's address? Then sleep came thick and heavy, loaded with whisky and accumulated night watches.

When I finally woke, a beam of sun was lancing through the porthole, printing a yellow disc on the cabin bulkhead. The alarm clock said six-fifteen. In the saloon, the settee where Dean had slept was empty. The blanket was neatly folded. There was a note on the table.

Adelphi Hotel Strand.

I went on deck, into the early-morning chill of the Basin. The spots of blood were still there. They had dried overnight. But the motorbike was gone from the car park.

I slung a bucket into the harbour, sluiced off the deck and scrubbed away the blood. The sun sailed up over the grain elevator. You are getting slow, I thought. Three months ago, Dean would have told you things.

By breakfast, I had finished greasing the stern gear. I was halfway through the coffee when a Detective-Inspector Nel-

46

ligan arrived, dropped cigarette ash on the deck, and took a statement about the circumstances surrounding the discovery of the body of Lennart Rebane, an Estonian national. I told him I had no idea of the whereabouts of Dean Eliot or Marie Clarke, which was technically true. As his white Ford Fiesta was bouncing away across the car park, the telephone rang.

I picked up the receiver and said, 'Yes?'

'Hope I haven't disturbed your meditations,' said the voice on the other end.

'What do you want?' I said. The voice belonged to Martin Carr. He had been my editor for five years. He was the cue that blasted Bill Tyrrell the human billiard-ball into the hell-holes.

'You,' he said. 'I assume you've had enough of dead Russians. There's an election in Madrid. They're building barricades. Our guy down there is hiding in a bar, in case he gets his feet wet in a water cannon. Would you go?'

He would be sitting at his desk in front of his picture window with the London River winding behind him. He would have his bald head in his hand, and his big horn-rimmed spectacles on the end of his nose.

'No,' I said.

He would be sitting back in his chair, shoving the spectacles up his nose with his soft white forefinger. The smile would be off his face. 'Listen,' he said. 'If I was you just now and somebody offered me a chance to get out of the country, I'd jump at it.'

'Sticks and stones,' I said. 'Touchy Ministers and their paranoid Parliamentary Private Secretaries. It's all hot air.'

He said, 'Possibly you are out of touch. Possibly because you are sitting on your yacht playing Buddhists, you have not heard what people are saying about you.'

I said, 'I am a no-good piss artist who drowns Estonians, wrecks supranational fellowship, and drags the fair name of statesmen in the mire.'

He said, 'That's a little bit of it. The other thing is, we had a Major Saunders in, asking about you.'

'Who's he?'

'He wouldn't say. But he was asking some peculiar questions

47

about your politics, like were you or had you been at any time a member of the Communist Party.'

'Not since I was nineteen. I didn't think people worried about that any more.'

'Major Saunders did. So do his employers.'

'Who were?'

'You will remember George Samuels, on the spooks desk. George remembers the Major. He's been around a while. Last time he showed up was in 1979, trying to join the National Union of Miners under a wrong name.'

'MI5?'

'More than likely,' said Carr. 'In fact, George says definitely.'

'What the hell do they want?' I said. It was more or less a rhetorical question.

He said, 'I'd check into that dead Estonian of yours. Because there might be more to him than meets the eye.'

'And do you the story.'

'That would be nice,' said Carr. He listened to the silence, 'Well, give us a ring, one of these days.'

'I'll think about it.'

I switched him off. I walked forward into the hot sun, pulled sail bags out of the forepeak, and started going over the seams, stitch by stitch. I kept thinking about Major Saunders. I could not concentrate on sails.

A man in a nylon shirt with sweat-stained armpits was walking down the quay. He looked like a journalist. I went and hid behind the doghouse with the telephone, and dialled Andrew Croft.

Andrew was a thin man with cropped hair, a white face and thick glasses who produced a magazine called the *Leveller*, when he was not fully occupied fighting libel suits. In my *Tribune* days, I had sent him stuff Martin Carr considered too dangerous to use. He asked me if I was having a relaxing time. I told him that he should try it himself. Then I asked him about Major Saunders.

'Umm,' he said. There was a silence. Andrew never wrote anything down, through justifiable paranoia. He kept his database in his skull. 'Used to be with MI5?' he said. 'There was a chap. Dodged around a bit. Counter-intelligence, industrial. Went on to specialize in Naval stuff. Haven't heard of him lately. Do you want me to have a ferret?'

'If you've got time.'

'Always got time for a friend,' said Andrew, with a touch of unction. 'If the friend is a bit notorious, and will do me a piece.'

'All right,' I said. 'If you come up with anything.'

'Lovely,' said Andrew. 'I'll call you back.'

The man in the nylon shirt had gone away. I pulled the staysail out of its bag. Dead Estonians would naturally attract Major Saunderses like flies. It was part of the rhythm of things. All I had to do was sit and wait for it to go away, mend the sails, get *Vixen* ready for the next trip.

I started to check the staysail. Marie had known the Estonian, who had been on his way to see me. Dean had been beaten up by security men seeking Marie's address.

And Christopher wanted to sell me up.

All unconnected. At least, that was what Bill Tyrrell, skipper of *Vixen*, thought.

Bill Tyrrell, late of the *Tribune*, was deeply curious. Bill Tyrrell was particularly curious to find out whether Christopher's sudden craving for respectability was anything to do with Major Saunders, and if so, what Major Saunders had told him.

Curiosity killed the cat, my mother said.

But curiosity had made me a living. And if the Major Saunderses were determined to be difficult, curiosity might save my skin.

5

I could exactly trace the origins of the instinct to find things out. It had started in the summer holidays before my last year at school. I had been upstairs in my room in my mother's house in Norfolk, reading. There had been the smell of burning eggs, the sound of her voice plaintive and reproachful at Christopher, who had got her up early to feed the pony on which he liked to pose. I was reading L.J.K Setright's column in *Bike* magazine, waiting for them to get out of the kitchen so I could breakfast in peace and go out to race my 505 dinghy at Brancaster. There had been the slam of the front door, and the whistle of the postman. Then my mother's voice, cracked and hungover, calling.

She was standing at the bottom of the stairs, holding a long white envelope. It was long before she had met Georgie in the bar of the Jolly Sailor, and given up cigarettes. The smoke from her Rothmans hung tangled in her chinchilla hat. 'For you,' she said.

I took the letter, and smiled at her. She did not smile back; I reminded her too much of the irritations caused her by my father for her to smile at me before the lunchtime gin had worked its sorcery. Not being smiled at hurt, the way it hurt most mornings. I took the letter back to my room.

The letterhead said MORGAN BUXTON, SOLICITORS.

It was short and traditional. It said that the firm had

instructions that they were to make themselves known to me on my seventeenth birthday. If I got in touch with them, I would learn something to my advantage. It was signed Henry Morgan.

When I went down to breakfast, the cigarette smoke was already seeping under the door of the room where my mother wrote her unpublishable operettas at a piano covered with the glass-rings of a thousand lunchtimes. I made toast, wedged the kitchen door shut against Christopher's flapping ears, and rang Mr Morgan.

'Ah,' said Morgan. He had a thin, dry voice that sounded amused by something. 'The Tyrrell boy. When will you produce yourself?'

'Produce myself?'

'Here in Maldon. In person. At the office.'

It was the summer holidays, and I was doing a lot of sailing, and riding a clapped-out BSA Bantam motorcycle with a top speed of thirty-five miles an hour. 'It's a bit awkward,' I said.

'Soon,' he said. 'Come soon.'

I said, 'What's it all about?'

He said, 'I can't tell you. Except that it's to do with your father.'

My father had died when I had been ten. I had loved him as sons love fathers. It was only when he had gone that I realized I had known nothing about him.

'What about him?' I said. My mouth was dry, now, my heart pounding. Maldon was a hundred miles away.

'We'll have to meet,' said Morgan, as if it was the easiest thing in the world.

I took a deep breath. A hundred miles. Three hours on the Bantam, flat out with a following wind. 'I'm on my way.'

Henry Morgan had cornices of white hair above his eyes, and a chin that nearly met his nose. Outside his salt-grey window, sailing barges lay like stranded rorquals in a muddy creek. He laughed when he saw me. Then he got up from behind his desk, and shook my hand with a most un-legal grip.

I was impatient, and tired, and too curious to be in any way overawed. 'What is it?' I said.

He laughed some more, loaded me into a highly polished Austin Princess, and drove down a lane that turned into a cart track between reedbeds and terminated in a huge wooden barn on the side of a creek. He stopped the car and unlocked the door in the side of the barn. 'Behold!' he said, flinging the door open.

The sun beat down on the grey-green marsh. Gulls shrieked in the huge East Anglian sky. I put my head inside the dark oblong of the door.

At first, there was only blackness. Then, as my eyes became used to the dark, I saw something rounded, high above me, like the belly of an elephant. More elegant than the belly of an elephant. The hull of a boat.

'Fifteen years,' said Morgan. 'Fifteen years, she's been in there waiting for you. He never told you, did he?'

I shook my head.

'There you are,' he said. 'That's your father for you.'

Fifty-five feet of cutter. Mast, boom and bowsprit slung in the rafters; everything good as new, kept that way by Charlie Williams the shipwright. Waiting all those years for me to turn seventeen.

Vixen.

I went round her like a seventeen-year-old who has recently been clubbed. I had spent much of my life in dinghies; I was a hot contender for the 505 Worlds, and coaches were already muttering about Olympics. But *Vixen* had a saloon bigger than my study at school, tiers of crew bunks in the fo'c'sle, a rudder six feet high, a keel eight feet deep. To a kid who was used to dinghies, *Vixen* looked the size of a small town.

'You've got a mooring,' said Morgan. 'And winter storage till you're twenty-five.'

I said, 'Glad to hear it,' dazed, but not wishing to give anything away. This was more than a boat. It was a message my father had left for me, a message from a past whose doors were shut tight.

So I said to Morgan, 'Did you know my father well?'

'No,' he said. 'Brought the boat in. Bought the barn. Had her hauled out. Came to see me, once, much later. Set up the Trust, which I'll explain. Left a sum of money, instructions for upkeep. That was that. Heard he died.'

'Weren't you curious?' I said.

'Doesn't pay, in my job,' he said. 'Must have been quite a chap.'

'I suppose he was,' I said.

He looked at me sharply. 'Suppose?'

'I didn't know him very well either.'

It was at that meeting with Henry Morgan that I grew up. To a child, a parent is merely a parent, even if he is dead. To an adult, a parent becomes a human being, about whose composition it is possible to feel curiosity. It was a curiosity that spilled over into an urge to explain the rest of the world.

During the next five years, I got used to owning *Vixen*, and asking questions. My father had been American. His American family lived around Boston, in considerable grandeur. I had written to them, and received answers that stopped only just short of being rude. Later, when I had been in the States, I had been grudgingly given an appointment by Henry Tyrrell, a first cousin of my father's in the bank in Boston.

There had been no family resemblance. Henry Tyrrell was a stout, soft-featured man who sat behind a big oak desk in a roomful of portraits. He had confirmed that my father's parents were dead. He had implied that they had died disappointed by the fact that their only son had run away to sea at the age of fourteen. Then he had politely but firmly showed me the door.

So he had set himself apart from his family in America. In England, he had used his Americanness to cut himself off. He had had no friends that I could track down, except during the war, and this only on his ship, which had been sunk during the Dieppe Raid. After the war, he had joined the Merchant Navy. Those of his shipmates I located had spoken of him as a man with an almost pathological reserve. He had met my mother in the Shetland Islands in 1949. She had been a Wren. In 1965 he had been working as Captain of MV *Proteus*, a tramp coaster. He had gone in one side of a storm in the Skagerrak, and not come out the other.

Apart from the bare facts, all I knew about him was that he had a romantic love of the sea surprising in someone who spent his life on it, and a brusque way with people who intruded on his privacy, including small children.

I remembered once when he was home from sea standing outside the study door, looking at the handle and wondering whether I dared turn it. I must have been very young, because the handle was on a level with my eyes. Finally, I reached up, twisted, and went in.

He was sitting at a desk, looking down at something in his hands. He said, 'Go away,' without looking up.

I summoned up the courage to say, 'What are you doing?'

His head stayed bowed, but his eyes looked up. 'Oh,' he said, 'it's you.' I got the idea he had relented. 'Tying a Matthew Walker knot.'

He held out a straight length of rope with an intricate knot in the middle. The rope ran unblemished on either side of the knot. I could see no way he could have tied it. 'How do you do that?' I said.

He laughed, a short laugh. 'You'll learn,' he said. 'Not yet, though.' Then he used one end of the rope to show me how to make a bowline.

That was one of the only moments I remember the study door opening. Later, after he had gone, I looked up the Matthew Walker knot, and taught myself to tie it.

The telephone chirruped. It was George Pinsley, a surveyor. He had a hearty voice, except when he forgot, and the cold underneath showed through. He had been requested by Christopher Tyrrell, MP, to take a look at *Vixen*, soon. I told him to come on over, with all the good grace I could summon up.

Then I called my bank manager, to find out what he thought about lending Bill Tyrrell enough to make him sole proprietor of *Vixen*. He did not seem impressed. The maintenance bills were bad enough, he said. Had I considered buying a steel boat, or a fibreglass boat?

The bank manager was a gardening enthusiast. I resisted the urge to ask him if he had considered planting plastic flowers, and said goodbye. If Christopher went ahead with selling *Vixen*, *Vixen* would have to go.

At noon, an Escort estate crept gingerly to the quayside. I had sent three reporters packing that morning. This was not a reporter, for a change. I would almost have been happier if it had been. This was Pinsley the surveyor. He was a squat man with disorganized teeth and an expensive gold Rolex. Unlike most people when they first see *Vixen*, he made no noises of awe and wonder. Instead he said, 'All right if I carry on?' and disappeared into the bowels.

I spliced a couple of new halyards. From time to time, knocking sounds made themselves heard. It was warm on deck. I put the Emperor Concerto on the stereo and began to sew up the doubtful seam in the staysail. After perhaps an hour, Pinsley's head came out of the forehatch. He said, 'Do you mind if I have a poke in the lockers?'

I said, 'Help yourself.' The lockers in *Vixen*'s saloon made a good inspection point for the hull planking.

It was hot on deck. I got thirsty. I went below to make tea. Pinsley was in the galley. The heat was getting to him too; his face was red and shiny.

'Am I in your way?' I said.

'No, no.' He gave off a smell of tobacco and last night's beer.

I took the tea back up and carried on sewing, shoving the thick needle through the slippery white sailcloth. I made the last stitch, hauled the thread tight, knotted it off, and cut it trim. Pinsley came up the hatch. He looked flushed. 'All done,' he said. 'Nice boat.'

I nodded, without enthusiasm. The nicer he thought the boat, the more expensive it would be. 'What's she worth?' I said.

He showed his jumbled teeth in a perfunctory grin, avoiding my eye. 'It'll be in the report,' he said.

'Let me have a copy.'

He scissored his thick legs over the rail and left. I collected up my tools and took them below.

The sail thread lived in a biscuit tin in a locker opposite the chart table. The thread came on a plastic spool; the needles lived in a plastic tube of oil, to protect them from pitting by airborne salt. I pulled the tin open, tossed in the thread, and took out the tube. Its barrel was slippery with spilt oil.

I frowned, and looked at it harder.

Oil rots sail thread. That is why I always screw up the needle tubes until a dot of paint on the lid meets a dot of paint on the barrel. This afternoon, the dots were out of line, and the oil was leaking.

I had closed the tube myself, when I had taken the needle out. Running a boat like *Vixen* is only possible if you pay meticulous attention to detail. There was no way they could be out of line.

But out of line was what they were. The only person who could have left them that way was Pinsley. You had to be a very conscientious surveyor to check the condition of the ship's needles.

I screwed up the tube, put away the tin, and went to the galley. There were other indications; tiny things, but things I would never have done myself. The tomato ketchup was the right way up. The sponge that padded the box of spare teacups was the wrong way round, abrasive side out, so it would rub at the paint when the boat rolled.

Either Mr Pinsley the surveyor was conscientious to the point of insanity. Or he had used his couple of hours below to make a thorough search of the boat.

6

I poured the lukewarm remnants of the tea into my mug, and dialled Christopher's home number. A woman answered, oozing charm that stopped just short of being erotic. The voice turned Christopher's constituents all runny inside. 'Ruth,' I said.

'Oh.' I could imagine the sharp face freezing, the sensuous lips compressing. The voice became cold and brittle as a washbasin. 'What is it?'

I said, 'Is Christopher there?'

'He's at a meeting in London,' she said. 'You could try tomorrow.' *If you insist*, was the unspoken message.

'Ah,' I said. Music was playing in the background; *Carmen*, by the sound of it. Her house was a magazine stylist's dream of La Vie en Dorset, loud chintz curtains and reproduction firebacks, soulless as her. It was not like her to play music before the sun was over the yardarm. 'Could you ask him to ring?'

'I expect he'll be rather busy,' she said. Again, there was the coldness I had noticed at Lydiats. 'He usually seems to be, nowadays.'

'There's something he should know. Then he'll be shot of me.'

She said, 'We should be so lucky,' and laughed, a laugh as soft as a brick through a plate-glass window. I rang off.

A voice on the companionway said, 'Are you being a

journalist again?' It was Claudia, in a waisted pea-jacket and short skirt that did fine things for her fine legs. 'A little bird told me you're making changes.'

'Changes?'

'Selling the boat.'

I stared at her. She stared straight back. Her eyes were wide and innocent, fringed by long lashes. Her hair was impeccably brushed, her lipstick only just not lip-coloured. This was working Claudia from Age of Sail, purveyors of classic yachts to the stinking rich. I said, 'Did Christopher send you?'

'He said you were thinking of selling the boat,' she said. 'Naturally, we'd like to be the brokers. I said I'd pop down and see you.'

'Is this love?' I said.

'It's business,' she said. 'Don't be nasty.'

'I'm not selling the boat.'

She lowered her eyes. Her shoes were espadrilles, suitable for walking on an important art object. 'Oh,' she said. She did not believe me. 'Buy me a drink.'

We walked past the stripped-out hulk of her eight-metre, round the quays to the Hole. They had laid in plenty of Bollinger.

Cyril the landlord sold me a bottle, and nodded at us affably, thirty-one times a minute. I ordered a pint of bitter for myself. We sat on the bench outside, looking back across the water at *Vixen*'s long, white hull, her great beak of a bowsprit, the lovely upsweep of her counter. 'God, she's pretty,' said Claudia. Her eyes were narrow, the way they were when she was making love. Sex and money and boats were all tangled up, where Claudia was concerned.

'Did you speak to the surveyor?'

'Can't say,' she said.

That was interesting. 'Why not?' I said.

'I'm in a . . . delicate position with you,' she said. 'Make friends of your clients, but don't make clients of your friends.'

'So you're not talking.'

Her hard, efficient hand squeezed my knee. 'I must get back to Southampton,' she said. 'I'll tell you one thing. If you

58

were hoping *Vixen*'s not worth anything, you're going to be disappointed.'

I said, 'I don't care what she's worth. She's not for sale.'

Claudia was good company and Claudia could make you laugh. But when Claudia sniffed a deal, Claudia was deeply serious. I had already watched her pour a glass of champagne over the balding skull of an inoffensive enthusiast who had changed his mind at the last moment about selling a restored nineteenth-century steam launch. When Claudia's lower lip began to look like a church doorstep, there was trouble for someone.

The lip began to stick out. She said, 'Christopher's already in negotiations.'

I said, 'He's going to change his mind.'

She laughed. 'Who's going to make him?'

I said, 'If you'll excuse me, I've got things to do.'

The lip was unmistakably petulant. She said, 'Pardon me for being alive.' I watched the red Alfa Romeo Spider shrink down the marsh road, heading inland, where people were making plans and doing deals. Out here at the Basin, I was in a sort of limbo, between sea and land; on the margins of both, and part of neither.

The first time I had had that feeling, I was just off the aeroplane from Central America. My ears were still ringing from the pounding of a Contra heavy machine gun, and there were crisp rusty stains on my trousers where Morales, my guide, had bled on them. Lying in the baked mud of a jungle road with big slugs kicking dust in your eyes is a very public feeling. What I had liked about the Basin was its privacy. Now, I felt as vulnerable as a barefoot blind man in a cellarful of scorpions.

I stowed the telephone below, twitched the leather jacket and the full-face Bellstar helmet from the hook at the bottom of the companionway, and jumped over the rail.

I had come a long way from the BSA Bantam. Nowadays, the bike was a Norton Commando, with a 750cc overhead valve engine that bellowed like a bull and shook like an iron blancmange. It had been built in 1971, and crashed outside a transport café on the A11. I had bought the remains from the café's owner, and spent two years on the restoration. A lot of people wondered why I bothered, because the Norton was old-fashioned, heavy, and bad-tempered. But then a lot of people wondered why I held on to *Vixen*.

Miraculously, the Norton started first kick. I took it gingerly across the car park. On the tarmac I twisted the throttle. The acceleration kicked me into the seat. On the main coast road I swerved left, and wove through a tangle of crawling holiday-makers towards Naylor Hill. From up here, Pulteney was a huddle of Boscastle slate roofs, terminated by the stone pincer of the harbour clawing into the brilliant blue of the sea. There was a park-and-ride car park on the hill, nowadays. The Norton's exhaust trailed thunder down Quay Street. Fat women with shorts and boiled-lobster legs made sour faces. At the bottom the crowds were thicker, milling round the ice-cream vans by the lifeboat house. Pinsley's office faced the lifeboat house. There were cards on the board outside, with idealized pictures of boats for sale. I parked the bike on the pavement, and went in. The secretary had creamy breasts, well jacked up under a sweat-damp silk blouse. She was wearing a tight skirt, and bright red lipstick. She looked tired and hot. I asked for Pinsley. She said, 'He left an hour ago.'

'When are you expecting him?'

'I couldn't say.' She did not like the jacket and the helmet.

'Today?'

'Oh, no,' she said. 'He's just left for Jersey. He's going on to Antigua.'

I thanked her, full of old-world courtesy. Then I shouldered my way through the crowds to a big granite-faced building on the quay. A brass plate by the door said CHARLES AGUTTER. NAVAL ARCHITECT.

Charlie was sitting at a big table in a hangar-like room with walls of whitewashed brick. A stereo was mumbling John Coltrane. There was a sketchbook beside the computer in front of him.

I said, 'Do you know a surveyor called Pinsley?'

Charlie said, 'I thought you'd given up being a journalist.'

'I have,' I said. 'What about him?'

He shrugged. 'He's a surveyor. Hasn't been here long.'

I said, 'What have you heard about him?'

Past experience with journalists had left Charlie with a powerful suspicion of the press. He looked at me with his brown-shaded eyes. 'Not for publication,' he said. 'He's got some bad habits. Thirst like a bilge pump. You see him at the bookies. Likes fast cars. He's messing around with his secretary, or so his wife says. He finds ways of . . . boosting his income.'

'Such as?'

Charlie looked uncomfortable. 'Depends whether you're buying or selling. If you're buying, slip him a couple of hundred quid and he'll find bad fastenings, something a bit nebulous that'll get the price down. If you're selling, another couple of hundred, and he'll overlook any little blemishes.'

'You sure?'

'He surveyed a boat for a friend of Scotto's, gave it a clean bill. First time out, the keel fell off.'

'I see.' I hesitated. 'Would it surprise you to know he's just spent a couple of hours on *Vixen*, and he searched her as well?'

'I'd be surprised if he's surveyed her, in two hours,' said Charlie. 'Searching sounds reasonable. Hundred quid, no problem, I should think.' He paused, tapped a button on his computer. 'What was he looking for?'

'Good question,' I said.

Charlie nodded. His was not an enquiring mind, at least not until it was asked to be.

'It'll die down. The talk,' he said. He was trying to be encouraging. Nice guy, Charlie. 'D'you want a drink?'

I shook my head. He said, 'Why don't you forget all this crap and come sailing? The fifty-footer's screaming for it.'

'One day,' I said. 'Not now.'

I picked up my helmet, started the Norton, and blasted off for London.

The Adelphi Hotel in the Strand was just down from the Savoy, on the other side of the street. That was about the best that could be said for it. The front entrance was blocked by hoardings, and the posters were an inch thick. The brick arch above was caked with pigeon droppings.

I chained the bike to some railings in a side street, snapped the padlock. The wall of the hotel rose like a soot-blackened cliff into the lowering evening sky. The air was hot and wet, with a promise of thunder. I walked back round to the entrance.

An old man was sitting in front of the hoarding. He was wearing three overcoats and a pair of baseball boots with no soles. There was no entrance door in the hoardings.

'What do you want, lanky?' His voice sounded like gravel marinated in British sherry.

'The way in.'

'Lucky you found me,' he said. 'I am Alfred, the doorman. You want to go round the back, the window with the box under it.'

I pulled out a fiver. He took it with the negligent stealth of a member of the Corps of Commissionaires. He was wearing cricket gloves. 'Well,' he said. 'The next one down, actual,'

I walked round. People slunk by in the hot night. They were wearing too many clothes, and they smelt as if they did not wash much. The window with the box under it was at the back, barricaded with corrugated iron. The one after it had bars. I pushed the bars with my hand. Someone had been in among them with a crowbar. They swung like a bead curtain. The window behind them opened easily. I got a knee on the sill, and went in.

I was in a storeroom. It was dark. I had guessed it would be. I had brought a flashlight. The beam illuminated a filthy carpet, worn into a track between the window and the door.

The ground floor was dark and derelict. There was something that might have been a ballroom. By the smell of it, it had been converted into an informal latrine. Three or four people brushed past me as I turned on to the stairs. Somewhere above, someone was singing a long, moaning song without words. The air was thick, as if it had not been changed for years.

The first and second floors were shuttered and uninhabited. On the third, the singing was louder, and there were open windows. The walls were covered in graffiti. One of the doors said DENS DEN in Dayglo spraycan. I pushed it open.

62

There were three men inside, sitting on mattresses round a hurricane lamp. Their faces gleamed with dirt. I said, 'Where's Dean?'

'Don't know no Dean,' said one of them.

'Tall kid. Black hair. Leather jacket.'

'Yeah,' said another of them. 'He's one of the spiders.'

'Spiders?'

'Up top,' he said, and laughed, a weird cackle. 'Seventh floor.'

The stairs were walled off after the fifth floor. There was a boy of about fourteen in the corridor, smoking a cigar. 'Where's the seventh?' I said.

'Out the window.' He pointed with the butt end of his cigar. 'You might be a bit 'eavy.'

I had no idea what he meant. The window he was pointing at was a big one, half open. Faded red letters on its lintel said FIRE EXIT. Outside was the rusty iron platform of a fire escape. I stepped through.

The platform drooped under my feet. Seventy feet below was the littered floor of a light-well. I took a deep breath, and started up the steps.

I passed a layer of windows. The steps sagged away from the wall. I began to understand why the inhabitants of these altitudes were called spiders. On the seventh floor landing, I climbed through the open window and stood for a moment to catch my breath.

Up here, the rooms were smaller and the air fresher. There was graffiti; but it was more controlled than the savage stuff downstairs. Someone was playing 'El Condor Pasa' on a sound system. Cross your eyes and hold your nose, and it could have been a university hall of residence. I knocked on the door.

A girl's voice said, 'Come in.' She was small, with nervous little eyes and unwashed fair hair and a wide slash of almost black lipstick across her mouth.

I said, 'Do you know Dean?'

'No,' she said. Her nervousness seemed to intensify.

I said, 'I run the boat he sails on.'

She said, 'What's your name?' I told her. She licked her lips. She said, 'Oh, *Dean*. Come 'ere.'

She led me down a corridor, to others. At last we arrived at a dead end. There was one door, marked FIRE EXIT. I opened it.

Dean was not there.

'Oh,' she said, as if she had stepped on a nail.

The room was a wreck. The mattress had shed its bowels all over the floor. An armchair lay in its constituent parts on the mattress. The carpet was up, and so were half the floorboards. There was a chimney, but the fireplace had been torn out.

It looked as if someone had been here looking for something.

I picked up a postcard-sized picture from the floor. It was a photograph of *Vixen*.

'Looks like he's left,' said the girl.

I would have done the same myself, if someone had searched my room like that.

'You don't know where?'

She shook her head. 'I gotta get back,' she said.

I pulled the window open, stuck my head out. The fire escape was a cobweb of rotting iron. Big sections of it were not there at all. Far across a dizzy cliff of wall, it merged with others that plunged into the shadows below. Only terror would put you on those rusty cobwebs. Even if you were Dean.

As we walked down the corridor, a door opened. A round girl's face peered out. 'Tyrrell,' it said.

'That's me.'

'Dean said, *Barbara Ann*, Powney's, on the Medway.'

'What about it?'

'That's it. He give me a fiver to tell you.' The door closed. There was the sound of a padlock.

I gave my guide another fiver. She thanked me in a way that combined shyness with ancient wisdom. Then I went down the fire escapes, through the reeking mausoleum below, and out into the clean air of the Strand.

I did not notice any of it. I was wondering. What I was wondering was whether it was a mere coincidence that someone should search Dean's bachelor apartment and my boat within the same twenty-four hours.

I had been to Powney's before, after a pair of bronze mooring cleats for *Vixen*. It was a semi-derelict boatyard. Things happened slowly at Powney's. Powney's could wait an extra half-hour.

I found a call box, and dialled Christopher's flat. Somebody who sounded like a butler told me Christopher was having a dinner party. I unchained the Norton. We thundered into Division Bell Land.

Christopher lived in a house in Westminster Square that (he never tired of telling people) had once been owned by an Archbishop. There were a couple of chauffeurs dozing at the wheels of ministerial Daimlers outside. When I rang the bell he answered the door himself. He was wearing a double-breasted dinner jacket, cut a shade too figure-hugging; he was proud of his slimness. His eyebrows arched on his smooth forehead.

'Good Lord,' he said.

I said, 'Can I come in?'

'The fact is . . .'

'Cabinet to dinner, is it? I won't be long.'

His mouth lost its cupid's bow curve, began to widen and straighten. '*Really*,' he said.

I said, 'Pretend I'm the motorcycle messenger.'

He opened his mouth to say something. Then he let me in.

The walls were Regency stripe. There were Turkish rugs on the floor, and blue-and-white vases that had sat on the hall table when we had been children. From down the hall came the smell of cigar smoke and flowers, and deep, studied laughter. It was difficult to believe we were on the same planet as the Adelphi Hotel.

'In here,' he said, and propelled me into a study lined with leatherbound editions of books he certainly had not read. 'You haven't got time for a cigar.'

I looked at his pale mandarin's face. It was innocent as a dawn sky. I said, 'Your surveyor turned up.'

'Good,' he said. He did not look worried. MPs very seldom do.

'Has he told you what he found?'

'I haven't heard. I hope the boat's in good condition?'

'It's got nothing to do with the boat's condition. I want to know what he was looking for.'

'Looking for?'

'He searched her. Stem to stern. What was he looking for?'

He put his palms on the desk, and leaned back in his chair. His mouth looked like a letter box. 'Am I to understand that you are accusing me of instigating a . . . rummage of *Vixen*?'

'That's right.'

'Why on earth would I do that?'

'That's what I'd like to know.'

'Look,' he said. 'I am a busy man. I have never even spoken to this surveyor. I leave such matters to my secretary.'

'How did she find him?'

'She rang Age of Sail. The brokers.'

I stared at him. Dear, loving Claudia.

I said, 'Are you suggesting that Age of Sail organized a search of *Vixen*?'

'Take it as you like.'

I said, 'Someone is making a mountain out of a molehill over this Russian business. The whole thing will blow over in a week. Why are you insisting on selling up?'

His eyes flickered nervously towards the door. 'You seem unaware that you have precipitated a major international incident.'

I said, 'What international incident?'

He straightened his immaculate bow tie. 'I am not at liberty to speak of it. You should know that. But you can take it from me that the boat is to be sold. My lawyers will be in touch.'

I was furious. I said, 'So I am not allowed to know what I am accused of?'

He said, 'If you don't know, I can't tell you. If you do know, I don't need to.' His hand was shaking. He was white as snow, and there was real hatred in his eyes. I had a sudden, disturbing thought. This man is your brother. He has always been jealous of you. Right now, if he could kill you, he would.

More to the dead Estonian than met the eye, Martin Carr had said.

I got up, and walked out of the smell of big shots, and into the sharp reek of the hot night.

7

I moved out through the southeastern suburbs of London at better than sixty miles an hour. The city peeled away, fell back from the road. The M2 was a snake of red lights. I wound the Norton up as far as she would go, and howled down the fast lane to the Chatham turnoff. At a hundred miles an hour, there are no questions.

They came back soon enough.

I cruised through the new cardboard estates on the outskirts of Strood, paused at a late off-licence. The sky was black and heavy. People were spilling out of a pub; half past eleven. The headlights lit a potholed road across marshy fields, a chainlink fence with a sentry box by the open gate. A notice on the gate said, THESE PREMISES PATROLLED – GATES CLOSE 12.00. Another, with less paint on it, said, POWNEY'S BOATBUILDERS MARINE ENG. Inside, the headlamp crossed piles of rubbish, a line of yellow dumper trucks standing under a crane which might have been going to load them into the rustbucket coaster slumped on the mud alongside the quay. Down the quay from the coaster, a group of masts stood tall against the dark sky, slashed by the huge, diagonal sprits of Thames barges. I heaved the bike on its stand and chained it to a mooring ring sunk in the stone of the quay. There were elder bushes growing in the cracks.

A light shone in my face. Someone said, 'Can I help you?' in an unhelpful voice.

I took off the helmet, looked away. The dazzle stopped. Behind the light was the dim shape of a thickset man in some sort of uniform cap and a tunic with silver buttons. I said, 'I'm looking for *Barbara Ann*.'

'Over there,' he said. The circle of light glided across black mud, found a floating jetty, followed its final twenty yards across a pool of inky water. At the end of the jetty, the beam rested on the cracked and blistered hull of a very old barge. 'What do you want?'

He had taken in the leather jacket and the uncut hair. I said, 'Visiting.'

He thought about that. Finally he said, 'Gates close in thirty minutes.'

'You'll let me out,' I said.

He said, 'Yessir,' in a ironic military voice. 'Careful of that jetty. Very slippery.' His footsteps crunched away across the littered gravel.

The smell of the mud rose thick and flatulent as I started down the jetty. The duckboards felt spongy underfoot, and the air was dank and chill. Behind me, the boats were a black huddle against the dirty red sky. A curlew howled its long, babbling cry, and rivulets of tide rustled in the mud. It was as if *Barbara Ann* had been isolated out here for reasons of age and disease.

A dim light burnt yellow in the barge's dark after end. I shouted, 'Hello!'

'Who's there?' said a voice. Its vowels were flat, Liverpudlian. Marie's voice. Last time I had heard it it had been strong and round. Now it seemed to involve too much breath, and a rough edge that might have been fear.

'Me.'

A flashlight beam nailed me. I could hear the whoosh of her breath. 'Come aboard, you.'

There was a wooden ladder nailed to the barge's side. Where my fingers touched the rail, I felt the slimy crumble of putrid timber. I said, 'Some boat.'

'Rotten,' she said.

We picked our way aft, down a deck littered with paintpots and old tyres. 'Mind the step,' she said.

68

The steps consisted of a painter's ladder with aluminium rungs, thrust into the ruins of a companionway. The cabin smelt muggy, nearly as evil as the Adelphi Hotel. There was a gas cooker, and a full-size sofa spewing damp stuffing, tucked up against a black pot-bellied stove. In the yellow glow of the paraffin lamp the bulkheads were poxy with bubbling paint.

'Not as nice as *Vixen*,' said Marie. She had recovered enough to be ashamed. 'Johnny's going to restore her.'

I nodded. *Barbara Ann* was going to be as easy to restore as a pile of wet firewood.

'Have a drink,' she said. She pulled a couple of tins of Special Brew out of a wood-grained locker, handed me one and sat down by the bunk. Her hair was lank and greasy, her skin a clammy grey-white the yellow lamplight could not warm. She sucked hard at her Special Brew. She said, 'How did you find me, then?'

'Dean left a message. Have you seen him?'

'Not for a couple of days.' Now she was over the fear she looked displeased, as if she was wondering what business it was of his.

'Whose boat?' I said.

'Bloke runs a scrapper,' she said. 'Met him in a pub before the Dutch trip. He'll never restore her, actually. But it's quiet.' The eyes under the heavy black brows flicked towards the hatch, returned to me. They were hiding something, those eyes.

I said, 'The Estonian. Dean said you knew him.'

'Lennart,' she said. 'Lennart Rebane. That was his name.'

'You were friendly.'

She pushed the hair away from her face. 'He was really nice,' she said. 'He wanted to talk. So did I. We went out in Amsterdam. Had a coffee. Went to a picture gallery. That's all.'

'I don't mind what you did,' I said. 'Have you got any idea why he would have been coming to see me?'

'He was crazy,' she said. 'When we was in Amsterdam he swam across one of them canals to pick me a flower.'

'So what was he up to . . . that night?'

She shrugged. 'He said he wanted to see me again. He said he wanted to meet you.'

I said, 'So why did he want to meet me?'

'He'd seen you on the telly. You did a film about Poland, right? He was dead keen on getting Russians and that out of Estonia. He said he liked what you said about Poland. He wanted to tell you about Estonia, get you to go there. That's what he said.'

I nodded, to give my head something to do. It was as clear as the mud on the tide. I said, 'Why did you run away?'

She looked straight at me, a little lamp-flame in each pupil. 'You spend six months in the nick,' she said. 'Then you try to sit still when the room starts filling up with busies.'

I thought of Dean on the run from security guards, his room in the Adelphi ransacked. I thought of Pinsley, searching *Vixen*. I thought of all the people who wanted Marie's address. I said, 'Rubbish.'

She rocked back on the sofa as if I had hit her. 'What do you mean?'

'Dean has had his head kicked in by people who were looking for something. Those people were looking for you, too. What were they after?'

'I don't know.'

I pulled my chair closer. I said, 'These are big, heavy people. They are not playing games. You can't stay here till the boat sinks.'

She looked at me. She saw someone who was fifteen years older than her; the authority figure. But she had been a watch leader on *Vixen*. She saw someone she had trusted, who had got her out of trouble before, and might again. She said, 'He gave me a parcel.'

'Who gave you a parcel?'

'Lennart. Lennart Rebane.'

The excitement started. It was a relic of the old Bill Tyrrell, that excitement. We were getting somewhere. I said, 'What was inside it?'

'I didn't open it.'

'Start at the beginning,' I said.

'It was in Amsterdam,' she said. 'He wanted me to bring it to England for him. He said if he had it on his own ship, someone would find it.'

'So you brought it.'

She nodded.

'Where is it?'

She said, 'I didn't like having it. I told Dean about it. He said he'd look after it.'

The security men had come and searched Dean's squat. They had tried to kick Marie's address out of him. I said, 'Has anybody come looking for this parcel?'

She shook her head. 'Nobody knows where I am.'

'Except Dean.'

'Except Dean.'

'So this Lennart Rebane was coming to see me. And to pick up the parcel. And to see you.'

She nodded.

'And he didn't say anything about what was inside it?'

'He said it was important. That's all.'

'Drugs?'

She shook her head. 'Not big enough. Too light.' Marie knew all about drugs. 'It was little, smaller than a packet of fags. All done up in tape and brown paper. Anyway, I asked him. I don't like all that stuff. Not any more.' She was looking at me, now. She said, 'It's like a bloody terrible dream. Dean says I ought to be frightened. So I'm frightened. But I don't know what of.'

I said, 'Go to the police.'

There were tears on her face, glittering in the dirty yellow glow of the lamplight.

I said, 'They can't hurt you.'

'They can always hurt you.'

I said, 'I'm going to Finland in *Vixen*. I need a watch leader. Can you come?'

Her face changed as if someone had turned a light on inside it.

'Police first,' I said. 'Volunteer to make a statement. Then come down to Fleet on the train.'

'Yeah,' she said.

'Tomorrow morning,' I said. I got up, shoved five ten-pound notes into her hand.

She stood on tiptoes and kissed me on the cheek. 'Thanks, Bill.'

'Get a taxi to the station,' I said. 'Welcome aboard.'

I slung my leather jacket over my shoulder, went up the ladder out of the rotting cabin and into the mixture of mud and sulphur that passed for night air.

The tide had risen. The jetty was a matt black line across the water. I walked up the ramp on to the quay, and turned to look back. The sky had cleared. There was a fingernail of moon up there, balanced like a canoe shooting rapids. Under the black-and-silver sky the river shone with a faint, metallic gleam. *Barbara Ann* was the clumsy black cross of a spidery T. The yellow glow from the cabin light had gone; Marie would be curled up in the grubby sleeping bag on the bunk, staring into the dark, thinking about dead Estonians, and a white-tiled police station in the morning.

And a parcel. I did not like the sound of parcels that Estonians gave ex-junkies in Amsterdam.

The thick heat of the night had passed with the blanket of cloud. I found that I was shivering. I shrugged into my leather jacket, turned away, walked to where I had left the Norton.

The Norton was gone.

I shut my eyes, opened them again.

The Norton was still gone. Moonlight glinted on the ring-bolt and the severed links of chain.

Thirteen years, I had had the Norton. I had wheedled parts out of back-street shops from Peterhead to Penzance, spent hundreds of hours in the shed getting it just right.

And some bastard had come down to Powney's bloody marine graveyard, and wheeled it away.

The gates were open. The sentry box stood silhouetted against the red glow of the horizon. Where had the security guards been?

I started across to ask questions. The sentry box was empty. I walked down to the knot of barges. They were dark and dead. Water gurgled sullenly in the crevices of their hulls.

I shouted, waited for an answer. No reply. I walked the other way, into the heaps of aggregate and piles of scrap metal that made a mountain range between me and the water, looking for a hut where they would be sitting drinking their tea, waiting to tell me it was all a horrible mistake.

It was a maze of rubbish, back there. I blundered round in the dark for what must have been ten minutes. There was no hut. There were no guards. There was only silence, broken by the yodel of curlews.

A starter motor coughed. A car was reversing out of a parking slot between two derelict workboats. After the moonlight, its headlights were dazzlingly bright. They lit a pile of rubbish. I started to run, to catch it before it turned away.

The lights did not turn away. They turned towards me.

My Norton. Thirteen years out of the junkheap behind the transport café. The guard must have seen something, I was thinking. Of all the places to get a bike stolen –

The car's engine roared. Its tyres spat gravel. The lights leaped straight at me.

I jumped backwards. My heel hit something. I went down hard on my back in a pile of stones. I rolled sideways, off the pile and into the headlights. Drunken bastard, I thought, with a mind still half on the bike. Careless idiot.

The car reversed. The blazing white eyes of the headlights came at me again.

And I knew like a bucket of water in the face that whoever was driving it was being the opposite of careless.

I started to shout, then. I should have saved my breath. Dazzled, I stumbled over something else in the dark. This time I hit my head a crack that made it ring. I found I was on the granite coping of the quay. The car lights had gone out. Big red suns floated in my retinas. The rubbish on the quay was a series of blacked-out lumps. Somewhere, a car engine ticked as it cooled.

The breath roared in my chest, and my ears rang. There was no other sound.

But there was light.

Out of the corner of my eye, I saw a yellow-orange pinprick. It was at the end of the jetty, at the aft end of the dark lump that was *Barbara Ann*.

Fire.

I started to shout. I got my mouth open, but that was as far as I got.

Something hit the back of my head. It hit it so hard that I

73

knew it was going to come off the neck. The orange glow out there on the boat spread all around the inside of my skull, and my legs turned to water and pitched me forward. I knew I was going to hurt my face on the stones, but there was nothing I could do to break the fall, because my arms would not work.

I landed with a bang. Feet scuffed grit near my head. I could hear breathing, hoarse and heavy. There was a grunt. Something hit me again. Pain exploded in my neck and the hinge of my jaw. Hands were fumbling in my pockets. I tried to roll over, but I could not move. Something landed on my head. It smelt of leather. Crash helmet. My crash helmet. Then the hands picked me up, pulled me to my feet. I could not see. Blind, I was thinking. I could hear my breathing. The visor was open. Vaguely I knew I was being walked, but I could not tell where. There was a grunt in my ear, and the hands let go. I was falling.

Something slapped my face hard, and yielded. Something flowed into the hole in the front of the helmet, and around my face. For a moment I knew I had fallen off the quay and face down into the mud.

Then I did not care what I had fallen into, because I needed to breathe. But I could not breathe, because there was no power in my neck, and the helmet kept my face pressed down into the stuff, and it was flowing into my mouth and my nose.

I tried to pull my head up. But my ears were roaring, and my neck was a patch of agony, and it would not come. So I had to lie there, face down in the mud. And I could not breathe.

In the part of me that was still conscious, a voice was howling with panic, telling me to struggle, and kick, and get out. *Breathe*, howled the voice. I breathed. Mud flowed instead of air, gritting between my teeth and in my throat. Somewhere, my chest struggled and jerked. Red light in my eyes.

Fade to black.

8

My head was a billet of white-hot steel, slung from a crane, glowing and pulsing. Pain roared into my throat with every pulse. There were hammers at my ribs, trying to shape the metal, forge it the way they wanted it. I did not want it shaped. What I wanted was for the crane to let go, drop the hot block into cool black water.

The prospect was so delightful it made the saliva flow. The saliva tasted gritty and foul.

The hammer started again. This time it hit me below the ribs. What air was left in my lungs rushed up and out like the charge of a cannon. Something went with it; something that tasted like mud. New air flowed in.

'Come,' said a woman's voice.

I opened my mouth, tasted rotten wood. I opened my eyes. It was dark.

'Quickly,' said the voice. Hands tugged at the shoulder of my coat. The head banged disgustingly as I struggled on to hands and knees. I gasped for breath. There was a big orange light at the end of the jetty. I knew it was a jetty, and I knew the orange light was no good.

'Up.' The hands were strong. My legs buckled as I rose. There were old boats, lit with jumping flames reflected in water.

The strong hands dragged me to a quay. Somewhere, people were shouting. There were sirens. The woman with the voice had hair that shone gold in the flames. The light caught a straight nose and a round, determined chin. They reminded me of Greek sculpture.

Then I was in a car. The engine was roaring. My head rolled on my shoulders. It would not stay still. The horizon formed a perfect circle with a vortex at its centre. I fell into the vortex and was sick, partly out of the window. I tried to apologize, but my voice did not seem to be working.

There was a radio, tuned to a foreign station. The night became a long, revolting dream. Streetlights tore red and silver stripes in a blood-red sky. I was sick again. The road developed bends that threw me around in my seatbelt. I could still see the black metal water, and the big orange flower blooming from the hulk at the end of the jetty. It had been *Barbara Ann. Barbara Ann* had been burning. I started to sweat. Oh, no, I thought. Oh, bloody hell, no. I said, 'Did she get out?' It came out as a whisper, because my throat was raw with mud.

The woman in the driver's seat said, 'Nobody got out.' Her voice sounded American, but not American. Marie, I thought. Marie. The name rang like a clapper of a big bell.

Then there was another phase, in which I might have been asleep. The next thing I knew, she said, 'Have you any money?'

I pulled out my wallet and gave her a handful of notes in fingers that felt like frankfurters.

There was a kid in oily dungarees, face lard-white and grease-black in the fluorescent lights of a garage forecourt. A blonde woman was giving him money. Her shoulders were straight and square in a blue jacket. She climbed into the car. A faint waft of perfume penetrated the mud in my nostrils. To the best of my recollection, I had never seen her in my life. I said, 'Who are you?'

'This is not important,' she said, and turned her Greek-sculpture profile to me, looking at the road.

Then I passed out in good earnest.

Next thing I knew, there were bumps, and sky outside the car window, blue as ink. It looked paler at the bottom than the top. Dawn. The car began to bounce on its springs. The bouncing hurt my head. Little luminous specks sailed in the sky. My brain was producing the specks. But it was not my brain that was producing the other things standing against the sky. Masts. The masts of sailing boats. One in particular: tall, double spreaders, new port lower shroud.

I struggled upright in my seat. My clothes were covered in mud, and my head was red-hot. 'Who the hell are you?' I said.

Because the mast belonged to *Vixen*.

She ran her hands through her hair, stretched, eyes closed. She said, 'If you have the key to your boat, you should get in your bunk.'

Dried mud fell off me in clods as I struggled out of the door. Fleet Basin, cool and fresh with the dawn, spun round my head like a plate on a stick. The strange woman took me by the arm, and led me over *Vixen*'s rail, and down the companionway, and into my bunk.

'Now,' she said, 'have you coffee?' She asked the question as if coffee was somehow rare and strange, like frankincense.

'In the galley,' I said.

I went to sleep. When I woke up, my head was thumping like a badly oiled steam engine, but I knew where I was and who I was. The bulkhead clock said two-thirty. Sun was pouring through the porthole. I kicked off the duvet, and swung my feet on to the deck. The jar nearly took my head off.

As the pain subsided, I thought: Marie is dead. It settled on me like a lead blanket. Marie, who had beaten smack. Burned alive on a rotten dock.

Clinging on to the grabrails for support, I navigated into the head. The face in the mirror on the door had dark red eyeballs and ivory-coloured skin. The hair was matted with mud, and there were mud-coloured bags under the eyes. I did some work with flannel and brush, and lurched into the saloon.

The woman I did not know was sitting at the table, polishing the enamel Nazi eagle on the sextant my father had acquired from the captain of a U-boat at the end of the war. She looked up at me and smiled. It was the smile of a child in a toyshop. 'Are you well?' she said.

77

I sat down, carefully. I said, 'Who are you?'

She said, 'Nadia Vuorinen.' She put out her hand. It was narrow, with long, elegant fingers, strong and brown. I shook it, with a strong sense of unreality. Last night's clothes were lying in a pile on the skylight. Suddenly there was the taste of mud in my mouth, the panic that I could not breathe. I said, 'Thank you for what you did.'

She shrugged. The smile had gone. Her face was still and serious. The skin was tanned, the cheekbones high. Her yellow-brown eyes had a Slavic tilt. She said, 'I saw that you were in the mud, so I pulled you out. You were choking, so I performed the Heimlich manoeuvre.'

I said, 'How the hell did you know where I live?'

Her face was a golden mask. She said, 'Maybe you told me. I don't remember.'

Last night was a collection of jumbled fragments. This morning was not much better. But I had a memory of surprise at seeing *Vixen*'s mast against the indigo sky. I was nearly sure I had not told her.

She got up. 'I will make some coffee.'

She went into the galley. She was wearing a little blue jersey, with buttons up the front, and an odd, old-fashioned collar. Her skirt was longer than was fashionable; her legs were bare, and her flat-heeled brogues looked much newer than the rest. There was something wrong with the whole effect, but my head was hurting too much for me to work out what. I rested it on the buttoned leather, and shut my eyes.

I was on the quay. I could see the orange glow on the boat. There was pain, the helmet. And the fingers, fumbling in my pockets. Then the mud.

It was the fingers I remembered. The fingers, and what Marie had said. A parcel. A little parcel. Smaller than a packet of cigarettes.

The woman came back with a cup of coffee, left me alone again. She made good coffee.

I pulled myself upright and took the telephone out of the locker. Directory enquiries gave me Powney's number. It rang a long time. I could almost smell the place; mud, and the

78

ashes of *Barbara Ann*, and no hope at all. Thinking about it made me think about Marie, which made me want to weep.

A voice answered. It had a strong Kent accent, and sounded none too bright. I said, 'I want to speak to the security man on duty last night.'

'Security man?' said the voice. 'What do you mean, security man?'

'There was a security man on duty last night,' I said. 'At eleven-thirty.'

'No security men here.'

I said, 'Just give me the name of the firm, and I'll check myself.'

'Werl,' said the voice. 'Guv'nor took them off two weeks ago. Blue Van Patrol, they was called. Reckoned there was nothing in the yard to bleeding nick.'

'Have you got their number?'

He read it to me laboriously. I dialled.

'Yes,' said a more intelligent voice. 'I know Powney's.'

'I'd like to speak to someone from your patrol.'

'No patrol at Powney's,' said the voice. 'Not since two weeks ago.'

Something very cold was crawling up my back and bringing out goose pimples on my shoulders. I said, 'Who took over?'

'I drove past last night,' said the voice. 'Whole place is wide open. They've still got the notices up. But there's no security at all.'

I said, 'I met a security man there.'

'Well,' said the voice. 'Whoever he was, he wasn't being paid by Powney's. Anything else I can do for you?'

I put the telephone down.

The woman came back in.

I said, 'You must have been on the quay last night.'

She said, 'Yes. I was.'

'What did you see?'

'I heard a noise,' she said. 'A splash. And you were with your face in the mud. So I pulled you out.'

'Did you see anyone else?'

'There was a car,' she said.

'Did you see what kind?'

'You were with your face in the mud. You had not very much time. So I did not go to look at the car.' She sat on the settee, hands folded. As if she pulled drowning men out of the river every day of her life.

I said, 'Thank you very much.'

She said, 'It was not a problem.' Again, there was that matter-of-fact competence about her. And it struck me that she must be enormously strong, to pull a prostrate body out of the mud, kick the breath back into it, haul it on to a jetty. 'I have been taught this,' she said. 'First aid.'

'Where?'

'In my country. In Estonia.' She watched me calmly, as if she was an anthropologist observing the reaction of a member of a primitive tribe.

'So what are you doing in England?'

'I am enquiring about the death of Lennart Rebane, of course.' Her eyebrows had risen a couple of millimetres. What else did you expect? they said.

'And how did you find Marie?'

She smiled, her bland, golden smile. She said, 'Have I saved a policeman?'

'If you knew about Marie Clarke, you know who I am.'

'Bill Tyrrell,' she said. 'A nice guy. Your crews admire you.' No sarcasm, no enthusiasm. She was repeating someone else's judgement.

'Who told you all this?'

'Marie Clarke made a telephone call to Lennart's mother. She told her many things. I think Marie did not have a mother of her own. Lennart's mother is a friend of mine.'

'So how did you know where I live?'

The smile became a notch brighter. 'You told me,' she said.

Sand or no sand, last night was becoming clearer in my mind. I knew I had not told her.

A car's engine sounded outside. She got up, stood on the settee in her bare feet, looked out of the skylight. Her legs, I could not help noticing, were very pretty. 'Excuse me,' she said. She went forward, into the girls' cabin, and quietly shut the door.

The boat rocked. Leather soles ground the deck. A voice said, 'Anybody home?'

Detective-Inspector Nelligan and another man came down the companionway. Nelligan was wearing a powder-blue safari suit. His companion had an anorak and black moustache.

'This is D-S Coombs,' said Nelligan, pulling a packet of John Player Specials from his breast pocket. 'Got a minute for a chat?' He sat there looking keen, and earnest, and appreciative of his surroundings.

I focused on him as best I could. 'Of course,' I said. My voice felt strange and thick.

'Had another call from Medway,' he said. 'They found a motorbike, registered in your name.'

'Oh?' I said. 'Where?'

'In some mud,' said Nelligan. 'End of a quay. Place called Powney's.' He frowned at me. 'You feeling rough?'

The gears in my head ground so loudly I was surprised he could not hear them. The woman was in the girls' cabin. Perhaps she did not want to see the police. I did not want to see the police either. The gears kept grinding. Hide the cards until you can see the pattern of the game. Keep it going. If you let anyone in, heads will go down and the game will go dead.

Like Marie.

Be reasonable, I told myself. It's not your business any more. Tell this man Nelligan what you know.

But the gears ground on.

I said, 'I was on the bike when it went off the quay.' The lie tasted flat and tired in my mouth.

His eyebrows made black arches on his pale forehead. 'Oh?'

'I went down to see a girl called Marie. One of my crew. She lives on a barge. I was asking her to make a statement to your colleagues.' That was true enough. 'I was meeting a friend there.' Sorry, Marie, I thought. All in a good cause. 'And on the way back I started up, took a skid, drove the bike off the quay. So my friend gave me a lift home.'

Nelligan was writing. He looked up from his book. He said, 'Read your papers this morning?'

I shook my head, gently, so my eyes would not fall out.

'Bad news about your friend Marie Clarke.'

'What?'

'Her barge burned out. I'm afraid she was inside it.'

'My God.'

'She had an oil lamp, it seems. We think she dropped it.' He paused. 'Did you have a drink with Miss Clarke?'

'Can of beer,' I said.

'Did she have a drink?'

'Yes.'

Nelligan said, 'You could have informed us as to her whereabouts.'

I said, 'She trusted me. I wanted her to come of her own free will. She was an ex-junkie. She didn't like policemen.'

Detective-Sergeant Coombs said, 'Not so ex.'

I stared at him. He stared back aggressively from under his thick brow-ridge. I said, 'What are you talking about?'

Nelligan cleared his throat soothingly, stubbed his cigarette out in a saucer. 'She was a junkie.'

I said, 'That was two years ago. She'd cleaned herself up. Completely.'

Nelligan said, 'When they did the post-mortem, there was a bit of alcohol in her blood. But there was enough heroin for the spoon to stand up.'

My ears were ringing, and the gears of my mind were suddenly made of rubber.

'But you don't know anything about that.' Coombs' voice was hard. His eyes looked like half-sucked aniseed balls.

Nelligan frowned, at him this time.

I said, 'No.' I had been ashore, wandering in the hill of rubbish behind the quay, looking for a security guard, to complain about my bike being stolen. While out on the end of the jetty, in *Barbara Ann*'s filthy cabin, someone was doing it. They would have knocked her down first. Then they would have tied up her arm, so the veins came up blue. She had showed me, once: the silver scars, like a shoal of tiny fish swimming up the white skin of her forearm. The needle going in, and the plunger. Marie on the deck, limp as a doll. Shadows flying as the lamp swung. The reek of paraffin soaking into the overstuffed sofa. And the dirty yellow flames, licking.

I hoped she had not known anything about it.

I realized my head was in my hands. When I looked up, Nelligan and Coombs were a blur.

Nelligan got up. 'There'll be another inquest. We'll take a statement later.' He paused, looked across at Coombs, a little shamefaced. 'By the way,' he said. 'I used to enjoy seeing you on the telly.'

I twisted my face into something I hoped was a smile. Their footsteps receded up the companionway.

I laid my forehead on the cool mahogany of the table. It got worse. I staggered into the head, and was sick.

It lasted a long time, the sickness. I had very little idea how long, because I was delirious. Somebody kept bringing me soup. The person looked a lot like the woman Nadia Vuorinen. But I was not sure it was her, because I was not sure she even existed. The only thing I was sure about was a nightmare. In the nightmare I was face down in the mud, and somebody was standing on the back of my head, and I could not breathe. And when I wanted to yell, I could not, because of the mud. It was a very hard nightmare to wake up from.

But after what might have been a couple of days, I did wake up. I stumbled into the saloon.

The skylight was open. Warm breeze was pouring in, full of the herbal smells of the marsh. Someone had filled a bowl with red roses, and put it beside the pile of letters in the middle of the table. A note in a neat foreign-looking script said *I am in Shop*.

Outside, there was the ripple of water, the shouts of a couple of children playing in a boat. Summer in the Basin. But there was no summer aboard *Vixen*.

I pulled out *Vixen*'s crew book. There were contact addresses for everyone who had sailed in her. I found Clarke, Marie, and dialled the number in Liverpool. A woman's voice answered.

I said, 'Mrs Clarke?'

'It's Beth. Her sister.' The voice was thick Irish, as if it had been crying. 'Margaret's not very well.'

'No,' I said. 'I suppose not.'

She said, 'Are you the police?'

I said, 'A friend of Marie's.'

The voice changed. 'Dirty no-good things.' The thickness was drink, instead of grief. 'The funeral's Thursday, if you're interested.'

The anger in the voice brought it home as nothing else had. No more Marie. Guilt flooded through me. Twenty minutes longer, I thought, and perhaps I would not have been making this telephone call. I said, 'It's a terrible thing.'

The woman at the other end sniffed contemptuously.

I said, 'I'm sorry to trouble you at a time like this. But I'm looking for a Dean Eliot. A friend of hers.'

'We don't know any such person,' she said. 'You could try the gutter.' The telephone went down with a bang.

I disconnected my end. The saloon was full of winter. Poor Marie.

I tipped coffee into the tin pot, and started on the pile of letters.

The one I opened first was on thick cream paper, with the Youth Venture galleon sailing across its wavy blue sea, and the letters after the other Trustees' names filling two lines of type under the address.

Dear Bill,

A recent meeting of the Trustees has come to a conclusion that I fear you will find disagreeable.

As I am sure you are aware, there has been much concern over certain events connected with *Vixen* while under charter to the Trust. The tragic death of the Estonian Naval cadet Lennart Rebane was, of course, an accident, and accidents do happen, particularly in the world of sail training. But it is important to minimize such occurrences.

One means of doing this is to observe rigorous standards of safety, and hence discipline. This the Trustees feel you have failed to do. Furthermore, the facts of the case have been widely publicized, to the detriment of the Trust's good name. Your presence at the inquest will only serve further to publicize these regrettable events.

We have therefore decided that the Trust must revoke its charter of *Vixen* under the machinery provided for by our agreement, as from the date of this letter.

It was signed with Dickie's neat Naval scrawl.

I read it twice. The ideas in it were not complicated. Nor were they unexpected. But I thought of the way Marie's face had lit up at the idea of coming back aboard. And I thought of the eight kids who were meant to be coming to Finland in a fortnight. Dickie would never get hold of a substitute for *Vixen* in the time. So they would kick their heels in hot concrete boxes, instead of getting the chance Marie had had.

My crime was not carrying drunken delinquents. It was carrying drunken delinquents close to a Cabinet Minister, and getting them into the news. What was at stake was Youth Venture's good name, second. First, in Dickie's mind, was Dickie's knighthood.

I poured another cup of coffee. Nadia Vuorinen came down the companionway, carrying a box of groceries. Her eyes were not so much brown as amber. They had a disconcerting tendency to look right into you, as if you were made of glass. She said, 'You feel better?'

'Yes,' I said. Without Youth Venture's charters, Bill Tyrrell was no better than a boat bum. Thanks to Christopher, he would soon be a boat bum without a boat. 'Have you made progress with your enquiries?'

'Enquiries?'

'Into the death of Lennart Rebane?'

She shrugged. 'Sure,' she said. I got the impression she thought the question scarcely worth answering.

I said, 'It was very kind of you to stay and look after me.'

She smiled. There was a surprising amount of warmth in the smile. 'It is better than a hotel,' she said. 'I have never lived on a boat before.' Again there was the flash of glee I remembered from the first time she had asked for coffee; a childlike excitement that made you want to reach out and hug her. She would be no problem to hug.

Easy, Tyrrell, I thought. There are questions round this woman like moths round a lamp. I said, 'What were you doing at Powney's?'

She said, 'I was going to see Marie.'

I said, 'One evening. I visit Marie. You visit Marie. Someone else visits Marie, and kills her.' I watched her face.

There was no surprise. She had been listening at the cabin door when Detective-Inspector Nelligan had visited. 'A lot of visitors, for one evening. Big coincidence.'

'No,' she said. 'Not a coincidence.'

I stared at her. 'What do you mean?'

'Someone was waiting for you,' she said. 'In the car that attacked you. A man in uniform.'

'How do you know?'

She shrugged. 'I was watching.' Her face had become blank, a smiling gold mask.

'Why?'

She said, 'Curiosity.'

'Based on what?'

'Curiosity.'

We were not getting anywhere. I said, 'I never told you how to get to *Vixen*.'

She said, 'Oh? I thought you had. Now I must take a swim, it is so pretty.' The face became eager again. 'Please can I stay longer?'

'Of course,' I said. I wanted to keep her where I could ask questions again, in new ways, until I got answers. And I wanted to see that excitement on her face again, because it was beautiful.

She came back through the hatch wearing a one-piece bathing suit of some shiny material. The muscles slid under the gold-brown skin. Her body looked firm and elastic, as if she was an athlete. I watched her walk up the companionway, heard the splash as she dived in. I wanted to go up there into the sun, swim with this beautiful woman in the cool black Basin.

Instead, I picked up the phone and dialled Otto Campbell.

A horsey woman's voice answered. 'He's up a mountain with the Sales Force of Aprochemical,' she said. 'Oh no. Here he comes.'

He said, 'Where the hell have you been? I've been trying to telephone you.'

'Tell you later,' I said. 'Can we talk?'

'Too right,' he said. 'What about, in particular?'

'Youth Venture. Dickie Wilson.'

He said, 'Dickie's been going mad.'

'He's sacked me,' I said. 'Politicians are putting the pressure on him and I want to know why. I'm going to have to sell the boat.'

Otto said, 'I think I might just be able to straighten you out.' His voice dropped, became confidential. 'Not over the telephone, though. Can you get up here?'

'Tomorrow evening.'

'Good,' he said. 'I'll fill you in, and you can give me a day's work, in exchange. Got a chap down with flu.'

I put the telephone down. I pulled out the account books and the log, and made some notes for the maintenance schedule, trying to pretend that none of this was happening.

I heard the creak as Nadia pulled herself up on the bobstay, the slam of the forehatch as she padded below. The door opened. She had a towel wrapped around her breasts. She said, 'I heard your telephone call. You must sell this boat?'

I did not know her. For all I knew, she had killed Marie. 'No,' I said. 'I'm not going to sell it.'

The hatch rattled. A voice said, 'Oh, yes, you bloody well are.' A pair of brown legs came down the companionway. Claudia's legs. She said, 'God, it smells like a tart's boudoir.' Her dark-fringed grey eyes started an auctioneer's walk round the cabin. They checked the roses, the polished table, finding fault. They settled on Nadia. The lower lip was out. There was another smell in the saloon, besides the roses. Claudia had been drinking. She said, 'And I suppose this is the tart.'

Claudia was a deeply tolerant human being, but only when confronted with things she could tolerate. I knew that she had been listening at the skylight. And what she could not tolerate was a strange woman advising me not to make a sale.

Nadia said, 'What is tart?'

Claudia ignored her. 'I've been in the pub,' she said, unnecessarily. 'I was watching. She's been sunbathing on deck. Starkers. Nice tits, I grant you.' Her eyes were narrow with rage. 'Good legs. Terrific screw, I should think. Like me.'

I found I was staring at her with my mouth open.

'Pratting about,' she said. 'I turn my back for one minute and the place is crawling with floozies and you're not selling your boat. You're a *bastard*.'

I was gaining control of my faculties. Claudia emotionally involved was not convincing. Claudia jealous was. She had been sitting over there drinking herself into a frenzy of righteous indignation. Now, the church doorstep lip was all the way out.

Nadia said again, 'What is tart?'

Claudia swung the lip at her. She said, 'Who the hell are you?'

'A visitor,' said Nadia. She was still smiling, but her eyes had a detached look, as if none of it had anything to do with her.

'Visitor with a suitcase.' I had never seen her this angry. 'Christ,' she said. 'Roses.' Before I could move, she had picked the bowl off the table and dumped the flowers in the gash bin in the galley.

Nadia stood up. I stood up. I said, 'Behave yourself.'

Claudia was supporting herself on the galley stove, half crying with rage. 'Knickers drying all over the bloody rigging; naked tarts wriggling around on deck. And she's dusting and sweeping for you as well. It must be bloody love.' She pulled open a locker, hooked her fingers and tore the contents out and on to the deck with a splintering crash.

The flour jar hit the deck like a bomb, covering the planking with a white cloud. A smaller container, perhaps a carton of pepper, bounced into the brush locker under the stove.

Nadia said, 'Stop this.'

Claudia said, 'Nobody treats me like this.'

I said, 'Come on deck.'

She sat down on the settee, folded her arms. 'I'm not moving.'

'All right,' I said. 'I'll say it here. Your Mr Pinsley made a search, not a survey of my boat. I'd like to know why, and what for?'

She said, 'Rubbish.'

I said, 'I'll be visiting. I'll ask him.' She was cooling down. She knew she had made a fool of herself. She did not know what to do next, so she would act stubborn. I said, 'I should go back to your office and have a cold shower. Then I'll ask you again.'

'You *shit*,' she said.

'I think you'd better go.'

She did not move.

Nadia said, 'All right. Now you go.'

Whatever Claudia had been going to say turned into a wail of pain and shock as Nadia shoved her right arm up between her shoulder-blades and propelled her violently towards the companionway. Claudia was shouting, Nadia grimly silent.

By the time I got up the steps, Claudia was lying in a spraddle of legs on the quay, and Nadia was standing at *Vixen*'s rail, sucking a scratch in her left hand. Claudia raised her head and looked at me for a moment with death-ray eyes. Then she scrambled to her feet, brushed grit off her skirt, and stalked away down the side of the Basin.

Suddenly, I felt intensely sorry for her. I had assumed that she saw me as an unusually active form of hot-water bottle. Perhaps there had been more to it than that.

I jumped over the side and ran after her.

She said, 'As far as I'm concerned everybody's right, and you're nothing but a bloody liability.'

Her skin was polished with rage, hard white marble with red lips and cheekbones.

In the car park, a car's engine whirred. It was a red Cavalier. The woman driving it was Nadia. She turned to look at me. There was no expression on her face. There was a white smudge on her blue jacket. She raised the fingers of her right hand in a small, economical wave. Then the wheels kicked dust out of the hardcore, and she was accelerating violently down the marsh road.

The van was in the shed, and the key was on *Vixen*. I would never catch her.

I said to Claudia, 'Lend me your car.'

'Certainly not,' she said.

The key was in her hand. The hand went behind her back. We stood there, furious. 'Please,' I said.

'Break my arm, then,' she said. Her teeth were bared. I could feel the heat of her breath on my face. 'Make like your lady friend.'

The whirr of the Cavalier's engine vanished behind the

clang of halyards and the sigh of the wind in the grasses on the marsh.

Claudia smiled, a mean stretch of her face. 'Looks like you're on your own,' she said. 'Look at our Billy, the only one in step.' She walked to her red Alfa, swinging her hips.

I turned away from that mess, trudged back to the mess aboard *Vixen*.

I filled the gash bin with broken jars. There had been plenty of casual affairs; but it is not easy to construct a solid home life when at any minute the telephone can fire you off to the far end of the planet. So I had shot for a new, simpler life. I had given up the job. Now I had lost Youth Venture, and Claudia, and it looked as if I would lose *Vixen*.

As I grovelled on the deck with the dustpan and brush, I felt an acute sense of loss. Not for Claudia, or Youth Venture, or even *Vixen*. What kept coming up before my eyes was the smile that lit the face of Nadia.

I went over the floor twice for glass splinters, because there are a lot of bare feet belowdecks at sea. The blood banged in my head. Finally, I lay flat on the deck and groped for the pepper carton under the stove.

The brush locker under the stove is one of *Vixen*'s many awkward crannies. It is a slot a little wider than a letterbox, and perhaps three times as long. I pulled out the brushes and fetched a flashlight from the chart table. Its beam lit planking. There was no carton.

I gave the beam a final sweep. Wedged in a corner was a small cylinder. I raked it out with my fingers. It was a film can, dusted with white powder. Flour.

My mouth was suddenly dry. I rested my back against the cooker, and looked at the film can, and let it tell me stories.

Vixen did not carry pepper or anything else in film cans. George Krukas, who had taken photographs of Cambodia while I wrote the words, used to carry most of his luggage in old film cans. I do not take photographs, so film cans had no place in my life. But it had been the film can that had jumped out of the locker when Claudia had raked out the contents.

During the past few hours I had gone all the way to the back of the locker. There had been no film can then.

Unless, of course, it had been in the flour jar. And if it had been in the flour jar, that would have been because somebody had hidden it there.

I thought of the tap and knock of Pinsley the surveyor, making his search. I had interrupted him in the galley. He had failed to go through the flour jar.

A parcel, Marie had said. *Smaller than a packet of fags.*

About the size of a film can?

Lennart Rebane had given it to Marie, for safekeeping. Marie had given it to Dean. Rebane was dead. Dean had come down to *Vixen* after he had been in trouble with security men. He had promised to stay, then left in a hurry. He had left the film can behind. Very soon after that, someone had ripped his squat apart, looking for something. Then someone had killed Marie. And tried to kill me.

Security men.

Nadia Vuorinen had picked me up on the quay at Powney's. She had brought me home. She had wormed her way into my life. I remembered the white smudge on her jacket. She must have found the can in the flour jar, and now she had gone off with whatever had been inside it. I had no right to feel betrayed. But I felt betrayed anyway.

I rolled the can in my fingers. It was grey plastic, with a faint chemical smell. People like Dean used film cans as stash boxes for their dope. Not this one though. This one smelt of film.

Suddenly I felt an intense urge to talk to Dean, while he was still alive.

While I was still alive.

9

The Norton came back from Medway on a lorry. It needed a month's work, so I set off for Otto's in the van. I was pleased to be on the open road, moving. Whoever had dropped me in the mud at Powney's might not have cared whether he killed me or not. But it would be unwise to bank on the fact that he would not try again.

At four o'clock in the afternoon, the black cliffs of Cader Idris were trailing rags of cloud above and to the left. At half past, I swung the wheel under an arched sign, gold on forest green, that said LEADERSHIP CENTRE. The track was less elegant than the sign; by the look of its water-polished boulders, it did double duty as a stream in the winter. It climbed tortuously between sullen pine woods, and terminated in a flat grit clearing with buildings on three sides. At the centre was a small grey farmhouse with a long, institutional-looking clapboard wing. The sky was the colour of cement. A group of men in grey tracksuits was jogging across the yard. They looked flushed and overweight, as grim as the sky. Behind them, wearing a blue jersey with canvas reinforcements at the shoulders and elbows, camouflage trousers and mountain boots, was Otto Campbell.

As usual, he looked as if he had been woven out of rawhide and whipcord. 'Get a shower,' he said to the men. 'See you in the morning room, ten minutes.'

They shuffled into a door in the wing. 'First day,' he said. 'Three-mile run. Taking it easy.' He was not even panting.

'Who are they?' I said.

'Sales director and area managers of Globe Industrial,' he said. 'Let's get a cup of tea.'

He lived in the grey stone farmhouse. The ground floor walls had been knocked out. There was a long refectory table with benches, a Jotul wood burner, and a couple of kitchen units down at the end. Otto had told me years ago, when he had been a soldier and I had been a journalist pumping him for information, that the happiest time of his life had been three months spent in a pine-branch shelter in the Yukon. He would have been right at home in old Sparta. At the same time, he was completely relaxed about living virtually without privacy. It did not occur to him that there was anything odd about sharing his living quarters with half-a-dozen businessmen bickering with exhaustion and terror. There was a fit-looking, dark-haired man and a big-faced, broad-shouldered girl by the stove, wearing jeans and jerseys and heavy boots: instructors. Otto's only personal space was a tiny bedroom-cum-office upstairs, about as comfortable as a badger's sett, looking out over Cader Idris.

We went up. There was a small, tidy desk, an iron bedstead, two armchairs and a wood stove. On the walls were black-and-white group photographs: Otto in his regiment, Otto aboard *Wilma* with a bunch of sail trainees, Otto at school, with a rugby ball and a tight, self-confident grin. There was a photograph of a woman, a demure, long-nosed British face, blond hair done up in a black velvet bow. That was Melissa. Anybody but Otto would have spotted that the demureness had been entirely superficial. She had spent his gratuity and run off to Wentworth with the managing director of Dubai Filling Stations two years ago. Apart from Melissa, it was the room of a man who was either a schoolboy or a schoolmaster. Out there, someone was setting fire to boats, and dropping people in the mud. In here, you were safe with Otto. It was impossible not to feel safe with Otto. That was what made him so good at what he did.

He made dark and violent tea. There was no whisky before seven o'clock, ever. 'Better,' he said. He tilted his hard chair back on its legs and closed his eyes. His face was lean and hawklike, seamed with deep lines. He had hardly changed in the ten years I had known him. He was one of the younger sons of an Ayrshire farmer who came from a long line of Ayrshire farmers. Unlike most farmers, he came straight to the point.

'What's eating you?'

'Youth Venture's cancelled my contract.'

'Oh.' He fingered his chin. 'Is that bad?'

'No kids. No money. No boat.'

He said, 'Nasty.'

I said, 'You had something to tell me.'

Otto was not just your average retired soldier, into all forms of hard man's fun. He had done service with the Sultan of Oman, and guarded the skins of other potentates less easy to identify: politicians, dealers, bagmen. He had spent time in the shadowy areas where violent people do the dirty work of democratically elected governments. When I had met him, he had just presided over a deal that had led to Youth Venture's acquiring *Wilma* from a harbour in Guadeloupe, as a gesture of gratitude from a French general for services rendered.

What those services were I had never properly discovered, since Otto was pathologically discreet. We had become good friends almost immediately, and he had persuaded me to take *Vixen* to work for Youth Venture. We had sailed together, and worked together. I liked him, despite his discretion. He had been back on the other side of the fence for years now, but he still had lines of communications into the shadows. Very occasionally, he dropped hints about messages that came down those lines.

He said, 'Bill, I want your assurance that you've retired.'

I said, 'You've got it.'

He sipped his tea, made a face. 'All right,' he said. 'You've made a bit of a cock-up. Several cock-ups.'

'So people keep telling me.'

'You've got to understand about Dickie,' he said. 'He's put a lot of effort into building up Youth Venture, since that *Arpeggio* business. He doesn't want to see it all torn apart in a press riot.'

I nodded. Five years ago, *Arpeggio*, a ship under charter to

Youth Venture, had sunk off Newfoundland, with a lot of deaths. Soon after that, Dickie's predecessor, Sir Clement Jones, had drowned on a Round the World Race. There were strong suggestions that *Arpeggio* had sunk through Jones's negligence.

'The organization's only just coming round,' Otto said. 'He doesn't like it. But there's more to it than Youth Venture.'

My boat had been searched. Marie Clarke had died in a suspicious fire. Dean Eliot and I had been beaten up by security guards. I said, 'I was rather thinking there might be.'

He ignored the irony.

'I had lunch with Johnny Dymock in the Guards Club the day before yesterday,' he said. 'My old Colonel. He's moved on . . . elsewhere. You know.'

I knew. He was a spook, was what he meant.

'About that little Lennart chap,' he said. 'Johnny said he was a bit of a wild one, which I dare say you already knew. He also told me that he was getting a breath of fresh air.'

I said, 'What the hell are you talking about?'

'He wasn't always poncing around in Tall Ships,' said Otto. 'He was a submariner. A nuclear submariner.'

'So?' I said. The Soviet Tall Ships fleet is notoriously stuffed with submariners.

Otto closed his eyes. 'Nowadays it is fashionable to believe that Soviets are nice and charming, but a little disturbed. They've still got a bloody good Navy, though. In particular, some bloody good submarines. And what we know about them is roughly bugger all, so we would love to find out. Your Lennart had just learned to drive one, and he was going to come and tell us all about it. In fact, there are those who think that he was on his way over when he landed up wrapped round your propellor.'

There seemed to be an obstruction in my throat. 'Oh,' I said.

Otto said, 'So you can understand why some people are not too keen on you. The way I heard it, there were a couple of reputations staked on bringing Rebane over. There is bound to be tittle-tattle, to shift the blame.'

I said, 'What exactly does this tittle-tattle consist of?' I had a pretty good idea. 'Drunk in charge of a boat?'

He fingered his hard red chin. 'Bit worse than that,' he said. 'There are discreet murmurs that ... well, you did the Soviet Navy a bit of a favour. The idea was that you could be doing a little part-time work for them. Apparently this Rebane'd been talking about coming to see you. Your brother isn't too delighted, I hear.'

'So I told him to be out in the Medway, and ran him over on purpose.'

He shook his head. 'Mad,' he said. 'Bloody stupid. All that. But these people want to punish you.'

The world was suddenly floored with quicksand. I said, as steadily as I could, 'I think I would like to meet these people. Who are they?'

He said, 'Don't be stupid. That drink business was bad luck. Call it careless, at worst. Nobody who counts thinks any different. So just you sit still and try to hang on to your boat and keep your lip buttoned. The whole thing'll blow over.' It was dark outside. His face swam in a yellow pool of lamplight. 'Dickie's a good ally. Keep on his good side. He'll give you your contract back.' He yawned. 'Suppertime,' he said. 'Early start tomorrow. OK?'

I stood up. 'Of course,' I said. I did not want to hang around in Wales. But then he had not needed to tell me what he had told me; to go as far as he had was a supreme gesture of friendship.

We ate round a long table, with the businessmen. Later, they started to build a suspension bridge out of cardboard mailing tubes, to sharpen up their teamwork.

I walked under the blaze of the Milky Way to the van, climbed into my sleeping bag, and lay open-eyed in the grey starlight.

Otto saw my problems as the result of a few spooks sulking about losing a defecting submariner. I had not told him Marie was dead, because it was part of the story he did not need to know. He did not need to know somebody had tried to kill me. By his own lights, he was right: if I kept my head down, it would all blow over. That had been the way when I had been a journalist – chase the story while it was hot, and drop it fast when it started to drift.

But I was not a journalist any more. I had seen the light in

Marie's eyes, a mere half-hour before someone had shot her full of heroin and burned her alive.

Rain pattered faintly on the van roof. I was very grateful to Otto. But in the circumstances, I was not interested in keeping my head down.

10

Someone was shaking me by the shoulder. I opened my eyes. It was still dark.

'Time to go,' said Otto's voice.

I swung my feet into my jeans, pulled on three jerseys, and stumbled out of the van and into the yard.

It was raining, a grey drizzle that cut off the mountains below their shoulders. The trainees formed up into pairs, running on the spot while Otto trotted round them, harrying them like a sheepdog. They set off at a jog, uphill.

I did not follow. Otto could go cross-country running before breakfast if he wished. Personally, I was in favour of short, effective routes.

So I wandered into the kitchen, and breakfasted off a jam sandwich and black tea. Then I slithered down through the darkness under the pines until I hit the brook that rattled along the valley bottom, and followed it downstream to the beach. At the back of the beach was a boathouse and a slipway that led down into the huge lagoon-like estuary the river made before it flowed across the sandbar into grey Cardigan Bay. Down here the rain was lighter, but the wind was stronger.

The joggers straggled in five minutes after me.

Otto unlocked the boathouse doors. Grunting, the men hauled the twenty-six-foot gigs on their trailers out of the shed, and on to the slip, and pulled up the masts with a lot of fuss and no skill at all.

'Race begins,' said Otto. 'When I say *go*, you get the boats into the water, the trailers into the shed. Then you get out past the breakers any way you like, and you get round the yellow buoy bearing 258° magnetic, and then you come back to the buoy off the beach. Ten miles. Then a little climb.'

They were made of wood, those gigs; they must have weighed the best part of half a ton. There was very little wind in the lagoon. They rowed, until we hit the Channel buoys.

The buoys were painted red. They curved away ahead and to port, marking the tortuous groove in the bar.

The lugsail went up, a tan oblong of canvas on a gaff. It hung empty, clattering. Ahead, beyond the lee of the point, a gust was dragging white horses from the sea.

Across the bar, the wind hit. Water started to come aboard. The Sales Force got cold.

It was not an interesting race. We flogged out to sea, hard on the wind. The gig lurched and corkscrewed in the steep, cold seas. The Sales Force, blue and shivering, took it in turns to steer. They were all certified winners, but that did not stop them being sick.

The buoy was five miles out. We rounded it seven or eight lengths ahead. As we started back the sun came out. On shore, the mountains went up to the sky like huge purple-green pillars, dappled with the moving shadows of clouds. Half the crew lay in the bilges, eyes shut. I said to the nearest salesman, 'Why are you doing this?'

'Learning to work as a team,' he said. 'Leadership.' He lapsed back into silence, teeth chattering.

The mountains came up. We rounded the inshore buoy. Everybody cheered, a thin cheer. Instead of heading back into the lagoon we went north, for a shoulder of mountain that plunged a steep thousand feet on to a beach of boulders. One of the salesmen, a fat man with black hair, was looking worried. He was right to be worried.

Otto led us into a patch of sand at the foot of the cliffs. We put the gigs on tripping lines.

'Right,' he said. 'Lunch.' Their eyes swivelled at him. They were hungry. 'It's up the cliff.'

'Up the cliff?'

'On a ledge.' Otto grinned at them, a boyish grin with a hint of wolf. 'Two hundred and fifty feet up. We're in pairs.' He emptied a snake's nest of ropes from a big kitbag he had brought ashore. 'Ready. Steady. Go.'

There was a moment of stunned silence. The man with the black hair said, 'I don't like heights.' His name was Gwyn.

Another man said, 'No climb, no eat.' His name was Tom.

'You got it,' said Otto.

It took them five minutes to untangle the ropes. Otto said to me, quietly, 'There's pitons up there. We'll find them.'

I roped up with Tom.

'Done much of this?' I said.

'Quite a lot,' he said, not meeting my eye.

We gathered round Otto. He showed us how to belay to the pitons in the cliff.

I am not much of a climber; but then the cliff was not much of a climb, if you used your common sense. The first part was a scramble over rubble. A hundred feet up it became a series of slabs, tilted back at perhaps sixty degrees to the horizontal, liberally provided with hand- and footholds. I swarmed up, keeping the body away from the rock in classical style, trailing the rope behind me. After twenty or thirty feet, the pumping heart began to drive the blood round the body, and the chill of a ten-mile open boat journey succumbed to the glow. Fifty feet up I stopped, belayed, and called down to Tom.

He started up, foreshortened against the narrow apron of the sand. He had not been lying when he said he had climbed before. He kept his body well off the rock, and he did not seem fazed by the rope attached to his climbing belt. As he went past me for the second time, I began to feel vaguely confident. Over to my right, fat Gwyn was roped to a Sales Manager who had done a little climbing, making heavy weather of it. I called across, told him to lean out, stop clasping the rock, transfer his weight from his belly to his feet. The face he turned to me was greyish-white and terrified.

Still, he made his belay. The Sales Manager climbed past him, and shouted down. I started up. Above me, Tom was yelling something about coming in last. I paid no attention. I was watching Gwyn.

Gwyn had managed to get himself into one of the few bad places on the cliff. Now, he was stuck.

He had his toes in a crack. His hands had no hold. He was pressing them against the rock, palms flat, as if he hoped they might grow suckers.

All he had to do was edge sideways a step, catch a handhold, and it would be like going up a ladder. But that step might as well have been as wide as the Grand Canyon. It looked as if Gwyn had an excellent imagination. I knew as sure as if I was inside his head that what Gwyn's imagination was showing him was Gwyn pitching back into the emptiness, seventy feet on to the jagged boulders at the cliff's base.

His little pudgy head turned left, then right. And he saw that four feet to his right, the crack in which he was standing widened into a ledge.

Suddenly my mouth was full of cotton wool, and sweat pricked on my body. The rope attaching him to the Sales Manager was taut. It would not let him move on to the ledge.

He began to untie it.

I shouted at him. But the terror must have been roaring in his ears. The rope fell away and to the left, beyond his reach. He started to move a foot sideways.

Then he realized what he had done.

For a moment, he teetered outwards from the wall, swinging his centre of gravity over the drop. Then he shot his arms inwards again. Gradually, he teetered forwards. I heard the slap of his palms on the stone even above the sigh of the wind. And I heard him yell.

There was nobody else within range.

He was yelling at me.

I looked up. Tom was waiting. I said, 'Have you got a good belay?'

'No piton,' he said. 'Fine, though.' I did not like the shake in his voice. But I would have to put up with it. I told him, matter-of-fact, what I was going to do.

Then I started.

There was a horizontal gap of perhaps fifteen feet between me and Gwyn. The rock was vertical, but there was a good crack for the fingers, and some bumps for the toes. I swung across, talking to him the way you talk to frightened kids on *Vixen*; normal, conversational stuff. The fingerholds ran out. The toeholds were further apart. Balancing delicately, the way Gwyn should have, I tiptoed along. The crack began. It was all easy, now.

I was close enough to hear him breathing. He was hissing like a Muscovy duck. 'All right,' I said, soothing as you can be with a throat dry as flannel. 'No problems. We'll have you out of there.'

His face was milk-white above the black stubble of the beard. His mouth opened and shut. No sound came out.

I moved up beside him. High above, Tom was looking solid.

'We'll just tie you on,' I said. 'Get your stomach off, so I can reach the belt.'

He looked at me, then away to the other side. 'Oh, Christ,' he said. Then he moved his left hand. I thought he was going to press his hip into the wall, so I could reach the loop on his belt.

That was not what he did.

What he did was put his left hand on my shoulder, and give himself a shove that propelled him right, to where the crack became a ledge wide enough for him to sit down and have a good sob.

It was a big shove. If I had been expecting it, I could have braced my feet in the crack. I was not expecting it, and I was out of practice. I felt myself being peeled off the rock, falling backwards into space.

Suddenly, the cliff was alive with yelling voices. *Good belay?* I thought. Then I was at the end of the rope's slack, and my right shoulder slammed numbingly into the rock, and there was plenty of pain.

Pain and something. Something was wrong.

My face was against the cold, rough surface of the rock. Below, the beach was a yellow ribbon gnawed by hungry little waves. With a horrible lurch of the stomach, I knew what was wrong.

The rock was moving past my face.

I twisted round. Grit fell in my eyes. Grit kicked off by a

pair of boots. Tom's boots. *Bad belay*, I thought. *Slippery hitch.* I brought my clawed fingers on to the rock.

But the rock was vertical here, and there were no holds.

My heart was walloping in my chest. He was sliding down his earth slope, up there. I could hear his voice, a heavy barking, shouting for help. But all I could see was the black rock with its yellow lichen, sliding past, faster and faster –

I stopped sliding with a jerk. I was dangling, turning slowly in the void. It was perfectly silent, except for the cry of white gulls below, and the distant mutter of the sea. Then a voice came from above. Otto's voice, calm and competent. 'I've got a rolling hitch on the rope,' he said. 'We'll pull you across to the ledge on your left. Look for it.' I looked. It was a beautiful ledge, wide as a motorway. 'Then you can come up, and maybe somebody will give you a bit of their lunch.'

I went up the cliff with wobbly knees. Someone had pulled Gwyn up. He offered me most of his sandwiches. He took me aside, looked round to see no one was listening. He said, 'Thanks, Bill. I'm really grateful.' He meant it. 'If there's ever anything I can do.'

I slapped him on the shoulder, and told him not to be a fool.

But later, when we were back at the house, I thanked Otto. He had unquestionably saved my bacon, and Tom's.

'Nope,' he said. 'You saved me. What'd I do for a living if I'd killed him?'

I went to bed early. People saving my life made a nice change from people trying to kill me.

11

I woke to a clammy morning. The Globe team were doing physical jerks in thick grey drizzle. I squirted easy-start into the van, twisted the key and rolled down the window. Otto was standing outside. I said, 'See you in Finland.'

He grinned, a kind, wide-open grin, the drizzle beading his hard face. 'Not if you've got any sense,' he said.

I tramped on the throttle and left them coughing in the black exhaust. The main road was already a death-trap of holidaymakers gawping at the clouds and wondering where Cader Idris had gone.

I drove north, fast. My shoulder hurt where I had hit the cliff with it. But I was not thinking about boardroom boy scouts. I was thinking about what Otto had told me, and the more I thought, the angrier I was getting. He had talked to me off the record. That would not stop me following up leads, off the record.

By lunchtime, the filthy water of the Mersey was showing between spraycan-blasted blocks of flats. The telephone in the van was broken, as usual. Just before the Birkenhead Tunnel, I stopped and found a call box that had not been torn apart. From it I rang Martin Carr's private number at the *Tribune*.

He said, 'Hello?' The telephone box stank of urine and chips. He would be leaning back, feet on the desk, London River winding away beyond the window behind his cosy leather chair.

I said, 'I seem to have a story. Can you put me on expenses?'

He said, 'Why the hell should I?'

'I will sell you newspapers.'

He began to grumble. I let him get on with it. Finally, he said, 'What is this story?'

'Can't tell you, just yet.'

'So I pop along to the proprietor and tell him Tyrrell wants a new jacuzzi on his yacht, on expenses.'

I said, 'Dead Russian nuclear submariners.'

'What about them?'

'I killed them,' I said. 'That's what your Major Saunders was sniffing for.'

'Oh, *that*,' he said. 'Tell me more.'

'Not yet,' I said.

There was a new note in his voice. It might have been caution. 'I heard you got the sack from that Youth Venture outfit. Are you sure you're not trying to use my paper in your private battles?'

'Yes,' I said.

He sighed. 'I will trust you. Millions wouldn't.'

After I had come back from the Gaza Strip that last time, the *Tribune* had met me off the plane in a stretched Mercedes with blacked-out windows. Martin had been in the back, with an odd expression on his big, soft face: pride mixed with shame, I thought, as he put the first glass of whisky in my hand.

Entering London had had a strange quality of nightmare. I was leaning back in the seat, whisky in hand, wrapped in the cloying softness of the expensive car. But my mind was still in the shattered white walls, and the stink of sewage, and the blasted fig tree where the children darted out of the black shadows and threw stones.

Martin had led me straight up to the boardroom. I had been a little muzzy with whisky and exhaustion; I remember the hollow echo my feet made on the white marble floors of the executive suite.

Downstairs, where people wrote and edited newspapers, they called the executive suite Versailles. The boardroom had oak double doors. Martin fell back. I pushed them open.

The world went mad.

Camera shutters rasped, and flashguns flickered like lightning. The clapping and cheering and the bang of champagne corks were a roar beyond the red suns the flashguns had lit in my vision. Slowly, the clapping died, and the suns faded, and one man started to talk.

The room was full of people in suits. The long table in the middle was covered in bottles. Six chandeliers were burning. The light of their candles glowed on the suits of the thirty men grinning at me, glasses raised. The only thing missing was the banner that said HAIL THE CONQUERING HERO.

The man who was talking was in the middle of the room. He was Aidan Murphy; he owned the *Tribune*, and two tabloids, and papers in America, and Australia, and anywhere else the public could read and had money.

'Tyrrell,' he was saying. 'Our Bill Tyrrell. Other papers have made the Middle East a turn-off. But our Bill Tyrrell goes and he gets his fingers in the stuff of life, ladies and gentlemen, the rich, thick warp and weft of this our human condition. And you know what this means? It means one hundred thousand plus extra newspapers sold daily since he started to run the Gaza Strip stories. Serious money. Serious newspaper sales. We're *very* pleased. Bill Tyrrell, welcome home.'

Someone had put a cold glass in my hand. There was an expectant silence. I was meant to make a speech.

But all I could hear was the voice of Hassan, the stone-throwing kid from the Gaza Strip. *They burned the village. My brother has a bullet in his head.*

I dropped the glass on the floor, turned my back on the pigs in suits, and walked out of the room. The following day, I wrote my letter of resignation. Martin Carr refused to accept it, told me I was on sabbatical. I did not have the strength to argue.

And three months later, here I was, back on the telephone to the office.

I put the telephone down. After the call box, the approach to the Birkenhead Tunnel smelt like a rose garden. The rain had started again, harder now, making millions of little craters in the concrete. I paid my toll, and yanked the van's rusty nose towards the real world. This afternoon the real world was Allerton Cemetery, where at three o'clock they were burying Marie Clarke.

Allerton Cemetery cannot be a comforting spot for anyone who believes that the souls of the dead hover round the body's physical resting place. It consists of a soot-black Edwardian chapel and some dingy Leyland cypresses, presiding over a lot of acres of close-packed marble and polished granite. There were four hearses, and a flock of black limousines, and a lot of men and women standing around in knots, avoiding each other's eyes.

Marie's party were not hard to find. There were three of them, not counting the chipboard coffin in the small hearse: two men in black suits, and a woman in a headscarf, cheap Dayglo wellingtons and a damp-patched fawn raincoat below whose hem a crescent of pink petticoat sagged. The men had the smooth, blank faces of undertaker's assistants on a cheap job. Under her damp scarf the woman's face was a blowsy version of Marie's. As I got close to her, it was impossible not to notice that the grief was getting a lot of help from gin.

I introduced myself. Her yellowish-pink eyes did not register. I said, 'I'm sorry.'

'Ah, Gods,' she said. As far as she was concerned, I was just another hole in the rain. 'Bloody Terry.'

A priest materialized out of the cypresses. 'Mrs Clarke,' he said. She nodded at him, hardly registering. He smelt the state of her and turned to me. 'Father Quinlan,' he said. ''Tis a terrible pity.'

I agreed it was a terrible pity. I took him aside, and said, 'Who's Terry?'

'The father,' said Quinlan. He had a black-haired, white-skinned Irish face, with two chins and a sharp nose from which the rain was dripping. 'He's not with us, I fear.'

'Why not?'

He looked at me with little black gimlet eyes. 'He feels his daughter let him down,' he said. 'So he'll be in the pub.' There was a world of tiredness at the back of his voice.

107

I looked at the blond-veneered box in the black hearse. I said, 'I think she did pretty well, considering.'

A faint expression of surprise ruffled his lard-coloured brow. 'Do you?' he said. 'Do you know, I think I quite agree?' Which was about all the obituary Marie was going to get.

We shuffled into the chapel. The service was over quickly. The grave was in a far corner of the cemetery, by the high black boundary wall. Ultraviolet had faded forgotten plastic wreaths to the colour of dishwater. I stood in the mud, and watched the undertakers' wet black shoes slipping in the wet black grass, and wished I hadn't come. There was nothing to be learned here. Better to remember her on watch on *Vixen*, grinning with pleasure in the wind, gangling denim legs adjusting to the deck's jump as the boat surged through the North Sea . . .

Over by the wall, a man was standing. He was dressed in black; but not the smooth, prissy black of the undertakers. He had a black leather jacket, a black T-shirt with a white device on the front, and black jeans, cut tight; the kind of jeans that Marie used to wear. On his feet were black Doc Martens. A greasy mane of black hair hung down the jacket. The only thing that was not black was the face, which was a gypsyish tan, peeling on the nose.

He began to walk away. I edged sideways from the grave to cut him off. When I was far enough, I said, 'Dean!'

He stopped. He looked over his shoulder. The sooty boundary walls formed a corner. Nowhere to run. He said, 'Hello, Bill,' and smiled. His teeth were dirty. His eyes kept shifting, looking for the exit.

I said, 'Come and have a look.'

He shook his head. He was frightened.

'You've come all this way,' I said. 'Do it.'

He was a hard man, Dean, in his leathers and his boots. His Adam's apple bobbed in his scrawny neck. His eyes stopped shifting. He nodded. Together, we moved to the graveside.

The priest finished. He moved away, with the mother. One of the undertakers made a joke, low-voiced. The other sniggered. Dean jerked round at him with an aggressive hunching of his shoulders. He said, 'Shut the fuck up.'

The undertaker's mouth sagged in his pasty face. Dean bent down, and said, 'Get an end.'

We pulled the astroturf off the mound of earth by the grave. There were a couple of shovels leaning discreetly behind a slab of mirror-polished black granite. He began to fling earth into the grave. It hit the chipboard with a hollow *whump*.

The undertaker said, 'There's a tractor for that.'

Dean said, 'Fuck off,' and kept shovelling, sharp, savage strokes. I helped him. After ten minutes, the grave was full. 'They can do the rest,' he said, leaning on the shovel.

I said, 'I'll give you a lift.'

There were the tracks of tears by his hot black eyes. 'All right,' he said, and flung the shovel flat on the raw earth. We walked back through the rain into the car park, into the cold, lonely world where people probably wanted to kill both of us.

I waited till we were on the motorway. I had been watching the traffic. Nobody was following from in front, or from behind. The tyres made a dirty hissing in pools of black rain. I said, 'Last time you came down to *Vixen*, what did you want?'

His face was invisible behind the greasy curtain of his hair. 'Sorry,' he said.

'You don't have to be sorry. Why did you come?'

'I was pissed off with London.' He was rolling a cigarette. His hands were shaking.

I said, 'You told me you being chased by security blokes. You didn't tell me why you were being chased.'

'They wanted me out of the squat.'

'Rubbish,' I said. 'They were looking for a film.'

He dropped the cigarette. His head snapped round. He said, 'What film?'

'Do me a favour.' The van's wipers were bad, and the stuff the lorries' wheels were blasting off the motorway stuck to the windscreen like glue. 'They wrecked your room looking for it. You put it in the flour jar on *Vixen*. People have been looking for it ever since.' I braked hard, to avoid a management consultant bound for glory in the fast lane. 'And you. They didn't find you. But they found Marie.' He had picked up the cigarette. He was blowing smoke at the windscreen, drumming his nail-bitten fingers on his knees. 'They put Marie in Allerton. What was on the film, Dean?'

'What are you talking about?'

'Listen,' I said. 'Unless you tell me, I will drive you to London, and I will take you down to that stinking tip where you used to live, and we will wait till the security boys come round, and I will hand you over. Marie got killed because she knew about the film. That was enough. Think about it.'

He thought about it. We ploughed on down the middle of England. The M6 became the M5.

I said, 'You're being looked for. Got any plans?'

Dean looked at me sideways behind his hair. He had been chewing his lips. 'I'm going down Southampton,' he said.

'What for?'

'Geezer I want to see.'

'Why?' None of your business, Tyrrell. Don't push it.

Dean said, 'There's a party.'

I said, 'Long way to go for a party.'

Dean said, 'You was asking about a film.'

He fell silent. I knew that was as close to a definite statement as you got out of Dean.

'Why are you going?' I said.

'Geezer I want to see,' said Dean.

That was it, for the moment.

The Dean I had met for the first time had been wild as a stoat. He was in the final month of a six-month sentence for taking and driving away. Two prison officers had shovelled him out of a black van at Fleet Basin, bundled him over *Vixen*'s rail, and blasted off down the marsh road as quick as they could. I had introduced him to the other seven layabouts and misfits in the crew, and cast off the shorelines with a view to putting as much English Channel as possible between him and the road back to London.

He had sulked for two days, vomiting at intervals into his bunk. Then one morning he had come on deck and before anyone could tell him aye, yea or nay, he had swarmed up the mast, all seventy-five feet of it, to collect a halyard. Then he had cleaned out his bunk, and cooked the lunch. After that, he had been treated with respect. Respect was something Dean had had very little of in his life. The more of it he got, the better he liked it. Going ashore after a *Vixen* trip was hard on him. But he had been learning.

He must still have been learning, because I got him through a gas station in Bristol without him jumping out of the van door. I knew he could change his mind. So I kept going south, towards Pulteney. He wanted to go to Southampton. Southampton is next door to Gosport, where Claudia had her office. Claudia was due to answer some questions. Once I got him on *Vixen*, he would have trouble getting off. And anyone who was after either of us would have trouble getting on.

I said, 'I'm going down to *Vixen*. I'll take you over to the Solent.'

A faint, enthusiastic gleam lit his face. 'Yeah,' he said. 'Thanks, Bill.'

It was eight o'clock by the time we reached Pulteney quay. Elegant young things in white shorts and long-peaked caps were leaning on the rails of the Yacht Club terrace, shrieking at the windsurfers weaving among the lobster boats in the harbour. A clutch of more serious citizens was gripping its pints outside the Mermaid. I squinted through the van window. Charlie Agutter was leaning on a big anchor with a glass of whisky in his hand, talking to Scotto Scott, a blond New Zealand bear of a man who operated as his factotum and general purpose boat nigger. I said, 'Come here,' to Dean, jumped out of the driver's seat and took him across.

Charlie looked him over with his dark, intelligent eyes.

I introduced him to Dean, said, 'He's a watch leader on *Vixen*.' I could feel Dean's confidence grow. He read a lot of sailing magazines. He knew Charlie's name. 'Get him a drink, could you? I've got to go off for twenty minutes.'

Charlie said, 'Of course,' as if he had read about Dean, too.

'I'm looking for Pinsley, the surveyor,' I said.

Charlie gave me an address up Naylor Hill. I jumped into the van and caned it between the floral hanging baskets, heading inland.

It was a bungalow, in a row of bungalows, with a picture

window that had once been full of sea and was now full of bypass. Nobody answered the doorbell, so I went round the side of the house. There was a BMW standing by a timber garage; the house might not be too good, but the bent surveying business was evidently brisk. A woman was sitting at an iron table, listening to the Mike Sammes Singers and knitting something in pink mohair. She looked up sharply when she saw me. She had grey hair, tightly curled, and a mouth that looked as if it was full of lemon juice.

I gave her my best smile. 'Mr Pinsley in?' I said.

'No.' The voice was flinty. 'What did you want?'

'A little surveying matter,' I said, still using the smile. The smile was meant to convey that while I was six foot four, built like a tank, and in bad need of a shave and haircut, I was cuddly as dammit. It had been one of my professional advantages that it worked surprisingly often. 'Are you Mrs Pinsley?'

'That's right.'

'Any idea when he'll be back?'

'Mr Pinsley comes and Mr Pinsley goes,' she said. 'It is none of my damned business. After all, I am only married to him.' Her voice dripped bitterness like a runner drips sweat.

'It's just that your husband . . . well, he's left me with a problem.'

She sighed, and looked very slightly happier. 'What is it *this* time?' I remembered what Charlie had said: '*He's messing around with his secretary, or so his wife says.*' And I knew we were fine.

I said, 'I've got to go abroad. He was to send me a copy of his report. Do you know where I can contact him?'

'Antigua,' she said. 'He's doing a charter fleet. His secretary's gone out to join him in case he needs her.' I remembered the secretary's too-tight skirt, her thick red lipstick. Mrs Pinsley's face was cold and grey as stone, without hope.

'Oh dear,' I said. 'So the office is closed?'

'Closed,' she said.

'Have you . . . I mean, is there any way I can get at this report?'

She shrugged. 'Not until he comes back.'

'That'll be too late,' I said. 'He was to send it last week.' I ran the hands through the hair, and tried to look frenzied. Under the circumstances it was not hard. 'I mean, have you got the office key?'

She looked surprised. 'Yes,' she said. 'Why?'

'I don't suppose I could take you down and have a look? For the report, or notes, or anything?'

'Oh,' she said. Her eyes were nervous. 'I don't think he'd like that.'

'I'm on the spot,' I said. 'I've got to talk to the insurance company first thing tomorrow.'

She frowned. Then she said, 'Don't I know you?' I gave her the grin again, and let it happen. 'Of course,' she said. 'You were on TV. In Ethiopia, wasn't it?'

It had been the Sudan, actually. I kept the grin going anyway.

'Bill Tyrrell,' she said. Her face was pink now, and she looked almost excited. 'Of *course*. Those poor people.'

The poor people had been dying of hunger. They had had their moment of glory in front of the cameras. Then the cameras had gone back to the Jeeps, and they had carried on dying.

'Come on,' she said. 'We'll go to the office.' She led me out to the van with a positive skip in her stride, come all over schoolgirlish. At the office she unlocked the door, and said, with a return of her woodenness, 'I never come here. The filing cabinet's over there.'

She waited in the reception area, by the desk. I went through to the office and started on the cabinet. When I looked back, she was going through the secretary's diary.

Mr Pinsley led a simple life. The files were arranged by boat's name. Under *Vixen*, there was a sheaf of notes, and a letter. There was a photocopier behind a screen in the reception area. I switched it on, and copied the lot, grinning at Mrs Pinsley. Then I ostentatiously sorted the copies from the originals, switched off the photocopier, and deposited her among the glutinous noises of the Mike Sammes Singers.

Dean had been into the Special Brews. His eyes were thickly glazed as he climbed into the van. That suited me fine.

I said to Charlie, 'Do you want a sail?'

He shrugged. 'Where to?'

'Gosport,' I said. 'To visit Claudia. Then Southampton.'

'Long as there's a station,' he said. He was a sucker for *Vixen*. He and Scotto climbed into the Transit. A big red sun was settling into the marsh as we pulled up to the Basin. There were people about; it was now August, after all. I looked at them hard, recognized all of them. Paranoia, I thought. I had been driving for two days, fallen down a cliff, been to a nasty funeral. Time I was at sea. I put the Transit in the shed, told the lock keeper we were off, and went aboard *Vixen*.

They were already rolling back the mainsail cover. I twisted the key, and the heavy chug of the old Perkins coughed back at me off the face of the grain elevator. Dean cast off the bow line. The bowsprit swung away from the quay, over the bloodshot mirror of the basin. People were watching now, tins of beer halfway to their mouths, cigarette smoke hanging in the still air. It was always like that with *Vixen*.

It was high tide, so the lock gates stood open. The walls slid by. We moved out on to the broad, flat sheet of the Poult. I moved the spokes through my hands, and she turned to starboard, the tide swirling under her long nose. The engine was a distant purr, the Poult a broad metal road winding glass-black and fire-red at the dark, sharp slash of the horizon. Past Neville Spearman's marina; past the throng of plastic yachts, lights lit, moving busily home to their snug little berths with the shore power and the plug-in TV aerials. And on to the wide, flat sea, with the night-shadows rolling in from the east, and the Start Point light blinking to the sou'west.

The sky darkened. The stars came out. Dean sat with his back against the coachroof, gazing at the shore, where the town lights sagged tawdry yellow across the loom of the land, and there were people who would smash you to pulp for the sake of a roll of film.

I rattled down the companionway into the cabin, hacked out a course for Portland Bill, and called it up to Charlie, at the wheel. Then I pulled the copies of Pinsley's file from my pocket, and spread them on the table.

Charlie came down. He said, 'It's a beautiful night. You're not allowed to do your filing.'

I grinned at him. Pinsley's file was going to be more beautiful than the night. Because it was going to tell me for sure who it was had sent him to search *Vixen*. And whoever that was had been the person who had turned over Dean, and pushed me into the mud, and murdered Marie.

12

Pinsley had done a survey, of a sort. He made a couple of suspicious remarks about the state of the fastenings, and pointed out that since the boat was in the water, the scope of his inspection had been necessarily limited. Like most bad surveyors' reports, it told the reader more about the surveyor's wish to cover his back than about the condition of the boat.

The interesting bit was at the front of the file, in the shape of a letter requesting Mr Pinsley to make the survey.

The letterhead bore a picture of a pilot cutter, as seen on nineteenth-century yachting prints, with a border of Turks' heads embossed in gold. The letterhead of Age of Sail. Claudia's company. Claudia was a firm believer in presentation. It was a straightforward enough letter: a request for a survey, and an agreement on a fee. The good part of it was the final sentence.

In view of some special stipulations, I should be grateful if you would call in person at my office before conducting this survey.

It was less than I had hoped, but enough. I was looking forward to finding out what those special stipulations were.

Charlie came down the hatch again. 'Got some breeze,' he said. 'Where d'you keep the whisky on this thing?'

I showed him. I said, 'Give some to Dean, would you?'

'He's had a lot already. You trying to get him pissed, or something?'

I said, 'Yes.'

116

He shrugged. Then he shoved the bottle into the pocket of his baggy blue canvas trousers, and went on deck. The halyard winch croaked like an old metal frog as the sail went up, and the mainsheet blocks groaned. The settee on which I was sitting tilted downhill, and the tremor of the engine gave way to the creak and sploosh of *Vixen* on a reach. Normally, it soothed me. Tonight, nothing was soothing.

I could believe that Claudia would conspire with Christopher to prise me loose from *Vixen*. But there was no reason I could imagine why she should arrange for clandestine searches. Furthermore, as one who was living aboard, she could have done all the searching she wanted herself.

I got up, and went on deck. The land had gone. We were well out in Lyme Bay now, cutting a thin black groove in the water. A full moon shone flat and hard on the white tower of the mainsail. The oil running lights glowed port and starboard and the wake ran straight as a ruler.

'Goes great,' said Charlie. I saw the white gleam of his teeth in the moonlight.

Dean was slumped against the coachroof, emitting a reek of tobacco and strong lager.

I said, 'Dean. Speak to me.'

The big, lean hull whooshed through the water. Out to seaward were the red port and all-round green-over-white lights of someone trawling. I said, 'You hid a film on the boat when you came down. What was on it?'

His eyes rolled under the moon. Whatever he saw, he caved in.

'Photographs,' said Dean.

'What of?' A puff hit. *Vixen* dipped, the gurgle of her wake becoming a small roar. Dean said nothing. I said, 'You're on your last sail, Dean.'

Dean said, 'You know the geezer.'

'What geezer?' I said.

'They was photographs,' said Dean. 'They was took at one of Dmitri's parties.'

The night was suddenly quiet enough for the beating of my heart to sound like a muffled drum.

'Who's Dmitri?'

117

'Feller lives down Lambeth.'

'And?'

'A bloke I was in the nick with took me down to see him,' said Dean. 'He's a big bloke. Dark. Greekish looking. I used to find him a bit of blow for his parties.'

'Blow?'

'Smoke. You know.'

'But not any more.'

'Nah,' said Dean. He was lying, but I did not mind who he was selling marijuana to. 'But I kept on going down these parties.'

'So they're a lot of people in paper hats.'

'Not exactly,' said Dean. 'At least, if they was wearing paper hats that was all they was wearing.'

I said, 'Who were the people?'

'The Russian kid. Him we run down.'

I said, 'Start at the beginning.'

He hesitated. Then he seemed to take the mental equivalent of a deep breath. 'When we was in London, before the last trip started,' he said. 'St Katharine's Dock, right? Before the Parade of Sail. You was at some reception. That Rebane turns up on board, visiting, like they do. So me and Marie went back on *Soyuz* with him. He started out asking all these questions about you. Then we got to talking, you know. About parties. And this geezer Rebane, he seemed well eager. I knew Dmitri was having one of his, so I took him down there.'

He was hanging his head. This was Dean the Fixer. Helpful Dean, ready with the answers. Confidential Dean, who never told anyone anything, unless he had an angle. If you wanted a smoke, or a woman, or a boy, Dean would help you out. Judges thought that he was in it for the money. I knew he only wanted to help, and nobody had ever bothered to tell him what was helpful and what was not.

'Go on.'

The dark mass of his shoulders moved against the glitter of the moon on the water.

'We were in a pub. Marie went back on the boat. She was angry. Said we was hammered. But old Lennart kept at it, and I kept at it with him. So we got well drunk, and I remembered there was this party on. So we went down there. And this geezer started talking to him. And then they disappeared off.'

'Off?'

'Upstairs. Lennart was no poof. He was a bit simple, really. And well drunk. But this old bloke was a talker, you know. Mr Johnson, they called him. Probably told Lennart that he wanted to show him his butterfly collection, Christ knows. So Lennart trots up the stairs, and there they are in a bloody great room with a mirror on the ceiling.'

I said, 'How do you know there was a mirror on the ceiling?'

He said, 'I saw him going. I went after them.'

I said, 'Why was that?'

He said, 'The place was full of poofs. Nobody upstairs had nothing on. I didn't want old Lennart to get ... well, you know.' His profile was dark and rigid against the glittering water. Too rigid; he was not telling the whole truth.

I said, 'Tell me it all. Why did you go after him?'

He said, 'Do me a favour.' His voice was suddenly childish, desperate; as if he was about to admit something about himself. 'I knew you'd be well unhappy if Lennart got into trouble in a place I'd taken him.'

I said, 'That is most considerate of you.'

'Yeah,' said Dean, immune to the sarcasm. 'So I go up after them, but by the time I get up there all the doors are shut. And one of them opens, and this horrible old poof with make-up and a camera pops out, and says that if I want a free sight of a bit of hello sailor I should get inside. The door was open. There was like a window into the next room. And there was this old geezer tugging at Lennart's boxer shorts.'

'The man had a camera?'

'I told you Lennart was well drunk.' Dean seemed not to have heard me. 'He didn't know what he was doing. I thought it wouldn't be too handy if this geezer with the camera was going to come round the skipper of *Soyuz* and say, look at these snaps, this boy of yours is up for a bit of the other with this poof that could be his grandpa, and the bloke who introduced them is on *Vixen*'s crew. So the geezer with the camera's standing there, giggling a bit. So I swipe the camera, and about then Lennart starts yelling bloody murder and he comes out of the room hanging on to his underpants. And we run off from there, throw the camera out of the cab window, but we've got the film out of it. And Lennart wants to toss the film out too, but I reckon we'll hang on to it.'

He was staring out at the dark sea. Good old Dean, I thought. Never miss an angle.

'Anyway,' said Dean. 'The day after, this security geezer comes round to the boat.'

'To *Vixen*?'

'That's right. You wasn't aboard. He got well heavy, so we seen him off.'

'We?'

'Me and Marie.'

I said, 'You and Marie.' Persecuted Dean, and dead Marie. 'Did Marie know what he was after?'

He shook his head.

'I gave the film to Lennart, because Marie says he's a nice bloke. He's a bit of a tearaway, this Lennart. By this time he's worked out that it might be worth a bob or two, but he doesn't want it on *Soyuz*, because they're always nosing around, there. So he gives it to Marie. And Marie gave it back to me, to look after, like. Then we come up the Medway, and there's Lennart, dead. So I keep hold of it, and get off back to the squat.'

'And the security people came looking for it.'

'Yeah.'

'You brought it down to *Vixen*.'

'Yeah.'

'Why *Vixen*?'

He said, 'We was off the boat. It was like, a posh place. I didn't reckon anybody'd look for it there.'

'And you were going to come back, and get it, and sell it.'

'Yeah.'

'Who to?'

'The bloke who was with Lennart.'

'Mr Johnson.'

'That's what they called him. It ain't his real name, though.'

'How were you going to find him?'

'He's always at them parties. And I've seen him before.'

The breath suddenly stuck in my throat. 'Where?'

'On *Vixen*.'

'*Vixen*?'

'He's always on the boats, this year, last year. He was hanging around down Chatham. Nobody introduced us, like. But his name's Wilson.'

'Wilson?' It came out as a croak. 'Dickie Wilson?'

'Little geezer. Sharp dresser.'

For a moment the world was frozen.

There were things that were possible, and things that were not. This was not.

Until you stopped to think about it. If Rear-Admiral Richard Wilson had been photographed indulging in homosexual orgies with Russian nuclear submariners, it was not at all surprising that he should want the film back.

If.

I sat down on the hatch cover and looked at the silver road the moon was paving over Lyme Bay.

Dickie was well aware of the power of rumour. If he put it about that I had blown the defection of a Russian submariner, other people would repeat it. If enough people repeated it, people of a nervous disposition would start to believe it, never mind whether it was plausible that I would commit a political assassination using a fifty-five-foot sailing cutter as the murder weapon.

It was not even important that people believed it. It was enough that people would repeat it. After enough repetitions, the name Bill Tyrrell would stink to high heaven. So Bill Tyrrell was finished as a journalist, because nobody was going to tell him anything. And he was finished as a yacht proprietor, because his brother Christopher was anxious to wash his hands under the eyes of the party's influence brokers. Best of all, nobody was going to believe in the existence of dirty photographs of Dickie.

Unless the dirty photographs turned up.

Nadia Vuorinen had the dirty photographs. She was an Estonian, like Rebane. It was possible that she would destroy them, out of regard for his family.

It was also possible that one day Harrods would open a branch on Mars.

I got up, went and stood on the stern, elbow hooked over the backstay, bending the knees to the long lift and plunge of the seas.

Dean came aft. He said, 'It's true.'

I said, 'I don't believe you.'

'You'll bloody see.'

I did not answer. Dickie's sexual proclivities were his own business. A man in his position would not enjoy publicity about his association with rent boys and petty dope dealers. I could understand him spreading rumours. But I could not believe he would murder in cold blood.

'All right,' said Dean. 'You wait till the next party. He'll be there.'

'Are you sure?'

'He's always there,' said Dean. 'There's one on tomorrow night, down Southampton.'

'Geezer you want to see?' I said.

'That's right.'

He went below. I went aft, and took the wheel from Charlie. *Vixen* was tracking clean and hard as a railway locomotive, her bowsprit pounding into the darkness to seaward of the glow-worm flick of Portland Bill.

I said, 'What do you know about Dickie Wilson?'

Charlie said, 'Personal friend of the extremely famous. Patron and benefactor of British youth.'

'Personally.'

I saw his narrow shoulders shrug against the sinking moon. 'Doesn't have a private life. Wedded to the cause. Why?'

I had known Charlie for twenty years. We had met on the 505 racing circuit. It had been he who had told me about the house in Filmer Canonicorum, five miles inland, that my mother had bought when she had moved from Norfolk after she had married Georgie. Charlie knew more secrets than most family solicitors, and kept them better. I said, 'Would you believe that he's a regular at homosexual orgies?'

Charlie squinted up at the luff of *Vixen*'s mainsail, and eased the sheet six inches. He said, 'Why not?'

122

'And he's being blackmailed?'

He eased the sheet another three inches. *Vixen*'s nose cut the upslope of a wave in two glossy halves. He said, 'They usually are. Where did you get that idea?'

I said, 'They were photographed at it.'

'Blimey,' said Charlie. There was a pause. 'If it was Dean told you, I wouldn't credit a bloody word. Nice enough bloke. But he's pissed, and he's a liar.'

He had a point.

'You should have stuck to racing,' said Charlie. 'Very political, this sail training. Any time you change your mind, give us a ring.'

Vixen surged on. And I found myself thinking of my father.

I had been perhaps eight years old. It was before I went away to school, before he had begun to fade out of my life. He had been at home a lot, then. He had had a shed by the marsh, where he used to build timber boats, very slowly, for anyone who wanted them. My mother had not liked the shed. As far as she was concerned, building boats was manual labour, and manual labour was for . . . well, manual labourers.

Christopher agreed with her. His ambition, at that moment, was to write musical comedies like she did, and compete in horse trials. Up at the house the piano thrummed and the pony shifted its feet under the curry-comb. Down in the dark, resin-smelling shed, I sat in the corner with a bit of scrap timber, and whittled, and watched my father peel shaving after deliberate shaving off the planks.

Wooden boats were passing into history, and so were the natural fibres of the ropes, and the knots we used. He certainly did not make anything like a living out of it. But through watching, and his occasional laconic instructions, I learned some boat-building, and a lot of basic marlinespike seamanship, the manufacture of the intricate machine of rope that held together the sails and spars of ships in the Age of Sail.

On the occasion I remembered best from that era, we were sailing one of his heavy clinker dinghies he had kept on a mooring at Burnham Overy. He was on the helm, his beard, still black then, fluttering in the cold east wind. We were racing, and we were in front; my father was usually in front, when he raced. Over the transom, the water was brownish, swirling with the eddies of the dinghy's wake. The next boat astern was Jack Labouchere's. Jack was the nearest thing my father had to a friend. On hot days in the long, parched Norfolk summer, I sometimes saw them on the bench outside the Lord Nelson, pints in hand, silent, watching the road. To my eight-year-old eyes it looked boring. But there was no question that they liked each other's company.

My father looked back at Jack over the oiled-wool shoulder of his blue jersey. 'Bastard,' he said.

I thought that was a nasty thing to say about his friend.

'Let's do him,' he said, and shoved the tiller away. I saw Jack's face purple with consternation as we shot across his bows. I heard him curse, saw the wind rattle out of his sails as he took evasive action.

My father turned back to me. His big yellow teeth were grinning in his beard, and his nose was hooked like the beak of a bird of prey. 'Rule one,' he said. 'Get the brutes before they get you.'

It was one of the only bits of advice he gave me. Soon after that, I had been sent away to school. A year or two later, he had given up the shed, and gone to sea.

We hit Portland Bill dead right for the tide, and kept it under the counter all the way to Christchurch Bay. Then we flogged through the crowds of plastic boats milling in the Solent, picked up Spit Sand Fort and tied up at one of the big-boat berths on the end of the jetty at Camper and Nicholson's marina in Gosport.

I said to Dean, 'Stay on board, if you want to keep alive. There won't be any fire escapes.'

He looked at me hard, to see if I meant it. What he saw seemed to convince him.

I ran down the pontoon and up the steps to the coffee bar. A couple of sightseers were already gawping at *Vixen*. We needed a nice, anonymous boat. I ordered coffee, and called Harry Featherstone at Reuters. Harry kept a fat Halberg-Rassy ketch at Camper's. He said how the hell was I, and of course I could borrow it. So I finished the coffee, and got his keys from the office. Charlie and Scotto climbed on to the Portsmouth Harbour Ferry.

I walked into Gosport in search of explanations.

The office of Age of Sail was discreet in the way that Bond Street auctioneers are discreet. The window was painted out in Rifle Brigade green, with the name in a frame of gold-leaf Turks' head knots. Inside, two women sat at mahogany desks that looked as if they might have come out of the captain's cabins of tea clippers. There were schooner portraits on the walls, the kind painted by the yard in the nineteenth century, with Vesuvius erupting in the background. There were sail-makers' chairs and photographs of big, glossy yachts.

The women looked up as I came in. They were both blonde, pretty with a high-gloss, expensive prettiness. One of them was Claudia.

The one who was not Claudia got up. She said, 'I've got some shopping to do,' and gave me a look that left me in no doubt that what she had to do was get out of the way while Claudia told me what she thought of me.

Before the door had properly closed, Claudia said, 'You've got a nerve, coming in here. Foreign floozy tossed you out, has she?'

Her eyes were hard and direct. She was ashamed of the way she had behaved. She had decided to tough it out. I said, 'I'm here on business. Would you rather I talked to your partner?'

She recognized her own line. She said, 'I think I can manage, thank you very much.'

'Fine,' I said.

'You commissioned a survey of *Vixen*,' I said. 'What brief did you give the surveyor?'

Her cherry lips opened to tell me to mind my own bloody business. Then her brain registered that as holder of three-quarters of the *Vixen* Trust, it was my bloody business. 'I told him to assess her condition,' she said.

'And you're happy with what you got?'

'Quite.' The cherry lips closed like a rat-trap. The jaw stuck out.

I said, 'I saw a copy. He could have written it without leaving the office.'

She said, 'If you don't like the survey, get one of your own.'

I sat down in a sailmaker's chair. I said, 'Do you normally use Pinsley?'

'Sometimes.' Her grey eyes shifted.

I said, 'He's as bent as a nine-bob note.'

'We trust him,' she said.

I pulled my copy of her letter from Pinsley's file. '*In view of some special stipulations,*' I read, '*I should be grateful if you would call in person at my office before conducting this survey.* What stipulations?'

She said, 'Where did you get that letter?'

'From Pinsley,' I said. 'Because Pinsley searched my boat. Which is an illegal act. I want to know who asked him to do the search, and what he was looking for. And if I do not get evidence to the contrary, I shall have to assume that searching the boat was a special stipulation. And I'll go to the police.'

The golden tan had paled a notch. She said, 'Don't be ridiculous. You're just paranoid. You couldn't prove anything anyway.'

I said, 'We are not talking seafaring antiques. We are talking murder and extortion. And you will be delighted to hear I'm writing a story all about it for the *Tribune*. If you don't tell me what you know, you're part of it.'

She laughed. It was a bad laugh, and it did not work. She said, 'You're mad.'

'You said I was mad when I wasn't working. Now I'm mad when I am working. Choose one.' This time, she believed me. 'What special stipulations?' I said.

She said, 'I can't tell you.'

'Why not?'

'It was . . . government business.'

I stared at her. I thought about Otto's old Colonel, the spook. On government business.

'Someone rang,' she said.

'Who?'

'I can't tell you.'

'Oh yes, you can.'

She thought about it. She said, 'It was a man. From the Department of Trade.'

I said, 'Oh, yeah?'

'D'you want his telephone number?' Her face had become red and angry. 'He left it.'

'Of course.'

She pushed a piece of paper across to me. I copied the number off it. She said, 'That's all?'

'That's all.' The anger had gone. She looked grim, and in control. It was the bitter end of me and Claudia. I wanted to say something to soften it. But there was nothing to be said. She said, 'I hope I never see you again.'

I left.

13

Back on *Vixen*, I rang the number.

A man's voice answered.

I said, 'Engineers. Who am I speaking to?'

'What do you want?' said the voice. It sounded efficient and suspicious.

'We've had reports of a fault,' I said.

'We haven't noticed one,' said the voice.

'What's your address, there?' I said.

'Look it up,' said the voice. The telephone went down, faster than telephones usually go down in the Department of Trade, or any other government department.

I called London. There was a man on the *Tribune* who knew how to trace the owners of telephone numbers. He was on holiday. I folded the paper in my pocket, jogged down the jetty, told the Camper's people to keep an eye on *Vixen*, took Dean aboard Harry Featherstone's Halberg-Rassy, and motored back round to Southampton, to see about Dean's Mr Johnson.

We tied up at the waterfront, a huge, grim marina dredged out of an arm of Southampton Water. The hot August sun glared down. Clouds of chip fat rolled over the pastel-coloured plastic boats jammed into the trots of its marina. Crop-headed brats stuffed burger cartons into the muzzles of the derelict anti-aircraft guns with which a hopeful landscaper had sought to decorate the twenty-acre car park. It was a dirty, cheap, unprepossessing place.

Over to the west of the glass-and-graffiti Waterfront Centre, things changed. Behind a high brick wall crowned with rolling spikes was New Venice. Its only point of resemblance to Old Venice was its proximity to very dirty water. It was a tangle of houses in the Developer's Fishing Village style. There were minarets, obelisks, and a campanile that marked not a church but a real-estate office. The houses overlooking the harbour were not inhabited by fishermen, unless the fishermen could afford half a million pounds. Their owners were businessmen, and lawyers, and plastic surgeons. Or, in the case of 21 Harbour Walk, Rear-Admiral Dickie Wilson.

I sat there in the cockpit, raised the binoculars to my eyes for what must have been the five-hundredth time. Dean ripped the top off a Heineken and rolled himself his fifteenth cigarette of the afternoon. Dickie's front door was shut tight. It had been shut tight all afternoon. We had a hired car in the car park, ready to follow him when he went out. My faith in Dean was beginning to waver.

We waited.

At six o'clock, Dean went below for a beer. A window opened on the first floor. For a moment I saw Dickie's bushy black eyebrows, crisp dark hair and silver-grizzled temples. Dean came back with his beer. The window stayed open. Nobody left the house, that I could see.

I said, 'He's at home. You sure he'll go?'

Dean said, 'I'll go the other end and wait for him. Thirteen, Lanark Way.' He picked up his leather jacket from the cushions.

'Careful.'

He winked. He had got a lot of his confidence back, had Dean. 'Course I will,' he said. He lifted the folding bicycle we had brought from *Vixen* over the lifelines, climbed on, and wobbled off down the jetty, no hands, cigarette stuck in his face.

I nearly called him back. Then I thought of the violence with which he had filled in Marie's grave. He had told me too much to run away, now. In his own mind, Dean had nailed his colours to the mast.

As far as you could be certain, with Dean.

So I opened one more lager, and told myself to make it last.

The sun dropped towards the buildings. The jolly denizens of the plastic boats clattered down the pontoons towards chemical beer and fast food ashore. On Harbour Walk the street lamps began to glow, electric filaments flickering electronically in the fake gas globes. Lights came on in number 21.

Dickie stayed indoors.

By the time my watch said eleven o'clock, it was properly dark. I had eaten a cheese sandwich, and finished the beer and drunk a litre of Malvern water. I knew the door off by heart. I could see its top left-hand panel. The rest was hidden behind a brick pillar. The harbour began to exude a clammy vapour that smelt of stagnant water and very old rubbish. It made me shiver. With the shivering came the doubts. Stupid bastard, I told myself. You spend fifteen years as a journalist, and you fall for a story from a junior hoodlum like Dean, who probably bears Dickie a grudge anyway. Marie would have told him how Dickie had shouted at her in Chatham.

A yellow crack appeared at the top of the blue door. Light streamed on to the brick pillar. There were figures inside, in silhouette. Dickie facing outwards. Another one; a woman. I trained the glasses on her. She said what must have been goodbye, slung her bag over her shoulder. The door closed, with Dickie inside.

But I was no longer thinking about Dickie. I was out of the Rassy's cockpit and over the side, feet hammering the teak slats of the pontoon as I ran flat out for the shore.

The New Venice car park was in front of the gate, lit with sodium glare. On the other side of it, a woman was standing by the driver's door of a car. The movement must have caught her eye. She looked round, stared at me. Then she turned quickly away. Behind me, an official voice said something. I began running again, between the cars, panting for breath. The woman had the car door open now. She turned back and looked at me again, her eye-sockets shadowed black in the red light of the street lamps which sucked the gold out of her hair and left it dead, metallic grey.

'Nadia,' I said.

'Excuse me, madam,' said a voice behind me. 'Is this man causing you a problem?' I turned. It was a security man.

Nadia smiled. The lights caught her white teeth. 'No,' she said. 'In fact, I am very pleased to see him.' She turned to me. 'Now,' she said. 'Are you getting in, or do we stay here all night?'

The security guard's head turned left and right. He had a pale, stupid face. 'Oh,' he said. 'Well.' He walked back to his sentry box, frustrated. I got into the car.

'Do you know,' said Nadia, 'it is true, I am most pleased to see you.' She reached out her hand and touched my head. 'Are you well?' she said.

Her fingers were firm, but gentle. I liked the way they felt, and the solicitousness in her voice. For a moment, I was pleased to see her, too, for the wrong reasons.

I summoned up the right reasons.

I said, 'Then why did you run away?'

'I did not run away.'

'With something that belonged to me,' I said. 'A film.'

The face she turned to me was hard and rectangular in the cold light. 'What film?' she said.

'The photographs of Lennart Rebane being . . . interfered with by an older man.'

'What are you talking about?'

The telephone chirruped in my pocket.

'Yes?' I said.

It was Dean. 'Cock-up,' he said. 'Twenty-five Lanark Drive. Pick us up, can you? Quick,' he said. His voice was frightened and breathless. There was noise in the background; yelling, and sirens.

'On my way,' I said. I did not want to lose Nadia. 'A friend is in trouble,' I said.

'We go in my car,' she said. She drove very fast, as if she was used to people getting out of her way. Southampton flashed past.

I said, 'I want to talk to you.'

She was staring across the wheel, eyes narrow, arms straight, like a racing driver. 'Later,' she said. 'I drive.' Then I was being flung forward into the straps as she stamped on the brakes. We came to a halt under a blue light that said POLICE. I stumbled out, and the desk sergeant gave me directions to Lanark Drive.

Ten minutes later, we were there. It was a wide street of ill-built executive homes, winding in and out of designer scrubland on the fringes of the New Forest. Nadia slowed, tyres squealing.

Ahead, the picture windows were flickering with reflections of blue lights. Beyond a black screen of trees there were other lights; dirty yellow flares, pouring from rectangular apertures. Windows. A house was burning.

We were moving slowly, now. The blue lights were on four police cars, two ambulances and three fire engines. One of the fire engines had a man up a ladder, blasting water into a hole in the roof. Round the cars was a thin crowd of men and women. Some of the women were in dressing gowns. I rolled down the window, and spoke to one of the women. 'What number's this?' I said.

'Thirteen,' she said.

'Anyone hurt?'

'Fingers burned,' she said. She giggled. Her dressing gown fell open. I caught a glimpse of dead-white thigh above black stocking.

'Looks like I missed the party,' I said.

'There'll be another.' She put on a fake American accent. 'Another time, another place.' She laughed again, a hollow, metallic laugh, full of gin.

Beside me, Nadia said something short and violent in a language I did not understand, and stamped on the throttle.

Once we were clear of the crowd, I got out of the car. I could still feel the heat of the flames on my face. The house that should have been number 25 was dark and silent. There was a wrought-iron gate, a path lined with dark cypresses. I walked down it to the front door and rang the bell. Chimes sounded. Nobody came.

Wrong number, I thought.

Then I saw him.

The bomb shapes of the conifers were black against the glow of the fire. A lanky figure was moving across an open patch of lawn between them. Its hair was long, dangling to the shoulders in greasy strands. It moved stealthily. It slid into the shadows of another cypress.

Dean.

I opened my mouth to shout, shut it again.

There was another shadow, motionless on the grey lawn. At first, I thought it was part of a tree. But it moved; a small movement, perhaps a hand going into a pocket. It seemed to me that there was something furtive about the movement. I stepped on to the lawn.

Everything started to move very quickly. The shadow detached itself from the bush. It was a man in some kind of uniform, wearing a flat-topped cap. I heard the rasp of his breath as he ran. His right arm was swinging free. Then he had plunged into shadow again. The same shadow as Dean. Someone said, '*Bastard.*' Then there was a horrible noise, halfway between a crack and a thump. I started running, because the shadows had stopped being shadows, and become solid people. Dean was crawling on the grey lawn, making desperate retching sounds. The man in the uniform drew his foot back, and loosed a rugby-player's place-kick at his belly. Dean fell over, and lay twitching. I found I was yelling.

I could have been ten feet away when the man in uniform turned. His black coat glinted with silver buttons. The peak of his cap came low over his eyes, casting them into a trench of darkness. A badge on the front caught the moon, two little glinting blobs of silver. I ran at him. My deck shoes skidded on the dewy lawn, and I landed with a thump in some sort of rockery.

Dean screamed.

The scream brought me on to my hands and knees. There was grey lawn, black cypresses, the distant orange glow of the fire. And two figures. The man in uniform, black and upright; and another, bent awkwardly forward because the man in uniform had him in an armlock. I got up, and yelled at them.

The man in uniform paid no attention. Dean was struggling. He screamed again. I saw him go down on his knees, twisting away from the armlock. The man in uniform yanked at him. I was still on the rockery. My foot hit something hard. I had been walking across a bed of ornamental heathers. The hard object was one of the edging stones. My fingers closed on it, and I stumbled forward across the grey lawn.

Dean was shouting now, a meaningless string of swearwords that made ugly music with the sirens down the street. The shoulders of the uniformed man lurched as the boot went in again. I heard him grunt, Dean's breath go between his teeth.

Then I was there, on top of them. The man looked round, this time. The moonlight hit him slam in the face. It was a big, white, round face. The eyes were narrow and the teeth were bared. With the clarity of extreme terror, I saw that the right upper canine was missing. Then I hit him.

I hit him with the rock, a big roundhouse swipe on the side of the head. Something squashed. It must have been his ear. He bellowed and clapped his hand to his head. I grabbed Dean by the arm and said, 'Car!'

He was making disgusting noises, as if he was trying to be sick. I dragged him towards the gate. Our feet kept getting tangled. When I looked over my shoulder, the man in uniform was staggering in a circle, clutching his head. The gate's iron was cold under my hand, and the lights of Nadia's car were coming on like white suns. Tyres yelped as she stopped.

The back door flew open. I shoved Dean in. He flopped face-first. I climbed after him.

'Which way?' She seemed completely calm; not, 'What happened?' or, 'Are you all right?' Just, 'Which way?'

I could not seem to speak. My heart was beating like a machine gun.

Into the glare of the lights there staggered the man in uniform. His arms were up.

'Him,' I croaked.

She drove straight at him. He dived out of the way. There was a sharp *thud*.

Dean struggled upright.

Nadia put her foot down. The road swooped left. The shadows of evergreen trees swept across grey lawns like ghostly windscreen wipers. The speedometer needle hit seventy-five.

The road swung right. Fifty yards ahead, it widened and came to a full stop.

Rubber squealed as Nadia stood on the brakes. She did something with her left hand. Suddenly we were moving sideways, then backwards, in a stink of burning rubber.

Then she was heading back the way we had come, engine howling. I tried to marshal my scrambled thoughts. The blue lights swept down on us. 'Slow,' I said. 'Police.'

She nodded. Suddenly we were driving at twenty-five, three suburbanites, good as gold. There were policemen everywhere, but they seemed more interested in the crowd outside number 13 than passing motorists.

'Bloody knocking shop,' muttered Dean.

'What?'

'Where the party was. Kicked over a candle.'

'Who did?' The house was sliding by the window. Flames were roaring through the door, spitting sparks at a navy-blue skyful of stars.

'Me.'

'You?'

'Them geezers come after me. It was an accident.'

'What geezers?'

We drove. Dean did not answer. I caught my breath. After perhaps five minutes, Nadia said, 'Somebody chases us, I think.' Her accent had slipped, but her profile was still cool and perfect.

Through the back windscreen, I could see headlights and fog lights; a Jaguar or a Daimler. We changed lanes. The headlights changed lanes, too. They were fifty yards back. Dean had slid down below the level of the back window. Outside and above us were the trees of the Inner Ring Road, solid and reassuring. The cars were thickening; there were passers-by.

'Ask them what they want,' I said. 'They can't do anything, with all these people here.'

Dean said, 'Don't do that.' His voice was shaking. I remembered that savage place-kick to the belly.

Nadia must have caught his tone of voice. She braked, hard. I heard the squeal of the car behind's tyres as it pulled over, accelerated up on the inside.

'Christ,' said Dean.

There were four men in the Daimler. The face I was looking at was looking back at me from the driver's window. It was round, and white, and it wore a peaked cap. It had a grin, that left the eyes as friendly as a couple of patches of black ice. There was a web of black blood running from its ear. The right upper canine was an empty black stripe.

Suddenly I knew it would be madness to ask them what they wanted, witnesses or no witnesses. The sweat burst out on me. Any minute now, I thought, he will tread on his throttle, and get in front, and stop us. And we are dead.

Nadia accelerated. She got the Cavalier's nose in front of the Daimler. Then she swung the wheel hard left. There was a big, terrible bang, and a howl of maimed bodywork. The Daimler left the road.

I started to say something. Then I saw the tree.

It was a big sycamore, every leaf perfect in the rushing headlights. The Daimler was trying to slither back into the road, and nearly succeeding.

Not quite.

Its front left headlight went into the trunk at fifty miles an hour. The tail slewed out, slamming us sideways down the road. A car coming the other way blared its horn, tyres squealing as it dodged. The world spun outside the Cavalier's windows, came right again. In the back window, the Daimler was pouring steam. Cars were stopping. Soon the police would be there. I said, 'Where the hell did you learn to drive like that?'

She did not answer.

I said, 'Leave the car. Someone will have taken the number. The police will be looking for you.'

She considered that. Then she said, 'Fine.'

We left the car in a commuter car park, near the station, injured side to the wall, just another Vauxhall in a city full of Vauxhalls.

Suddenly I was eaten up with anxiety for *Vixen*. We could leave the Rassy at the Waterfront; Harry Featherstone would collect it. We ran into the station, Dean staggering between me and Nadia, another of Southampton's myriad drunks, and caught the train for Portsmouth Harbour.

14

Dean's face was white, except where the bruises were rising. His left eye was a blackened slit. His right was too wide open, glazed with shock. You are meant to give shock patients a rest, with hot, sweet tea if there are no internal injuries. I gave Dean whisky, and repeated the prescription for myself and Nadia.

He said, 'Mr Johnson didn't bleeding show.'

'So what happened?'

Dean gulped at his whisky. He said, 'I got past the geezer on the door, told him I was waiting for some punters. I hung about a bit, said hello to Dmitri. So then I thought, maybe Mr Johnson come in the back way, and went upstairs already. So I went upstairs, and had a look.' He shook his head, carefully. His voice was thick, as if he was drunk. 'They was at it everywhere. I couldn't see him nowhere. It's meant to be private up there. I stuck my head in this one room, and a bouncer come at me from the corridor. So I went in the room, locked the door. They had a four-poster bed in there and candles and that. I seen I couldn't get down the corridor, so I went into the room. The bird started screaming blue murder for help, and the bloke she was with was hiding under the bed, and the bouncer was trying to kick the door down. So I went out the window, but I knocked the bloody candles over on the way out, and the curtains started burning. Then them geezers come after me. Security geezers.'

I had been thinking about that. There was no reason the security men should have been there. Unless they had been following Dean. And if they had been following Dean, they must have watched him all the way up to Lanark Drive from New Venice. But how had they found him?

'Oh yeah,' said Dean. 'I read the label on this one's uniform. They're called Equipoise.'

'Equipoise?'

'Weird name,' said Dean.

He finished his whisky. His head lolled sideways. He was asleep.

I remembered the silver buttons on the black uniform. There had been silver buttons in the moonlight the night Marie had burned. I dragged Dean forward into the bunk room. How the hell had they found him?

They had lost contact with Dean after he had gone out of the window of the squat. But they must have been following Nadia. That was how they had come to be at Powney's, tracked down Marie. They had lost Nadia and me at Powney's. They had been helping Dickie out with his little photographic problem, and she had walked straight into them this evening. And I had walked into her; and they had picked up Dean's trail again.

I wondered what they found so interesting about Nadia.

I was beginning to find her very interesting myself.

When I came back into the saloon, she was sitting upright, square-shouldered, gazing at the whisky in her glass.

I said, 'You pulled me out of thick mud and on to a high jetty without assistance. You bounced a large woman up a vertical companionway. You drive like someone has spent a lot of time teaching you how to. You act as if you own the place.' I tipped a quarter-inch of whisky into my glass. 'You work for the police. Right?'

She shrugged. 'Also somebody has taught you how to ask questions. If I tell you, I ask that you tell nobody?' She was sitting up very straight, her hands folded in her lap, her eyes large and golden and earnest.

I said, 'Last time you left, you walked out with a film that belongs to me. I don't see why I should trust you.'

She said, 'You don't understand.'

I discovered I was very pleased to see her again. Sitting in the warm glow of the mahogany panelling, she radiated the kind of feeling of at-homeness that you get from a cat sleeping on a sofa. It was infectious, that feeling. Nadia and me and *Vixen*, I found myself thinking. A good trio –

Stop it, I thought. She has a beautiful face and a beautiful body, and you have already seen that she is prepared to use them. I said, 'Explain.' My voice was harsher than I had meant it to be.

'I am a Lieutenant of the criminal police of the Republic of Estonia. I speak English, so I am asked by my senior officer to make enquiry into the death of Lennart Rebane.' She shrugged. 'So this does not make me a bad person,' she said. 'In Estonia we have laws, same as here, to protect society. I am not a spy, or a secret police person.'

'Who knows you're here?'

'I am in England with a visa to attend a European conference on private and public safety in Imperial College in London. So now you know.' She was watching me with an odd expression in her eyes; as if she wanted reassurance. 'I am not here as an official, of course. You can send me away.'

I said, 'You wouldn't go.'

She smiled. It was a big, dazzling smile. 'I think we are both looking for the same thing,' she said.

I said, 'Why were you talking to Dickie Wilson?'

She shrugged. 'Investigation,' she said. 'I am collecting statements. I told him I was a journalist for an Estonian newspaper.' She batted her eyelashes at me, made a kissing movement of her lips. 'He was very pleased to talk with me.'

'Did he tell you anything?'

'He is a difficult man,' she said. 'Very hard, I think. He pretends he is caring for his young people, but he is a bureaucrat. In my country we know about bureaucrats. They are interested only to look splendid themselves.' Her analysis of Dickie was so exactly right that I found myself warming to her again. 'He told me that your crew was not sober,' she said. 'He blamed a certain William Tyrrell.'

It was all good anodyne stuff. It might even be true. But there were important things missing.

I said, 'You'd better stay on the boat.'

'Of course.' She seemed to hesitate. Then she said, 'You know, it is a great pleasure for me to be back?' She took my hand. 'OK, so I am working for the police. But I am a person too. I have never been on a boat like this.' She lowered her eyes. 'Or with a man who looks after a boat like this. I am very pleased I have met you, William Tyrrell.' She leaned forward and kissed me quickly on the cheek.

It added up. I found myself very pleased, indeed. Half a policewoman, and half a woman. It made sense.

I said, 'Welcome aboard,' and showed her to my cabin.

Then I locked her in.

I put my feet up on the settee berth in the saloon, and went to sleep.

Someone was battering on wood. The wood was a coffin lid. Marie was in the coffin. I had to let her out, because I knew that she was alive, that the fire had all been a mistake, but they had screwed the lid down anyway. But I could not move. So I started shouting for help, loud as I could –

'Easy,' said a voice. It was Dean. His left eye was swollen shut. His right was alight with the will to please. He said, 'Her in there wants to come out.'

I lay for a moment in a bath of sweat, letting the dream go away. Then I rolled off the settee and unlocked the door.

Nadia's hair was tousled by sleep into a blond mane. She looked rumpled and cynical. She said, 'There is no need to lock me in. I will not run away again. Now please coffee. Shower.'

She had brought a bag from the car last night. Ten minutes later, she walked into the saloon, neat as a Fortnum and Mason parcel, in a white blouse and long white shorts. Her eyes watched mine. She continued to look cynical.

She threw a brown envelope on to the table. 'So you do not trust me still,' she said. The smile broke through. 'It is hard to blame you, of course. But now, we work together. You will maybe like to look at this.'

It was thick and stiff and heavy, the way photographs are heavy. My fingers fumbled as I tore open the flap.

There were thirty-six colour prints, developed like holiday

snaps. I leafed through. My heart was beating hard. I said, 'Dean,' and shoved them across the saloon table.

He picked them up, bruised hands clumsy. 'That's it,' he said, and pushed them back.

Marie had been killed for these photographs. Someone had smashed me on the head, gone through my pockets, searched my boat for these photographs.

The negatives were in the envelope. They matched the prints. They were numbered one to thirty-six. The numbers were consistent.

The pictures were rubbish.

In one, there was a face that someone who already knew Rebane might have recognized as his. There were shots of flock wallpaper, a bare foot, a blurred print of Dean. That was it. Rubbish.

I put the pictures back, shoved them across to Nadia.

'Nothing,' I said. 'Did you show these to Dickie Wilson?'

'Of course no,' she said. 'I found them so I can take them to the mother of Lennart Rebane. He wrote her a letter from London, when they were taken. He was worried there would be disgrace. I have found them so I can show her there is no problem, nothing to fear.' She smiled at me. 'Well, what do we do now?'

15

At nine o'clock, I got out the address books and started on the telephone. Yellow Pages said nothing about Equipoise. So I started calling people.

There was a lot of explaining to do. They were people I had known when I was on the *Tribune*, and they had short memories. Most of them thought I was dead, or retired, or wished I was, because they had read their newspapers. Most of them told me without sincerity how much they envied me. None of them had ever heard of anything called Equipoise, though one of them told me there was a neo-Hindu sect of that name operating out of Des Moines, Iowa. But at eleven-twenty, when I was on my third cup of coffee, I got lucky.

I was ringing Jerome Feuerbach, a forty-year-old scourge of the hypocrite who wore silk suits and had retired from a TV news programme to edit a popular encylopaedia by day and indulge in the wilder type of conspiracy theory by night.

'Bill,' he said, 'Superstar.'

'Subversive,' I said.

He laughed. We went through the usual retirement and sailing jokes. Then I trailed Equipoise across his nose.

'Equipoise?' he said. 'What d'you want them for?'

'I'll tell you when I find out.'

'You'd better.'

'So tell me about them.'

'They're a security firm,' he said. 'Also very private investigations.'

'I know that.'

'Yes, yes.' His voice had become testy, which meant he had run out of persiflage and was diving into the crammed filing-cabinet of his mind. 'But not your usual kind. A bit Jermyn Street. Very hard to get close to, and not given to answering questions.'

This was merely a preamble, to impress me with the super-human feats of spadework involved in his research. I kept quiet, as was expected.

'You will remember the mid 1970s,' he said. 'A lot of old buffers running around telling each other Western Civilization in melting pot, arming the tenantry and generally forming private armies. Well, most of that lot went back to hunting foxes, but a couple hung on. One of them was a bloke called Varley Fitzgerald. He'd been in the Paras, and he did not take kindly to socialists of any kind. So he started something called the Chevron Foundation, to safeguard the freedom of the individual. First it was a baby army, with a few ex-SAS hard nuts in charge of some volunteer loonies. When they all went off to work for Ollie North he started a sort of think tank, which sent pamphlets about the place and provided ready-made speeches for a lot of MPs on the far right; some US senators too, I believe. Then the Tories got back in, and the people who had been giving Fitzgerald his money decided they didn't need him any more. But he's an adaptable cove, so he decided he'd put all that muscle and aggro to sensible use. So he started Equipoise.'

'A security agency.'

'Of a new kind. What Varley reckoned was that the onward march of free enterprise was beset right and left by the trade unions. He reckoned that Thatcher's union legislation didn't go far enough. So he set up as a freelance strikebreaker.'

'You can't be a strikebreaker in England.'

'Yes you can. Example. There was this company, Wavecrest Homes, building one of those marina villages in Wales; owned by David Lundgren, Swedish money man. Wavecrest wanted a non-union site. The local union boys objected. He bussed in guys from Ireland and the North, ready to work for half union rates because there wasn't any work to do at home. There were punch-ups. Lundgren brought actions under the trade union laws. Problem was, none of the people he sued had any money, so they weren't worth suing. So he called in Equipoise.'

He paused. He would be lighting a Gauloise, tipped.

'And then?'

'They're not just thugs,' he said. 'They do their homework. The chief negotiator had a mistress. That came out when he was found under her bedroom window with two broken legs. He said a couple of guys had done it with iron bars. His mistress said he had fallen, but then she seemed very frightened about something. A couple of other union guys seemed to have car crashes, pissed as rats, which was odd because they were impeccable Chapel. By the end of it, five union men were in hospital, badly hurt, with their reputations blown wide open. And the local union boys sort of lost interest.'

'I would,' I said. Blackmail and violence, I thought. It had a familiar ring. 'Didn't the police get curious?'

'One has one's theories about whose side the police are on, in cases like that,' he said. 'Besides, they were pretty thorough frame-ups.' He yawned. 'Sorry,' he said. 'New girlfriend. Does that answer your question?'

I said, 'Thank you, Jerome. Where does this Fitzgerald of yours hang out?'

'He's in the Hampshire telephone directory,' said Jerome. 'Watch out for baseball bats.'

We rang off. At the time, I thought he was joking.

Nadia was watching me from the far settee. 'So?' she said.

'I am going to visit some people,' I said.

'Security people.'

'Correct.'

'You will maybe get hurt.'

I said, 'Journalists don't get hurt in daylight.'

I called directory enquiries, and asked for the number of Fitzgerald, V. I wrote it down on a page of my notebook.

Stopped dead.

I turned back to the page where I had stuck in the number

Claudia had given me: the number she had said was the Department of Trade.

It was the same as Varley Fitzgerald's. Fitzgerald, or someone working for him, had hired Pinsley to search *Vixen*.

For a moment, I considered sending them the film. They would see nothing on it. The violence would stop.

But if Equipoise had searched *Vixen*, terrorized Dean, killed Marie, all for the sake of a strip of celluloid, I was not going to let them get away with it. In fact, I was going to blow them wide open.

I dialled the number.

The voice on the other end was clipped, faintly military.

I asked for Captain Fitzgerald.

'Who's that speaking?'

I thinned out my voice, smoothed it down. 'Christopher Tyrrell,' I said. 'MP.'

'Stand by.' He was military, all right.

There was a pause. A new voice said, 'Mr Tyrrell?'

Sweat broke under my shirt. If he had called me Christopher, that would have been that. I said, 'Good morning. I've got a chap here who'd like to meet you. I said I'd ring you as a matter of . . . introduction.'

'Quite.' The voice was soft as a hammer in an Angora hat. 'Who's this chap?'

'He's running a business,' I said. 'He's got some difficulties with security. I said you might be able to help.'

'Ah,' said the voice. 'Yes.'

'He'd like to come out today, if possible.'

'Three o'clock,' he said. 'For quarter of an hour.'

'That's very good of you,' I said.

'Not at all,' he said. 'I've got some South Africans I'd like you to meet on the sixth. Lunchtime. Boodles. Do come.'

'Delighted,' I said. One good turn deserves another, in the upper echelons.

I ordered a car from Hertz, and pulled the blue linen Noriega suit out of the wardrobe. It was somewhat crumpled – *Vixen* did not run to an iron. I put it on anyway. I knotted a Royal Ocean Racing Club tie round my neck, and stepped into a pair of black shoes. Then I greased my hair back behind my ears and slid my little Sony tape recorder into the jacket pocket. When I went into the saloon, Nadia smiled and put her hand over her face.

I said, 'What's the problem?'

'You are a businessman?' she said.

'That's right.'

'Too big, too brown.'

'We come in all sizes,' I said. 'Goodbye.'

She had changed out of white shorts into a knee-length blue skirt. She picked up a matching jacket from the settee. 'I am coming with you.'

'You bloody well are not.'

Her smile did not flicker. 'You need a partner,' she said. 'All businessmen have them.'

I said, 'The man I am going to see is not a nice man.'

She said, 'I am a police person.'

It was one o'clock. She was capable of arguing all day. I said, 'Come on, then.'

We picked up the car and drove northeast out of Southampton. We had lunch in a pub.

It was a sunny day, with white cotton-wool clouds trailing their shadows across a beech wood on a round hill. The pub was half-empty, the bar a cool cavern of black oak. We ate smoked salmon sandwiches outside and drank half-pints of Dunkertons Kingston Black Cider at a wooden table in the back garden.

A man was fishing in the chalk stream that wound through the willows in the bottom of the valley. Nadia said, 'It is a soft country. Not like Estonia.'

We were on our way to ask questions about perversion and death. But for the moment, none of that existed. The sun shone, and the lunch had been a good one, and Nadia was a beautiful woman.

'Rocks and trees,' said Nadia. 'Great cold, and mosquitoes in the summer. Only the people are the same.'

The moment flickered, began to disappear. She smiled at me, the big, surprised smile I had seen when she had found the coffee on *Vixen*. 'But you can forget, no? This feels like a holiday, not business.' She put her hand on mine. 'Thank you for bringing me.'

A lark was singing high above the hillside. The moment was back. 'Glad you came,' I said.

Deep down, a nagging voice said, *Can you trust this woman?*

I ignored it. The lark worked its way up into the sun's eye.

Then it was time to go.

North of the pub, the countryside became steadily more expensive. Gold-thatched cottages with prominent burglar alarms nestled smugly in the bosom of soft chalk hills. After thirty-five minutes, I pulled the nose of the car between two pillars crowned with fat stone pineapples. There was a lodge festooned with honeysuckle. The man who came out of the porch was by no means apple-cheeked. He had hair like black suede, and a black eyebrow moustache. He walked with a dangerous spring in his step. 'Morning, sir,' he said. 'If you'd like to proceed on?'

'Soldier,' said Nadia, as we passed along a beautiful tarmac drive across a billiard-table-green park studded with pollard oaks. The perfect trimness of the place was beautiful, but chilling. Lovely from the point of view of a story; but stacked up against one man and his boat, it verged on the frightening.

The drive passed through a sun-splashed beech copse. The house came into view. It stood on a low rise of ground, a pocket castle in Strawberry Hill Gothic, a rich man's whimsy from the age of duels. Another springy man opened the front door. We went into a hall two storeys high, walls covered with pictures.

There was a lot of cannon-fire in the pictures, and blood and dead horses. I did not have long to look at them, because the door opened and Fitzgerald came in.

He had a small, brown face, the nose and chin horned towards each other like nutcrackers. Despite the weather he was wearing a three-piece heather mixture suit, cut close but not tight, that gave him a vaguely horsey air.

'Afternoon,' he said. His eyes were a surprise; hard and bright, but deeply pouched. They were the kind of eyes that took in a lot.

I thumbed the RECORD button of the tape recorder in my pocket, introduced myself as Harry Wallace, and Nadia as Nadia Orlov, a co-director.

'Russian?' he said.

She simpered, something I would not have believed her capable of. 'My grandparents,' she said.

He lost interest, glanced at his watch, and stationed himself against the mantelpiece, under a portrait of himself in the uniform of the 17th/21st Lancers. He said, 'I hear you've got a difficulty.'

I said, 'Yes. Tell me about your organization.'

The eyes rested on me like a couple of bright ice cubes. 'We specialize in security and intelligence,' he said.

The tape recorder was running in my pocket. I said, 'Can you give me some idea of your track record?'

'I should have thought Christopher Tyrrell would have given you some idea.'

'He was very . . . discreet.'

He caressed his jaw as if he loved it. 'You have my word that my methods are effective. We operate on a no cure, no pay basis. For reasons of security I cannot discuss individual cases.'

The portrait to his left was of the Fascist leader Oswald Mosley. I was not getting anywhere. I said, 'All right. I've got a factory in Swindon. I've got a director who's telling the competition what he oughtn't. And the competition have got one of my shop stewards in its pocket, I think. I want someone to find out exactly what's going on. Report, and act.'

'Why don't you just sack them?'

I said, 'They've hurt me. I want to hurt them.'

'Hurt them?'

'Accidents will happen,' I said, and did not take my eyes off him.

His face did not move. He said, 'Yes.'

'Good,' I said. 'There are two things I'd like to ask you. First, references. Who have you worked for in the past?'

'Martin Williams, solicitors, Bristol. Globe Industries. They'll give you an idea.'

In the sudden silence I could hear the whine of a chainsaw, the chink of someone stacking plates at the far end of the house. Globe Industries had been at Otto Campbell's adventure school, learning how to fall down mountains. If it was a coincidence, it was a spectacular one.

I did not believe in coincidences that spectacular. 'Thank you,' I said. 'Now, as to . . . *modus operandi*?'

'Meaning?' He was gazing at the moulding in the corner of the room.

'I want this chap sackable,' I said. 'But I don't necessarily want him to be able to walk to his next job. If you get my drift.'

'I see.' His eyes returned from the moulding to mine. Suddenly they narrowed. His face was carved from brown wood. He said, 'Have we met before?'

'I don't think so,' I said. 'So what will you do?'

'Will you excuse me a moment?'

He went out of the room, walking fast. A door slammed. Nadia said, 'What is he doing?'

I shrugged. My stomach felt hollow.

'I think we have trouble,' she said.

Fitzgerald came back into the room. His back was straight as a poker. He was carrying a leatherbound book, quarto size, open. It was a cuttings book.

We had trouble.

He smiled at us, a smile that missed his eyes by a mile.

He went back to the marble fireplace, rested his elbow next to the smart black telephone that stood beside an animalier bronze of a wolf rampant.

He said suddenly, 'Do you know Dickie Wilson?'

I could see the page in the book. There was a newspaper photograph of me and Dickie on the quay at Chatham, both of us looking angry, heads turned towards the camera. My stomach sickened. What I saw in Fitzgerald's face was recognition. I said, 'I've come across him.'

He said, 'Do you know, I think you're wasting my time?' His hands came out of his pockets, and he stepped away from the mantelpiece. I stood up. He looked small, and hard, and dangerous. There was a new buzz in the air, now. It made the pulse pound and dried out the mouth. Violence.

I said, 'What are you talking about?'

He said, 'You have conned me, Mr Tyrrell. I don't like that.'

So we were rumbled.

He said, 'Please leave.'

I said, 'I would like the name of the client who requested that you instruct Mr Pinsley to search my boat.'

'I have absolutely nothing to say,' he said. 'You are trespassing. Get yourselves off my property.' He picked up a mobile telephone. 'I am calling the police.'

'Thank you for your time,' I said courteously.

He said, 'You are going to regret this,' in a quiet, conversational voice.

I said, 'The client's name.'

He said, 'Get out.'

We left.

As we drove through the park, the smell of new-cut grass wafted through the open window. Nadia was flushed. She said, 'This is a violent man.'

I smiled at her. 'You don't have to worry. He'll be frightened of newspapers. He won't hurt us.'

We passed under the hard black eyes of the lodgekeeper with the eyebrow moustache. As we turned on to the main road, I was not at all sure I was right.

16

When we got back to Gosport, Dean was up the mast, oiling sheaves.

The more I thought about Fitzgerald, the less I liked what he had said. *Vixen*'s mast was very tall. I could feel it sticking up like a lighthouse, saying *here we are*. Equipoise had good eyesight. So I got Dean down to deck level, and cast off, and motored across to the Portsmouth side, where I begged my way into tying up alongside a tramp freighter in the commercial docks. Tucked away among the commercial shipping, I felt a little less naked.

I fetched the telephone and sat on the deck, looking across at the truncated mast of HMS *Victory*, getting some sun on the face. I punched the buttons. The voice said, 'Otto Campbell.'

'Otto,' I said.

'How the hell are you?' he said. 'You saved my life with that Globe bunch, and no mistake.'

I said, 'The Globe bunch was what I was ringing about. How did you get hold of them?'

'Usual thing,' he said. 'Friends of friends.'

'Who?'

'They turned up at Youth Venture,' he said. 'Dickie was having one of his fund-raising evenings. He got talking to that bloke Tom Stibbard, the one who tried to drop you over the cliff, and recommended the Centre.'

'Good old Dickie,' I said.

'He's still plenty angry with you,' said Otto.

'I'm sure,' I said.

'I've got ten of them waiting for a long-distance swim,' said Otto. 'Got to go.'

'See you in Finland,' I said.

He laughed. 'Never give up, do you? See you there, then.'

I switched off. Scratch the surface, and what pops up? Dickie Wilson, every time.

When I called Globe Industries, Tom Stibbard was out. His secretary told me he would call me back at six. I was not so sure.

'So what now?' said Nadia.

'Keep the boat afloat.'

'At this time?'

'At all times.'

I spent an hour pulling apart the generator that makes *Vixen*'s spare electricity when she is at sea. At five, we hitched the dinghy up to the main halyard, and winched it down over the side.

It had a tan lugsail, the dinghy, and a little jib. It had been the last boat my father had built in the shed. The centreboard case had a slight wave on its right-hand side, where my ten-year-old hands had planed off too much. He had laughed, a thumping big noise behind his black beard, grey-streaked by then. 'You spoilt her,' he said. 'You'd better have her.' It was the kind of boat most children sailed twenty years ago, clinker-built from pine planks on ash ribs, fat, jolly and obsolete as a wicker shopping basket.

I put the mast up. Nadia climbed in. I pushed off into the harbour.

The breeze slapped into the dinghy's sail. The water rippled under the nose. We made off northwest, in the general direction of Fareham, dodging the Cherbourg ferry gliding out into the grey channel. I started to teach her to sail. She had light hands, and a good memory. She seemed to get Fitzgerald out of her mind.

By the time we had turned to go back to *Vixen*, the harbour was a mass of sails. She brought us alongside, reasonably neatly. Dean took the painter.

On deck, the telephone rang. It was Tom Stibbard. I reminded him of our meeting in Wales.

I said, 'I wanted to ask you a favour.'

'I suppose you could say I owe you one.'

'Strictly voluntary,' I said. 'I've just been to visit a security firm called Equipoise. I wonder if you could give them a reference?'

'Oh,' he said. 'Yes. Why not?'

'What did they do for you?'

'Pilferage,' he said. 'We've got a CD pressing plant in Dagenham. Half a million ... that is, a sum of money ... went missing. We called in Equipoise. It stopped.'

'How did they do it?'

'I didn't ask.'

'How did you get on to them?'

'Youth Venture had a presentation in London, a few months ago. Showing a film about sail training. They were looking for corporate donations. There are attractive tax aspects, you know. I was there in my capacity as Group Sponsorship Officer.'

'And?'

'I was talking to a gentleman there, about responsibility, realization of goals, probity in the workforce. I mentioned our Dagenham problem. He told me about this agency called Equipoise, how they were based on libertarian principles, specializing in the eradication of corruption and encouraging the individual to face up to his responsibility to the group. He recommended them personally.'

I was listening to the public face of Equipoise. I thought about the private one, skulking in the dark, spreading violence and death. 'Who was this gentleman?'

'Very nice man,' said Tom. 'Rear-Admiral Richard Wilson. Your President.'

'Thank you,' I said. 'Thank you very much indeed.'

So there it was, wrapped in a nice neat bundle. Dickie wants his film. So Dickie tells Equipoise to go looking for it. Dickie did not have to kill anybody. The firm took care of all that.

The light thickened with dusk, and the wind died. The

dinghy's fenders bumped gently against the side. Out there in the channel, a deep-laden rustbucket was pushing a hillock of bow-wave up towards the harbour. It was towing a leprous-looking punt. The thud of its engine was a busy mechanical heartbeat.

'Coming a bit near, isn't he?' said Dean.

The sound of the tramp's engine had changed from a busy heartbeart to a loud clatter. It was perhaps half a cable's length away. The hull was foreshortened. There were no hatch covers; the holds were full of big lumps of something that might have been scrap metal. Navigation lights burned red and green on the wings of the wheelhouse. I watched idly, waiting for the helmsman to bear away across the tide.

He did not bear away. He came straight on.

The sound of the engine had become a monotonous hammering. My tongue was suddenly made of felt. I was on my feet, gripping the steel rope of the lifeline, yelling.

The hammer of the engine filled the universe. My voice made no sound.

'Fenders,' I yelled to Dean. But Dean was no longer on deck.

I scrabbled in the locker, caught a handful of fenders. The heads of the men in the wheelhouse were stolid and unmoving, looking straight ahead. They're blind, I thought. They wouldn't be doing this if they could see. The bow was twenty yards away. I could see the white-painted Roman numerals of the load marks, chipped and flaking on the rusty plating.

The shoulders of the man in the middle moved, turning the wheel. The bow began to swing away. Nadia was shouting something, clutching my arm. She sounded relieved.

That was because she did not understand what was happening.

A boat does not follow its nose round a turn, like a car. When a boat turns the rudder swings the stern, and the stern pushes the bow, and the whole length of the hull pivots around a point about two-thirds of the way aft from the bow.

I ran for the dinghy. Too late.

The scrap barge's side was six feet away from *Vixen*, moving sideways, fast. The gap narrowed from six feet to four, then three. Nadia was screaming. The hammer of the diesels was like a big metal drum. The rusty iron wall touched the side of the dinghy, gentle as the brush of a butterfly's wing. Something happened to its shape. It became narrower, deeper, pressed between the barge and *Vixen*'s side like half a pea pod.

I was shouting. Above the shouting there was a big, nasty *crunch*. The dinghy folded up and disappeared. And the side of the scrap barge, five hundred tons of metal, drove remorselessly on to *Vixen*'s seventy-year-old hull.

The fenders were big air-bags, made of inch-thick polythene. The one closest to me squashed. I felt the evening air in my mouth, waited for it to bounce the scrap barge off again.

It did not bounce.

The tramp freighter next to *Vixen* was moored tight against a solid concrete quay. When the fenders went flat, the scrap barge was going to smash *Vixen* like her dinghy.

I had my hands against the barge's side. I was pushing like an idiot, trying to shift five hundred tons with God knew how many horsepower of diesel screwing it at me.

There was a heavy detonation, then another. Nadia shouted with surprise. I did not, because I knew what it was. The fenders were exploding. They went off one after the other like a battery of field guns.

We were pushing perhaps a third of the way down the barge's hull from the bow. It was deep-laden; the deck was level with my eyes. When I looked down at the wheelhouse I could see the helmsman's face, pale in the dusk, behind the windows.

He was laughing.

I thought of *Vixen*'s mast, towering above the shipping. A beacon. Damn you, *Vixen*, I thought.

Nadia shouted something, her voice high. She was up towards the bow, feet braced against a hatch coaming, shoving iron.

'Going!' she yelled.

She was right.

Dead ahead were the lights of the ferryport, strung like agates down the pier. Four of them were showing to the right of the barge's bow. As I watched, another one popped out, and another. I was shouting, swearing incoherently.

The tide was ebbing hard. The ebb had got under the barge's nose and was prising it away from *Vixen*, towards the middle of the channel. The only way the helmsman could get it back was to apply right rudder, which would swing his stern out as well.

A black ribbon of clear water appeared between the hulls, widened to a stripe, then an alley. The remains of the dinghy wallowed like a dead seal. I ran aft, hung more fenders between the hulls where they touched. There was very little weight in him now, because the tide was taking him away from us. The helmsman's teeth were bared as he spun the wheel. He'll go away, I thought. He's finished.

White water boiled round his rudder as he spun his wheel to starboard. The sickness returned to my stomach. He was coming back.

I bent down and pulled from a cockpit locker the two-foot iron bar I used as an extension to the bilge-pump handle. *You will regret this*, said the small, crisp voice of the man in the heather mixture suit under the pictures of cavalry battles.

The barge came in again, yawing, as if the helmsman was not sure of what he was doing. I gripped the iron bar hard. The rusty hull was a foot away now, bow in, moving slow but horribly purposeful.

I put one foot on *Vixen*'s lifelines, and stepped aboard.

The deck was a narrow catwalk round a hold full of metal chunks. It lurched as the barge's side met *Vixen*'s. I heard the bang of another fender, the crack of a stanchion tearing out of *Vixen*'s deck, and a big, nasty creaking. The wheelhouse windscreen was swimming with the blood-coloured clouds of the sunset. The hammer of the engine rattled the teeth in my head. I pulled back the arm with the iron bar in it, and flung it into the centre of the screen.

There was the sound of breaking glass. Above the rattle of the engine, someone began screaming. Edges of sharp metal tore at my hands as I scrambled into the hold and out the other side.

There were terrible grinding noises where the two hulls joined. I did not look back. I jumped on to the side deck and yanked the wheelhouse door open.

It stank of oil and cigarette smoke. There was a man lying on the deck. His hands were over his eyes. What I could see of his face was a wet red mask. He was moaning. The other man had been bending over him. As I went in he straightened up. He had a wide, white face with slit eyes. His teeth looked big and yellow as a horse's. The right upper canine was missing. The left ear was a red, raw mess. He had been there last night, hitting Dean in the garden, silver buttons gleaming under the moon.

There was nobody at the wheel.

I grabbed it and yanked it hard to port. The man with the missing tooth came at me.

It was like running into a thrashing machine. I am big, but I have made a speciality of staying out of fights. Now, I wedged myself against the wheel and did what I could.

He was grinning. I took a swipe at the grin, felt my knuckles slide on tooth enamel. Something hit me impossibly hard in the stomach, and everything turned red and nasty. I locked my arm in the wheel, kept it down to port. I knew I had to stay on the wheel.

The next bang was somewhere around my ear. It hurt a lot, in a vague, foggy way. The grin meant pain. I lurched away from it, realized too late I had abandoned the wheel. My right knee exploded. I pitched forward, tripped over the body on the floor, found myself hanging on to a handle of some kind.

A door handle.

I heaved it downwards. He was coming at me crabwise, hands clawed. The door swung inwards. I was in cool air, sprawling against the barge's rail. He grunted, kicking. I twisted. The boot that had been meant for my groin caught me on the outside of the left thigh. *Dead leg*, shrieked a voice from my schooldays. Both legs gone, I hung on the rail.

He moved in.

Someone had hold of my useless legs, and was lifting them up over the rail. My fingers twisted free of the steel. The hammer of the engine was like the roar of artillery. I knew enough to realize that I was going over the side. But my legs were not working. All I could do was yell.

Then I was falling.

Propellor, I thought.

I hit the water. It was cold, spinning. It cleared my head instantly. I paddled frantically with my arms, waiting for the bite and chew of the big bronze blades, spinning like a mincing machine by my legs.

It did not come. The punt whipped past my head on its tow-rope. Then the barge was turning, broadside-on, a black cliff against the bloody clouds. My legs were hurting, badly. But it was a useful pain, because it meant they were still there, and I could use them to swim.

Swim.

The surface was a sheet of black glass, seamed with the creases of the ebb. The tide was sweeping me out; the lights of the shore were moving, fast. *Vixen*'s mast slid away upstream, tall and black against the sky.

Over to the west, the fiery upper limb of the sun was oozing down through the chimneys of Gosport, making a red lane in the sea. I trod water, getting the feeling back into my legs.

The barge's engine-note changed. I looked round, quickly. What I saw set my heart thumping, and hollowed a pit of fear under my breastbone.

The barge was no longer a cliff. It was an island, squat and solid. My head must be in the middle of the lane of blood from the sun. It was coming to run me down.

I dived, swam sideways through the flat, mud-tasting water. Dirty water, I thought. Heavy metals. As if five hundred tons of barge would give me time to die of slow poisons.

I came up in his bow-wave. I felt the lift of the water before my eyes got used to the light, cringed away from the rasp of the hull. It swept by ten feet away. It was a small triumph, and accidental. But it made me feel better. Missed, you bastard, I thought.

The sun had gone. The water was dark. He would not see me now. But there was not much more swimming left in me. Before I got back to *Vixen*, I would drown.

The wheelhouse was coming past. I made my decision.

Hard as I could, I swam for the white ghost of the propwash at the barge's stern. It drew ahead of me. Behind it, skittering at the end of an overlong towline, came the punt.

I put up my hands and clawed at the gunwale. It was travelling at five knots. Splinters ripped the flesh of my fingers. *Hold on*, I told myself. *Hold on*.

The yells kicked at the back of my teeth. But I held on to the flare of the dinghy's bow. My feet came up, dragging in the water. My legs ached like teeth. All right, I told myself. Two choices. Rejoin the human race, or sink like a brick. And with a grunt of pure agony, I hooked my right leg over the gunwale.

I waited, hanging there in the rushing dusk; waited for the boat to capsize, and for me to roll under with it. It was a big, fat, evil old harbour punt. It heeled, but it did not capsize.

I had done it dozens of times, heaving myself out of the water and into boats. It is exhausting even after a day of fun in the wind. I had never done it with my legs kicked in, and my head ringing, into a dinghy being towed by a man who had tried to kill me twice in the past twenty minutes.

I clamped my teeth together. Then I heaved, leg and hands, dragging my body over the gunwale.

Water sluiced in. Gone, I thought. That's it. Then it slammed back on to an even keel, rocked violently, steadied. And for a long, blissful second I lay absolutely still and rested.

Only for a second. It was getting dark, but not so dark I could not see oars under the seat, and rowlocks strung under their holes.

My knife was still on its lanyard. Leaning forward, I found the eyesplice which attached the towrope to the ring on the punt's stem.

I began to saw at the cheap polypropylene. It parted with a thump. The dinghy yawed, and slowed, and drifted free, rocking in the barge's wake.

17

I pulled out the oars, and began to row back towards *Vixen*. I had time to think now. I did not even know if *Vixen* was still afloat. I looked over my shoulder. Her mast was still there. I felt hot with relief.

Then I heard again the crunch of the dinghy I had made with my father, the terrible creaking as the barge had squeezed *Vixen*'s hull.

The anger returned.

I was angry that violent, ignorant people should try to wreck something beautiful to achieve their dirty ends. I was furious at the ignorance of them, to think that they could brush away my friends and my past, because it was an irritation to them.

Down towards Gosport, the barge turned suddenly through 180°. Its long nose searched the water, one eye red, the other green. Looking for me.

A ferry was easing off its dock, a brilliantly-lit city sliding on the glassy tide. It passed between us. When it had gone, the barge was closer. The eyes had seen me. He was coming in.

There were six inches of water in the punt. I was dripping wet. I should have been shivering, with cold if not with fear. I was neither. Come on, you bastards, I thought. Come after me.

We were in the main channel now. I spun the dinghy and

rowed northwest as hard as I could against the ebb, splashing and catching crabs. Make fear, I was thinking. Create the atmosphere of terror. Beyond the dinghy's transom, the red eye and the green eye slid down the night, easing wider apart as they came closer.

My shoulders were hurting now, and my splinter-ripped hands were on fire. The fear nibbled at my mind. *Too late*, it told me. *You've left it too late*. The ebb sucked and swirled at the waterline. The iron ram would pound over the transom, roll the dinghy under, mince it in the whirling bronze blades.

The tide was too strong. I was not making progress. I had miscalculated.

The engine was a big noise again. The eyes had disappeared behind the loom of the blunt bow. I could hear the wash and roar of the bow-wave.

The water changed.

One moment it was alive and turbulent, plucking at the oars with its swirls. The next it was quiet and flat and dead. Over to starboard a light flicked, a green cat-blink. Channel marker.

I started to grin. It was probably more like a snarl than a grin, and it hurt the battered muscles of my face. Ten more big strokes, and the barge was a mere twenty feet away, its bow-wave roaring in long white combs on either side of the blunt nose, breaking on the shallows.

And suddenly it was falling behind, and the bow-wave shrank and disappeared. I rested on the oars, panting. The engine howled and clattered. Water churned. The barge did not move.

I prodded over the side with an oar. The bottom was two feet down: black, viscous mud. I turned the dinghy, and rowed gently past the barge.

It was hard aground, propellor spewing black mud. Fifty yards beyond its stern, the channel buoy tilted to the suck of the tide. He had chased me past it, out of the deep water, on to the mudbank. An hour from now, he would be high and dry.

Slowly, like a very old man, I pulled back towards the glare of the commercial docks and the tall black loom of *Vixen*'s spars. The adrenalin had left me. I ached all over. The barge was on the mud for ten hours, and its crew would not get far if they tried to walk away from it.

Ten hours' grace was better than none.

Vixen's white side bore long scratches. My fingers told me they were deep. I said, 'Dean?'

A head appeared over the side. A flashlight shone in my eyes. 'Skipper?' said Dean's voice.

'Get me up,' I said.

He gave me a hand. My muscles yelled as I scrambled over the lifelines.

He said, 'Jesus, I hate that geezer.'

Nadia came up from below. She watched silently as we hauled the remains of the dinghy on deck.

'Off,' I said. I was shaking like a leaf, past talking.

Dean untied the shorelines, working double time to make up for being frightened before. *Vixen* pointed her sharp, elegant nose into the tide, swung and headed into the yellow-and-white dazzle where the lights of Gosport swam in the water.

Nadia stood beside me. I could feel that she wanted to say something. I was too tired to help her. She put her hand out and touched my arm. It was enough.

The city lights fell astern. The red wink of the channel buoys curved into the dark Solent. The breeze was small and sou'westerly. I put her on autopilot, and Dean and I cranked up the main and staysail.

Nadia said, 'They try to wreck your boat, kill you. Do you not go to the police?'

'No,' I said.

'But you must.' It was too dark to see her face.

'In Estonia, maybe,' I said. The anger was back. 'Not here.'

'But what will you do?'

'Find out the truth,' I said. 'Write about it. Then go to the police.'

She was quiet after that. Which suited me fine.

We headed south and a little east until we picked up the flash of St Helen's Fort, off Bembridge.

'Anchor,' I said. Dean padded forward.

The anchor went down. We hung a lantern in the rigging, bagged the staysail, bundled the mainsail along the boom. Then I did the thing I did not want to do.

Under my cabin is the deepest point of *Vixen*'s bilge. With a boat *Vixen*'s age, you keep a firm eye on the water she is making. I lifted the floorboards and pushed the old carpenter's rule into the pond of black water below.

The pond was nine inches deep. Nine inches was about right. The sweat of relief broke on my body. I dragged my aching limbs on deck, and went over the side with a flashlight to look at the damage.

The fenders had done a good job. There were three or four long grooves, with splinters. None of them was more than a quarter of an inch deep. *Vixen*'s planking is an inch thick. The rest of it was dirt and rust, ground in along the side, and two stanchions, the uprights that hold the lifelines, torn out of the deck at their bases. It could have been a lot worse.

I clambered up the ladder and on to the deck, lowered myself down the companionway and lit the cabin lamp. The brass chronometer on the wall said ten-fifty-five. Two and a half hours ago, we had been sitting in the sun, listening to the approaching hammer of the barge's engine. It felt like a year.

Nadia came out of the cabin. When she saw my face, in the lamplight, she said 'Jeesus.'

In the glass front of the barograph was the reflection of an unsuccessful boxer. Both eyes were puffed and blackening. There was a graze on my right cheekbone. Blood had run out of my hair and dried on my face.

'Sit,' she said. Her fingers were cool and firm. She got water and Dettol, and cleaned Portsmouth Harbour out of the wounds.

I sat there in a half-coma, eyes closed. The smell of the disinfectant carried me back to Norfolk, ten years old, after we had launched the dinghy the barge had smashed; the day I bought the BSA Bantam out of the scrapyard. Front brake first, my father had said. Used to my pushbike, I had jammed on the back brake. I could still feel the horrible slide as the back wheel came round and flung me into the gravel, then the pain as he tweezed the sharp stones out of my knees. And after that the yelling two closed doors away as my mother let him know what she thought about fathers who were stupid enough to give children motorcycles; and his voice, deep and final, explaining.

Final in more ways than one.

Six weeks later, there had been a telegram from Tromsö Lines. My mother had read it, dropped it, gone to her room. Christopher had picked it up; even then, he had been reading other people's mail. REGRET MV *PROTEUS* LOST WITH ALL HANDS, it said.

At first, it had been as if he was away on an unusually long voyage. Little by little, it sank in that this time, the voyage would last for ever. And then the loneliness came.

He had been a pathologically silent man. Until he had gone, I had not realized that in his study and in the shed, fumbling with rope or hacking at a plank with a plane, I had been closer to him than children who could actually talk to their father. My life became a dreary round of work, and books, and staying out of the way while Christopher and my mother had the endless shouting-matches that kept them close. Nothing had ever been the same again.

The fingers stopped moving on my face. I opened my eyes.

The lamplight was gleaming on Nadia's tawny skin. She was sitting propped against the table, watching me. Her cheeks glistened in the lamplight as if they were wet. When she saw my eyes open, she smiled. It looked too brave to be quite right, that smile. She had been crying.

I said, 'You must be getting fed up with sticking me together.'

'It is a pleasure.' She put a hand on each of my shoulders, bent forward, and kissed me on the mouth, where the man in the wheelhouse had hit me. It hurt. But it was the thought that counted.

'Come,' she said. 'Now you go to bed.'

I went. My head hit the pillow, and lay there, banging like the scrap barge's engine. My mind was full of fog. But not foggy enough to hide the fact that someone else had climbed in, too. A pair of arms went round my neck. I could smell her Chanel. She whispered in my ear, 'You must be careful, please.' Her lips were soft as duckdown.

Sleep came down like a manhole cover.

Next morning, in daylight, it was all different. I woke alone, and dragged my aching legs on deck. *Vixen* was lying on a sea of blue glass, the Isle of Wight a low green animal sweating haze to the west. There was no extra water in the bilge. We had the anchor up before the sun was properly out of the sea, hoisted all three foresails, and took off down for St Catherine's Point, hard on a small southerly. The forecast said the southerly would go southeasterly, which was fine.

Dean took the helm. I sat and drank coffee below on the settee, and felt a hundred years old. I could hear Nadia clattering in the shower.

She came out of the shower with her head in a towel, wearing a T-shirt and jeans. The towel showed the good bones of her face. Dimly, I remembered her sliding into the bunk last night.

She sat down beside me, poured herself coffee. I put a tentative arm round her shoulders. For a moment, she stiffened. Then she let herself lean towards me, and her long fingers smoothed my knee. And she went on deck.

It was just like being on holiday.

Except for the aches, and the man with no canine, who would be off the mud bank by now, ready to finish what he had started.

I drank my coffee and climbed laboriously on to the settee. The skylight was ajar. Nadia was on the foredeck. She had taken off her T-shirt. She was wearing a bikini top, doing sit-ups. Her skin shone with good health. The muscles of her shoulders slid smoothly as she exercised. She looked well, and happy. *Bastard*, I told myself. *You can't do this*.

But I had done it before, for the greater glory of my employers. I knew how.

I swallowed nothing. Then I went forward, through the galley and into the girls' crew cabin. There was a table in there, the double tier of bunks on either side. Her bag was on the bottom bunk, starboard side. It was black leather, with pockets on the outside. It was not locked. I went down on my aching knees, and unzipped it.

There were dresses and underwear. The underwear was

practical stuff: no frills. Her make-up kit was a quarter the size of Claudia's. The shoes were good, plain Italian, with a couple of pairs of espadrilles. There were several books, all in English: A. G. Macdonell's *England, Their England*, Cobbett's *Rural Rides*, Nicholas and Charlie Hurt's *Quest for the Perfect Pub*. The books of a foreigner trying to find out what made Brits tick.

I repacked it, started on the outside pockets. There was a notebook bound in black boards. The entries were in a foreign language, in her small, neat handwriting. In the same pocket as the notebook was a combined address book and diary, big, with a heavy leather cover. It looked new. The diary entries were abbreviated, in what looked like the same language as the notebook. The address book held four or five telephone numbers in London, and was otherwise blank.

In the back cover of the diary was a sort of flap. There was a bundle of paper in there: typewritten sheets, folded in half, a London tube map, leaflets from Hertz and Holiday Inns of the kind handed out in airports. And a photograph.

My heart gave one big wallop in my chest. I crouched on my aching legs, steadied against the heave of *Vixen*'s drive southwestwards, and stared at the photograph.

It was a ten-by-eight print. It looked as if it had been taken with an old-fashioned, large-format camera; the grain was fine, and the black-and-white had a hint of sepia. There were five men gathered round a ship's wheel. It was a sailing ship; a fat mizzen mast rose abaft the wheel, a sail flaked untidily along its boom. The ship looked as if someone was varnishing it. The brass binnacle was covered with newspaper, and one of the men had a paintpot in his left hand. In his right was a brush, which he was brandishing theatrically at the photographer.

The men were bearded. The ones on the outside were wearing woollen hats and big, dirty jerseys. The man in the middle had a cap and dark pea-jacket buttoned tight to the chin; he would be the captain.

I had never seen the men in the jerseys before. But the man in the cap was my father.

I moved the photograph into the yellow beam coming

through the porthole. My hands were shaking. Not because a woman I barely knew was carrying a picture of my father in her suitcase. What was making the hair at the back of my neck prickle like an icy steel comb was on the newspaper on the binnacle.

They had used the front page of the *Svenska Dagbladet* to keep the varnish off the brass. The headline was huge and black. It yelled at me across the years. MARTIN LUTHER KING DÖD. Martin Luther King dead.

Martin Luther King had died in 1969.

Which meant my father was standing on deck, gazing across his beard at a photographer, four full years after my mother had opened the telegram that told us the MV *Proteus*, Captain Joshua Tyrrell, had sunk in the Skagerrak with all hands.

18

I stayed below, and repacked her suitcase, except for the photograph. I got on the VHF, and warned Spearman's boatyard that we were coming in for slipping, and told them that Pete the shipwright was urgently required. I wrote up in my notebook what had happened yesterday. Then, almost reluctantly, I climbed up the companionway.

When I went aft to check the course, Dean said, 'Very tasty.'

I nodded. The wind had freshened, and *Vixen* was creaming along through a sea which was beginning to look ruffled and slaty.

Nadia was lying on her back by the forehatch. She had finished her exercises. There was a faint gleam of sweat on her skin. She opened her eyes when my shadow fell across her.

I took a deep breath. I hardly wanted to speak. Her face was grave, perhaps because of what she saw in mine. I said, 'What are you doing?'

'Sunbathing.'

'In England,' I said.

I pulled the photograph out of my shirt pocket, flicked its edge with my thumbnail.

She sat up fast. Her face was dead serious.

'Where did you get this?' I said.

Vixen ploughed through the dark-blue sea.

She said, 'In Tallinn. From the mother of Lennart Rebane.'

I stared at her. I said, 'My father.' I was finding it hard to keep my voice steady. I did not want to ask the next question. 'He was alive in 1969. Is he alive now?'

She shook her head. 'You must ask Mrs Rebane,' she said.

I looked at the clear blue horizon as if it would settle the whirlwind between my ears. 'The mother of Lennart Rebane,' I said. 'What would she be doing with this photograph?'

Nadia said, 'I cannot say.'

'Can't say or won't say?'

'All right,' she said. 'I tell you what happens. In Tallinn, I was called to the office of my superior. He says to me, this cadet Lennart Rebane is dead, killed. We want you to go to England, go to this conference, find out what you can about his accident, or was it an accident. And you go and see his mother. I already know this woman a little. We have the same political ideas; independence for our country. Even, we are friends. But she was not happy to see me. Nobody in Estonia is happy to see the police. But I spoke much with her. She was sad and sorry for her son, of course. Very. So we became better friends. But in Estonia, even now, you say very little, even to your good friends. She told me only that she had this photograph. And she told me that Lennart had seen you when you worked in the television, and had a big interest in you, and wanted to meet you. This he had said in a letter from London, two weeks before.' She shrugged her shoulders. 'That's all.'

Vixen heeled to a puff whipping across the water from the general direction of France. The breeze was freshening.

I said, 'That's not all. You found out a lot of things about me.'

'I have been trained to find out,' she said. 'We are a small, poor country, but we have excellent training.'

My father had been put in front of me, then snatched away again. There was a nightmarish remoteness about things. All those years we had thought my father was dead, but he had been alive. He might still be alive. Resentment bubbled in my mind, mixed with guilt and sadness.

There was a way of dealing with chaos and disaster. You learn it, in the hell-holes, or you go crazy. *Think of the story.* Tyrrell the journalist engaged autopilot.

I said, 'You know a hell of a lot. How did you find out?'

'Rebane's letter reported his first conversations with Marie.'

I looked at her. Her face was sad, her eyes lowered. I wondered whether she was telling me the truth, about Rebane's mother. There were other ways she could have found out: even in these enlightened times, Russian ships carried a KGB man, just in case. KGB men might communicate with police. Or with other KGB people . . .

I said, 'You arrived at Powney's at a convenient moment.'

She said, 'I had been there a day, watching who came, who went.'

A day, I thought. Time for Equipoise to find Marie, organize an overdose and a fire. 'And who did?' I said.

'You did.' She smiled. This time it was more tentative. 'I am glad I did.' She dropped her eyes. The pink of her cheeks deepened. 'Very glad.'

I did my best to smile.

'And now you will send me away,' she said in a small voice.

I opened my mouth to say yes. But I shut it again.

Her eyes were Baltic amber. They held mine without a shadow of guile. I could see my reflection trapped like a fly in each pupil. On your guard, I told myself.

But it is not easy to stay on your guard when you cannot even remember which way is up.

'You will be going to Helsinki with the Tall Ships,' she said. 'You must come to Tallinn, and meet the mother of Rebane, and she will explain the photograph. Is that what will make you happy?' She paused. 'I would be most happy to see you, in Tallinn.'

I bet you would, said Bill Tyrrell the journalist. You and your pals in the KGB. Let's get him over here, and lock him up, to show them that nobody knocks off our nuclear submariners. Visit Mrs Rebane, and get arrested.

But it had been a while since I had been a journalist. Bill Tyrrell, Joshua Tyrrell's son, wanted to go to Tallinn. And all the Bill Tyrrells looked deep into those amber eyes, and said, 'I would be most happy to come.'

Then I got up abruptly, and walked aft, to hang on to the backstay as *Vixen* corkscrewed through the southern fringes of the St Catherine's Point overfalls, and try to do some serious thinking.

Mostly, I thought about my father. The worst day of my life had been the day that telegram had arrived from Tromsö Lines. The day I found out that he had been alive afterwards, without getting in touch, should have been the second worst. It should have made me angry and resentful.

It did, a little. But above all, it made me curious.

There was a thought that kept picking at the edge of my mind, a thought I could not let through, but which elbowed in anyway, and left no room for any others.

He had been forty-eight when the telegram had arrived. He would be an old man now. *What if he were still alive?*

Don't be bloody stupid, I told myself.

But it would not go away.

I went below, pulled out the telephone, dialled Dickie Wilson in Southampton. He answered quickly, his voice warm and brown as toast.

I said, 'Dickie. I want you to know that I'm coming to Finland, whether you like it or not.'

He said, 'I don't.' His voice was cold.

I said, 'Also, you can tell your people to stop bothering me. I'm on my way to the police.'

He said, 'What are you talking about? Where are you?'

'Mid-Channel,' I said. I was not going to the police. On the strength of the evidence I had, there was no case. I hoped Dickie would not work that out for himself, but I was not confident. 'Damage slight, superficial. You know what I'm talking about.'

He said, 'You're obviously mad.'

I switched off the telephone, and shoved it in its locker. Then I took the wheel from Dean. The 1355 shipping forecast said winds south veering southwest, force four to five, seven later. Down to the south, an edge of grey cloud was moving up the sky. *Vixen* heaved her way across Christchurch Bay, left St Alban's Head five miles to starboard, and drove a straight groove across a Weymouth Bay full of the sails of yachts running for shelter from the dirty bits of the forecast and into the hot, snug bars of the town.

She was steady as a rock under my hands as she dug her knife-sharp groove in the water, heading for Portland Bill and the grubby cotton-wool clouds massing low over Lyme Bay. It was cold now, with flurries of rain. The seas were bigger. From time to time the nose went up a steep one and came down with a *crunch* that drove half a ton of water along the lee rail, raising white plumes on the bottle-screws and slopping against the cockpit coaming. The day became hard and hurried with the crack of wind-driven spray, and the bar-taut straining of overpowered sails, and the vertiginous dip and heel of *Vixen*'s seventy-five-foot mast.

Halfway across Lyme Bay the tops were coming off the waves and the wind was veering. Dean and I banged a reef into the main and took off the yankee. Then we thundered on across an empty grey sea.

We hit the Poult at the top of the flood. I steered up the lines of foam the wind had left on the water, and swung the bowsprit between the red and green lights on the entrance of the New Pulteney Marina, where Neville Spearman had his yard.

We tied up at the fuel dock. It was eleven o'clock, and I had arranged for *Vixen* to be on the slip as early as possible on the morning tide. I hoped that Dickie would believe we were at sea, and call off the dogs. So supper was a quiet, cold business of corned beef and stale bread in the yellow pool of the cabin lamp.

Nadia sat next to me. I could feel the pressure of her knee on mine, light but deliberate. Dean ate quickly, and said, 'I'm shagged out. Night-night.'

He shut the door into the crew cabin. We were alone.

She said, 'I want you to know this. I am not trying to make you come to Tallinn to accuse you.'

'No,' I said. I did not know what to believe. But I knew what I wanted to believe.

'I want you to come because I want you to come.' She took my hand. I kissed her. She kissed me back. Her mouth was soft.

Someone was banging on the hatch. 'Mr Tyrrell!' a voice was yelling. 'Telephone in the office!'

She held on to me, arms round my neck. 'Make them wait,' she said.

'I'll call back.'

'It's a Mr Glazebrook,' said the voice. 'Urgent.'

Bill Tyrrell the journalist stood up.

Nadia looked flushed and desirable in the lamplight. But I was already halfway up the companionway.

When I had first come to Pulteney, Spearman's office had been an electric kettle and a few notes scrawled in an exercise book on a table in the corner of the workshop. Nowadays it was made largely of plate glass, the occasional patches of solid wall bearing photographs of successful boats he had built. I inhaled the aroma of new carpet and fixed my eyes on a photograph of me and Charlie Agutter in the cockpit of *Thunder Gulch* the year we came second in the Clear Island race. Then I picked up the telephone.

Neville Glazebrook's fruity voice said, 'You've had your telephone switched off.'

'How did you find me?'

'My boat's been in. Spearman told me you were on your way.'

There was a wet kissing noise; he was sucking a cigar.

'I want to make you a proposition,' he said. 'I've got a new boat this year, y'know.'

I said, 'Charlie told me.'

'We're sailing a scratch crew,' he said. 'In the Cherbourg Race. I'm looking for a helmsman. Charlie said you'd be free. I'd be pleased if you'd come.'

He was a politician. I was a boat bum, who had got him plenty of dreadful publicity. Asking me sailing was not the obvious thing for him to do. He would know that as well as I would.

I said, 'To what do I owe this honour?'

He said, 'Two things. One, that business on the Medway was a bloody awful accident, but it was an accident. The gossip's doing nobody any good. If you do a decent job in the race, I might even get Dickie to take you back on.'

'Dickie?' I said. I was dazed.

'With Youth Venture. I can put some funds his way. Override him. And you might find that if you're back with Youth Venture, your brother takes a better view. Particularly if you're off in Finland. Out of sight, out of mind, eh? Best all round. Specially after the Rebane inquest.'

'Is there a date?'

'Tuesday week, I hear. Now, then. The other thing. The reason I want you on this race is because I want to win it, and Charlie says you're the best helmsman he can think of, besides him.'

I said, 'Your daughter won't like it. The press won't like it. Why are you doing it?'

'I want to win the race,' he said. 'And as a Minister of the Crown, I'm used to doing my own worrying.' *Squelch*, went his lips on the cigar. 'So eat the meat and drink the vodka, and get your blood pressure up. See you Friday lunchtime.'

'There are a couple of things,' I said. 'Bits of information –'

'Tell the staff.' The warmth was going out of his voice. His mind was moving on to the next thing. 'They'll do what they can. See you on board.' The quid pro quos were established. The receiver was already moving away from his mouth as he said goodbye.

I sat down on a bollard outside the office.

So Glazebrook wanted to win the race, and he wanted me out of the way while things settled down.

It suited me fine.

The night air was cool, heated by the yellow glow of lamplight from *Vixen*'s skylight. I took a couple of deep breaths. Nadia was down there, waiting.

I sat on a bollard to think. She had put herself in my way. She was investigating the death of Rebane. She had done her level best to get me to go to Tallinn, in pursuit of people for whose existence I had only her word.

My friend Terry Falconer had jumped into bed with a young lady in Czechoslovakia in 1981. He had been Central European correspondent for a US TV network, until he got the photographs, and the carefully worded request to drop the

174

story he was working on about Czech arms sales to South Africa. Nowadays he was editor of *Home Woodworker*, a job he did not enjoy, but the best he could get under the circumstances.

I sat on the bollard, and swore at newspapers, and television companies, and politicians, and the rest of the bastards who twisted the world's emotions to suit their bank balances. Bill Tyrrell the private citizen would have gone down to the cabin and continued where he had left off. But Bill Tyrrell the working journalist was going to do nothing of the kind.

I got up, checked the mooring warps. They were fine, as I had expected. I was making time, putting off the decision. There was a yardstick. The yardstick was the photograph.

Photographs could be faked. And Bill Tyrrell was going to have to keep his hands to himself until he had found about this one.

I went below, stumbling on the companionway, and leaned against the door frame. Nadia was on the settee, smiling a new, soft smile.

'Tired,' I said. 'Bang on head. G'night.'

I caught a glimpse of her face, slack and disbelieving. Then I went into my cabin, and locked the door, and dozed and swore at myself alternately until dawn came creeping between the serried masts.

19

At seven o'clock I got up, and I got out. Pete the shipwright was already in the yard. I told him what I wanted done. He gave me a lift up to the Basin, and I climbed aboard the van, and turned its nose towards Plymouth.

I had a bacon sandwich in a café, washed it down with tea, parked in the multi-storey and walked the concrete maze to the mauve-lettered façade of Maurice Paul Studios.

Maurice Paul's real name was Den Sloggett. He had a short, spiky haircut and snooker player's spectacles which failed to hide the suitcase-sized bags the gin had stitched under his sharp black eyes. 'Billy!' he cried, tossing aside a contact sheet of a dough-faced girl gazing hungrily at a white kitten. 'Long time no see!'

Once, Maurice had been one of Fleet Street's most talented ambulance chasers. What he did not know about photographs had not yet been discovered. I shook him by his small, soft hand, and pulled Nadia's photograph out of my pocket. 'I was wondering,' I said. 'Is that a fake?'

He frowned at it. Then he pulled a fat magnifying glass out of a drawer, and squinted through it. 'Looks all right,' he said.

'Sure?' My mouth was dry again.

'No.' He lit a Silk Cut, coughed, and blew smoke at an engaged couple in a vacuum-moulded gold frame. The fiancé was wearing a kilt. He made a face at it. 'I seen a film the other night,' he said. 'Margaret Thatcher doing it with Colonel Gaddafi. Marvellous thing, computers.' He picked up his magnifying glass again. 'But this one's a good print. Old plate camera. No retouching. Very fine grain. Bugger to fabricate.'

I swallowed hard. 'Impossible?'

'Nothing's impossible, these days. But as near as makes no difference.'

'Can you do me a couple of copies, quickly?'

He pressed a button on an intercom. 'Dilys?' he said. 'If Mrs Rogers turns up with her bleeding kid tell her to bleeding wait.' He switched off. 'Half an hour,' he said.

I went and had another cup of tea and read some newspapers. The prints were ready to the second; the habit of deadlines died hard. He asked for a fiver. I borrowed his telephone, and dialled Christopher's number.

Ruth answered. I asked for Christopher. She said, 'He's not here.' Her voice was cold and sullen.

'When are you expecting him?' I said.

'When it suits him,' she said. 'He's seeing your mother.'

Christopher was Member for a market town in Dorset largely inhabited by retired colonels and their ladies. The ladies liked his boyish charm. The colonels liked the fact that he was Neville Glazebrook's son-in-law. Lately, I was getting the feeling that neither of these was cutting much ice with Ruth.

I climbed aboard the Transit and drove up into the hills and down into the fudge-coloured stone suburbia of Lydiats Manor.

My mother was prodding a flowerbed with a trowel. Georgie was sitting on the terrace reading page three of the *Daily Telegraph*, his lips moving under his white moustache.

My mother straightened up from her flowerbed, her face red with bending. 'Darling!' she said. 'How wonderful! Christopher's just this minute gone.'

I had a cup of coffee. They had pink gin. Georgie began to speak approvingly of Christopher's recent achievements in cutting aid payments to the smaller West Indies. My mother did not need much persuading to show me her phloxes, which were at the opposite end of the garden, out of earshot.

'Lovely,' I said, and pulled out the photograph. 'Have you ever seen this before?'

'Goodness,' she said. 'It's your father.' She stared at it for perhaps a minute. 'He really did have a terrible beard,' she said eventually. 'I was always telling him to shave it off.'

'Do you know the people with him?'

She shook her head, as if she did not care. My father's love of the sea had amounted almost to an infatuation. My mother had been jealous at the beginning, then slid into an accommodation with it, as she might have accommodated herself to a mistress.

I said, 'He always told me his ships were diesel.'

'What's a diesel?'

'As opposed to sailing ships.'

'Oh,' she said. The gin was getting to her. 'I don't really know.'

I said, 'After you were told he was lost at sea, did you ever hear anything else?'

'Hear anything?' She looked suddenly blank. This time, it was not the gin. It was as if she was looking inward, at something she did not want to look at. 'No,' she said. 'I don't *think* so.'

'But you're not sure.'

She said in a faint, restless voice, 'Stop bullying me.'

I felt guilty, as she had intended. I said, 'I'm sorry. Things have been a bit strange.'

The gin rocked her back on an even keel. 'I know,' she said. 'Poor Bill. You did miss your father dreadfully. I've always held that against him. With all the rest of it.' She squeezed my hand. Her skin was hard as leather from gardening. 'There was a letter. That was all.'

'A letter?'

'Some madwoman. Somewhere in Eastern Europe. She said she'd met your father, and he was ill, or something.'

'When was this?'

'Oh, I don't know. Some time after he died, anyway. I told you, she was mad. People do it after accidents. Quite a lot of people wrote and said they'd got messages from the spirit world, that sort of thing. It was rather distressing.'

There was silence. Rooks cawed in the ash wood, and bees whined in and out of the phloxes. I said, 'Did you keep these letters?'

'Oh, no,' she said. She started to walk back across the lawn.

The sun was high and hot, pulling last night's rain out of the black-hedged lawn in a thick, vegetable steam. I could not breathe. 'You burnt them?' I wanted to shake her.

'No, no.' She looked shocked. 'When we moved I gave all the letters to Christopher. He's got those huge attics.'

Georgie had finished with the sex murders in the *Telegraph*. 'Sensible chap,' he said. 'Put down his roots, bought a house, got his directorships.' He put a hand on my shoulder. It was meant to be paternal. 'When are you going to give up all this sailing rubbish? Find a nice girl, settle down?'

My mother's hand tightened on my arm. I gave Georgie a skull grin, kissed her goodbye, climbed into the van, and headed for Dorset.

Christopher lived in what his agent called a modest farmhouse. There was a modest swimming pool in one of the modest barns, and garaging for a modest four cars. His modest Daimler was not at home, but his modest Porsche was parked in the sweep. Two gardeners were spraying roses as the van rattled on to the gravel.

The house was long and low, with a pantile roof and brilliant herbaceous borders. The air was loud with bees. The French windows were open. *Don Giovanni* drifted into the hot August air. I went to the front door, stuck my head in, and called, 'Anyone at home?'

No reply. The Commendatore continued to bellow. The hall was tastefully furnished with the oak chests and portraits that Christopher had kindly offered to look after for my mother when they would not fit into the Lawn House at Lydiats.

'Ruth!' I shouted.

The stairs went up from the back of the hall. A door slammed up there. A voice said, 'Who's that?' It was Ruth's voice. It sounded breathy, not quite under control. If there was one thing Ruth prided herself on being under, it was control.

'Me,' I said.

179

She appeared at the top of the stairs. She was wearing a dressing gown of Chinese silk with big peonies on it. Her sharp-boned face was flushed. Her mouth looked big and bruised, like the peonies. 'Oh,' she said. She sounded jittery. 'You. What do you want?'

'There are some family papers in your attic,' I said. 'I was wondering if I could have a look.'

She said, 'Were you?' as if she did not understand the words.

'I won't disturb you,' I said. 'Didn't mean to get you out of bed.' It was two o'clock in the afternoon.

She said, 'I've got flu. I can't stand here all day in the cold. Talk to Christopher, would you?'

I stood and looked at her, and thought, things are not going well, I am about to be thrown out. She was chewing her lower lip. Her blue eyes were narrow.

Her heavily made-up blue eyes.

I said, 'I'm awfully sorry. Can't I get you some Disprin or something?' And I started up the stairs.

There was a dull sound behind her; a thump, as if someone had dropped a shoe on the floor. Her face became scarlet. She said, 'No.'

I stopped. She was wafting clouds of Joy de Jean Patou.

She said, 'Go away.'

Somewhere behind her, a window went up. I walked slowly past her, pushed open the door. She was saying, 'Get out.' Her voice was thin and shrill. The bedroom she shared with Christopher was huge, full of sunlight. The covers were off the bed; the bottom sheet was heavily rumpled. Women's clothes lay on the Chinese carpet, where they had been flung. The window was open. Outside, there was a fourteen-foot drop to a crushed clump of acanthus in the border below.

I turned back into the room. I was surprised to find I felt sorry for Christopher. Ruth looked hot and flustered. 'He does it too,' she said. 'He's got some floozy in London.'

'Don't worry,' I said. 'I won't say a word.' I grinned, a grin to mask the gloom. I took a deep breath. 'There's something I'd like to see. In the attic. I believe it came from my mother's house.'

'You'd better ask Christopher, then,' she said, barely polite. 'As you can see, he's not here.' She was suddenly very pale, and the make-up stood out on her face like warpaint.

I was getting angry. I had thought that Christopher and I were people on bad terms who happened to be brothers. Now, I was surprised to discover a hint of a sensation that we were brothers who happened to be people on bad terms. I said, 'I think the less fuss the better, don't you?'

She stared at me, gnawing her lip. It sank in. She said, 'You're despicable.' I walked into the passage. She stamped into her room and slammed the door.

I heard the click as the bolt went home. I was despicable, all right. I climbed the winding oak staircase to the attic.

Christopher's attics were the kind of attics you would expect of someone who had spent the past thirty-three years tying life into neat parcels. They were bone dry, and entirely free of spiders. Down one end was a tidy pile of furniture surplus to his requirements, padded with green baize. At the other were the cardboard boxes, labelled in black felt-tip.

There was a time when I would have given part of my right hand for a look at the private side of Christopher's political life. Not now. Three boxes at the right-hand end said MUMMY'S PAPERS. I pulled them under the fluorescent tube on the purlin, and started.

There were files, tied up with green ribbon. The first box was full of bank statements dating back to 1950, arranged in meticulous order. The second had photographs and letters from my father, with letterheads that ranged from Alaska to Cape Town. His writing was small and neat, with the pronounced forward slope I remembered from my schooldays. The letters dealt with the running of the house. There were many enquiries about my progress, rather fewer about Christopher's. I found myself thinking that it could not have been much fun being Christopher, playing second fiddle to Bill. There was no more affection for my mother than if she had been a steward, and he an absentee landlord.

The last letter in the bundle was dated 1965. The writing was the same, and the paper was the same: MV *Proteus*. It had been written in Reykjavik. He said it was raining, and bloody cold, and the depressions had been spinning across from Labrador, and he did not expect them to stop. He mentioned school fees, and asked after the roof of the house. There was no mention of Christmas, although it was November; but he had never paid much attention to such matters.

Two weeks after it had been written, he had sailed into his storm in the Skagerrak and not come out the other side.

I looked through the other bundles. There were letters of sympathy after the telegram had arrived; my and Christopher's letters from school; and a bundle labelled *Misc*.

It was at the bottom of the bundle, with an envelope. There was a Russian stamp on the envelope, with a picture of a steelworker toiling in front of a furnace. The writing was sprawling and female.

Dear Madame Tyrrell [it read],

This is a sad letter I must write. A man who once was dear to you is ill. I have seen him. He could not write himself, and was sorry for this. He sends you his affection. Also, he sends his greeting to Christopher and William, and asks William to tame the fox.

A woman who knows you.

There was no signature.

I folded it, and put it in its envelope, and slid it into my breast pocket. My hands were clumsy, as if I had woken up from a long, deep sleep. I tidied the boxes, turned off the light and walked down the stairs into the smell of pot-pourri and furniture polish.

Ruth was dressed, in jeans that fitted with an expensive looseness and an embroidered Mexican shirt. She smiled at me, showing her white designer teeth. It was an astonishingly affable smile, with an edge of anxiety and a faint aroma of sherry. She said, 'You get lonely, you know.'

I was so far away that it took me a moment to work out what she was talking about.

In the driver's seat of the van I read the letter again. There was no clue to the identity of the sender. Or the person who had been ill, except the reference to taming the fox. The fox had to be *Vixen. Vixen* the untameable. I felt sad and remote, as if I had been at a funeral. Then I felt again the vague, unreasonable excitement.

There had been no funeral.

At the end of the lane, trucks were hurtling along the main road. Christopher's perfumed garden might have been a dream. I was back in a world where Equipoise wanted to kill me. It was a world in which there was corroboration for the notion that Father had survived the wreck of the *Proteus.* Corroboration for the idea that Nadia had been telling the truth.

My foot went down on the floorboards, and the Transit coughed and roared its way westward. By Exeter, a new fear had taken the place of the rest of them. It sat in my mind and swelled like a toad as I clattered off the coast road under the sign that said SPEARMAN'S, and on to the neat gravel tracks between the palm trees.

Vixen was on the slipway, chocked, looking like a gigantic model yacht waiting for launch, her lifelines thirteen feet above the concrete. Pete was up the ladder against her side. The scars had gone. He looked round, beard fluttering in the breeze, recognizing the bronchial wheeze of the Transit's engine. 'Done,' he said. 'Checked, filled. Keep you going for the rest of the season.'

'What?' I said.

'The boat.' He slid down the ladder. He was frowning above his red beard. 'You put three bloody big scratches in, remember? With the grain, though. Very tasteful. And no damage to frames, neither. Bloody lucky.'

I said, 'Where's Dean?'

He said, 'On the boat. D'you want it back in the water?'

I said, 'Yes.' Dean's head appeared above me, silhouetted against the sky. 'Where's Nadia?'

'Gone,' he said.

'Where?' The fear had turned to a sort of numb sickness.

'Home,' he said. 'Via Helsinki.'

'So are you going to consent to giving us a hand to put your boat back in?' said Pete, with violent irony.

I did not answer. I clambered up and into the saloon, and switched on the telephone. The Finnair person told me in a polite, even-tempered voice that the flight had just left, and confirmed that there was a Nadia Vuorinen on the passenger list. I went on deck, and climbed down the ladder like an eighty-year-old, and ministered to the needs of the fox.

When she was afloat, I hit the starter button, and swung her out through the pontoons to the Pits, the berths by the entrance where they parked the racing boats and anything else Neville Spearman thought might bring him a little notoriety and increase his ice-cream and T-shirt sales. We tied her up, Dean and I, and I went below.

There were no flowers on the saloon table. Instead there was boatyard dirt: muddy bootprints on the deck, and greasy fingermarks on the panelling. The only trace of Nadia was the wraith of her scent mixed in with the sharp smell of raw diesel.

I took down the Bell's and poured myself half a tumbler-ful. My parents had vanished, to be replaced with people I did not know. People wanted me dead. And I was in love with an Estonian policewoman. Yesterday, life had been tough. Today, it was chaos.

There was a tentative knock on the door. Dean said, 'Anything need doing?'

I shook my head. The whisky was hot and thick in my mind. Everything needed doing.

'When the taxi came, she gave me this.' He handed me a sheet of paper. 'She was crying.'

It was an address in Tallinn, in her neat writing. Madame Rebane's address. I stood up. 'Thank you,' I said.

There was Neville Glazebrook's race. There was the inquest. And there was Finland, which was just across the Gulf of Finland from Tallinn.

20

We spent two days filling tanks, provisioning, tuning the fat bottle-screws that keep the mast upright. On the third day, Dean and I took her round to the Solent. Before we left, I had called Neville Glazebrook in Westminster.

I got through with gratifying speed.

'Bill,' he said. He sounded rushed. There were people talking in the background.

'I'll have to leave my boat in the Beaulieu River,' I said. 'I'm a bit worried about it. I'll need a mooring; not alongside. One of my blokes will be on board. Can we have a policeman, too?'

'A *what*?'

'Do you want me to explain?'

'God, no,' he said. 'I'm on my way into a Cabinet meeting.' I could hear him fading. 'I'll fix you up.'

Dickie thought I had police protection. Still, I was not taking any chances with Equipoise.

Eighteen hours later, *Vixen* was nosing between the oak woods that crept down to the Beaulieu River. Brown, glassy tide gurgled away from her counter. The hard-polished windows of designer cottages gleamed among the foliage. We picked up a buoy and pulled down the sails. A Zodiac buzzed out from a pier in the trees. A burly man in tennis shoes and an anorak climbed aboard. 'Detective-Sergeant Ellerton,' he said.

I introduced Dean as my bosun. Dean looked first startled, then proud. 'Three days,' I said. 'You're in command. Can you look after her?'

Dean nodded, as if he was given command every day of the week. I climbed down into the Zodiac.

Glazebrook's house was a big cedar bungalow, with a verandah covered in people. He gave me a wide smile that was several times more raffish than anything he gave his public. Some of the people were neighbours. He walked me past them to a knot of brown men with big shoulders, square chins and mole-wrench handshakes. One of them had sailed as mainsheet man in an America's Cup boat, and three of the others had trimmed and ground winches on the winner of last year's Fastnet Race. 'The crew,' he said.

Lunch featured salmon mayonnaise and Sancerre. I did justice to neither. I was nervous. Things seemed less cut and dried than they had at Spearman's. If Glazebrook did not like the way I sailed his boat, there would be no Finland.

After lunch we drove in convoy to the Berthon Marina at Lymington. Glazebrook's boat was called *Blue Murder*. It was your classic state-of-the-art racing sled. Peacock blue, sharp of bow and retroussé of transom, it lay alongside a jetty like a formula one racing car, mast a three-spreader whisker of pre-bent aluminium raking the overcast, deck a young playing field studded with winches the size of oildrums.

Charlie was on board, with Scotto and another gorilla, getting the boat ready. I thanked him, quietly. He said, 'Nothing to do with me. He asked for you.'

Charlie's mission in life was to make people feel at home. It was hard to know whether he was telling the truth, or whether he had fought like a barrister to get me on to the crew. Whichever way, I was there.

'Let's go,' said Glazebrook. The engine whirred. He shot off the jetty, smiling for the benefit of the photographers on the pierhead.

Out in the river, he roared, 'Let's get some sails on this thing!'

They went up the mast at a speed that would have horrified *Vixen*'s trainees; big ochre-and-white Kevlar wings, with fans of tape running from tack and clew and head, corsets for precise control of the aerofoils.

'Your turn,' said Glazebrook. He handed me the wheel.

On *Vixen*, the helmsman looks past a doghouse, a chocked dinghy, a hatch cover, two skylights, and a spider's web of shrouds and jib and staysail sheets. On *Blue Murder*, I was looking over a rainbow spaghetti of control lines on a flat white plastic deck. For a moment it seemed improbably clean and tidy. Then the rudder started sending its signals to the wheel, and I ran out of time for making comparisons.

The ancestry of racing fifty-footers contains very few cruising yacht genes. The dominant influence is the racing dinghy, like the 505s in which I had whizzed round the buoys of coastal England in my teens. In the days when *Vixen* had been built, racing was an extension of cruising. When I was racing *Vixen*, my mind was half on the race, and half in the boat, probing at her weaknesses like a tongue at a sore tooth. *Blue Murder* was a brand-new flat-out racing machine, and there was no need to worry about weakness. The wheel said she wanted to go. So we went.

The bow went up, and the stern went down. She heeled, and the wake came hammering out of the downhill side of the hull like the jet of a municipal fountain. The trimmers worked their magic on the winches, cranking in the last iron-hard inches of jib and main until the sails were taut aerofoils sucking the boat up into the eye of the wind.

Glazebrook's plump shoulders appeared in the hatch from below. He was navigator and tactician; a good job for an owner, particularly if he is a politician too. His face was red with pleasure and wine, glowing like a sun over his Lacoste shirt. 'Filthy forecast,' he said. 'Sou'west six, seven. Big depression. Eight, maybe.'

'Do you want to go?' I said. The Cherbourg Race course takes you all the way to Cherbourg and back. Fifty-footers generally do their racing round buoys and go home to nice safe marinas at night.

'Of course we want to go,' he said.

I could feel the ripple of adrenalin as the body got itself geared for battle. The mouth was dry, and the hands showed a tendency to sweat. I sighted down the deck across the Solent, at the ochre wedges of sails leaning on the water against the dull green of the Island. The boat was a living thing under the hands. Over there was the enemy; the only enemy, for the next twenty-four hours.

Wrapped about by the heavy roar of the wake, we slid through the blue-grey seas towards the start line.

On the way, we did some practising. The crew were very good; frighteningly good. When *Vixen* went about, her thirty tons took a long time to get going again. *Blue Murder* spun like a mustang on her fin keel, and her big sails picked up her featherlight Kevlar hull and blasted it forward with a dinghy's acceleration.

Sails were thickening on the line. Charlie had come to stand next to me. He was wearing faded blue shorts and a pair of Polaroids mended with a salt-greened paper clip. 'Look at 'em,' he said. There were multihulls and cruising boats down there, slewing around in the starting area like pigs on an ice rink. 'Family racing.'

I nodded. Today was the kind of day when artistic man-oeuvres got the boat bent.

The time said twenty minutes to the start. We looked at the other boats. There were three other fifty-footers; they were hanging back from the pack too, watching each other and us.

'Everyone wants a bash at the Cup,' said Charlie.

'The Cup?'

'Captain's Cup. Selectors watching. The Cherbourg Race's an unofficial qualifier.'

Unofficial or not, it cranked up the stakes.

Someone put a cup of tea in my hand. 'Don't worry,' said a man with a black crewcut, 'I don't mind losing.' He grinned. He had no front teeth. 'The other guys do, though.'

'Thank you for your support,' I said. Over his shoulder, the timer was coming down the seconds. A gun banged on the committee boat. I said, 'Genoa, main.' The sails stopped spilling air. The boat seemed to leap forward, squeezing lumps of water from its lee side.

'Tacking,' I said, and spun the big hidebound wheel.

The boom smashed over. Water roared as we went for the

committee boat. Up to windward, the other fifty-footers were right with us, moving ahead in echelon. There was no jinking, no barging. Under the boom, the helmsman of the boat to windward was perhaps twenty feet away. I could hear the slosh and rattle of the wakes in the gulch between the hulls.

'Too far over,' said Glazebrook, frowning.

I hardly heard him. The shakes were gone, now. It was all in the big moving map in my head; over the line, the little boats, jostling and luffing each other to a standstill. Behind them, the line of big boats, one beside the other. And over to the right, beyond the flags fluttering on the committee boat's halyards, the almost imperceptible shadow on the water that meant more breeze, and more tide.

'*Thunder Gulch*'s coming after us,' said Charlie.

Thunder Gulch was two lengths astern and to windward. She was red and sleek, another fifty-footer, a descendant of the *Thunder Gulch* in which Charlie and I had sailed the Clear Island, designed by Ernest Slevin of Hamble, one of Charlie's principal rivals. She was being helmed by James Dixon, another Pulteney hotshot.

'Beat him,' muttered Charlie. 'Or the bloody Minister'll get his next boat from Slevin.'

The blue hull of the committee boat flashed past. A man with a white beard and blue cap waved. Charlie was the only one who waved back; excellent manners, Charlie. Then we were out there, and the heel steepened as we found that little bit of wind and took the extra half-knot of tide on the lee bow. It drew us fractionally ahead. *Thunder Gulch*'s sails shivered as we fed them dirty air. Now we were in the tide, our lead was up to three lengths, but we were a long way to the right of our course. I kept it going until we were a couple of hundred yards out. 'We'll try one on,' I said.

Charlie's eyebrows went up, semi-circular arches under his spiky black hair.

'Ready to tack,' I said. 'Helm's a-lee.'

The wheel swung. The boom clanked. We were on starboard. Astern, *Thunder Gulch*'s crew were yelling that we had tacked in their water. But we had been well clear, and they knew it. And now we had right of way, starboard tack, and one after the other opposition was having to duck under, give ground. By the time the Needles were rising from the sea like broken teeth, we were four lengths ahead.

'Sorry I spoke,' said Glazebrook.

We rattled out through the tiderip that sweeps past the Needles. The fifty-footer went through with a long, hollow burble, bow thumping in the short seas.

Thunder Gulch's crew had been practising hard. She had worked her way up to a couple of lengths astern. She had slipped down to leeward, looking for speed to go past, but not finding any. East of the red-and-white sugarstick of the lighthouse we turned south, off the wind, for Cherbourg. *Thunder Gulch* held her position.

The gulls followed us. So did the fleet. After an hour, the gulls went away. The fleet stayed, strung out now, wisps of white canted against the navy-blue sea. Now we were on the reach, Charlie took over the wheel. I went up and sat on the rail next to Scotto, who moved over deferentially. I had been awake most of last night. The roar and bubble of the sleek hull in the water was lulling. I folded my hands on the top lifeline, and laid my head on them. The crew were beguiling the long, tedious wait by watching the big knotmeter on the mast. They did not think much of Charlie's helming. I thought about Nadia, gone. I thought about my father, gone. Beyond reach. The ache in my legs spread until it was an ache in the mind. I dreamed.

I was ten again. We were in Felixstowe docks. My father had brought me down to see him off. I had been looking forward to seeing the ships. I had not bargained for the fact that he would be going away on one of them, and I would be staying behind. My father was high above me on the wing of a ship's bridge. I was waving. He did not see me.

In the dream, he looked as he did in the photograph, peajacket buttoned under his patriarch's beard. He stared straight ahead, into a future I was not part of.

The ship slid away. I knew I would never see him again. I could feel a hot pressure behind my eyes. I was crying.

Something woke me. The dream vanished. I was sitting on the weather rail of Glazebrook's yacht with a dozen of the baddest apes in boat sailing, with the tears streaming down my face.

The wind fixed it for me. It flicked the top off a wave, and kicked it up in a fat, drifting clot, and suddenly the hot salt water on my face was cold salt water.

The wind had gone round to the west and freshened. There was a new, colder feel to it. The sea had changed, too. The blue had gone out of it. Now it was a dead grey like concrete, under a low sky of stone-coloured cloud.

'Looking dirty,' said Scotto. '*Thunder Gulch*'s gone through.'

I looked at him, wondering how much he had noticed. His wide brown face was stolid as ever. 'Forecast?' I said.

'Six, seven,' he said. 'Maybe eight.'

I twisted my head to look at the bend of the four-spreader mast, the set of the huge, semi-transparent foresail. I had been through some big blows in some small boats. But after *Vixen*'s thick wooden spar and belt-and-braces rigging, this spider's web of steel and alloy looked very insubstantial.

Scotto muttered, 'The Minister's not happy about *Thunder Gulch*.'

A voice behind me said, 'If you've had a nice snooze, maybe you could get back on the helm?' Glazebrook was in his usual spot, the best place on the boat, head and shoulders out of the cabin hatch. He was chewing one of his thick cigars, holding out a cup of coffee in his white paw.

There was brandy in the coffee. It spread around me like a blast of napalm, pushing away the misery. The elkskin cover of the wheel was jumping under the hands, the boat a half-wild animal scarcely under control. It was as if *Blue Murder* was a cherry pip, and the blast of the wind and the resistance of the sea were two giant fingers, squeezing, shooting her forward. She had a lot of sail up.

The sun had dipped low towards the western horizon. Charlie had his binoculars on *Thunder Gulch*, off the port bow. A single beam held her pinned in a patch of turquoise. The sail was a triangle of ochre the size of a folded postage stamp. As I watched, it seemed to grow. 'He's depowered,' said Charlie. Even with the naked eye, I could see the ripples running through the sail. 'Taking a reef.'

There was a moment's silence. The blink of sun went out. The sea was the colour of the gravestones in Allerton cemetery, where Marie lay among the washed-out plastic wreaths.

'We'll hang on,' said Neville Glazebrook.

'Could break the boat,' said Charlie. His spiky black hair blew into his eyes as he propped himself against the pushpit.

'Never mind the boat,' said Glazebrook. 'What about a kite?'

Charlie shrugged. 'It's your mast,' he said.

'Will it break?'

'Depends on the helmsman.'

Glazebrook shifted his eyes at me. 'He's used to steering dodgy boats,' he said. 'Go on, then.'

It was not spinnaker weather. But like Charlie said, it was Glazebrook's mast.

The mastman and foredeck man shuffled around the lurching triangle at the front end. Even with the wind on the beam there was a lot of water about up there.

'Bloody stupid,' I said to Charlie.

'Owner's request,' said Charlie, poker-faced. There was a hard *crack* of wind slapping into sailcloth. *Blue Murder's* fifty-foot hull lay far over to leeward as she tried to broach, nose seeking the wind. I hauled at the wheel, fighting tons of water pounding at the rudder. A wave came under, brought her upright, knocked her back into the groove. I kept her there.

It was an exciting ride. She charged along, sliding on hard wings of white spray that roared and drummed from her big, hollow hull. I could feel the ponderous weight of the wind in her sails. There was a lot too much of it. All I could do was watch the darkening heave of the water, anticipate, and ease the rudder a millimetre, to keep her in the groove. *Steer small*, my father had said up there in Norfolk. He would have been proud of me. Steer any larger, and those big hammers of wind whooping out of the northwest would tweak the rig out of her like a cocktail stick out of a sausage.

We went past *Thunder Gulch* as if she had been standing still. The worries began.

My face was aching with squinting ahead, groping for any hint I could get about what the sea was planning. Some of it

192

came by magic, through the soles of the feet and the cartilages of the knees. Some of it had to come through the eyes. But the wind was going up, and the night was coming down. And the eyes ceased to function.

By ten o'clock, it was blowing force seven, and the seas were sharp-edged mountain ranges that shed avalanches of white water into their troughs. The people on the rail had stopped making remarks about the readout on the mast. We had been up above thirteen knots for two hours, well over hull speed, which was remarkable. But up on the rail, it was dark and wet, and the only thing that was remarkable was the cold.

Ahead and to starboard, there was a faint lightening in the sky. Somebody pointed it out. Somebody else grunted. There might have been relief in the grunt, because the light was the nuclear power station behind Cap de la Hague, which meant we were coming up to the Ch. 1 buoy, the turning mark. Halfway.

Neville Glazebrook came up from below into the scream of the wind. He said, 'Nearly there.' His cigar had gone out. His lighter flared briefly in the pitch black.

Not briefly enough.

The flame left a bright blood-coloured patch in front of my eyes. Round the patch the night turned black, impenetrable. There was no gleam in the upslope of the next wave. For that moment, *Blue Murder* tore through the sea with a blind man at the helm.

The wheel lurched as she caught a wave wrong. She tripped. Her nose came round. The wheel spun hard, spokes smashing at my fingers. Broaching, I thought. She's broaching. The wind smacked beam-on into the big kite. I was yelling, 'Mainsheet!' The deck's heel was steepening underfoot. Things were rumbling below, a big, hollow landslide. People were bellowing. The deck was vertical, the mainsail a big, pale triangle, flattened towards the black water.

'Spinnaker!' someone was yelling.

The mainsheet was flying. The spinnaker was full of water, holding her over on her side. As vision returned, I could see a knot of people up by the mast.

The spinnaker winch was down to leeward, six feet under-water, where the sea was chopped up like the inside of a washing machine. The people by the mast would be at the halyards, trying to drop the sail.

I found I was standing on the downhill wall of the cockpit, which was horizontal. Next to me, Charlie's voice yelled, 'Look out!' The water was in the cockpit. It would be running into the hatch. That was why a dark, bulky figure was struggling with the cover. Neville Glazebrook.

Someone shouted up by the mast. There was a dull, heavy *twang* that made the hull vibrate like a plucked bass. The mast came upright, fast. I found myself sprawling on my back.

Neville Glazebrook had not heard the warning shout. When the deck came horizontal, it caught him bending. I saw his body go down and his legs go up. Struggling to my feet, I waited for the safety harness to catch him.

He was not wearing a safety harness.

He bounced once, and slid under the lifelines into the boiling sea.

Instincts took over. I shouted, 'Man overboard!', heaved the lifebuoy out of its clips and into the water. The wind howled, the sea roared, but the voices stopped. Suddenly, nobody was racing. The dan buoy's strobe blinked out there in the night. The wind towed it down, carting it away to leeward in spite of its drogue. My stomach felt cold and hollow.

'He's got a lifejacket,' said Charlie.

He was thinking aloud. With that wind kicking those seas in your face, you were going to drown in ten minutes, lifejacket or no lifejacket. 'Trailing lines?' I said.

'Spinnaker's still overboard.'

Someone said, 'Shit.' It would take time to get the spinnaker aboard. Until the sail and its cat's cradle of sheets and guys and halyards was inboard, there was no point in starting the engine, unless we wanted a foul propellor.

Something banged the deck by my feet. I looked down.

Blue Murder had an open transom, so the cockpit could drain quickly when it needed to. There was something down there, sticking through the open aft end, silhouetted against the white plastic deck. I stared at it with a headful of cement.

It might have been a squid; tentacles on end, long, dark body. It began to slide, overboard, back into the sea.

The cement in my head shifted. I knew what it was. I bent and grabbed it.

It was cold and wet. But it was a human hand.

A wave came under, kicked the back end high into the air. The hand was intolerably heavy. I hung on anyway. Charlie was with me now, latched on to the arm. A head came up the transom. Someone shone a big flashlight. The head was Neville Glazebrook's, the colour of plaster of Paris in the sudden glare. He was alive.

I found myself on autopilot again. We pulled his clothes off, dragged his stout white body below, got him into crackling silver survival blankets, tipped boiling tea between his teeth.

'Gimme a cigar,' he said. Someone gave him one. He looked at me. 'Just as well someone on this boat's got bloody eyes,' he said. 'Are we racing, or cruising?' Then he lay back on the pipe cot. His face had lost its plumpness. You were lucky, I thought. Bloody lucky.

Then I went back up the companionway. After that, we put three reefs in the mainsail, and pulled the number five jib up the forestay, and went for the flash of Ch. 1.

We got round. We went on the wind, heading for Bembridge Ledge, the next mark, sixty-odd miles up there in the screaming black. My shoulders were burning with the pull of the wheel, and my knees were showing a tendency to buckle. Shock. The spinnaker had put us ahead, and the whole Minister-overboard episode had only used up five minutes. Charlie took the wheel. 'Get your head down for an hour,' he said. It was all I was good for. I stumbled below.

It was white plastic down there, running with condensation, thundering with the racket of the big hull pounding up to windward. I ate some glucose tablets, climbed on to one of the uphill pipe cots with an armful of blankets, and clipped up the lee cloth to stop myself sliding on to the deck.

The Minister was in the bunk below, strapped like a foil-wrapped mummy. My eyelids began a slow, heavy downward slide.

The voice below said, 'Thank you.' Neville Glazebrook's voice. 'I couldn't have hung on. I was going.' He laughed. 'So your brother wheels me around the House, and you stop me drowning at sea. Your father would have been pleased.'

The hull was full of the boom of the sea, the amplified moan of wind in tight wire. The curtains of sleep whipped back. 'My father?'

'Worked with him,' he said. 'After the war.'

'He wasn't interested in politics.'

'No.' There was silence, except for the mad hammering of the sea and the rhythmic crash of cutlery in the locker. 'Not parliamentary politics, anyway. But Europe, after the war . . . well, it was a funny place.'

I thought of the photograph. I said, 'Particularly the Baltic States.'

He laughed, a single, ironic bark. 'Journalist,' he said.

I said, 'Did you tell Christopher you knew my father?'

'He never asked.'

'What was he like?'

'I didn't know him. Nobody knew him. He made sure of that.'

I was disappointed. *Blue Murder* wound and thumped her way through the seas.

'He said something to me once,' said Glazebrook. 'He was talking about you and Christopher. He said your brother needed all the help he could get, and you needed just as much as you would accept.'

'So you helped my brother.'

'He helped himself. To my daughter.' His voice was not ministerial. It had a thinness to it that I had heard before in bad, dangerous places; men and women who are very tired or who have been very frightened. They do not think it is worth wearing whatever disguise they use to protect themselves from the truth. 'He's been very . . . useful.'

I found myself feeling defensive for Christopher's sake. It was a surprising sensation. 'What exactly was the work you were doing with my father?'

'Can't tell you.'

'Did you know anything about . . . when he died?'

'No,' he said. 'We lost contact in, oh, the mid-sixties.'

'I've got a photograph,' I said. 'Could you tell me if you recognize anybody in it?'

'I won't,' he said. His voice was blurring. 'I might know someone who would, though.'

'I'll send it to you.'

Ten seconds later, he was snoring.

I lay there glaring at the deckhead with eyes that felt like red-hot golfballs. As far as I knew, there were very few kinds of politicians at large in the Eastern Baltic in the 1950s and '60s. There were the Stalinists. There were the scattered shreds of the Baltic nationalist movements.

And there were the spooks.

21

We won the race by five miles. Someone had been on the radio to the press. They were waiting at the end of the jetty at Berthon's. Glazebrook pumped my hand, and told them that I had saved his life as well as winning the race for him. He had been vomiting as we came alongside, but as he bounded into the black Daimler, he could have been a football player off for another training session. He winked at me, for the benefit of the cameras, and said, 'I'll be in touch!' I saw the bald patch on his head slump wearily to one side as they drove him away.

Mike Snape from the *Mirror* was there, his long, questing nose scorched by the sun or the drink that was on his breath. 'Bit of a change since Chatham, innit?' he said. 'Best pals with the Minister. And the inquest on that Russian kid next week.' His little eyes were gleaming with malice. 'Any connection?'

I wanted to walk away from him. But walking away would mean that he would write what he liked. 'Of course not,' I said.

'Oh,' he said, 'dear. It was just that I was wondering. I mean, you run over that kid, and the Minister's around. And your brother's his PPS. And after all, your crew was pissed. So what I wondered was, what if all these important blokes got together and told everyone else at the inquest to take it easy, so as not to tread on any important toes?'

'Fascinating,' I said. 'For your information, inquests have juries. When you find out how to fix a jury, perhaps you will tell me how you do it, so I can write a story about it?'

'Very clever,' he said, with a twist to his face.

'Law of the land,' I said, and walked past him to the slip where the Minister had left his Zodiac.

Next morning was a travel poster day, high pressure over France, winds light southerly. *Vixen* was sitting in the Beaulieu River, proud as a swan, her tall mast wavering in the green reflection of the trees.

Dean had made friends with Detective-Sergeant Ellerton.

'Your bosun can certainly play pool,' said Detective-Sergeant Ellerton.

'Cleaned him out, down the pub,' said Dean. There was a dazed expression on his face, like a cannibal who finds himself friends with a missionary.

I took Ellerton ashore and left a copy of Nadia's photograph with Neville's Filipino butler. When I came back, Dean said, 'Oh, yeah. That Admiral Wilson called.'

'When?'

'Night before last.'

Dean and I moved *Vixen* down the river and into the Solent, where the white sails were gathering for another Sunday of VHF abuse and insurance claims, and threaded our way eastward. Once we were out of the big traffic, I got on the telephone.

Dickie was in Southampton. He would be on his balcony, folding his *Sunday Telegraph* away as the telephone rang, dabbing with a linen napkin at traces of boiled egg round the corners of his mouth.

And the little worms of fear would be gnawing.

'Dickie,' I said. 'You rang.'

'Bill,' he said. 'Listen, old chap, we've had our differences. But I'll come straight to the point. I'd like *Vixen* to do the Youth Venture trip to the Baltic.'

His voice positively glowed with friendliness. I was taken aback. I had expected something a lot more grudging.

'Goodness,' I said, mildly. 'This is all very unexpected.'

'Things change. I've had . . . well, I've received assurances. Now, then. What plans?'

He was feeding me the lines. 'I'll go into Ramsgate,' I said.

'I'll arrange for the crew to join me there at noon. We'll be in tomorrow morning. Eleven o'clock for sure.'

'Marvellous,' he said. 'Absolutely marvellous. We'll have two more boats up in the Baltic. *Wilma* and *Xerxes*. I'll be there. Neville Glazebrook's coming for a week.'

Oh, is he, I thought. You bloody old hypocrite.

'Charter terms as before,' he said.

I said, 'Could you do me a favour? Ring my brother Christopher, tell him what you've just told me.'

Mission accomplished, I thought. I rang Pete, and told him to round up the crew.

We were alongside at Ramsgate by eight the following morning, and tied up next to a noisy boatload of Poles from Gdansk. At nine, a blue Transit minibus rolled along the quay. The doors burst open, and eight kids spilled on to the stones, followed by Pete.

He jumped on to the deck. 'Got your crew,' he said. 'Nice type of brat.'

I watched as Dean, swaggering slightly, showed them over *Vixen*. They eyed her with a suspicion that gradually began to look like enthusiasm.

It was all very wonderful. Dickie and I were friends again. Both he and Neville Glazebrook had pointed out to my dear brother Christopher the merits of his owning a share in the *Vixen* Trust. Claudia would be most disappointed. The inquest would be a formality. Everything had blown over.

Or so I was meant to think.

But it left out of account two real dead bodies. And it meant that Bill Tyrrell, who knew a lot, was in a specified place at a specified time, known to Dickie Wilson.

I said, 'Take 'em sailing. We'll talk later.'

I slipped a portable VHF in my pocket, climbed into the van and drove to the station.

I parked in the middle of the car park, and spent a long time asking a man in the ticket office all possible permutations of return tickets to London. He would remember me.

The train was one of Network Southeast's relics of the 1950s. The first-class carriage was empty. I climbed in and sat slumped in the seat on the far side from the platform. There was nobody on the opposite platform. Very gently, I opened the door, slid out, dropped to the tracks, and walked quickly along the train until I was level with the end of the platform at the far side. Then I strolled up the slope and into the car park, and summoned a taxi.

The driver played Radio 1 as he drove me through the rotting streets. I told him to drop me in a cobbled alley. Ahead and to the right, a sign said CAFE in red letters on a rust-streaked white board. I had eaten breakfast in here before, stormbound in Ramsgate. A thin slick of grease floated on the tea. I took it over to a table by the window.

It was made of plate glass, the window. Below it, the ground dropped away vertically. Seagulls quarrelled in the void. Beyond the seagulls was the marina, and beyond the marina the harbour, with six or seven yachts tied up at the visitors' pontoon. *Vixen* was out there, hovering in the entrance, waiting for the cross-Channel ferry to get out of the harbour.

I had four cups of tannic tea, and a couple of stale doughnuts. The waitress was bottle blonde, with an addiction to her own doughnuts and forearms like pillows. She obviously liked tall dark strangers. I told her it was a hot day, and agreed that it was a really nice summer. *Vixen*'s sail was a tilted white dunce's cap against the blue slash of the Channel. A red Rover pulled up to the dock gates, parked on the double yellow line. Two men got out and started down the quay.

My mouth became dry, with a dryness that had nothing to do with tannin. The waitress kept talking. I failed to answer. She went away, piqued.

The men went down to the pontoon. I put my binoculars on them. They were heavy-set, crop-headed. They started asking questions of the yacht crews. When the bigger of the two spoke to the Polish boat, I got a look at his face.

He had wide, flat cheeks. One of his canines was missing, and there was a bandage on his left ear. Dickie had been the only person I had told we were stopping in Ramsgate. Dickie, you conniving little bastard. I pulled the portable VHF out of my pocket, clicked to Channel 72, ship-to-ship. 'Pete,' I said. 'Flush. Over.'

'Flush,' squawked the portable. 'Out.'

Vixen's sails shifted against the horizon, narrowed as her nose pointed north and east.

'Ooh,' said the waitress, eyeing the radio. 'You a policeman?'

I grinned at her, the kind of grin policemen on TV give waitresses. Then I walked down to the Avis depot, rented a car, and drove out of town.

Vixen was on her way to Flushing, where it would be hard for Equipoise to find her. I was on my way to the inquest of Lennart Rebane, where it would have been easy for Equipoise to find me, if they were still looking.

As I had known they would be.

22

I spent the night in the Capistrano Guesthouse, Whitstable, writhing on nylon sheets, in a room as airtight as a bank safe. Next morning I wrote up the notes for my article, climbed into the blue suit, and left for the inquest.

It was held in Chatham Magistrates' Court, a grim grey building full of grim grey policemen. The press were there. So, presumably, were the men from Equipoise. I did not wish to see them, so I stayed in the thick of the Kent constabulary.

Wallace Holt, my lawyer, found me making stilted conversation to a lady CID person. Wallace's small red eyes had a bloodhound-like gloom. 'Press don't like it,' he said. 'Coroner's standing for the County Council, wants to impress. Tin-hat time.'

I smiled at him. I did not feel like smiling. When people are trying to murder you, legal process becomes a minor worry. As we filed into the court and the coroner seated himself under the Lion and the Unicorn, I was out of range of murder. But in exchange, I had the unpleasant feeling that I fed myself into a big, hungry machine.

My palms were sweating. I sat down in the chair provided. The jury came in. It was a hard, upright-looking jury; not the kind of jury to sympathize with a skipper who fed booze to a crew of delinquents, then ran down an innocent foreigner.

The coroner put on a pair of half-moon spectacles and confirmed the dead man's identity as Lennart Rebane, of

Tallinn, Estonia. The pathologist confirmed that the dead man had died by drowning, and that there had been alcohol in his blood.

I leaned across, whispered to Wallace. Wallace rose. He said, 'What time did he drown?'

'Difficult to say, to within an hour,' said the pathologist.

'We have heard the body was caught in the propellor of my client's yacht at approximately eleven-thirty p.m. The night before the discovery of the body.' There was a stir in court, a craning of necks. 'We would like to establish whether he was dead before he became so entangled.'

The pathologist was young, with a mop of black hair and a slightly worried expression. He said, 'He was dead by the time the propellor caught him.'

'Long dead?'

'Impossible to be precise.' The pathologist's voice took on a told-to-the-children tone. 'Bruised tissue changes in behaviour when the blood ceases to circulate. Circulation had ceased by the time an attempt was made to start the engine. I'm afraid we can't be more precise than that. The fingers of the left hand appear to have been jammed in the, er, hinge of the rudder. I am of the opinion that this was caused by the action of currents.'

Wallace thanked him, and sat down. I sat there and wondered whether I should be feeling relieved. But it was too early to feel relieved, because Superintendent Robertson was on his way to the stand, steely and compact in a grey suit. Wait for it, I thought.

The Superintendent cleared his throat, moistened his lips with a tongue the colour of his suit. My ears were ringing with what he was going to say, my heart thumping so I could hardly hear. His voice was thin and dry.

Then I heard what he was saying. 'In this case,' he said, 'it seems clear that what we have is a most tragic type of accident, in which no blame can attach to anybody.'

Next to me, Wallace Holt's mouth was hanging open like a trapdoor.

'Ah,' said the coroner. 'Statements, then.'

They read the statements. The coroner polished his glasses,

shaking his head. There was no mention of booze, or delinquents.

'Tragic,' said the coroner, when it was all over. 'No blame
attaches to any person *despite*' – he scowled at the press in the
gallery – 'uninformed speculation.' Then he directed the jury
to return a verdict of accidental death.

We got up. It was thirty seconds before Wallace could talk.
'Well,' he said at last. 'Well, I'll be *buggered*.' We were leaving
the courtroom now, shoved and jostled by dozens of shoulders.
Dickie Wilson was there. He raised a hand, waved. Little
bastard, I thought. Butter wouldn't melt. But Equipoise would
be there, somewhere.

Something brushed against my hand; something cool and
crisp, with square edges. I found I was holding an envelope.
The press were at me now, baying in a ring. Wallace was
saying, 'No comment.' I caught the eye of Snape from the
Mirror. His prehensile nose was wrinkled. His mouth made
the word, 'Fix.'

I looked away. I did not like agreeing with Mike Snape, but
on this occasion it seemed the only way to go. Stuffing the
envelope into the pocket of my suit, I got Wallace by the arm.
'Thank you,' I said.

'Not at all,' he said. He had recovered enough to take the
credit, but he still looked dazed.

'Drink?'

'Brilliant,' he said, clutching the notion as the one fixed
point in a world gone mad.

I took some time to choose a pub. The layout was important.
Eventually, we discovered a dark-brown gin palace whose car
park had the right characteristics. Wallace ordered a large gin
and tonic. I drank whisky; I needed it. Wallace said, 'You've
got friends.'

I shrugged. I pulled the envelope from my pocket. It was
made of thick, heavy paper. A portcullis device was printed
on the flap; the crest of the House of Commons. Inside was a
single sheet of paper, without a letterhead. Typewritten in its
centre were the words AMYAS TERKEL, NÄMANÖN,
SUOMI.

'Posh friends,' said Wallace.

I laid the envelope in an ashtray, got a match from the barmaid, and watched the orange flames flicker in the dark, hot bar. 'All square now,' I said. When you saved the life of a Minister who had been a spook with your father in the old days, the Minister showed his gratitude. It was called practical politics.

'Another?' said Wallace.

I said, 'I'll have a pint.'

He ordered the drinks. 'I don't suppose you can tell me what the hell's going on?' he said.

'Not yet.'

I sipped the rank, tepid beer. Outside the back window of the bar, the car park was empty, except for a couple of delivery vans and Wallace's Mercedes. I said, 'Finish up. You're leaving.'

He looked at me sideways, across the bags under his eyes. He finished his gin. I told him what I wanted to do. 'Why?' he said.

'You're my lawyer.'

He shrugged. We shook hands, elaborately. He left.

I sipped my beer, and stared at the Edwardian leaf-patterns ground into the mirror behind the bar. The mirror gave a view of the window overlooking the street. There was a red Rover out there. The Mercedes drew away. A man got out of the Rover. He was thickset, with a bandaged ear. He had been in Ramsgate this morning. His mouth was shut. If he had opened it, the right canine would have been missing.

I took another sip of beer, and strolled through the door marked TOILETS. There was a door to the car park. I went through it. At the back of the car park was an alley, with a couple of dustbins and some dog muck. At the bottom of the alley, Wallace was waiting in his silver Mercedes. I climbed into the back and lay down on the floor. 'Sheerness,' I said. 'Ferry terminal.'

'Yassuh,' said Wallace. We drove.

We turned on to a dual carriageway. Cardboard houses were petering out into rubbish dumps. There were no red cars in the rear-view mirror.

'Are you sure you know what you're doing?' said Wallace.

'Of course,' I said. I was not not telling the truth.

He nodded. All his chins nodded too. We turned between the concrete gatehouses of the Sheerness ferryport.

'There you are,' said Wallace.

I shouldered my bag, bought a ticket with a private cabin in the name of Henry Vandervelde, and walked on to the Flushing ferry. There were a couple of hours before the boat left. I stayed in the cabin, finishing my notes for Martin Carr's article.

The notes read like the libellous ravings of a paranoid maniac. Except that it was all true.

What I needed to sew it up were two interviews. One with Nadia Vuorinen.

And one with Amyas Terkel.

The ship's fabric trembled. The quay slid away. The ferry moved out into the Medway. I yawned, stretched; there was no air in the cabin. Last time I had sailed over this water, it had been a sheet of black glass full of winking red eyes, and Lennart Rebane and Marie Clarke had been alive.

I called the steward, and bribed him to buy me a cheese sandwich and a bottle of The Macallan in the duty-free shop. When he came back, I locked the door and poured myself half a toothmugful.

The thick, strong taste of it took me back to the Basin, to races with Charlie, and evenings outside the Hole with Claudia. I finished the first glass, poured another. Claudia's face kept turning into Nadia's.

I slept hard and deep behind the firm lock of the cabin. Bad dreams came; restless dreams, me running across the viscous surface of a purple sea that caught at my feet and slowed me down so I could not get away from the rusty barges that ground after me under the livid sky.

I woke, mouth dry, heart hammering, blanket down around my waist. The luminous hands on my watch said three-ten. It was black as coal in the cabin. I had the impression that the door had opened and shut. My skin felt hot, but every hair on my body was standing on end as if I was freezing cold. I sat up and turned on the light. Pale blue Formica walls. Spare bunks folded up against the bulkheads. Nobody there. Whisky dreams, I thought. I hit the light switch and lowered the lids over hot eyeballs.

Sleep would not return. My mind clanked round the old questions: Nadia, my father, Dickie Wilson, Christopher. I could see their faces with peculiar vividness, floating in the blood-coloured world behind my eyelids.

Something was happening in the red world. The red was turning mauve. The mauve was the sky in my dream. Once again I was running on water that sucked and dragged at my feet. Behind me, the engines of the barges were clattering like road drills. I looked round. In the wheelhouses, the helmsmen stood thickset, immobile, as if carved from granite. I started to shout at them.

Normally, if you shout in a dream you wake yourself up. Under the mauve sky, in the clatter of the barges, I had a horrible moment of truth.

My shouting was echoing in the cabin. I was not dreaming. I was still awake.

I swung my feet on to the floor. My legs felt weak and spongy, as if I had pins and needles. When I turned on the light the mauve sky cleared, and I could see the cabin again. But it was oddly blurred, and the fluorescent tube of the cabin light was bright enough to send spears into the back of my skull. The cabin was intolerably hot. Air, I thought, muzzily. Must get air. I pulled on my underpants. Not the whisky. Not the food. What the hell is happening to me?

Someone was knocking on the door.

There was a voice, booming, 'Telephone for you, Mr Tyrrell.'

I said, 'Thank you.' My tongue was several sizes too big for my mouth. Something was wrong, but I could not remember what. My fingers fumbled with the lock. The fog in my head lifted for a moment.

Not Tyrrell. Vandervelde.

The fog came down again.

The far wall of the passage appeared, speeding towards my head. Red sparks drifted around the black space in my skull. Someone had hold of my arm, a reassuring, confident grip. I could see a gold watch on the arm. The arm belonged to a

208

man who was wearing a white-topped hat. One of the crew. Off to the radio, radio, radio, radio, radio *room*. Damn civil. The civility made me want to laugh, but we were going up stairs now, empty stairs, to the top of the sleeping ferry, the only sound the distant bleep of a fruit machine in a frowsy bar –

The night air hit me as if I had walked into a wet curtain. Suddenly I was shivering, freezing cold. The man holding my arm said something. The pressure of his hand faded. Something clicked, wood and metal. It was dark out here, with wind, pools of yellow light that bled into fog. In the light I saw the white-topped cap of whoever had brought me on deck. Below the brim was a slice of shadow that hid his eyes. Below his eyes was the mouth, smiling. A polite, helpful smile. With a gap in it. The right-hand upper canine tooth was missing.

I frowned. My face felt as if it belonged to someone else. It should all mean something, and so should the banisters around me. They kept growing in my mind, those banisters, forming orchestral harps, stairways to heaven.

A puff of breeze hit me. The fog in my mind lifted for a second. It let in terror. *What is happening to me?* I thought. In the same moment I knew that the man in the white hat was the man who had been driving the barge. And that the banisters were not banisters. They were the ship's rail. The man with no tooth was inside the rail. I was outside it, on a lifeboat platform.

The fog came down again. I swayed like a tree. I swayed away from the rail, so my blurred vision swept across rust-pocked deck and beyond, into a pit of blackness that wrinkled and gleamed. The sea. I knew I was a tree, though; I had roots. I swayed back. The man in the white hat said, in a low voice, 'Get over, will you?' Metal squealed. He came through the gate. The clouds of euphoria shifted, darkened. Black horns sprouted from the white top of his cap, and electrical discharges played in the gap where his tooth should have been. Terror came down like a storm of rain. I would have shouted, but my lips were numb, and what came out was a nasty blubbering, weak as a kitten. I laced my arms through the rails, and hung on.

He raised his hand to hit me. Then he lowered it again. The fog receded. No marks on the body, I thought, when they pulled it out of the sea. If they pulled it out of the sea. A face appeared; a drowned face, bloated, eyes eaten out by crabs. My own face. Someone was fiddling with my feet. Gripping my feet. Pulling. My arms were hurting, because they were stretching like rubber, miles long.

I wriggled. It was about all I could do. A foot came free, I stamped backwards with it, hard. Someone grunted.

The grunt took me back to the black cypresses in the garden by the burning brothel. He had made the sound when I had hit him on the ear.

I twisted my head. 'Come on,' he said. He was a tall blur. 'Or I'll break your bloody fingers off, one by one.'

The top of the blur had a gap in it. A mouth.

'You're not going to cause no more trouble,' he said. 'So don't make no fuss.'

I lashed out with my foot, to the right of the gap. My bare heel skidded on shaven jaw.

Hit ear. The ear I had smashed with the rock in the garden.

He made a high sound, and let go of my legs. I kicked him. Tried to kick him. It turned into a weak shove. The whimper became a bellow of horror. There was a very nasty scraping.

I could see fingers on paintwork, looking for an anchorage. At first I thought it was in my mind. Then I realized I was stooped over, watching a pair of hands with the intentness of a lepidopterist watching a rare butterfly. The hands were gripping the place where the deck joined the side of the ship. Down inside, a kettledrum was sounding. *Boom, boom*, it said. 'Help me,' said the man with the gap tooth, as he hung over the ship's side.

I wanted to help him. But I could not move, or shout. *Boom, boom*, roared the kettledrum.

The fingers slipped, caught again. Then they vanished over the side. I craned my neck over the edge. I peered into the dark sea, eighty feet below. There was water, the roar of the wake. The sound of the kettledrums filled my head, made it heavy. I swayed out over the black abyss, caught myself, swayed back, began to crawl inboard, to where the white cabins rose like icebergs. The kettledrums were constant now. They were my pulse, forcing blood into my congested brain. I thought: *What the hell is wrong with you?* There was a sound; an exclamation of horror. The drums swelled to a roar. I fell forward on the cold metal deck, and passed out.

23

There was a cream ceiling. There was a smell of antiseptic, and a face with spectacles above an open-necked khaki shirt. All this I could see, but not well, because of the blur in my eyes. I had a headache, too, and a taste in my mouth as if I had been gargling with sewage. But I felt better.

The face said, 'He's back with us.'

I began to remember things. My brain was fuzzy, but it remembered almost everything. It did not remember this face.

'Lie down,' said the face. 'Don't move.'

There was a woman there, too, wearing a dark-blue uniform and a petulant expression. One of the ferry stewardesses.

I said, 'What happened?'

The woman said, 'You're lucky Dr Gillibrand was on board.'

The doctor said, 'I know it's not much fun being seasick, but that was ridiculous.'

'What the hell happened?'

Even in the blur, I could see her face stiffen.

'You used hyoscine plasters.' The doctor smiled. 'Next time, you ought to read the packet. Use one at a time.' He held out a dish. In it were about a dozen circular pieces of used sticking plaster. 'One's enough,' he said. 'You're lucky you didn't kill yourself.'

I laid my head on the paper pillowcase. 'Accident,' I said.

The doctor shrugged. 'Twelve,' he said. 'All the way down

the spine.' He held out the packet. 'Can't you bloody well read? Look here. *Apply one, as needed. It is dangerous to exceed the stated dose.*

I had been asleep, full of whisky, in a hot cabin. The man with the white cap must have followed me to the ferry. He would have put the plasters on one by one, soft as a whisper. Hyoscine is a powerful drug. It passes quickly through the skin. Accidental death.

'Used to use it as a truth drug,' said the doctor to the woman. 'Heavy alkaloid. Comes from deadly nightshade. Look at the pupils, the way they're dilated. Same family as the stuff Italian women used to drop it into their eyes, make the pupils big. Hence *bella donna*.'

The woman sniffed.

'Fascinating,' I said.

'You've caused the doctor great inconvenience,' said the woman, like a school matron.

But I lay there, and paid no attention, because I was thinking of the rake of fingernails on paint, and the black void beyond the white edge of the deck. And the man with the missing tooth, who had tried to kill me twice, and would not be getting another chance.

'Well,' said the doctor. 'All over, eh? If I were you, I'd resign yourself to being seasick in future.'

'Don't worry,' I said. 'I will.'

They helped me back to the cabin, gingerly, as if I was a drunk who might throw up on them. It seemed nobody had noticed that they were a passenger short. They would not notice until the morning, if then.

The relief wore off. In its place came horror. *Help me*, he had said. I had not helped. The water would have been cold. If he had escaped the suck of the propellor, he would have trodden water, watching the lights of the ship shrinking towards the horizon while the salt stung the ends of his ruined fingers . . .

My watch said four-twenty. He would be dead by now. If he was lucky.

Next morning, I leaned on the rail and watched the Flushing pierhead grow against the flat banks of the Schelde. Under the lifeboat on my right, there were brown specks that might have been rust, if I had not known they were blood.

Beyond the pierhead was a tall brown mast. As we came round, the lock gates to the inner harbour opened, and *Vixen* slid into the Buitenhaven. I found I was grinning foolishly.

The ferry came alongside. I put my bottle of The Macallan into my overnight bag, strolled down the gangway and through the Customs. Ten minutes later I was standing on the old familiar teak of *Vixen*'s deck, and the crew were casting off the shorelines, and Pete was pulling her nose round to point at the flat, open horizon of the North Sea.

'Nice trip?' said Pete.

'Quiet,' I said.

And that was that.

The Schelde is the southernmost arm of the Rhine Delta. That night, we pulled out into the stream of ships that pours up through the Straits of Dover, bound for Rotterdam, the busiest port in the world. We moved up the low Dutch coast over a sea as flat as a green silk bedspread. All around the horizon, the ghostly white upperworks of tankers and bulk carriers faded in and out of a whitish murk.

It was a brute of a place in bad visibility. But today, I did not worry about it. I had a pounding headache, and other things on my mind.

See you in Finland, Dickie.

The wind stayed westerly, and freshened. An August depression was making life unpleasant in the Faeroes, and we got the benefit of it. *Vixen* stirred up her old bones and ploughed her narrow groove towards the Friesian Islands. The new crew began to settle into their four hours on, four off.

We began to train them up.

Dean had left behind his last-of-the-technicolour-wide-boys persona. His pony-tail had become a pigtail, secured with a Turk's head. If we had had any tar aboard, he would have tarred it. Pete spent his time in a state of acute gloom and disbelief that *Vixen*, pride of his life, was being sailed yet again by eight kids who did not know a belaying-pin from a compass needle.

The seasickness had passed. The crew were eager to learn.

So we taught them.

They knew about pavements and pubs, and the workings of the probation system. Out there on the grey-green North Sea, we taught them the names of standing and running rigging, and the purpose of it. We taught them to steer a course, and to hoist and drop a sail so nobody got hurt, and how to haul in a big sail without a winch when the helmsman luffed. At first, there was plenty of shouting from Pete and Dean, and the crew shouted back. Then, after two days, they began to fall under the spell, and the shouting stopped.

It was the same spell *Vixen* had spun round me, the season I had taken my tentative steps in her, out into the North Sea, and finally down-Channel to Pulteney and beyond. The magic of it was that *Vixen* ceased to be a mere machine of wood and rope and canvas. She became a world, that occupied your full attention, or you were in trouble.

By the time we were leaving Heligoland to the south, their city-pale faces were red with sun and wind, and they were listening so hard that you could give orders in a conversational tone of voice. They were a team.

At noon two days after we had left Flushing, we emerged from the short, murky waves of the Elbe's mouth and slid into the right-hand lock at the entrance to the Kiel Canal, the short cut across the bottom of the Jutland Peninsula from the North Sea to the Baltic. It takes eight hours to motor its length. In a yacht, you blast along thirty feet from the right-hand bank, and do your best not to get sucked under one of the continuous stream of merchant ships, tall as apartment buildings, hurrying down the middle.

That evening, we tied up outside the British Army Yacht Club at Kiel, and the crew went to have a look at Germany. Dean went with them. He loped after them like a gangling sheepdog loping after sheep, and came back with them at ten o'clock, sober. I did not congratulate him. Instead, I got him a beer, and we drank it by the rail, looking at the spars of a big German barque easing down the lock approach, outward bound.

Dean said, 'I wish Marie was here.'

It was the first time I had heard Dean worry about anyone

but Dean. I wished I could tell him that whoever had killed her was at the bottom of the North Sea.

We finished the beers. I told the starboard watch to light the big kerosene running lights, red and green in the port and starboard shrouds, white on the transom. The port watch cast off the shorelines, except a single stern line. Pete told them to pull up main and staysail. The wind was from the east, offshore. A crowd gathered on the quay. I made the crew cheer. Then, in the silence, we made up the staysail sheet, and *Vixen*'s bowsprit swung off the quay.

'Mainsheet,' I said.

The blocks clacked as Dean hauled. The boom came in, and the sail filled. *Vixen* hung a moment in the water, heeling. The stern line came off. Water gurgled from her transom, and she began to move.

The compass card swung gently in its bath of green light. We slid smooth as paint down the winking avenue of buoys, between the lights of the shores of the Kieler Fjord, and into the coal-black Baltic.

In the early morning on the fourth day out of Kiel, I had the wheel, for the pleasure of it. The light was low over the water, and the sea was a deep, clear blue, touched at its eastern edges by the pink remnants of the dawn. There were no other sails. Baltic sailors put their boats away early in the year, and nobody sails all night, unless they have to.

There was a knot of excitement in my stomach. These were waters my father had sailed. And up there, over the northern horizon, was the man behind the name on Nadia's photograph.

Pete brought coffee into the cockpit, and a spiral-bound book of charts. His eyes were bleary with sleep, his beard matted. *Vixen* churned on, reaching to the fifteen-knot westerly.

The coffee was strong and sweet, and acted directly on the backbone. Pete opened the chart. 'God almighty,' he said. 'Looks like the bloody measles.'

I had spent a lot of time over those charts, these last few days. Just over the northern horizon were the first rocks of the Archipelago, the belt of islands that spreads from the west coast of Finland, across the neck of the Gulf of Bothnia to the east coast of Sweden. The biggest island is Åland, less than thirty miles from end to end. The smallest scarcely breaks the surface of the water.

'Where are we going, then?' said Pete.

The islands lay scattered across the chart like a spilt jigsaw. Directly north of our present position, a wedge of open water drove between two clusters. It was marked Gullkronafjärd. To the east of the fjord was a tangle of channels, specked with the black triangles of rock cairns and the dotted lines of leading marks. I put my finger on the long island marked Nämanön. 'Right there,' I said.

The crew cooked breakfast. As they were washing up, the first of the rocks came out of the blue horizon. A black-and-green gunboat nosed around us, made curious by the red ensign flapping at *Vixen*'s counter. They welcomed us to Finland, sheered off again. The islands closed in.

At three in the afternoon we were in the islands, turning hard-a-starboard between two great grey cliffs crowned with pine trees that shone unearthly green in the low sun. We came to anchor in a semi-circular bay with shores of ice-planed granite. Pines and maples grew right down to the water; a squirrel scuttled away from a narrow beach.

I slipped the photograph I had found in Nadia's luggage into my pocket. We swung the tender over the side. Two of the trainees rowed me ashore. The bow grounded with a soft crunch on the beach. A path wound through big, mossy boulders and into the trees.

A hundred yards up the path, a fat man was gathering sticks in the undergrowth. I said, 'Amyas Terkel?'

He looked up. He had a wide, copper-brown face. He said something in Finnish. I said, 'English?'

He said, 'Amyas Terkel,' and jabbed a dirty finger down a path I had not noticed. 'All way,' he said. 'All way.'

The path was narrow. It wound through pine woods thick enough to blot out the sun. Its surface was moss and dry twigs, undisturbed by feet. Mosquitoes whined in the shade. I could have been the first person to walk down here in a year.

After half a mile, the trees began to thin. The pines had given way to silver birches, with brown, slimy-capped boletus mushrooms round their boles. Through the birch trunks was something straight-edged and green. I had been stumbling towards it for perhaps five minutes before I realized it was a roof of wooden shingles, thickly grown with lichen.

The roof belonged to a log cabin, overlooking a minute cove with a wooden jetty. Tied up at the jetty was a battered aluminium boat with an outboard. Squatting by the boat, mending a net, was a brown, stringy man wearing a pair of shorts. I stepped out of the trees. It was hot. Sweat ran stickily down my face and inside my shirt. I said, 'Amyas Terkel?'

The man's head snapped round with the speed of a wild animal's. I was thirty yards away, but I could still see that his eyes were an extraordinary sky blue. He said nothing. He scrambled into the boat and yanked the start cord of the outboard. I started to run.

The motor did not start on the first pull. By the time he gave it a second, I had my foot on the painter. I said, 'I've come a thousand miles to talk to you.'

His nose looked as if he had been a boxer. His lips were thin to the point of non-existence. The whites of his eyes showed all the way round the irises. Sign of madness, I thought. Like Mussolini.

His hand dropped. 'Good Lord above,' he said. His voice sounded rusty, as if he did not use it much. 'You're the son.'

24

He climbed out of the boat slowly, as if the shock of seeing me had cost him his strength. We walked towards the cabin. Woodsmoke was drifting from a stovepipe. There were neat piles of firewood the size of houses, stacked in the sun. Outside the front wall was a homemade table with a single chair. He said, 'Sit down,' and went inside. There was a crucifix on the wall, with a little roof to keep the snow off. He brought coffee in an enamel pot. It tasted as if the grounds had been used before. He sat on a rock. He said, 'I don't see many people, nowadays. Not many at all.'

'No,' I said. I pulled out Nadia's photograph, and pushed it across the table.

He held it far away, as if his eyes were no good in close-up. 'Ah,' he said. 'The old *Åland.*' He fell silent. I did not prompt him. If he was going to tell me anything, he would tell me in his own time.

The pause lasted a full two minutes. My mouth was dry, and not only because of the vile coffee. When he finally spoke, it was as if he had come up from deep water. 'I remember that,' he said. 'We were in Gotland. Varnishing.' He said 'warnishing'. His accent was as rusty as his larynx. 'That was the bad trip. The trip they drowned.'

My stomach sank. 'Who drowned?'

'Sven and André.' My heart began to beat again.

He dabbed a gnarled finger on the men in jerseys and

woollen hats, moved it to the figure waving the varnish brush. 'And that was me. I was happy then, I think. It was a wild time. Before the Lord Jesus told me I must take myself from the world, and think on the torment to come.'

I could not restrain my impatience. 'My father,' I said. 'What about him?'

He shrugged. 'Your father?' he said. 'A crazy man. He appeared with this ship, a schooner, I do not know from where, in perhaps the year 1967. He wanted to make money, trading. But of course it was a time for motor ships; the years of sailing ships were gone, and nobody was interested in them as things of beauty the way they are now.' His voice was gaining strength as use knocked the rust off it. 'So he could not make a living carrying corn, or timber, as before. He had to make his money carrying . . . other things.' He looked at me sideways. 'You are the son,' he said. 'You have the look of him. I can tell you the truth.'

The skin was crawling on the back of my neck. I said, 'What other things?'

He threw a crumb of bread to a chaffinch, and swivelled his disconcerting eyes on to mine. 'Men,' he said.

'Men?'

The eyes dropped. 'To the southeast of here are countries that were once free.'

I said, 'Lithuania, Latvia, Estonia. All that is changing.'

'Maybe,' he said. He did not sound convinced. 'Your father used to deliver spies. He knew people in England, in America. Me, I worked for the English, for wages. He was what you could call a freelance. Nobody suspected anything about this antique ship he was driving. He used to catch some fish, move around. A wooden boat doesn't show up good on radar. Everyone thought he was crazy. But he was very good. He could tell you where he was in fog, big wind, you name it. He'd cruise up the edge of territorial waters. He had a couple of open boats on deck, with sails and oars. He'd drop people over the side, they'd go ashore.'

I had been noticing the past tense. 'But he got caught,' I said.

Terkel's face twisted. 'Not by the Russkies,' he said. 'Lazy bastards. They couldn't catch snails. It was bad weather, and the ship.'

'What happened?'

He picked up the photograph, gazed into it as if it was a window. 'Picked up an Estonian in Gotland. We were all drinking except your father. He did not drink. He had his ship, you know? We had been all day varnishing. It was spring, but a bad night, wind and snow.

'Your father was mad for his ship. Always, the varnishing, the remaking of old, broken parts. But he had little money. There were parts of the ship, masts, the keel, that he could not afford to mend. So we went off in a blizzard. A late blizzard: the sea-ice was gone. The Estonian, the man we had to land – the spy, you understand – he was frightened. Your father said no problem, the snow was good cover from the Russkies. We left.' Terkel stopped. He put his elbows on his knees, and stared down at the rock.

Bloated yellow-black clouds leaning on a black sea, a west wind screaming in the shrouds as the old bow blasted spray from the heave beyond the island. Ice stiffening sheets and halyards. Ice matted in my father's heavy black beard and eyebrows.

I did not want to hear what came next. It came anyway.

'Sven had a bottle,' said Terkel. 'The more he drank, the more frightened he got.' Terkel looked up. His eyes were reminiscent, but sane. Seaman's eyes. 'It was a blizzard, all right. But it wasn't a too terrible night. Just bad, and bloody cold. There were those two boats on the deck. Like dories, big dories, you know that they have in the Newfoundland cod fishing, that your father put overboard when he needed to land someone. Sven and André told your father to put back into Gotland. Your father would not go. So they took one of these dories from the deck, and put it in the water alongside, and got in. They were shouting. A wave came. The ship fell on them. That was the end of them.'

The low black island, coming and going between horizontal whips of snow. The masts of the trader scribbling huge, jerky words in the sky. Two men wrestling with a frozen halyard, lowering the boat overboard, climbing down the side, yelling above the scream of the wind, shaking with fear. The man with

221

the wind-torn black beard putting up the helm, angry, but making a smooth for them, a patch of water where they could at least get a start. Then, over to the westward, the humping up of the horizon that signals a big wave; the rearing of its smooth, coal-black face; the lift of the trader's hull. The man at the wheel, heaving the spokes. Too late; the downward drive of the trader's fat side into the trough, the great blossom of white spray mingling with the snow downwind; and in the boom and roar of the hull's fall, a harder concussion, wood on wood.

'We never found them,' said Terkel. 'Then the wind got up. The main topmast came down, it was rotten. There was no sailing to windward. We were driven east. There was a fishing boat. Your father saw his lights in the night. He put us aboard, me and the Estonian. Two seconds alongside. We both jumped. He stayed there, on his beloved boat.'

My father, head bowed, alone on the big wooden ship in the dark. A ship he could not control alone; the wind screaming in the rigging, digging up lumps of icy water, flinging them at him until he was soaked and freezing. The sounds of a wooden boat: the groaning of the masts as the gusts walloped home, the hollow, sinister boom of water in the voids of the hull. And at the centre of it all, the great silence of his thoughts. What had he been thinking?

'It was fifty miles upwind of Hiiumaa,' said Terkel. 'Estonia. When a ship goes ashore there in a big wind, there will be very little left of it. Even if the Russkies do not shoot it, eh?'

I tried to see the ship hitting the shore, rolled by the breakers, smashed to splinters. But all I could see was darkness.

'He was a good man, your father,' said Amyas Terkel. 'But his love was for ships and the sea. And in loving them too much, he lost sight of the Lord.'

He looked at me sharply with his brilliant blue eyes. 'Although . . .' He hesitated.

'Yes?'

'I heard that the *Åland* went ashore. And I heard he did not die.'

Suddenly, everything was still. I said, 'Did you?'

'A man I know said he met him afterwards. In western Estonia.'

'When?'

He shrugged. 'Five years ago, ten. Who knows? The man is dead, now. He died of cancer in Uppsala.'

'Who was this man?' My heart was pounding violently.

'One from our . . . old profession. Who can tell if he told the truth?'

'There was a letter,' I said. I could feel him slipping away. 'From a woman in Estonia. She said my father was ill, and she was looking after him.'

He shrugged. 'If it was God's will.'

I said, 'I want to know about my father.'

He said, 'There is nothing else I can tell you. It is a time I wish to forget. If you want more, you must go to Estonia, I think.'

I said, 'You wish to forget. I wish to discover.'

He did not answer. He was staring at his crucifix.

I said, 'Is my father alive?'

He did not move or speak.

I said, 'My father.'

'I did not hear he had died. Please. I would rest.'

'Is he alive?'

'You are persistent,' he said. 'Like your father.'

'In Estonia?' I said.

'Very well,' said Terkel. 'Go to Estonia.'

He is alive, I thought. *You shifty bastard, you are telling me he is alive.*

I got up and walked into the dim woods. In the fringes of the trees, I looked back. He was squatting on the jetty again, mending his nets. He might never have moved.

That evening, we sailed south and east, outside the Archipelago, to Helsinki. It was a bleak, beautiful landscape of tree-clad islands, with goshawks overhead, and low, ice-smoothed rocks. I paid it very little attention.

I had a father who had steered a merchant ship into one side of a storm with a wife and two sons. He had emerged from the other with no dependants, and a Baltic trader full of spies.

I sat in *Vixen*'s saloon, and got the pencil lines I was drawing on the chart wrong three times running, which was something I had not done for fifteen years.

It was called rejection; long delayed, but rejection all the same. The thing that was blurring the chart and mixing the numbers in my mind was anger. How could a sane man go and play pirates on the skinny edge of the Baltic, and leave his children, who loved him, to think he was dead? He and my mother had led separate lives. But it was hard to forgive him for Christopher's sake, and mine.

I heard Claudia's voice: *You can do better than sailing round Europe with a lot of juvenile delinquents.*

I liked juvenile delinquents. Perhaps all that time ago my father had felt the same way about the spies he carried.

That was an idea that calmed me down enough to get the course straight.

I caught sight of my face, dimly reflected in the clear plastic of the Portland plotter lying on the chart. I had not shaved since we had left England. The beard was black and heavy. Terkel's first words came back to me. *Good Lord, it's the son.*

The son. He had known about me. The only person who would have told him was my father. My father had re-membered me. But he had stayed away.

I did not understand.

The anger had faded, but not gone. I wanted to know why he had done it, and I knew how I was going to find out. I had known since I had seen the uneasy sideways shift of Terkel's eyes.

I was going to find him.

I put away the plotter, hung the bearing compass round my neck, and ran up the companionway.

To the north, the coast was low and grey-green. To the south, the sea sparkled under the hot glare of the sun. Down there beyond the horizon was Estonia. In Helsinki, I was going to introduce Dean to Dickie Wilson, alias Mr Johnson. After Helsinki, the Tall Ships moved to Tallinn, the capital of Estonia.

Helsinki is a good town to arrive in. One moment you are threading your way through grey rocks towards an apparently uninhabited shore of trees and granite. The next, there are big black-and-white cardinal buoys bobbing like fishing floats

224

ahead, and the buildings of the city are sprawling out of the woods to meet you.

We were heading for a waterfront thick with ships. There was a huge cobbled square, flanked by ochre-painted buildings with white colonnades. In front of the buildings there were market stalls, and a crowd. Three or four cabin cruisers came out to meet us.

'People,' said Dean. He looked excited. Cities were Dean's element.

Alongside the quays, the Tall Ships were rafted one outside the other. In the doghouse, the VHF squawked berthing instructions and formal messages of welcome. I felt a moment of trepidation; last time we had come alongside at a Tall Ships gathering, we had found Lennart Rebane round the propellor the next morning.

I stood there at the wheel, feeling the solid power of *Vixen*'s rudder through the spokes, sighting along the bowsprit at the Norwegian barque alongside which we had been instructed to moor.

'They're all there,' said Pete.

Two Youth Venture battle flags were flapping in the forest of spars. One of them would be *Wilma*, Otto Campbell in command. The other was *Xerxes*. Dickie Wilson was aboard *Xerxes*.

'Family reunion,' I said.

'Engine?' said Pete. The sun had peeled the skin off his nose, yellowed his beard and bleached his eyebrows to invisibility.

'No,' I said. 'Hands to sheets.'

Pete said, 'Aye, aye,' with untypical formality. I wondered how many times my father had come alongside here in the *Åland*. The Norwegian's side was growing under the bowsprit.

Dean was standing by the binnacle, his pigtail flapping in the breeze, the late sun glinting in his newly-polished silver earring. 'Shorelines ready?'

'Ready,' he said.

The crew stood on the deck, pretending they did this every day, ignoring the crowd on the quay. The crowd was seeing fifty-five feet of gleaming timber cutting a white swathe through the sea, canted on its ear under full sail, hard on the little easterly that was blowing along the quay. Goodness, they would be thinking. All those sails up, all that speed. He's left it too late. They would be eagerly awaiting the crunch as the bowsprit pounded into the Norwegian's polished side.

'Let go all!' I said, and eased the wheel two spokes to windward.

Vixen's sails thundered as they let the sheets fly. She slid up on the Norwegian, losing momentum. Dean tossed up his stern line, got it back on a slip, snubbed it on a cleat to take off the last of her way. Someone had gone ashore with a line forward.

'Down,' I said.

The practice paid off. The sails came down with a whizz and a thump.

On the quay, the crowd began clapping.

We stowed the sails and tidied the boat. A Finnish cadet came aboard, saluted, and handed me a gold-edged invitation.

There was a reception in the Town Hall at six. At this particular event there would be a large British contingent, one of whose luminaries would be Dickie Wilson.

I walked into the town, found a library, and conducted some research into the geography of Tallinn. When I returned to *Vixen*, Dean was sluicing salt off the topsides with a freshwater hose.

I said, 'We're going to a party.'

He looked at me suspiciously. His teeth were greenish-yellow in his brown face. 'What kind?'

'Mr Johnson's going to be there.'

He said, 'Ah, *shit*.'

'Put on your glad rags,' I said. 'I'd like you to point him out to me.'

Dean thought for a moment, fingering a spot on his chin. Then he said, 'Yeah. Why not?'

I went below, pulled on a blazer and a Youth Venture tie. At five to six, Dean and I walked across the cobbled territory of Finland and up the steps of Helsinki Town Hall.

There was a big crowd milling around on the parquet floor of a lofty room with a ceiling like a wedding cake.

'Christ,' said Dean. 'I thought you said it was a party.'

'It will be,' I said.

He stared in horror at a Spanish Admiral with most of Fort Knox on his jacket, and collared us two glasses of vodka from a passing tray. It was not my kind of party either.

There were a lot of familiar faces. I talked to Otto Campbell.

'Glad you made it,' he said.

I said, 'I nearly didn't.'

'Told you, though,' he said. 'All you had to do was keep quiet, keep your nose clean. It blew over, didn't it?'

'Did it?'

'Saw my old Colonel again, last week. He said his blokes had decided Rebane wasn't any good anyway. You were off the hook.'

'Nice of him.' I wondered how much of that was down to Neville Glazebrook.

'Race tomorrow,' he said.

'Say your prayers.'

'You're not steering our Neville now,' he said. I didn't reply. I was searching the crowd for an iron-grey head, well below eye level, and not finding it.

A stout man with a paper-white face and a blue uniform with brass buttons climbed on to a stage at the end of the room, and started to bang a table with a hammer. There was an instantaneous hush, broken only by the surreptitious rattle of glasses against teeth. Dean had found some smoked salmon canapés. He was eating five at once. The man with the blue uniform started making a speech about brotherhood.

'And now,' he said, 'I would like to introduce to you some friends of sail training who have come from far away to be with us here.' A parade of luminaries marched on to the stage. Dean said, through the smoked salmon, 'Like bleeding Miss World, innit?'

And on he came; dapper as dammit in his blazer and sharply creased grey flannels, eyes twinkling like hard little sapphires under his big, reassuring eyebrows. Dickie Wilson.

I said to Dean, 'Well?'

Dean said, 'Well what?'

'Who's that?'

Dean said, 'Dunno.'

I looked round at him, quickly. I said, 'Haven't you seen him before?'

Dickie started to speak, bluff, hearty, charming. Dean watched him without curiosity. In the careful scaffolding of ideas in my mind, a pole buckled, then another. The structure bulged. The ground trembled.

'Nah,' said Dean.

I said, 'There's Dickie Wilson. Isn't he your Mr Johnson?' The structure swayed, started to collapse.

Dean said, 'If that's Dickie Wilson, I had the wrong Dickie Wilson. I never seen this one before in my life.'

And the walls came tumbling down.

25

Back on *Vixen*, I went at it from all angles. But for once in his life, Dean was unshakable. He had not even seen Dickie when he had come aboard at Chatham; he had been below at the time, making preparations to run for his life.

'Listen,' said Dean. 'He was on the quay down Chatham, Mr Johnson. He was a big shot, with all the others, right?'

'And he looked like Dickie.'

'Yeah,' said Dean. 'Well, he looked, you know, rich and old.'

I was beginning to understand. As far as Dean was concerned, anyone over twenty-five who habitually wore a jacket looked rich and old. There had been a hundred of them at Chatham.

If Dickie had nothing to fear from the film, that meant that the Equipoise campaign to silence me was being inspired by someone else.

Dean, I thought. Nowadays, he was the lion-hearted watch leader. But once a liar, always a liar.

How much of a liar?

I poured myself whisky, added very little water, and took a swig.

Dean put his head down the hatch. 'Going uptown,' he said.

I nodded at him, my face still with anger. 'Careful,' I said, automatically. There was no need to be careful, at a festival of international brotherhood, in a safe town like Helsinki.

The cabin door opened. Pete came in. There was sawdust in his beard. 'Parched,' he said. 'Those kids have gone uptown, drinking. I'm going after them, just in case.'

He was looking vaguely anxious. The Chatham business had left its mark on him. I said, 'I'll come with you.'

There was still light in the slots above the tall buildings crowding in on the street.

'The Chauffeur Svenson,' said Pete. 'That was the bar.'

We walked under the neon sign. The kids were in the corner. I waved, pretended to look surprised. Dean had tied a big band of coachwhipping round one of the girls' wrists. They were talking. Dean was talking. He was staying with the gang, nowadays. Ever since I had picked him up in Allerton cemetery, Dean had not spent a minute by himself. He was frightened. *Vixen* had kept him safe, the way *Vixen* had kept me safe.

There was another man, down at the far end of the bar. When I looked at him, he looked quickly away at the mirror behind the bottles.

I said to Pete, 'Wait here.'

I walked along the bar. The man was still looking at himself in the mirror. He had a dark, sharp profile. His hair was cut into black bristles. I said, in a light, relaxed voice, 'Haven't seen you for a while.'

He looked round. His cheekbones had a flattened look, as if at some time in his life he had been a boxer. He had a crooked nose above an eyebrow moustache. His eyes were narrow and aggressive. 'Can I help you?' he said.

'No,' I said. 'Sorry. Thought you were someone else.'

He smiled, a quick meaningless stretch of the mouth. Then he slapped money on the bar and walked out and into the road.

Pete said, 'Friendly sort of bloke.'

I finished my beer. 'Let's get going,' I said. 'Early start.' How to catch Dean when he would not lie. Early, I thought. No one can lie in his sleep.

We chased the crew back to the harbour. It was a warm night. They sang 'Mull of Kintyre'.

I had seen the man in the bar before, in the gate lodge of Varley Fitzgerald's toytown castle in Hampshire.

230

We kept an anchor watch that night. It was not technically my watch. But I lay awake and worried, all the same. At four o'clock in the morning, I got up and went on deck. The moon had set. The sea slapped against the sides. A grubby dawn was reddening the sky. It reminded me of the night Marie had died.

The parcel, she had said. Smaller than a packet of cigarettes. An odd way of describing a film.

Dean, you lying bastard.

I yanked open the hatch, went below. The boys' cabin smelt of socks, and the frowsy breath of sleepers. Dean slept top bunk, starboard side. I grabbed his shoulder, shook him violently.

'What?' he said.

'On deck.'

He stumbled up, reflexes trained by weeks at sea. He was wearing jeans and a T-shirt.

I said, 'What did you hide in the flour?'

'Film,' he said.

'How many films?'

'What?' His face was pale, his hair sticking out like a scarecrow's.

'One film?'

'I told you.'

I took him by the throat, slammed him back into a shroud. His breath smelt bad, night-stale. 'The truth,' I said. 'Or you're over the side. And they'll kill you.'

'*Christ*,' said Dean. He was awake, now.

'Five seconds,' I said. 'Four –'

'Two,' said Dean. 'There was two.'

I let go of his neck. I said, 'Why didn't you tell me?'

'Dunno,' said Dean.

Lying and breathing, I thought. One as natural as the other. You got Marie killed. You tried to make it better by going to the funeral. Then you went to Southampton to your friend Dmitri's party, to make someone a proposition, even though you didn't have the film. You wanted me there to look after you, hold your hand. So you told half the truth. If you get half rumbled, keep your mouth shut and hope the other half will go away.

231

'The geezer with the camera had one in 'is pocket,' said Dean. 'Lennart swiped it.'

It did not matter how it had happened. There had been a second film. Nadia had got them both. She had given me the first one to keep me off her back. She had taken the other one to Estonia. You could bet that she knew who Mr Johnson was. Tough luck, Mr Johnson.

I went below, and drank coffee till my ears rang. She had told me the reason she had wanted the film was to dispose of it, so it could not turn up to cause pain to Mrs Rebane. I had not believed her.

I still did not believe her.

Next morning, we left harbour in a Parade of Sail. Merchant ships in the roads blew their sirens. The shores crawled with thousands of people. Square-rigged ships like *Wilma* sent their crews aloft. As each ship reached the channel end buoy, clouds of canvas blossomed at their yards. They heeled to the westerly ruffling the Baltic, and began to surge into the blue southward, for the invisible shores of Estonia.

It must have been quite a spectacle, but I was not interested in spectacles. The only thing in my mind was Tallinn.

The Parade of Sail ended between two gunboats five miles offshore. The gunboats marked the start of the race to Tallinn. Coastguards kept away a spectator fleet that seemed to contain half the population of Finland.

The Youth Venture contingent were moving together, in line ahead: Dickie first, aboard the three-masted schooner *Xerxes*, then *Wilma*, square topsails set, Otto Campbell at the wheel, with his peaked cap pulled down almost to his long red chin, and Neville Glazebrook tucked away somewhere in the waist.

Pete said, 'What is this, a bloody procession?'

It was not supposed to be a procession any more. At the gunboats, it was to turn into a race. We were having to spill wind to keep our position in the line.

I said, 'Shall we do it to them?'

Pete nodded.

I said, nice and quiet, 'Yankee.'

The crew were getting fed up with pottering along being

admired. The yankee came out of the sail-locker as if it weighed two pounds instead of two hundredweight. It shot up the outer forestay, and three of the boys lay horizontal in the lee scuppers with the effort of sheeting it in. We got the jib up too.

A gun thumped on the right-hand minesweeper. 'Ten minutes,' said Dean.

I grunted at him. I didn't want to talk to him.

The wind was blowing straight at us from the other side of the starting line. *Vixen* heeled steeply as I put her on port tack, heading for a patch of water that had opened up behind the line. She had become light as a feather under the hands, like a thoroughbred horse. She settled in and rode for the gap, flying through the jade-green water, the four wings of her wake white as the wings of the cherubim.

Down to port, a couple of big barques had hove-to. There were other yachts coming into the starting area now. *Wilma* and *Xerxes* were up at the right-hand end of the line. *Wilma*'s square topsails were aback, and *Xerxes* was head-to-wind, hovering. They would wait. Otto knew that *Wilma* was fat, and stolid, and hard to manoeuvre. With Neville Glazebrook on board, he would be taking extra care. As for *Xerxes*, it was in Dickie's nature to take what he conceived to be the high ground, and hold on to it. Today, the high ground was the right-hand end of the line. They were unassailable. All they had to do on the gun was sheet in, and they would be on the starboard tack, with a licence to sail across the noses of the fleet.

'Not very close-winded, are they?' I said to Pete.

His eyes were narrow over his beard. 'You wouldn't,' he said.

I said, 'They've mucked us about. We'll muck them about.' He laughed.

'Watch it,' I said. A Swedish ketch was showing fight, rattling across us on the starboard tack. I swung the wheel. *Vixen*'s wake hissed as we ducked under, and her boom crashed as we went about. We were on the ketch's tail now. He was slower than us. I depowered the mainsail. He tacked, to get rid of us. We tacked, to follow. Canvas roared like a cageful of lions. The crew were sweating on the sheets and runners. We stayed on his tail like a fighter plane, following him out, away to the right of the course, beyond the gunboat.

'Five minutes,' said Pete.

Wilma and *Xerxes* were still head to wind, the best part of half a mile away. We were out on our own with the ketch.

'Ready about,' I said, and shifted the wheel slow and easy, so *Vixen* carved the turn like a skier, not losing any way. I kept her turning until the wind was just forward of the beam, and she was screaming along, the end of her boom dragging a V of wake out of the sea to leeward.

We came directly astern of the right-hand gunboat. 'Hardening up,' I said.

Pete yelled, 'In, in, *in*!' The sheets hardened as if there was one person trimming, not eight. *Vixen* came on to the wind. Her bowsprit was aiming like a rifle, bang at the stern of the gunboat. *Wilma* and *Xerxes* were up to starboard.

'Two minutes,' said Pete.

Vixen's lee rail was underwater. Her stanchions were tearing plumes of spray from the rushing green, and the sound of her wake was a long roar. I had the feeling that I could take my hands off, and she would do it all by herself . . .

'There they go,' said Pete.

Wilma's topsails had filled. *Xerxes* had backed a staysail, and her main was swelling.

'Too bloody late,' I said.

I had sailed on *Wilma* and *Xerxes*. They were big, fat things. To windward, they stopped dead an easy five degrees further off the wind than *Vixen*, and they were slow to pick up speed.

It was one thing holding the high ground, but while you were up there you had to watch your back. Which they had failed to do.

Vixen's log was up to eight knots. *Wilma* was in front, alarmingly big and alarmingly solid. People were looking at us off her deck. I could see mouths open.

Go on, I thought.

A puff came through. *Vixen* dipped, accelerated like a boat a quarter her weight. *Wilma*'s bowsprit crossed my line of vision. Her bow, too. Collision course.

'Our right of way,' said Pete. 'He's below his proper course.'

I got ready to bear away. If he forced us to bear away, we could protest. I did not want to protest. I wanted to show the other officers of Youth Venture with their crews of hooligans what *Vixen* could do with her crew of hooligans.

We were fifty yards away, now. *Wilma*'s bowsprit hung across our track like a frontier barrier.

'He's got *Xerxes* the other side,' said Pete.

The bowsprit moved, foreshortening.

'He's giving way,' said Pete.

I eased the helm a little. There was shouting up to starboard. The spotty cadet at the end of *Wilma*'s bowsprit watched slack-jawed as *Vixen*'s weather shrouds whipped past five feet from his nose. I kept my eyes straight ahead.

The start gun thudded. *Vixen* romped under the gunboat's side, and into open water.

Canvas was roaring astern. I looked round.

'Bloody hell,' said Pete.

It looked like a war. *Wilma* had gone back head to wind. *Xerxes* had been astern of her, and to windward. Once *Wilma* had cut her off, her options had been to collide with the start boat, or go about. She had gone about, and was struggling to get back up to the line, half her canvas flapping or aback. *Wilma*'s topsails were filling the wrong way. Down to the left of the course, the rest of the fleet was a mountain range of taut canvas.

'*Wilma*'s sailing backwards,' said Pete. The crew were cheering.

'Enough of that,' I said. And I eased her due south, for Tallinn.

Twenty miles off the coast, a pair of rust-flecked grey gunboats fell in alongside, and welcomed us on VHF to the Republic of Estonia. Two hours later we slid between the gloomy concrete pierheads of Tallinn, first by an easy mile.

A launch flying the hammer and sickle and driven by an unshaven man in a baggy uniform led us past the grey superstructures of a naval base. The buildings were grey, too, with tired-looking red lettering.

'Very picturesque,' said Pete.

Suddenly there was a quay ahead, lined with tall timber-framed buildings. Instead of the concrete, there were tall, elegant spires.

We tied up at a buoy. A Russian customs man came aboard, reeking of sweat, and left greasy fingermarks on the French polish. Pete gave him a packet of coffee. The customs man pocketed it without remark, spat on the deck, left a sheaf of forms, and went over the side. The rest of the fleet filtered in.

Otto had himself rowed over from *Wilma*. He was laughing. 'Wiped our eye proper,' he said.

'Strictly observing the rules.'

His eyes glittered with competitiveness. 'Revenge will be sweet,' he said. 'Glazebrook thought it was hilarious. I hope Dickie sees it like that. Coming ashore tonight?'

'Of course.' My throat was tight.

'The usual beer-up,' he said.

I nodded. I had more in mind than a beer-up.

Among the crowds on the quay there were several men in cheap suits. They were eyeing the boats, but they did not look like Tall Ships enthusiasts.

'Secret policeman's ball,' said Otto. 'I thought they'd given up all that kind of thing.' He laughed. I did not feel like laughing with him.

By five o'clock, *Vixen* was gleaming as if she had just come out of the yard, and three captains had come to take coffee in the saloon, as a tribute to us as the winner of the day's race. When they had gone, I called Pete below. He looked hot and bothered.

'Bloody Commies,' he said. 'Mary and Cath, they say that customs man's swiped two lipsticks and a pair of knickers.'

I said, 'Tell them we'll replace the stuff out of ship's funds.'

Pete's red beard fairly bristled with indignation. 'What about complaining to the bleeding Inspector of Customs?'

I said, 'I'd rather keep out of the way just now.'

'Why?'

'Have a cup of tea,' I said.

He knew me well, did Pete. He sat on the edge of the settee, and he looked at me sideways, and he said, 'What the hell are you up to?'

I told him. I told him what I wanted him to do.

He said, 'You're off your bloody block.'

I said, 'No.'

He said, 'You'll land up in bloody Siberia.'

I said, 'That's my problem.'

He pushed the mug of tea away from him. 'Put something in that,' he said.

I gave him two inches of whisky. He drank it. His dreadful teeth showed in his beard. 'Bloody madman,' he said. It was a compliment.

I handed him the ship's cashbox, in which I kept *Vixen*'s emergency funds. Then I went into my night cabin, pulled out the paper with the address in Nadia's handwriting and stuffed it into the breast pocket of my blazer. A private entrepreneur on the quay was selling plastic mackintoshes. I bought one, shoved it into my pocket. Then we marched off to the reception.

There was plenty of vodka. People warmed up fast. More skippers came up and congratulated me on the race. I grinned at them as best I could; my mind was on other things. Otto Campbell noticed. He asked me if I was feeling all right.

It was the chance I had been waiting for. 'Touch of flu,' I said. 'Excuse me.'

The lavatories were on the right of the stage. Beside the lavatory door was an emergency exit. I pulled the plastic raincoat out of its pocket, and put it on. Then I eased the door open. The door opened into an alley. It was empty. But I was taking no chances. I lurched up to the wall opposite, leaned my forehead against the concrete and pretended to relieve myself. Then I set off between the rows of tall, step-gabled buildings towards the quay.

I was hurrying now, the sweat popping in the mobile Turkish bath of the raincoat. Masts and yards gridded the sky at the end of the street. Nobody looked at me. My reflection in a window was stooped, raincoated, unshaven. It went well with the smell of cabbage and stale urine that rolled out of the alley.

I took the last turning on the right before the quay. There was a rusty bicycle leaning against the wall; *Vixen*'s ship's iron horse, left there by Dean on my instructions half an hour previously. I picked it up, climbed aboard, and pedalled away from the harbour, weaving through a group of Russian sailors. They were passing a bottle of vodka from hand to hand. None of them gave me a second glance.

I kept on riding. It was a damp, muggy evening. The air smelt of rain. There were other cyclists on the street. Cobbles battered at the front wheel, gave way to tarmac. The buildings became new, sullen concrete monuments. I stopped, looked at the map I had dug out of the *Great Soviet Encyclopaedia* in Helsinki.

The Paldiski Maante ran north-south, a mile back from the seafront. It was a huge, almost empty boulevard lined with grime-streaked apartment blocks. Between the blocks, narrow alleys formed crossways with the next boulevard back. There were no trees. It was as welcoming as a cement factory.

Number 1267 was precisely like all the others, a dirty tombstone rearing at the black evening clouds. The sweat on my face had mingled with road dust and turned to mud. My beard itched. My stomach was fluttering with nerves. Somewhere up there, behind those blank windows, the answers were waiting.

26

A boxy black car spluttered down the boulevard. Cyclists drifted wearily homeward from work. I stood my bicycle in a slot in the concrete, pushed open the steel door, and went into the lobby.

There were mailboxes, numbered one to forty. Some of them had spiders' webs over the slots. It smelt as if every one of the tenants was having boiled cabbage for supper. A ground-glass hatchway in the wall opposite the entrance shot open with a bang. The face of an old woman appeared. Her wrinkles looked as if they had been scientifically packed with grime. She said something in a voice like the bark of a terrier. I grinned at her. She barked again. I waved my piece of paper at her, said, 'Madame Rebane.'

A filthy claw appeared through the hatch, groping for the paper. Look out, I thought. If she gets that, there is documentary proof that you have been here. I snatched it away. She screamed like a harpy. I advanced to the hatch. Inside the room was a greasy sofa, a rack of keys and a smell bad enough to singe the eyebrows. No telephone.

I slammed the window in her face, found that the elevator was out of order, and started up the stairs.

The door of number 26 was a long way up. I hammered, waited. My heart was pounding, and not only from the stairs. Footsteps approached, and fingers rattled at the door handle. It opened a crack. It seemed dark in there. I could not see a

239

face. A young man's voice said something I did not understand.

I said, in English, 'I have come to see Madame Rebane.'

The door opened. The boy who opened it looked about sixteen, and fat. He was wearing a Motley Crue singlet, a studded belt, black jeans and engineer's boots. His hair was shaved, except on the crown, where he had a Taras Bulba topknot.

'Wrong house,' I said.

'No.' The accent was very thick. 'Come see my mama.' He beckoned me in. There were snake rings on his fingers.

The apartment was hot. The air felt wet, as if too many people did their sweating and breathing in it. I was in a living room, with a blue, white and black Estonian flag occupying the whole of one wall. On another wall was a sampler and a signed photograph of Ozzie Osbourne. There were other photographs, framed on the windowsill. But I did not have time to look at them, because the fat boy had said something, and a woman had come out of what must have been the kitchen, followed by a cloud of steam.

Her face was thin, the bones standing out so she looked beaky and predatory. What saved her from meanness were the eyes. They were huge, those eyes, set deep in brown-skinned sockets.

When she saw me, she stopped as if she had been frozen. Her hands went to her mouth. She said, '*Issand!*' and sat down suddenly on the floor. The eyes did not leave my face.

I bent down, and helped her up. She clung to my hand long after she should have let it go. Then with visible effort, she calmed herself, and said, 'Sit, please.'

Her son was watching me with sulky eyes. 'What you want?' he said.

The mother said something that had an angry sound. He shrugged, took my raincoat, hung it on the door.

Now I was here, I did not know where to start. I said, 'I came about the death of Lennart Rebane.'

She nodded, as if she had been expecting me to say it. She said, 'I am sorry. You reminded me of someone else.'

Her accent was good, but the words came out raggedly, as if she had once been fluent, but had lost the habit of stringing

240

together the phrases. She said something in Estonian to her son. He sucked air between his teeth, swaggered into the kitchen and began to bang pots and pans. 'Now,' she said, 'how did you find me?'

'I was given your address by Nadia Vuorinen.'

'Ah,' she said. Her voice held polite interest. I looked for wariness in her great brown eyes, saw none. 'Nadia.'

'A friend of yours,' I said.

'My son is dead,' she said. 'She went to England. You met her there. She spoke to me on the telephone.'

'That's right,' I said. 'I'm very sorry about the death of your son.' It sounded hopelessly inadequate.

She shrugged. 'He was on his way to visit you, when he was killed,' she said. She smiled. 'I am glad to meet you for his sake. And mine.'

I wanted to ask her what she meant. Later, Tyrrell, I thought. I said, 'Your son wrote to you about photographs.'

She stopped smiling. 'Yes,' she said. 'Nadia took the letter. She said that there were some pictures that might embarrass a man in England. She told me that she should hand them to the political police, but that she would not. We are friends, Nadia and I. Lennart said to me in his letter that these were shameful pictures. Nadia wished to spare me shame. We work together, Nadia and I, for the independence of our country. Perhaps these shameful pictures will be of value to the Russians. All my life I have fought the Russians. Lennart also.' She smiled, a sad smile, spread her hands. 'But of course the Russians took him, for their Navy. And now he is dead.'

There were a lot of questions to ask. I asked the journalist's questions first. 'So Nadia feels as you do?'

'Nadia is a democrat,' she said. 'Me, I have grown up in a free Estonia. I have watched the Nazis come. Then the Red Army, then the KGB. I went to the forest, joined the partisans. I am a nurse. With the partisans, I have pulled bullets from the body. I have shot Russians. It was in hot blood, fighting with the gun ... Nadia was young in a time when there were no bullets, only cold blood, the men at the door in the night. They took Nadia's father and her uncles to the camps. Nadia hates Russians also. We have fought the same war, but in different battles. Lennart was beginning to learn. But he is dead.' The tears pricked up on her lower lids, spilt into the tracery of wrinkles under her eyes. 'Excuse,' she said.

She ground the heels of her hands into the sockets of her eyes. Then she raised her head again. 'I cry for all lost children,' she said. 'For you also.'

'For me?' I did not want to ask. I asked anyway. 'What do you mean?'

'The father of Lennart,' she said. 'He was also the father of you.'

The pots clashed in the kitchen. Beyond the thin walls, the radios babbled. I was someone who had pedalled ashore from the boat that was my home, walked up the steps of a stinking concrete building, and met a complete stranger who was telling me that a man I had accidentally killed was my half-brother. I sat in a globe of private silence. Nothing was real. She said, 'This is why Lennart was coming to see you, on the night he was killed. He had seen you on television. He had asked people about you. He knew you were an honest man. He was in trouble. He wanted help.'

So, I thought. People knew Lennart was on the way. Who did you ask, Lennart? Who knew you wanted to see me, you and your photographs, besides Dean? Marie. Marie was dead. Did you tell anyone on *Wilma*, when you were there that night in Chatham?

Just at the moment, those were not the most important questions in my mind. The most important ones were the ones I did not dare even ask.

I tried. I said, 'You wrote to my mother.'

The question hung in the air between us. 'Yes,' she said at last.

'Why?'

She gripped the arms of her chair, as if to stop a gale blowing her away.

'From sympathy,' she said. 'Your father said she would not be interested. I could not believe this. So I wrote the letter. I thought that if she was interested, she would be . . . not reassured, but . . . well, I don't know what I thought.'

242

'You said he was ill.'

'Only because he missed you,' she said. 'But he would not admit it. He did not understand people, your father. Only the sea, and ships. I wrote the letter to make him more ... contented.' She shrugged. Her thin brown cheeks broke into a maze of wrinkles as she smiled. 'Who can tell if it worked?'

My mother had not been interested. By vanishing, my father had given her a quiet life, which was all she had wanted. Somewhere inside me, a ten-year-old child was raging: *You took my father away, and told lies so you could keep him.*

She did not notice. Her eyes were looking at things happening inside herself. 'We had Lennart. After, Lennart wondered always about his father. He wanted to visit you, he said, to find out more about him. But now Nadia tells me these things, I think also to get your advice about the photographs.'

'He would have known more than me,' I said. 'My father left when I was ten.'

She spread her hands. She said, 'Your father went from here when Lennart was two.'

I stared at her. 'Sixteen years ago?'

She counted on her fingers. 'Sixteen,' she said. Her eyes were hazy. 'The armies in the forest, the partisan armies, they stopped many years before. After the war, the spies and informers finished them. Some of us stayed in the forests, kept out of the way. It was a hard life. There was big talk about fighting, and how America could rescue our country.' There was a dull glow in her eyes, like the smoulder of a very old fire. 'But all the guns were buried and rusty, and nobody could remember how to use them. And there were very few of us. So I came out of the forest, to continue my life, and I met a man, and lived in Tallinn.

'After five years, we got news that the KGB were looking for him. So he went to the forest to hide, with some people from the old days who had never come back to the city. It was a false rumour; when you are afraid, there are many rumours, and most of them false. So I went to the forest to bring him back. The people there told me my husband was dead; he had fallen into a lake and drowned, poor man. They knew I had been a nurse. They took me to see a man who was in a barn, sick. His ship had come ashore in a gale.'

'My father,' I said.

'Of course.' She said it as if it was the most natural thing in the world. 'The people of the forest were worried. This was not a place where you can keep as a guest a foreigner. By now they were living a quiet life, and they wished no disturbance. I was worried, too. In those days, if your husband drowned, there were police who would arrest you, just in case you had something to do with it. Your father had a black beard. So did my dead husband. I brought him back to the apartment. Before he was well, we moved. None of my neighbours noticed anything. He was a kind man.' She dropped her eyes. 'Soon, he was my husband . . . not only in pretence.'

I was thinking of my mother in England, in mourning. I was thinking of Christopher and myself, sitting at school with great holes in our lives, not like the rest of the boys.

She shrugged. 'Then Lennart came along. Your father was registered as sick, which meant he did not work. We used to laugh together. But oftener and oftener he became quiet, as if he was thinking of other things. He loved the sea. This for me was a crazy idea. What man can love more than a woman or a child a thing that is grey, and cold, and will kill you?'

The hostility in me began to fade. This was not a woman who had lured my father away with her wiles. She was a victim, the way my mother and Christopher and I were victims.

'So,' she said. 'He did not want to live in the city. He went back to the forest, to some people I had met, by the sea. At first, I would see him sometimes. Then not at all. At first it made me sad. Then I met Jaan. He has a good job, as an engineer in the oil refinery. I had Vello with him.' She lifted her face. It was shiny with tears. 'But now Lennart is dead, and your father is I do not know where. And I have nobody to remind me of those good years. I wish you had not come.' Her hands came up. Her head went down.

China broke in the kitchen. The youth Vello came out, slammed the door. He started talking, loud and urgent. The mother's face whitened, as if someone had removed the blood with a syringe. She started to say something to me.

Behind me, there was a crash like an anvil falling on a wardrobe.

The front door jumped out of its hinges and slammed on to the floor.

27

There were four men. Against the fluorescent light on the landing, they looked the size of wrestlers. The two in front were carrying sledgehammers as if they were battleaxes. They were wearing the same cheap synthetic suits as the men on the quay. The suits were too tight. One of them had black chest hair that curled between the buttons of his shirt.

We stood for a split second looking at each other. Then the man with the hairy chest said something in a toneless policeman's voice. I did not understand the words. I did not have to. He was telling me I was under arrest.

Nadia, I thought. You have set me up.

Vello started shouting. They were big shouts, a pair of words repeated. The policeman with the chest hair moved towards him fast. Mrs Rebane flung herself between them. The policeman pushed her aside like an empty cardboard box, reversed his hammer, and slammed the butt end into Vello's big stomach. The air went out of him with a sound like a balloon emptying. The policeman turned the hammer round, lifted it. I thought, *He's going to break his leg*.

The thought woke me up. I kicked the policeman as hard as I could above the right knee. He grunted, turned on me. His face was high-blood-pressure pink, his uncomfortably shaven neck bulging over his white nylon collar. He stank of sweat and violence.

I kicked hard at his groin. He twisted away, caught it on his hip. My foot hit muscle like hard rubber. I felt sick. *Assaulting a police officer. Ten years.*

He tried with the hammer handle. I moved sideways. The handle grazed my ribs. The pain made me feel sicker.

There was shouting on the landing. The policeman's eyes flickered. I hit him on the cheekbone, hard. His eyes came back, black and piggy, hot with anger. The hammer came round, head first this time. I was in the corner of the room. There was nowhere to go. It hit the muscle of my upper arm, slammed me into the wall with a bang that knocked the breath out of me. There were other men in the room, fighting. Two people rolled in at the front door: a boy in jeans and a man in a suit, hitting each other. Women were screaming. Sirens were wailing outside.

The man with the hammer was not listening. The handle hummed in the air. Something exploded alongside my head. My knees buckled. I wanted to shout, but no words came. My cheek whacked the tiled floor. Rough hands jammed my arms in front of me. Metal closed on my wrists, too tight. I found my voice, shouted. A boot slammed into my right kidney. I shut up, concentrated on feeling I was going to die.

The policeman was screaming at me, face brick-red. No interpreter needed; same as before. *You're under arrest.* He was leaning over me. I curled myself into a ball, trying to protect my kidneys with my elbows, the handcuffs tearing at my wrists.

Something happened to his face. It went slack. The mouth opened. He fell forwards like a sack of coal, landed across my legs. A young man was standing behind him. He was wearing a leather jacket, no shirt, and grotesquely tight jeans. He was grinning. The grin showed that he had no front teeth. In his hand was a long chunk of four-by-two. 'Bastard Russkie cops,' he said, and something else in Estonian. He jerked his head at the door.

I was getting fluent. I dragged my legs from under the policeman, pulled my raincoat out of the wreckage of the front door, and limped, head buzzing, for the stairs.

There was shouting all the way up the stairwell. People were fighting. They paid no attention to me. I jogged down the stairs, awkward because of the handcuffs. The sirens were loud now, and there were a lot of them, the troughs and crests of their wailing cancelling each other out in a continuous scream. There was blood on the grey cement walls. My head was ringing from the hammer-handle.

As I went down, a new noise began in the street: a roaring, dull and ugly, like a heavy sea in rocks. I knew that sound well. It was the sound of the hell-holes, an angry rumour that floated through the double-glazing and the air conditioning, into the offices and bunkers where the big shots smiled their false smiles and fed you the official line.

Except that this time there was no story to write, and if there had been, I could not have written it anyway, because of the handcuffs on my wrists. Instead of the press credentials from the Ministry of the Interior, I had a British passport with a wanted man's name on it. Instead of the waiting driver and the open return air ticket, I had a rusty bicycle.

The tear gas in the lobby caught my throat and eyes. The place was full of policemen. I draped the raincoat over the handcuffs, and walked slowly, eyes streaming, a citizen trying to get a little peace while the hooligans rioted. Something wet was trickling down my cheek where the hammer handle had hit me. I hoped they would think it was a stray stone.

The police had long clubs and tight white crash helmets that made them look like vintage motorcycle enthusiasts. They had no gas masks. As in every riot squad I had ever seen, most of the faces were young and pale and savage with fright.

One of them took a half-hearted swipe at me with his truncheon as he ran for the foot of the stairs. There was a grey-painted steel door at the back of the lobby. I shouldered it open, stumbled into a fluorescent-lit corridor. There were doors in the side walls, boiler-rooms by the sound of them, and another at the far end. I ran for it. The fear was on me now. I was making plans. How the hell, I thought, do you ride a bike while you are wearing handcuffs? My hip hit the crash-bar on the door.

It swung open more easily than I had expected. I fell head-first down a couple of steps and landed heavily on my bad arm in a pile of rubbish.

There was a slit of lead-grey sky trapped between the concrete edges of two apartment buildings. It was raining, a light drizzle that cooled the tear gas. I lay in someone's potato peelings, and tried to work out where I was. In an alley, I thought. At the side of the building. The alley would run down to the next boulevard. What I had to do was to get down there, get back to *Vixen.*

But I could not walk back. The policeman with the hammer would come round or he would not come round, and the radios would be chattering for my blood. Tallinn was a bad city for a battered foreigner four miles from his ship, wearing Estonian handcuffs.

It would be better on the bike.

I turned my head towards the front of the building. There was light, a pale glare of floodlights in the rain. I put my hands down in a pile of rotten cabbage leaves and levered myself to my feet.

The bicycle park had been on the near side of the building, in the mouth of the alley. The police would be fixing their attention on the things happening in the boulevard.

I wiped my bloody face on my shirt sleeve, improved the drape of the raincoat over the handcuffs, and strolled towards the grey-white nimbus of the floodlights with loose bowels and a thumping heart.

When I had arrived an hour ago, the boulevard had been a concrete desert, empty under the gritty wind. Now, a crowd of people seethed in front of number 1267. Somebody was talking quickly through a loudhailer. There were stones rattling on the ground. I heard the smash of a breaking bottle.

I grasped the handlebars in the middle, near the upright, and rolled the bike out of its slot. Walk slowly, I told myself. The raincoat wrapped itself round the front forks. I shoved hard, to clear it. It tangled in the spokes. In pulling it free I let go of the handlebars. The bike fell over with a crash. I pulled again. Something tore. The coat came free. I threw it away into the shadows. I was sweating now. How to draw attention to yourself, I thought. A couple of dark-uniformed figures had turned to look at me. They were twenty yards away. The floodlights gleamed in their jackboots.

I got a leg over the bicycle. A sudden point of bright light shone by the policemen. A flashlight. It shone in my eyes, moved down the bicycle. It winked in the metal of the handcuffs. I got a foot on to the top pedal. As I trod on it, the shouting started.

The bicycle was old, high-geared. It is hard to steer with your hands chained together. In the mouth of the alley I wobbled, fighting for control. The shouting had stopped. The skin of my back crawled, waiting for bullets.

There were no bullets. But there was the crash of hobnails on concrete, close behind. The pedals began to turn. I achieved steerage way. The boots kept their distance. I passed the end of the building, got up speed. Three hundred yards away was the end of the alley, the next boulevard. My heart was hammering like a road drill. But I was going now, riding faster than men in big boots could run. Get to the end, turn left. Four miles to ride; then the quay, and *Vixen*'s workshop, and the toolkit for the handcuffs.

A car had turned down the far end of the alley. The white glare of its headlights filled my head. I could hear the sob of my breathing, the swish of the bicycle tyres on the wet concrete, the crash of hobnails behind. And the scream of an engine, accelerating hard in low gear. Then there was another light. A blue light, on top of the car coming towards me. It was a police car. I found my teeth were clamped together. The boots behind me had stopped. I rode on.

Rain spattered my face. There was a high wall to the right, buildings to my left. I pedalled hard, gripping the handlebars with my cuffed hands until my wrists ached. There were no turnings. When I glanced round, the two policemen were standing silhouetted against the floodlights on the boulevard. On the right-hand side of the alley there was a walkway, a pavement.

That would have to do. The car was so close I could see the corrugations in the glass of its headlights. I pulled the handlebars up and sideways. The front wheel hit the kerb with a solid *bang*. I felt my hands twisting. I opened my mouth to swear. The wheel turned sideways. Somewhere, tyres were screaming. I was flying through the air. Quiet air, except for the roar of the crowd, and the howl of sirens, and the scream of tyres. You stupid bastard, I thought. All because of you.

Then I hit the ground, and stopped thinking at all.

My shoulder went in first, then my ear, then the rest of me in no particular order. If I had been a parachutist, I would have known how to roll. But I was an ex-journalist. I slammed down like a dropped omelette, slithered along the ground, and hit the wall with a thump.

The pain was horrible. Then there was worse than pain.

A car door opened. I heard feet, squelching on wet concrete. Something pulled at my collar. I opened my eyes. I could not see. Blind, I thought. Bloody hell, you're blind. Panic rose in me, caught at my throat. Rotting in jail, not able to see.

Another tug at my collar, harder this time. Something was running out of my hair. My tongue tasted salt and iron. Blood. Running into my eyes. Not blind. Another tug.

I got up on to hands and knees. My palms stung, skinned. I pushed with my legs, came upright, the way a two-year-old child comes upright, straight-legged, most undignified. All the bits were working, except my eyes.

A car door opened. Something pushed me in the chest. The door-sill caught me in the calves. I fell in backwards, hit a seat, bounced. Another shove at my chest forced me down in the gap behind the front seats, between two sets of cushions. I was on the floor, grit in my mouth. I thought of the rolling clouds of tear gas, the hard grey floodlights, the policemen in their jackboots and their stupid white helmets, the black, boxy vans waiting to take you to concrete sties where you would never be heard from again.

Suddenly I was shaking with raw terror.

28

The driver trod on the accelerator. I screwed my head round, so I could see the reflection of the floodlights on the roof. I expected the car to go towards the lights. It did not. It went backwards. It went backwards very fast indeed. I could see the headlights sweeping the grey concrete faces of the buildings, hear the shriek of the transmission. Then the driver stamped on the brakes. The car screamed on to the boulevard, wheels locked, gears clashing as the driver rammed the stick across the gate. The lights went off. The tyres began to howl on the concrete.

I struggled up, got my head above seat level. I could see the driver's head and shoulders, a peaked cap pointing rigidly ahead. We were on a wide, empty boulevard, lined with apartment buildings.

'Get down,' said the driver.

My heart rolled over in my chest. I lay down on the floor of the car.

'You are bloody stupid,' said the driver. 'One day, you will get killed.'

The voice was speaking English. It was a woman's voice.

The voice of Nadia Vuorinen.

'And me too,' she said. 'Stay down there.'

I lay with my head on my hands. Not a trap, I thought. Not a trap. For perhaps a minute, that was the only thought I had room for. Then it began to sink in. When someone finds out,

252

she will be in real trouble. Big trouble. I said, 'How did your friends know I was here?'

'Not my friends,' she said. A radio chattered. She paused, listening. Then she said, 'You must understand that we have a war here. It is a quiet war, a little war, inside the police. Some of us think as I do, that Estonia is a republic on our own, and we must enforce the laws of our country. But there are others, maybe Russians, maybe left over from the *nomenklatura*, who want the old ways, where the police invent the laws.'

'The secret police?'

'Not so complicated,' she said. 'We are making a new state. As a police person, I serve the people. These others serve not the people nor the state; only themselves. *Jeesus*.' The car slowed. 'Stay down. Another police car.'

She drove on steadily, blipped her horn, waved. 'OK,' she said. 'Nothing on the radio yet. I drive.'

She drove. She drove very fast, the way she had driven that night in Southampton, except that tonight there were no cars on the road. After ten minutes, she said, 'Sit up now. We leave the bracelets on, in case.'

I struggled upright. The boulevard had gone. There were trees on either side: fir trees, black in the silver sweep of the headlights. Every now and then there was a clearing, with the grey whaleback of a rock outcrop.

For the first time, she turned her head. Under the cap's peak, her profile was the profile of a Greek sculpture. She smiled at me. It was a tight, perfunctory smile. She was worried.

I said again, 'How did your friends find me?'

She said, 'Do you think we are children, that a man in whom the police are interested can ride from the harbour on a bicycle, and not be followed?'

There was anger in her voice, hurt pride. I said, 'I see.' Her pride was not the only one that was hurt. 'What the hell happened?'

She said, 'You were lucky. That crazy kid, Vello. He is a member of an anti-social group. An anti-Russian group, yes. But anti everything else. They don't make time to think. They don't believe in thinking. So they make big activity, like a chicken with its head cut off. A lot of the kids in the big blocks are the same. They say, we are revolutionaries, so on, so forth. But in fact, they are only anarchists. Some of them are gangsters, making extortion. Some of them like to fight policemen. They attack the KGB, who had gone to arrest you. And the KGB had brought the civil police, in support. The civil police do not like the KGB. So now there are friends of mine getting hurt, because you started a riot.'

She was a different Nadia from the Nadia I had met in England; more matter-of-fact and professional, at home in her own country. I said, 'I'm sorry if I have caused you any inconvenience.'

She laughed. She laughed longer than the circumstances warranted, with an irony I did not completely understand. The radio crackled and started to gibber. I heard my own name, mangled in the middle of a torrent of Estonian. She stopped laughing. 'So,' she said. 'They know they have lost you.'

'And what about you?'

She turned, and smiled. I could see by the rounding of her cheeks that it was a real smile. 'They have lost me too,' she said. 'Here.' She passed the key to the handcuffs over her shoulder.

I unlocked them in silence. I felt stupid, and ashamed that I had suspected her of luring me into a trap. As it was, she had saved me from the consequences of my own idiocy. And it looked as if in the process, she had made herself an outlaw in her own country. I said, 'I am very grateful to you.'

I saw her shoulders move as she shrugged. She said, 'And I to you.'

Beyond the window, the forest was dark as a black velvet curtain. There were no more outcrops of rock. Now, the clearings were filled with rain-pocked sheets of black water that gleamed evilly in the headlights. I said, 'Where are we going?'

'We go to look for a ghost,' said Nadia. And she would say no more. I had been looking for ghosts myself today. I did not dare ask what she meant, in case she told me what I expected to hear.

During the next half-hour, the country became flat as a billiard table. The trees thinned into clumps separated by meres and reedbeds, and the smell that came in through the car window was flat and sulphurous, with overtones of rotting vegetation: peat bog. We turned off the main road on to a track surfaced with gravel, and off the gravel road on to something that might have been a cart track. The bad steel of the Lada's springs twanged in the potholes. 'Where are we?' I said.

'Nowhere,' she said. 'North of Haapsalu.'

I had seen Haapsalu on the map. It was perhaps eighty miles west of Tallinn, on the northwest corner of Estonia.

'Why?'

'There are no houses any more,' she said. 'No dachas for bloody Russians. Too many mosquitoes.'

Two objects loomed, one either side of the track. They were tall and cylindrical, mottled with something that might once have been white paint. Gateposts. Ahead, the ground rose gently. There were trees again; different trees. A couple of oaks loomed out of the rain, a stand of pines that were not the black, stunted pines of the bog. There was a new atmosphere. If I had been a dog, my hackles would have been bristling. At some time or other, this place been a garden. Bigger than a garden. A park. The presence of the dead hung over it, thick and heavy.

The road turned a corner. The trees shrank suddenly, became a low-lying hump of ivy and creepers. It could have been a hill. But it was too square to be a hill.

The road came to an end in a small, weed-grown clearing. Nadia cut the engine. The windscreen wipers whined. Inside the mat of ivy there were straight edges. Windows, and a pediment.

'The White House,' said Nadia. She opened the door. A gust of warm, wet night air blew into the car. 'We get out.'

I got out. She cut the headlights. It was very dark. She had two flashlights, one for each of us, heavy police issue. The beams flicked over lumps of fallen masonry, mats of bramble.

'No mosquitoes,' she said. 'It is the wind from the sea. They do not come. Also, now there is no blood for them here.'

We stood a moment. The rain swished down. Then she said, 'Come.'

A path, little more than a badger track, led through the ferns and into a grove of pines. I followed her down it. The smell had changed. The flat stink of the bog had gone. In its place was wind and pines, with open salt water.

As we entered the pine grove, I felt a gust of wind on my cheek, and the trees hissed overhead. I thought again of ghosts. Whose?

There were steps here. They went down ten feet. Now there was cut stone underfoot, a flurry of wind-blown rain in the face. The flashlight beam swept over water; water with waves that slapped and boomed against the masonry on which we were standing.

We were standing on a quay. There was a shed by the quay, a long, low shed, sunk into the ground. A boathouse. There was a door, with a finger-hole. I pushed my finger through, pushed up the latch. Nadia followed me.

There was a slot of water. In the slot of water was a boat: a rotten-looking thing, more bare wood than paint, about twenty feet long, with a stub of mast and a furled tan sail. There was six inches of water in the bottom. The stones of the quay looked polished by frequent use.

'Who uses it?' I said.

'The people of the forest.'

I remembered what Mrs Rebane had said, all that time ago; three hours ago; talking about my father. *He, too, had known the people of the forest.* Hope, bloody stupid hope, began to bubble. Nadia walked off the quay, along a little beach. She had turned the flashlight off, now. The rain had lightened. The clouds were moving faster.

I said, 'What was this place?'

She said, 'A house of the bourgeoisie. A summer house.'

'Why are we here?'

'We must be somewhere,' she said. 'It is a good place to hide.' There was something she was leaving unsaid. 'Also, we must keep you somewhere until it is possible to take you to Finland.' We had stopped walking. Something was crashing in the trees inland. 'An elk,' she said. 'There are many elks. Nobody knows this place.'

256

I said, 'You must come to Finland too.'

'Yes.' I could smell her Chanel. She must have put it on recently. 'I think that now I must.'

In the darkness, her hand went out, touched the stone of the boathouse wall. 'Once this was the home of my family. It will hurt to leave it.'

A glimmer of moon filtered through a crack in the clouds. I saw that the beach ran across the inshore end of an inlet, perhaps seventy yards across. At the far side of the inlet was a dark mass of trees.

'Come,' she said.

There was something waiting in those trees.

I walked slowly, putting one foot in front of the other with an effort of will, walking towards something I did not want to know about. The old story, I thought: damn foolish curiosity beats fear, with Tyrrell.

We arrived at the far end of the beach. The wind's sigh in the branches had become a hissing.

Nadia switched on her flashlight.

One of the trees grew right by the water's edge. It was tall and straight, grey, with no leaves or branches. It was not a tree. It was the mast of a schooner. Or what had once been a schooner.

It had sunk long ago; except that there had been nowhere for it to sink to. So it sat on the sand, with the waves sluicing in and out of the hull between its sprung planks, as if resting after its long work.

The disc of light from the flashlight settled on what had once been the rail, by the hawse hole. On the grey planking was screwed a wooden nameboard. It was weathered and grey as the planks. But its border still bore carved ropework, terminating in a Turk's head. And the shadows thrown by the flashlight beam picked out the grooves of what must once have been gilt letters. *Åland*, they said.

I stood and looked at it. I should have felt something. I did not. It was a slab of wood, carved. That was all.

'My father's ship,' I said.

'Yes.'

'You knew?'

She did not answer. She walked on, up a path into the wood. I followed her, reluctantly. The ship might have been my father's, but it was just a ship. Whatever it was that I did not want to see was waiting in the trees.

At the top of the hill there was a clearing. There was moss underfoot. At one end was something big and round. It might have been a rhododendron bush, except that on its top, silhouetted against the pale grey cloud, was a cross.

The hope turned heavy as lead. Nadia's flashlight beam moved over the moss, settled on a plank of wood jammed upright in the ground. There was writing on the plank. *Joshua*, said the writing. *R.I.P.*

My eyes burned with tears; not for me, but for him. His boat, which he had loved more than his wife, or his mistress, or his children, rotting in the harbour. I touched the plank. It was slimy, softening. Soon it too would be rotting. The end result of his grand gesture was loneliness. He was out of it now. But not my mother, and Christopher, and Mrs Rebane, and me. *A man's gotta do what a man's gotta do.*

Rubbish.

I stepped back from the grave marker.

It blew apart.

One moment I was standing there, gazing at the rotting plank that marked the finish of my hopes. The next I was flat on my back in the soaking moss, face pounding with the ache of a deep cut. And the woods to the side of the churchyard were spewing noise, tree-shadows dancing to a bright little blue-and-orange flame.

The flame stopped, and with it the noise. Darkness flooded back. There was only the hiss of the wind in the trees and the jumpy hammer of my heart. I was back in Beirut now, the Gaza Strip, Khartoum. *Machine guns. Bloody horrible machine guns.*

I put my hands under my shoulders, pushed myself backwards. The machine gunner would be dazzled. Nadia was by my side, pushing herself back too.

Then there was light.

It was brilliant white. It flung a corpse-coloured glare over the churchyard, laying the shadows of the headstones black as ink across the rain-silvered moss. A mobile searchlight. *And so we die.*

Not yet, though. We were in the lee of a ridge of moss, a low parapet against those lumps of lead that any minute would come whacking out of the night and tear us to pieces.

In the lee of my father's grave.

Something glinted to my right. I swivelled my eyes. Nadia had a pistol. She was holding it in her right hand, resting it in the crook of her left elbow. I could see the corrugations of her frown as she squinted along the barrel.

The night thundered three times as she fired. The light went out. 'Run,' she said.

I was already running. The machine gunner opened up again. He was firing blind. The bullets went high. My foot hit something hard. The flashlight flew out of my hand. I tumbled into the trees like a shot rabbit, twigs and pine needles pattering down. We scrambled through the wood, heading downhill, for the mutter of the sea. Next time the machine gun opened up, the sound of the shots was flat, muffled by the trees. *Why?* I thought. *Why are they shooting at me?*

'Car,' said Nadia.

'Who is it?' I said.

'Don't worry who,' she said. 'Run.'

We came out on to the beach. Over towards the house there was a light in the sky. An orange light, flickering. The light of something on fire. I had been in enough riots to know what burned like that. 'They've set fire to it,' I said.

Whump, said the petrol tank. The woods turned coal-black against the eruption of flame writhing up the sky, torn away by the wind. The beach was pale under our feet. It felt horribly naked and open. A gust tore the tops off the waves, splattered them at our shoes. Wet feet, I thought, running after Nadia. We will get wet feet in the peat bogs. I could feel those bogs inland, waiting, hot and stifling, humming with mosquitoes. If we got past whoever had burned the car, there were only the bogs. In the bogs, we would sink . . .

We were on the quay. Nadia started to turn left, for the steps, up to the house, inland, away from the blind alley of the quay. I grabbed her arm. She was trembling, the rapid, adrenal tremble of a terrified animal. 'Boathouse,' I said. Nadia found the pale oblong of the door in the stone wall, slid through. I followed her, jammed the latch with a stick. Nadia's flashlight batteries were fading. In its orange glow, the boat tied up in the slot of black water looked as old as Pharaoh's barge.

'Get in,' I said.

She looked at the boat. The reflections from the water made gossamer of her hair. She hesitated. 'In,' I said.

She went down the steps. I ran to the seaward end of the boathouse. The big double doors were bolted shut. The bolt was frozen with rust. I whacked it free with a stone, shoved the right-hand door. Wind roared in. It caught the door, tore it out of my hand, flapped it out and slammed it back against the outside wall with a crash like a bomb bursting. My flesh crawled, expecting the sleet of bullets. None came. I scuttled back, bent double, to the bollards that held the boat's mooring lines. There was an ancient bucket hanging on a nail. I grabbed it, tossed it down.

The old knots were tight, the rope flattened. God knew when they had last been untied. God knew when anyone had last used the boat. I hacked them free with my knife, bounced once on the steps, landed in the boat.

The water in the bottom came halfway up my shins. I said, 'Bail.'

'Sorry?'

'Get the water out of the boat.'

'With what?'

I pushed the bucket at her, shone the flashlight over the boat. There were oars. The halyards were old, but not entirely rotten. The sail was cotton, with the velvety softness of extreme age. There was a rudder. I jammed the rudder on to its pintles, pulled out an oar. The boathouse was full of purposeless lumps of air, tumbling and spinning, raising little wind-arrows on the smooth black water. I pulled up a rag of mainsail, three reefs. Then I took out an oar, shoved it into the notch on the back end, and sculled for the dark mouth of the night.

29

As the stern passed under the lintel, the sail filled and the boat heeled. I took the tiller, feeling it stiffen as we gathered way. Nadia had stopped bailing. The water in the bilge was down to a puddle. I said, 'Hold tight.'

The rock walls of the boathouse channel fell away on either side. I eased the tiller towards me. The sea was a dirty grey. On the far shore of the inlet, the trees were black and menacing. We were out of the shelter now. A clod of wind roared across the water and walloped into the lugsail like a fist. The boat lurched over to leeward. Water tipped over the downhill edge, and it shot forward. Too much sail, I thought. Three reefs were still too much.

Another gust crashed in. I let go the sheet. The rattle of the canvas sounded deafening. But the wake had a roar of its own, now. On the far shore of the inlet, the tall, straight mast of the *Aland* was falling behind. We were moving.

Another gust. The boat heeled violently. This time, we shipped a lot of water. But I said, 'Don't bail.' Weight on the downhill side of the boat could put us all the way over.

She said, 'Where are we going?' There was fear in her voice. I knew how she felt.

I said, 'What happens outside this inlet?'

'The sea,' she said.

'Which way does the coast go?'

'North,' she said. 'Then east.'

To starboard, the north shore of the inlet was falling away. We were still close in under the south shore; there were rocks and trees to keep the waves small and the wind light.

Ahead, there was only darkness. If there were rocks, they were invisible. That was good. If whoever was doing the shooting could see as much as we could, we were safe. Down by the shore, a whitish glare slid in the trees. The searchlight; they were looking inland.

I squinted over the bow, into the grey-black blur of the night. The wind was southerly, a heavy wind, near enough a gale as made very little difference. Right direction, wrong quantity.

Something black loomed in the grey ahead. The waves roared. I yanked the tiller towards me. The waves were suddenly short and steep, and the sweat was hot on my body, and I was yelling. The hull went up on a wave, came down again. In the bottom of the trough there was a big, terrifying *bang*. We sheered off. The waves became more regular.

I am a connoisseur of bangs. There is the bang that means you have hurt the paint. And there is the bang with an overtone of splinters to it, which means you have broken something important.

This bang had been the second kind.

Nadia said in an odd, flat voice, 'There is water coming in the boat.'

I said, casual as I could, 'I suppose we'd better bail, then.' I put the boat head to wind, went on my hands and knees in the bilges.

It did not take long to locate the problem. The rock we had hit had been sharp. It had smashed in a six-inch square of planking. Water was pouring in as if someone had turned on the cold tap.

I took off my trousers, made them into a tight roll and jammed them into the hole. Nadia kept bailing. She said, 'We must turn for the shore, or soon we will be in the open sea.' She sounded frightened. My legs were already getting cold. I ignored them; there was worse to come. I said, 'We can't go ashore.'

Cold grey moonlight was filtering between the squalls of cloud. Her face was a pale oval. 'Why not?' she said.

I said, 'They don't know we've got this boat. If we go ashore, they'll find us. They'll kill us. We're going to Finland.'

She did not say anything. There was very little she could say. Except that Finland was sixty miles to the north, and we were in an open boat with a hole in its bottom and a rotten sail, without water, food or compass. And that between us and Finland, *glasnost* or no *glasnost*, Soviet gunboats were patrolling their territorial waters.

I pulled the tiller towards me and let out some sheet. The sail was iron-hard with wind, and water roared away from the rudder. Sailing to Finland might be as lethal as a machine-gun bullet.

But at least it would be slower.

The wind had been blowing a good force five under the land. As we pulled clear of the north shore's lee it was six, seven in the gusts, kicking up a steep, ugly chop.

'We must bail,' I said.

'I'm frightened,' she said. Her hand was cold as marble.

I got her to hold the tiller, and scuttled forward, and took in the last reef. There was a lot of water in the boat. I bailed with the bucket, went aft and took the tiller again. The wind was blowing past my left ear, from the port quarter. Astern, the stretch of sea between us and the black line of the north shore grew wider. If they were using the searchlight, we were too far away to see it.

The night began to take on the wide, empty feel of open water. Lighthouses were winking ahead, casting a white glow on the grey cloud base. One was well to starboard of our course, another, fainter, a couple of hands' breadths on the starboard bow. We began to get the full force of the waves. The motion changed from a purposeful corkscrew to a long, winding roll. Ten minutes after I had bailed out, the water was ankle-deep in the bilges, slopping to and fro, intensifying the roll. I said, 'More bailing.'

Nadia groaned. She moved slowly for the bucket, filled it, tipped it over the side. She did it again and again. Then she was sick. Then she bailed some more.

Slowly, the first lighthouse came abeam. I remembered it from the big chart, at the top left-hand corner of Estonia. The chart had been in *Vixen*'s big, solid saloon, with its smells of polish and lamp-oil. The next lighthouse was on an island, a couple of miles of flat rock off the coast. After that one, it was all open sea.

I said, 'How did those people know where to find us?'

'Who knows?' She sounded as if it was too much effort to talk. 'Maybe they already suspect me. Maybe they fit a device to my car.'

'That was the police, shooting?'

'Russian police always miss,' said Nadia.

They bloody nearly didn't, I thought. But I did not say it. 'Why the shooting?' I said.

'We shoot spies,' she said.

'We're not spies.'

'You have friends who are spies. And one of them told Gruskin you are here.'

'Oh,' I said. We were on the sea. There was death everywhere. There were questions I should have been asking. But all I said was, 'Who is Gruskin?'

'A political policeman,' she said. 'A Russian. A man I fight, and my people fight. You would call him in a way my boss. In Gruskin's mind, you have friends who are spies, so you are a spy and I am a spy.'

The boat heaved, screwed its way down the face of a wave. Nadia hung her head over the side. 'What about radar?' I said.

'Don't know,' she said. Her arm moved mechanically as she bailed. The tiller tore at my bruised shoulder. I said, for the purpose of reassurance, 'We're made of wood. Radar's not much good on wood.' It did not work. A wave rolled under. I heaved the tiller towards me, fighting the nose as it tried to claw up to windward and broach. Last time I had broached had been with Neville Glazebrook. Water sluiced into my face. I licked it away. It was scarcely salty.

Neville Glazebrook, my friend. Who knew about spies; had been a spy, or at least controlled spies. Who had given me the address of Amyas Terkel. Who had sent me off to Estonia. Where the police had been waiting for me.

I sat there and glowered into the night, and heaved at the unrelenting tiller with muscles made of red-hot iron. I thought: Amyas Terkel, wish you were here.

There was water round my ankles. Nadia had stopped bailing. She was lying on the side thwart. It was too dark to see if she was asleep. She did not answer when I spoke to her.

So I bailed with one hand, and steered with the other. The second lighthouse went abeam, dropped astern. Over to starboard, the anthracite sky was showing a pale gleam of light. Dawn was on the way.

I did not want dawn. We had got off the coast without being seen because the mast was fifteen feet high, and the sail was a handkerchief-sized rag, and the hull did not show up in the troughs of the seas; but most of all because it had been a dark, dirty night. The front had gone through. The day was coming, and the breeze was moderating. I had not shut an eye for twenty-four hours.

I thought about my father. I tried to work out what it was about this grey, dirty sea that had made him give up family, job, the lot, and live the life of a hunted animal in a swamp.

I said, 'That was your family home?'

'A long time ago.' Her voice was a small monotone, as if she could not be bothered to move her lips. 'It burned in 1941.'

'But your parents lived there?'

'My mother lived there a long time in a cottage. Until five years ago. She was very old. She died.'

'How did she live?'

'Madame Rebane will have told you of the people of the forest. She was one of them. Perhaps she tells you that they were an army. That is not so. They were old people, full of memories of a time when they fought the Nazis, the Red Army. But it was all talk, at the end. Hot air.'

'Who buried my father?'

She was silent. The shrouds groaned as the boat nudged its way into a sea. 'My parents helped your father,' she said. 'When he came ashore, they took Mrs Rebane to him. Then they became ill, and my father died; it is a bad life for an old man. My mother could not move well. So when your father moved away from Mrs Rebane your father looked after her,

265

two years. Then he died.' A wave broke, hissing. 'I was not happy about my parents,' she said. 'I was busy, with my work. I did not see them for a long time. When you are in the police, you do not admit to yourself that your parents are people of the forest. I had changed my name, too. I was Naima Voore, a good Estonian name. For the police I changed to Nadia, Russian, and Vuorinen, Finnish. It was a bad life my parents lived; perhaps a bit crazy. Your father kept first of all his big boat. But there was no point, it was too much. So he kept only this boat. He died of pneumonia. After that, the people of the forest used it. But by then they were old also.'

I said, 'Why did you join the police?'

She said, 'I am Estonian. I want to guard my country against Russian bandits. It is a better way than being old, living in the forest with a bad gun, dreaming. But Mrs Rebane was a friend, through my parents. When my officer said, Lennart is dead, I said I would go into England. I never met your father. I think I was curious to meet you.' She touched my hand with hers. 'I am glad I did this,' she said.

The light grew. I could see the pallor of Nadia's face, the water slopping as the boat's stern rose to the big waves. And I could see the boat. It did not look as if it came from the Baltic. The hull had a hard chine, a flat bottom; like a coble, or a Grand Banks dory. I remembered what Amyas Terkel had said. *Åland* had carried two boats on deck. Like dories. I looked at it with a new interest. On the transom, beside the tiller, a wooden plate was screwed. It bore a gold-leaf phantom of the boat's name. *William Tyrrell*.

I had not been forgotten.

My eyes stung with tears. I blinked them away. The Baltic stretched away ahead, ridge on heaving ridge of metal-grey brine. Empty.

Not completely empty.

Down to starboard, perhaps two miles away in the half-light, was a grey, slab-sided ship. It had radomes aft, and a squat funnel leaking diesel fumes into the wind. The snouts of a pair of guns jutted on the foredeck. It was too far away for the ensign to be visible. But I did not need binoculars to know what it would be. It would be red, with a yellow star and hammer-and-sickle in the top left-hand corner.

Suddenly I felt sick as a dog.

I said to Nadia, 'Russian gunboat.'

She did not move her head, face down on her crossed arms, under the salt-matted coils of her hair. She said, '*Issand Jumal.*'

There was water in the boat again. My knees were showing a tendency to shake. The Russian made a ninety-degree turn to starboard, steamed away, slow ahead. He had his stern to us now. Nadia lifted her head, squinted blankly at the retreating ship. She said, 'He's going away.'

I did not answer.

He steamed until he was a grey matchbox, far down towards the peach-coloured glow on the eastern horizon. I kept my eyes ahead, looking past the flaking mast, over the high bow plunging in the short, squarish swells. We had been sailing six hours. Twenty miles, I thought. Twenty-five, even. Nearly halfway. Hope tried to rise. I did my best to ignore it.

I did not want to look round, but I looked anyway.

Down there on the horizon, the Russian's shape was changing. The ship came into profile: guns, funnel, radomes. The hope congealed. Now he had turned port ninety. He would turn port ninety again, and steam back towards us. He was using a technique standard in Search and Rescue operations and antisubmarine warfare. It is called a box search, and it is one of the best ways there is of finding a little thing in a big sea.

Suddenly our anonymity was gone, and we were as conspicuous as a traffic light on a pool table.

The fear was like a liquid, filling the limbs and the body, paralysing the mind. It was not for me as much as for Nadia. Me they would put in jail. She was a policewoman who had turned her gun on her own people. They would nail her to the wall.

Estonia was out of sight astern. Finland was out of sight ahead. All that existed was the paling dome of the sky, and the metal waves heaving, and the grey shape of the gunboat bustling towards us out of the dawn, full of eyes.

There was a thread of hope.

The gunboat was searching, all right. But if you are seriously

267

looking for something in the last ten years of the twentieth century, you do not use a ship. You use aeroplanes, helicopters.

In the twentieth century, searching the sea with a ship is like digging a ditch with a deer's antler. There are better tools for the job.

Inland, the flooded forest would be clattering with helicopters. Even if the people looking for us knew that the boat existed, they would not think we were crazy enough to try a sixty-mile sail in it. I clung to the thread. The gunboat was the backstop. He did not believe in us. And what you do not believe in, you do not necessarily see.

I wedged myself in the boat's bow, loosed off the forestay. The mast came down faster than I had meant. I scuttled aft. Nadia said, 'What is it?'

I scrabbled in the pool of water, found the sodden canvas of the wadded trousers, pulled. A small fountain came into being on the bottom-boards.

'We will sink,' she said. There was panic in her voice. 'Put it back.'

'No.'

She tried to tear the trousers from my hands. Seasickness had left her as weak as a bird. I grabbed her wrist. I said, 'Look.'

She turned her head. The gunboat was close enough for us to see the white water at its forefoot. She said, 'Oh, my God,' in a voice from which all hope had been wrung.

The water in the boat was up to the thwart. I groped on the bottom, found the hole. The pressure was less than it had been; it was equalizing as the boat sank lower in the water. I jammed the trousers back in.

We sat there in the flooded boat. I said, 'Put your cap on.'

She put it on, pulled it down over the wet tawny ropes of her hair.

The oars were trapped under a thwart. I pulled them out. 'Roll overboard,' I said. 'Swim. If the ship comes close, go under.'

The glow on the eastern horizon had turned lemon-yellow. The wind had dropped flat as a doormat. It was going to be a lovely day, for those who were alive to enjoy it. I pushed an oar at her. 'Take it,' I said. 'Stay between the ship and the sun.'

The water was cold, but not freezing. I kicked away from the boat, pushing the oar in front of me. Nadia's head was a small dark object on the sea. The boat was a straighter line among the confusion of glassy-sided swells. *Mustn't lose it*, I thought.

The sea changed colour, grey to green. I turned my head, rose on a wave. The eastern horizon shone brilliant saffron. In the middle of the saffron the upper limb of the sun floated, a white-hot chip of light that hurt the eyes.

I lay flat, resting my head sideways in the water. The gunboat looked like a big grey house, bristling with aerials. It was sliding along at fifteen knots, kicking a foam-edged wave away from its bow.

The sound of the propellors was a loud ticking. I put my face into the green water. Go past, I thought. Radio back that there's nothing here, waste of time, go and look for them in the peat bogs, with your dogs and your helicopters ... The ticking changed, slowing. My heart slowed with it. I raised my head. I did not want to look, but I had to see.

The gunboat had settled on to its wake. It was three hundred yards away, down-sun. A wave hid it from me. When I went up on the crest again, it had moved. The sharp grey bow was swinging towards me. For a moment, it was hidden by a shining hummock of water. When I could see it again, it was closer.

For a moment, I thought: they've seen us. Then I realized that it was not us they had seen. It was worse than that.

They had seen the boat.

The boat was perhaps a hundred yards away, down-sun. The ticking in the water accelerated. They were not going to pick it up. They were going to run it down.

The Baltic was a huge green disc. I wanted to yell and wave, anything but be left boatless in the middle of all this loneliness. But there was Nadia. If she wanted to wave, she would wave. It was her decision, not mine. I saw her rise slow and easy on a swell. She was not waving.

White water boiled under the gunboat's stern. It leaped forward. The dory lay wallowing in its track. I saw it rise on the bow-wave, the bow leave the water. Then the great grey knife of the gunboat's hull ploughed through it, and I could not see it any more.

There was a cheer from the gunboat's rail, and a burst of raucous laughter. It wheeled without slackening speed and surged away southward on a cushion of foam, golden in the light of the yellow sun hanging in the east.

I waited for it to go hull down. Then, from the top of a wave, I shouted, 'Nadia!'

Forty yards downwind, a hand went up, flopped down again.

Twenty miles from land, clinging to our oars, we swam slowly towards each other.

30

We did not say anything. We hung on the oars, and felt the water's insidious suck at the heat in our bodies. It would not take long, I found myself thinking. It would be better than a cell.

Nadia's hair was plastered close to her head. There were deathly black circles under her eyes, and her skull showed through the yellow-brown skin of her face.

Finally, I said, 'I'm sorry.'

She shook her head. 'Don't be stupid,' she said. She looked past me. Her eyes narrowed, catlike. She said, 'There's the boat.'

I kicked round. Twenty yards off, the glossy upslope of a wave was marred by a shape like the outline of a giant arrowhead. I was not sorry any more. I swam towards it.

There was perhaps a foot of freeboard. But the side of that boat was the solidest thing I had ever felt.

'Incompetent bastard,' I said.

'Sorry?'

'That Russian. He tried to run it down. But he bloody well missed.' I found I was grinning. We were not swimming twenty miles any more. We still had a boat. A half-sunk boat, with a hole in the bottom. But a boat nonetheless. I tumbled over the side, and set to, bailing hard, ignoring the cramps that were developing in my shoulders and upper arms.

Estonian police issue caps are high-crowned and capacious.

This one was not going to win any more points at an inspection before a May Day Parade. But it made a very good bailer. I used the cap. Nadia used the bucket. The water level dropped rapidly.

After a while she went to sleep. I finished bailing, pulled up the mast, shook the reef out of the sail. There was a breeze again, westerly now, across the line of the swells. I pointed my watch at the sun, found south, got us a course to steer. The sea was empty. The ship's boat *William Tyrrell* waddled northward, towards the free world.

I was thirsty. The last thing I had drunk was a tumbler of vodka at the reception in Tallinn Town Hall, twelve hours ago. It was a repulsive memory. A substance like dried glue coated the inside of my mouth. My head nodded over the tiller. Twice I woke to find the dory head-to-wind, sail flapping, without steerage. I got her sailing again. Then the drowsiness came back, and I was on the Norton, riding across a desert, except that unlike most deserts, it was full of oases with wide, sparkling pools of clear water. I was driving the Norton straight through the pools, and the water was shooting into the sky in glittering fans, making rainbows, falling back with a delicious liquid sloshing. The trouble was that the faceplate of my helmet was shut, and none of the water was getting in. My father was there, on the pillion, yelling at me to open the visor. But to do that I would have had to take my hands off, and if I did that the bike would crash. So I asked my father to do it for me. And he said he could not do anything of the kind, because he was dead –

Something was bellowing in my ear. I woke up with a jerk. A huge red wall was sliding in front of me. The hull of a ship, a bulk carrier. The bellowing was the siren. I shoved the tiller away, shot under the stern, muzzy with sleep. The red and blue quarters of the Panamanian flag flapped high on the superstructure. Close, I thought. Could have been killed. I swore weakly out of my dry throat. The ship slid away westward.

I stopped swearing. I shouted. I shouted for joy. It would have sounded like the shouting of an insect. But I meant it.

If it was going west, it would be on the north side of the

shipping channel. Down to port, there were more ships, in line ahead, going west. We were out of Estonia, and entering Finnish territorial waters.

The exhilaration lasted what must have been a very short time. After that, the haze came down again, assisted by the sun. It clamped the back of my neck like a set of red-hot vice grips, that sun. I hung on to the tiller, steering on a personal autopilot that depended on the feel of the wind in the sail, the angle of the corkscrew as we wound our way through the seas. I kept my eyes on the boat, because of the map unrolling in my mind.

It was a mixture of several maps. One of them was the chart, arranged on the well-worn mahogany of *Vixen*'s chart table, showing a splatter of islands up on the coast. But the one that was giving me the trouble had been at the front of an atlas in my desk at school. It was a salinity map. I could hear old Colonel Maxwell, alias Cursing Bertie, the geography master: *The Baltic is damn near fresh. Awkward bloody sea. Not salty enough for decent fishing, too damn salty to drink.*

But the Baltic was out there under the sun, cool and sparkling. It was coming up for noon, now. And neither of us had drunk any water for eighteen hours.

I was dipping seawater out of the bilges, pouring it over myself and Nadia. Most of what salt there was in the Baltic seemed to have dried on me, sticking to my skin and gritting inside my clothes. Nadia lay dead still, one hand trailing in the bilges. I hoped she was still alive. I hoped so very much indeed, with those small parts of my brain left over from the maps and the steering, and stopping the big dry balloon that had once been my tongue falling out of my mouth and flopping in the salt burn of the boat's bottom . . .

Which was why it was easier to keep the eyes in the boat.

It went on for what seemed like weeks. I could not remember a time when I had not been steering under the sun. There was only the red nightmare, the suck and roar of the Baltic an irregular heartbeat to drive the thick blood through the skull.

The roaring changed.

At first I thought it was the wind. But it was persistent, the change. So I pulled myself up, and looked over the side.

Fifty yards away was an island rocky-shored, pine-crowned, with a landing stage sticking out of a reed-fringed bay. We had already passed several other islands. They lay like basking whales to seaward. I moved the tiller hard over, went alongside the jetty and tied up with fingers like salamis.

Nadia did not stir. I shook her by the shoulder. She mewed like a cat. I said, 'Land.'

Her eyes opened. They were glassy, uncomprehending. Her legs came off the thwart and into the bottom of the boat. She said, 'Where?'

'Finland.'

'Oh,' she said. 'Water?'

I pulled her out of the boat. Her legs wobbled like rubber as we walked down the landing stage. There was a boathouse, locked. Inland, a shingled roof slanted in a grove of pines and maples green as an oasis. A weekend cottage. The owner would be away. Nadia was leaning on me, one arm around my shoulders, using me as a walking stick. My own legs were showing a tendency to buckle. It seemed like fifteen miles to the cottage.

There was a mossy lawn, a path edged with boulders leading up to an insect-screened verandah. The door was locked. The lock was small and flimsy. I picked up one of the boulders lining the garden path and smashed it.

There was a big room, with holiday furniture. In the corner was a sink and kitchen units. There was a tap. I turned it on. Nadia went straight for it. She started drinking out of the washing-up bowl, making sucking noises, like an animal. I filled a jug with water, drank it, refilled it, and went exploring.

There was a shower. I could feel the water from the jug creeping through the cell walls. My soul lusted for the shower. I turned it on. The water was lukewarm, from the roof tank. I went and fetched Nadia, and showed it to her. She pulled her clothes off, falling against the walls. 'Come in,' she said.

So I took off my clothes and went in too.

We stood there naked as babies, and let the water run. We were aware of each other only as someone to lean on.

'Better,' she said, after perhaps ten minutes.

I said, 'Yes.' The water's drumming on my skull was the most soothing thing I had ever felt. Sleep rolled in my brain like fog. I stumbled out. There was a towel on the rail. Through a half-open door I could see a bed. I lurched into the bedroom, drying myself as I went, fell on the bed, crawled under the covers.

Thoughts flitted in the mind. I did not know what day of the week it was. I hoped it was not the day the owners arrived, because that would mean waking up. But there was a better thought than that. It had to do with the hints dropped by Amyas Terkel, and Mrs Rebane's door caving in, and the tombstone by the burnt-out ruin. It was a knot; a great big Turk's head of a knot, all tucks pulled tight.

Except one. And I knew exactly what to do about that one, because the means of pulling it was waiting in Turku, on the west coast of Finland, start of the next Tall Ships leg. If Pete had arrived back there with *Vixen*.

Good old Dean.

A fly was buzzing. Light was creeping through the curtains. My eyelids came down, and stayed down.

When I awoke, I did not know how long I had been asleep. The light was still coming through the curtains. A fly was still buzzing. What had changed was that there was a thickness in my head. And that Nadia was in the bed.

Her eyes were open. They looked big and dark, almost purple in the dim light. She said, 'Thank you.' Her hand found mine under the sheet. She took it and put it on her breast. The skin was like satin, the nipple hardening to the touch. I moved towards her. Her fingers came up to the back of my head. She pulled my head towards her, and kissed me. It was light as angels' wings, that kiss, soft as clouds. I was falling. I found myself thinking, *These are the lips of a police-woman*. Then I was lost to rational thought, if you call that a rational thought. Because my hands were travelling of their own accord, round to the nape of her neck, so she sighed and shivered, and burrowed her way towards me. And from the back of her neck down, to where the muscles swelled into wonderful rollers, sea-waves of skin that shifted easily, like a sea, and stirred, opening. She moaned in my ear, the merest whisper of a moan. Her legs slid open, trapping me. I found I was raised up above her in the dimness.

Her head was sideways on the pillow, lips parted. For a second her palms were flat on my chest. Then she looked at me, and curled her fingers round my shoulders, and said, 'Now.'

Later we lay there, in the wreckage of someone else's bedclothes, and breathed each other's breath. After a while, she said, 'What happen when the person who owns this place will come?'

We rolled out of bed, and went into the shower together.

We did not care.

The clock in the bedroom was still going. It was six o'clock, but the sun was in the wrong place. We had slept for eighteen hours.

There was bottled herring in the kitchen, and dried rye loaves the shape of flying saucers, and instant coffee. We sat side by side at the kitchen table, and ate holding hands. All of a sudden there was a feeling that there was not long left; a frightening sense that we had already spent together what time we were allowed, and that we had scarcely noticed it pass.

For perhaps half an hour we did not mention it, though each of us knew what was in the other's mind. Then I said, 'Where will you go?'

'Helsinki,' she said. 'I have a friend who lives there.'

I did not ask the next question. She answered it for me.

'I go to the government,' she said. 'I think maybe I will need a new passport.' She would not meet my eye; she was looking down, rolling a breadcrumb on the red checked tablecloth.

I said, 'If there's anything I can do to help?'

She looked up shyly under her lashes. She smiled, with a returning hint of the confidence she had shown in the bed half an hour ago. 'Thank you,' she said. Her fingers were warm on my palm. 'You come to Helsinki?'

Her eyes were pools of amber. I was falling in. I said, 'Turku.'

'What in Turku?'

'*Vixen* will be there. There is a race. And people I must see.'

'Oh.' She sounded disappointed.

'There are things I have to clear up. About the problems we have been having. And about the death of Lennart Rebane.'

'Oh?' The disappointment was gone. She was a police-woman again.

'Enquiries I must make.' I was lying. It was not a matter of enquiries, any more. It was a matter of certainties that needed confirming.

She shrugged. 'OK,' she said. 'When can I see you?'

'A week,' I said. 'Sooner.'

Her lower lip came out. 'Then I must put up with it,' she said. 'How long till we get away from here?'

That was a good question. There was no telephone, and no radio. There was some writing paper, with a letterhead. We were on Tukkala, wherever Tukkala was.

'Back in the boat?' I said.

She said, 'The boat's no good, I think.' We walked down to the jetty, holding hands. The boat had filled with water. A little shoal of minnows rested in the shadow of its bow, out of the sun. She said, 'I don't want to go in the boat again.' She smiled. For a moment, we were wrapped in a common fantasy: cast the boat adrift, set up house on our desert island, wait to be rescued and hope that the rescuers never arrived.

But it was only a fantasy, and we both knew it.

I said, 'I'll mend the boat.'

She said, 'Will it take long?' apprehensively, in case it did not take long enough.

'Won't finish today,' I said.

She smiled, the smile of pleasure and surprise that trans-figured her. 'Oh,' she said. 'What a pity.'

I cranked the boat out with a block and tackle I found in the boathouse, made a tingle of copper sheeting and sealed it with tar, melted in a baked bean can. The sun was hot on my back. Nadia sang. I worked slowly and meticulously, not because I needed to, but because I wanted the moment to last. We went swimming, off the end of the pier, gliding over the black rocks of the bottom. Nadia's hair streamed like a mermaid's in the glass-clear water. We made love in the warm shallows, slipping in the silky mud. Then we swam slowly back to the jetty.

I hauled the boat back into the water. The sun was low in the northwest, the sky a bonfire. Nadia had dug a bottle of vodka out of somewhere. We drank it by the fire while legions of mosquitoes droned against the screen. I did not notice what we ate. But very soon we were back in the bed again, holding on to each other for dear life while the fire's reflected flames jumped and died on the ceiling.

And soon, far too bloody soon, it was the next morning.

We left a wad of rough-dried money in the cottage, with a letter. A flight of goldeneye rose and wheeled as I rowed the dory out of the bay. I had found a chart in the desk. Two hours later, we were sliding into a harbour of rust-red wooden houses that came all the way down to the water, and climbing on to a quay beside a pair of old diesel pumps. Then we sat in a bar, and drank coffee, and waited for the bus.

The Turku bus came first. Nadia kissed me. There were tears in her eyes. I bought tickets: her east, for Helsinki, me west, for Turku.

My bus wound through a landscape of forest and rock. Occasionally there was a flat, yellowish field and a cluster of wooden houses. It was the kind of country which looked as if human beings had arrived late, and were hanging on by the skin of their teeth. The man next to me was drinking Finlandia vodka fast and efficiently from a frosted glass bottle. He wished to make conversation. I wished to think.

I thought principally about the open boat called *William Tyrrell*. Not about the naming of the boat; but about open boats in general. And about the man with the eyebrow moustache who had made such a speedy exit from the bar in Helsinki.

I had seen him in the lodge at Varley Fitzgerald's house. And once before.

The vodka enthusiast went to sleep. In the middle of the afternoon, we were deposited at the bus station in Turku. I walked into the town, down a boulevard that rolled for what looked like miles to something that had to be the Town Hall. A soldier in a khaki uniform and black crocodile-skin loafers directed me to an international newsagent. I riffled through the yachting magazines, found a copy of the *Yachtsman*, flipped through the pages to the race reports.

It was there: top left-hand corner of the page, a black-and-white photograph, with caption. I paid, shoved the magazine into the pocket of my filthy trousers. Then I got a taxi to the quay.

There were a couple of Baltic traders, and three icebreakers. Down towards the mirror-glass ferry terminal was a forest of tall spars with tight-furled sails, house flags fluttering from halyards against the deep blue sky. The Tall Ships were in.

I paid off the taxi, walked down the quay, looking for *Vixen*. Maybe Pete had failed to get out of Tallinn. Maybe he was there still, hostage for the skipper –

The mast popped out from behind the mizzen of the Norwegian barque. I started to sweat with relief. I ran across the Norwegian's milk-white decks, and climbed over the rail on to *Vixen*.

Pete looked tired and worried. He said, 'What the hell have you been doing?'

'Tell you later,' I said. I did not quite know what to tell him. I was not sure he wanted to know the truth, even if he would believe it.

'They didn't want to bleeding let us out,' said Pete, aggrieved. 'We had to let them count the crew three bloody times, with someone dodging through the cabin. Luckily they was pissed. I thought we was all going to land up inside. I had to give the boss man all that money.'

All that money was a thousand US dollars from *Vixen*'s emergency fund. Never underestimate the power of valuta in the planned economy.

'Sorry,' I said. 'Where's Dean?'

'Below,' he said. 'Varnishing.'

I slid down the companionway. Dean was at work on a corner of the men's bunkhouse. 'Oh,' he said, cool as ever, faintly apprehensive. 'Hi.'

I pulled the copy of the *Yachtsman* out of my pocket. My

279

heart was going too fast. I turned to the page, and threw it on the bunk in front of him. 'Recognize anyone?' I said.

'Course I do,' he said. The picture was of me, at the wheel of *Blue Murder*, unshaven, glaring at the world from behind a mop of black hair like a bashi-bazouk's. Beside me, hand on my shoulder, grinning a proud owner's grin round a giant Montecristo, was Neville Glazebrook. 'That's you, innit? And that bloke you're with. The one with the cigar. That's Mr Johnson.'

'Sure about that?' I said.

'Course I am,' he said.

'Yes,' I said. 'Me, too.'

31

I changed thoughtfully out of my salt-crusted clothes. If Neville Glazebrook was partial to the companionship of his own sex, it was no business of mine. But for a Minister of the Crown to be photographed *in flagrante* with rent boys was something else altogether. Particularly if the rent boys were taking time off from driving the nuclear submarines of the Union of Soviet Socialist Republics. It was fair to assume that he would not have wanted anybody to know about it.

I had made some other assumptions, too.

It was time to test them.

I walked across to the shed on the quay that served as the race organizer's office. The girl in there was white-blonde, hugely efficient. It took her half an hour to have a mobile telephone delivered to *Vixen*. Thirty-five minutes after I had made my request, I was on the telephone to England.

The ringing tone sounded thin; portable phone. I could imagine them: Christopher and Ruth bashing away on the hard court, the telephone lying next to the jug of Pimm's on the table by the hard-clipped yew hedges. A few constituents on the Barcaloungers, basking in the glory of the MP and the Minister's daughter. And, invisible over the blue horizon, in Finland, the thunderclouds.

'Hello?' Ruth's voice, brittle, Sloane-Rangerish. I asked to speak to Christopher. She said, 'Can't it wait? He's in the middle of a set.'

I said, 'I want to talk to Christopher.'

The silence hissed across a thousand miles. 'Look –'

'Not about you,' I said. 'Or your boyfriend.'

'Wait.'

Christopher sounded out of breath, but it had not helped his pomposity. 'Look here,' he said. 'What –'

I said, 'Do you like being in the middle of scandals?'

'What –'

'You will write a letter to Neville Glazebrook,' I said. 'Date it today. Get a postmark on it. You will resign as his Parliamentary Private Secretary, now.'

There was a silence, as if he had been sandbagged. Then he said, 'Explain, please.' I noted the 'please'. The pomposity was gone. The voice sounded careful, the way hunted animals are careful.

I said, 'Lennart Rebane came to see you in Chatham.' It was a guess. But it was a good guess.

'Who's he?'

I told him he knew bloody well who he was.

There was silence again.

He said, 'So what?'

'What did he tell you?'

'Some ludicrous things about our father.'

'Ludicrous, but true. Did you also know that your father-in-law had tried to seduce him at a homosexual party?'

'Rubbish,' said Christopher. There was no conviction in his voice.

'Either you sent him away and ran for it, or you had to leave early anyway. Either way, you chased him off. I'd radioed to say we were coming in. He was on his way to see me. Glazebrook was on *Wilma*. Lennart was last seen on *Wilma* at about eleven-fifteen. At about eleven-thirty we ran down his waterlogged boat, with him inside it.'

Christopher said nothing.

I said, 'Someone held him under till he drowned, sunk his boat, and cast him adrift. Everybody was singing. Nobody heard a thing. It was going to look like an accident. But they were in luck. We ran down the dinghy, and Rebane got wrapped round the propellor.'

'Who could have killed him?' There was recognition in his voice, and terror.

'There is a security firm,' I said. 'Called Equipoise. They have tried to kill me three times, trying to recover photographs of Neville Glazebrook fiddling with sailors. The film is now in the possession of an Estonian policewoman who is at large in Helsinki. The Russians are after it. Bail out, Christoph.'

At last he said, 'You're sure?' His voice was tentative. He was adding two and two and getting results.

'Bigger than Vassall,' I said. 'Bigger than Christine Keeler.'

'I appreciate this,' he said. The arrogance was gone. Now he was the little brother, thanking the big brother for getting the playground bully off his back.

'Not at all,' I said. 'Quick word with Ruth?'

'Ruth,' he said. 'Oh, my God. Yes.'

Ruth said in a cold, sharp voice, 'What have you done to him? He looks like a stranded cod.'

'Boyfriend's name,' I said.

'Go to hell.' The words were an explosion of scorn.

'See you in print,' I said.

'You are *despicable*.'

'Makes two of us. Name?'

She told me.

'Thank you,' I said.

She slammed the telephone down.

The telephone rang. It was Nadia. Her voice sounded light, full of bubbles. 'The race office gave me your number. I am in Helsinki,' she said.

I told her where I was. I wanted to tell her I loved her. But there were other things that had to be said first. The knot was tied tight as basketwork on the outside, every bight and crossing in place. But there was an ugly tangle in the middle, and I wanted it explained.

I said, 'When we went to the place my father is buried. I must know how your colleagues knew to follow us.'

She shrugged. 'I told you before. An electronic device, in the car, maybe.'

'So they would have suspected you already.'

She laughed, a hard laugh. 'It was known I met you in England. It was in my report.'

'Why would they follow you?'

She shrugged. 'Nobody can tell you why Sergei Gruskin does anything. Maybe he makes a deal with someone. If he does not want to tell you, you will never know.'

I thought about that. Finally, I said, 'Call this Gruskin.'

'Do *what*?'

'Call him. Ask him what happened. As an old colleague.'

There was silence. She said, 'He's a bastard Russian. A very bad man.'

'He can't hurt you, now.'

She thought about it. Suddenly, she giggled. 'All right,' she said. 'Why not?'

'Attagirl.'

'Pardon me?'

'I love you.'

'That is good.'

'I must go sailing,' I said. 'I'll call you later.'

'I'll wait in.'

She gave me her number.

I went on deck. I looked up the line of ships. We had sailed in company three years running. They were as familiar as the keys on my typewriter.

There were two missing.

I could see the programme of events in front of me as if I had it in my hand. *Free cruise Turku–Helsinki. Helsinki, formal leavetaking.*

Wilma and *Xerxes* had left early for Helsinki.

Pete said, 'They was off for a pleasure cruise. Admiral Wilson stayed in Helsinki. Contact number's the Hotel Sibelius, he said to tell you. Neville Glazebrook's commanding *Xerxes*.'

I said, to Dean, 'Get the crew.'

He loped off along the quay, yelling. 'Vixens!' he roared. 'Vixens!'

Pete said, 'What is it?'

'Sailing.' I already had the ties off the mainsail.

'Already?' he said. 'We've only just arrived. I had a bird.'

'The other two have gone,' I said. 'Let's go.'

284

'What's the rush?' he said.

My stomach was jumping. I said, 'I want to catch them.'

'What the hell's wrong with you?'

'It's not me,' I said. The crew were dropping off the barque on to the deck. 'Count them.' No point in getting angry when you were dealing with Pete.

He sighed elaborately. He counted. 'All present and correct,' he said. They were already taking the springs off.

I hit the start button. The warps came aboard. I kicked the engine to full ahead. We moved out into the channel.

The town fell away fast. I opened the spiral-bound chart on top of the doghouse. It was two o'clock in the afternoon. The crew made sail, and I cut the engine. *Vixen* heeled to the westerly breeze, the same breeze that had blown us across the Gulf of Finland. The wake gurgled under the counter, roared away from the nose. We went down the channel at eight knots. At five o'clock, we burst into the wide blue Gullkrona-fjärd. The islands on the far side rose steadily from the sea, turning from deep indigo to jewel-green, like islands in a dream. At six-thirty, we rounded the point in front of the island on which stood the cottage of Amyas Terkel.

The bay was empty, except for the wind, and the sun on the water, and the mirror-images of dark pines. I was glad it was empty; so glad there was sweat on my hands where they held the wheel. The roar of the anchor going down seemed muffled by the trees. The tender gang swung the dinghy over the side. I climbed aboard, started the engine.

Pete said, 'Do you want me to come?' His face was grim. Perhaps he was sensitive to atmospheres, after all.

I said, 'I'll manage.' As I twisted the outboard's throttle, I was thinking of my father's tombstone, blown apart by a torrent of machine-gun bullets. Nobody on *Vixen* deserved to get in the way of bullets.

Except me, for being a fool.

I buzzed round the headland. Terkel's cottage crouched in the fringe of the pines, flanked by its stacked logs. The peace was so deep that the air seemed viscous as syrup. I tied up at the jetty, stepped ashore, and walked to the cabin. The only sound was the whisper of the wind, and the hum of the flies.

The hum of the flies.

Under the crucifix on the cabin wall, there was a black pile of something. When my shadow fell on it, the blackness rose in a buzzing cloud. What was underneath it was a lot of different colours of brown. There was brown skin, and brown shorts. And there was brown dried blood, from the wound in the chest. There was a knife in the wound. The blood around it was still red and sticky. Terkel's hand was on its hilt. It looked as if he had killed himself. That was how someone had meant it to look.

The someone who had told Terkel to give me the idea my father was still alive. The someone who had made good and sure I was not going to be able to check back.

The smell of new blood was raw and disgusting in the hot, still air. I walked down to the jetty, climbed into the dinghy, cast off. The snarl of the engine drowned the flies. I was glad about that. Cocooned in the noise, it was even possible to put the nausea aside, and think a little.

Amyas Terkel had been told to tell me my father was still alive. That would have been to make absolutely certain I went ashore, and went looking for him. Bill Tyrrell disappearing in Estonia would have been a convenient form of accidental death.

Amyas Terkel was the last accident. Now, the accidents were going to start happening the other way round.

'Everything all right?' said Pete, as I went up the side.

I grinned at him. It would have looked like a skull grinning, but I did not trust myself to speak, just yet. I pointed at the anchor, jerked my thumb upwards. Then I went below, and the cosy wood and leather of the saloon wrapped itself around me.

The noise of the anchor chain rattled down *Vixen's* old timbers. We could have been having a nice picnic in Newtown Creek. I concentrated on Newtown Creek. Not that I liked Newtown Creek. But anything was better than thinking of that horrible thing with the flies all over it, lying in front of the cottage in the bay.

Pete stuck his head down the hatch. 'Into the channel,' I said. I thought of radioing the police. But the police would mean delays, and thousands of questions. Things were moving too fast for questions.

I picked up the telephone, and dialled the number Nadia had given me. The call started to go through, was cut off. We were a long way out, in the middle of some big rocks, far from any transmitters. The VHF aerial was on top of the mast. I called the coast radio station. The ether was full of the spit of lightning. The operator put me through.

I said, 'Did you ring your friend Gruskin?'

She said, 'Yes.'

'So?'

'It was as I said. He put an electronic tracer on my car because he had been warned to follow us by a countryman of yours.'

'I knew that.'

'But the fellow-countryman was not a private individual.'

'Oh?'

'He knew your exact movements. He said that you were a spy. He said his . . . agency wished to get rid of you, they did not mind how, because you had destroyed a good set-up.'

'And your boss agreed.'

She hesitated. 'My boss only agreed when he found out that I was with you. He is an angry man. He wishes revenge. I think I am not so safe here.'

I said, 'Don't move.' I rang off, and asked the coast radio station to get me the Hotel Sibelius, Helsinki.

When they answered, I said, 'I'd like to speak to Rear-Admiral Richard Wilson.'

I chewed a pencil while I waited for him to answer.

Finally, the brown voice said, 'Bill. I hope you're ringing to apologize for that start.'

I said, 'No.'

He laughed. 'All right,' he said. 'Blow me, I must be getting old. Good stuff, that.'

The bluff jovialities were too sudden to be heartwarming. I said, 'I need your help. There's a woman in Helsinki needs the protection of the British Embassy.'

'*What?*' he said. Lightning spat in the ether.

'She's an Estonian national. She's in danger of abduction.'

287

His voice became jovial as a polar bear's snarl. 'Are you trying to be funny?' he said.

'If you want confirmation, ring my brother Christopher.'

There was silence. I could almost hear his mind stripping its gears. Finally he said, 'I'll do that.'

I gave him Nadia's number, and disconnected. Then I twisted the VHF dial to the call channel, and said, '*Xerxes, Xerxes*, this is *Vixen, Vixen*, over.'

More lightning. The set said, '*Vixen, Vixen*, this is *Xerxes, Xerxes*, over.'

'Evening, all,' I said. Get jovial, I thought. Ooze with cooperation and teamwork. 'Where are you, over?'

'Having a lovely time.' The operator sounded young, full of the joys. 'I hope you're bloody miserable after that start of yours, over.'

'Yes.' I was sweating with impatience. 'What is your position, over.'

Lightning roared in the speaker. '. . . over,' said the operator.

'Say again, over.'

'Twenty miles short of Hanko,' said the voice. 'We both stopped for lunch at Nämanön. We're on the inside channel, over.'

And at lunchtime, Amyas Terkel had received his last visitor. 'Pity,' I said. 'We're going round the outside. We'll miss you, over.'

'Rather you missed us than hit us,' said the operator, giggling. The lightning drowned the rest.

I disconnected, ran up the companionway. *Vixen* was motoring smoothly down a narrow gut between two rocky islands, sails slatting in the still air. A gold-lined edge of black cloud was gliding steadily in from the west.

'Coming towards us,' said Pete.

I shoved him the chart. The channel curved round to the left, snaked through rocks and islands. There was a ten-mile buoyed dogleg round a mass of ill-marked shoals. We could not be more than two miles behind them. 'Let's catch up,' I said.

'Going to get wet,' said Pete. The clouds had slid closer,

lost their golden edge. There was a constant mutter of thunder.

'Never mind,' I said. I went back to the VHF, and called Nadia's number again.

A man's voice answered. 'No,' he said. 'She is not here. She has left.'

'Left?'

'Who is this?' said the voice.

'Bill Tyrrell,' I said.

'Ah. Good.' The voice was as precise as a digital door lock. 'Some Russians came to the front door. Nadia left the house by the back door. Could you tell me, please, what is happening?'

'No,' I said.

'She asked me to tell you if you called that she is going –'

'Don't tell me!' I yelled at the microphone.

The crackle stopped. 'Hotel Sibelius,' said the voice, and faded into the roar of the atmospherics.

I kept the set on. The sound of lightning was continuous. Keep going, I thought. Keep going. Crackle your heart out. Like a bloody fool I had called Nadia by VHF, not cellphone. Someone had been listening in. Someone had sent the Russians. And that someone was going to send more messages to the Russians, and make sure they were waiting for Nadia at the Hotel Sibelius.

Rain clattered on the skylight. I pulled two waterproofs from the hooks, one for me, one for Pete, and went back up the companionway.

The rain was falling in big drops that hit the deck with a thump I could feel through the soles of my shoes. I pulled up my hood. Dean and the crew were crouched by the hatch covers, hoods up, laughing. They did not know how little there was to laugh about.

Ahead, beyond a black-and-white South cardinal buoy, a lane of ripples crossed the channel from right to left.

'Spinnaker,' I said. The engine pushed us into the ripple. I wound the wheel to port. The wind arrived.

It came bang on the stern. The mainsail filled. On the foredeck, they were struggling with the spinnaker pole. The huge balloon of sailcloth went up the mast, waved, filled. *Vixen* accelerated smoothly past the buoy and down the channel.

The rain was hissing over the sea in heavy grey curtains. Ahead, the world closed down to a hundred-yard circle. Lightning flicked. The thunder came three seconds later.

'Going to lose the wind,' said Pete.

But it held. It held long enough to take us through a narrows, past a lighthouse with steel-latticed legs crouching on a rocky island. It held long enough to blow the rain past us, and open a blue crevasse in the inky sky, walled with billows of cloud that wrung like hands. Along the canyon of cloud blazed a shaft of sun that cut a brilliant blue-green path across the wide sheet of black sea that had opened out ahead. The thunder boomed like cannon all round.

'There they are,' said Pete.

At the end of the path, perhaps a mile away, the light glowed on two white mountains of canvas. They were perhaps a hundred yards apart. *Xerxes* was down to port, goosewinged, *Wilma* with her square topsails set, studding-sails on the tips of the yards.

I pulled the handbearing compass out of its clips on the doghouse bulkhead and took a quick bearing.

The sun went out as if someone had switched it off. The rain came.

It roared down in poles of water that turned the scuppers into miniature salmon rivers and deafened the ears with their thunder. It knocked the wind out of the sails and brought a new wind, an icy wind that came from a new direction and caught the spinnaker aback. Dimly, I could hear Pete bellowing at the crew to get the spinnaker off. I could hear it, but I was not listening. I had shut it all out of my mind: Nadia, everything. I was concentrating on the steering compass. It hovered on 083°, the bearing of the two ships ahead.

The spinnaker came down. The wind had gone southwest.

Pete said something to me. Lightning illuminated him, frozen, mouth open, blue-white. The thunder came right on top of the flash, a giant concussion that left the brain stunned and the ears ringing. Wind screamed in the shrouds. *Vixen* lay

290

over on her ear and rushed, decks streaming, down the channel.

Water ran up my sleeve as I looked at my watch. Ten minutes, I thought. Ten minutes to catch up. In the flicker of the lightning, I saw the crew looking upwards. They had noticed that the masts were high, and the clouds were low.

I said to Dean, 'Tell them it's all right.' He scuttled forward.

The next flash was a giant blue spark that fizzed out of the black murk and balanced itself over the sea like a devil's trident. It must have given a full half-second of light.

My scalp crawled.

Wilma and *Xerxes* lay a hundred yards ahead. Spouts of blue fire shone from *Wilma*'s yardarms, and her shrouds were picked out in a ghastly electric glow.

'Stone me,' said Pete. 'St Elmo's fire. Never seen that before.'

And suddenly nothing was eerie or supernatural. It was simple and matter-of-fact. The weather was bad. But we were chasing a man, and we had almost caught him.

'What's he playing at?' said Pete.

Xerxes had paid off, eased sheets. She heeled, white foam flashing from her counter as she boomed away down the channel. There was a stocky figure by the wheel, dressed in what even at this range were distinguishable as expensive oilskins. From the hood there jutted what was unmistakably a big cigar. Neville Glazebrook.

I was not watching *Xerxes*. I was watching *Wilma*.

She was moving away, too. But she was edging south, out of the channel. The channel ended at Hanko. The deep-water route was ten miles, two sides of a triangle. The chart showed the short cut as six miles of shoal water, crudely marked.

'What the bloody hell's he playing at?' said Pete.

'He needs to make a telephone call,' I said. Then I rammed the helm hard over, and *Vixen* shot out of the channel in *Wilma*'s wake.

'What do you mean?' said Dean. He had come aft to stand in the lee of the doghouse, shoulders hunched round his ears.

'His VHF isn't working,' I said. 'Too much electrical

interference. He's looking for a telephone box so he can ring some friends.'

Pete said, 'Do you know where you're going?'

Wilma was two hundred yards ahead. I peered at the chart through the rain on its plastic envelope. I said, 'We're going to stop *Wilma* from getting ashore.'

'What for?' said Pete.

'Do as you're bloody well told.'

Ahead, beyond *Wilma*, low humps of rock reared out of the rain-flattened sea. The rain made it all hazy, like a seascape in a nightmare. There were no buoys.

The lightning flashed blue in *Wilma*'s sails. She was heeled far over to port, great foam-crested waves tearing from her bow and quarter. Ahead of her was open water. I checked with the bearing compass. There was a way through the shoals; narrow, but a way.

'Yankee,' I said.

The crew squelched forward down the deck, hauled up the high-footed triangle of sail. *Vixen*'s deck heeled hard as she squatted down. The gap separating us from *Wilma* started to narrow.

I told Pete what I wanted him to do. He said, 'That's bloody stupid.'

'Do it,' I said.

He shrugged. 'It won't be my fault,' he said.

I went aft, to my usual place, on the counter, holding on to the backstay. The rain was inside my coat, and I was shivering. Some of it was cold. And some of it was good, old-fashioned terror.

I was going to meet the man who had killed Lennart Rebane, and Marie Clarke, and Amyas Terkel. I was not looking forward to it at all.

I looked down *Vixen*'s deck, at the sweet curve of the planking, the old faithful web of rope and wire and spar. I did not want to leave it.

Pete looked round. His beard was whipping outside his hood. 'Going through,' he said.

We were ten yards from *Wilma*'s stern. There was a man leaning on her taffrail; the man with the eyebrow moustache who had walked out of the bar in Helsinki. The man from Varley Fitzgerald's gate lodge. *Vixen*'s nose lifted as it came over *Wilma*'s quarter wave. We were on her windward side. Her mainsail flickered as we caught its wind. There were rocks down to port, now, and thirty yards to starboard.

The wakes roared like lions between the hulls. *Vixen* was moving past *Wilma* at an easy knot, Pete narrow-eyed at the wheel, judging his distance. He said something to Dean. I was gripping the backstay so hard my hand hurt. Dean nodded to me. *Vixen*'s counter edged in towards *Wilma*'s until there was a mere foot between the two boats. The chainplate of *Wilma*'s starboard shroud came up to me, slow and elegant.

I stepped aboard.

32

Vixen sheered away. I grabbed a shroud in each hand and climbed up over the bulwark and on to the deck. *Wilma* was a ship, not a yacht. Her crew were hunkered down behind the bulwarks, looking for shelter against the lash of the rain. Her deck was a broad wooden dance-floor, running with water.

I ran aft towards the hooded figure at the wheel. The lightning was flickering like a stroboscope. The world moved in a series of silent-movie jerks. The thunder was sledge-hammers on a kettledrum. Nobody moved.

The man at the wheel had a beard. Nobody I was interested in had a beard. Behind, the man with the eyebrow moustache was leaning on the companion hatch. It was the same attitude as the first time I had seen him: wearing instructor's kit, heavy boots and a jersey, leaning against the stove in the Leadership Centre in the foothills of Cader Idris.

He saw it was me. He came at me.

He was small, wiry and light on his feet. He hit me hard, aiming for the neck, made contact with the shoulder. I hit back, a big round swing that missed. My arm was numb. I could feel the tilt of the big schooner sliding solid as a rock down the channel. The crew watched, open-mouthed, numb with rain and thunder. He came at me again. I was angry. I caught him by the coat, and swung him at the man who was steering. The helmsman flinched. The man with the mous-tache slammed into the wheel. The spokes caught him in the back. He screamed, a hoarse, nasty scream, lurched into the helmsman, knocked him to leeward, down the slope of the deck. The wheel spun. Canvas rattled. *Wilma* heeled, slewed off the wind and on to the reach. The rustle of her wake deepened to a roar. I caught a glimpse of pine trees on the shore. I backed to the rail, pulled a belaying-pin out of the rack. The man with the moustache was up again, coming at me, slowly, as if he hurt.

I hit him hard in the face with the belaying-pin.

The world came to bits.

The deck lurched under my feet, sailed on, tipped again. I fell on my face, shouted, 'Down!' There was a rending crash. *Wilma* slowed, stopped. Out of the corner of my eye I saw the steeple-high topmasts bend like fishing rods, a couple of yards break loose, float in the air, accelerating, slam into the deck in a terrible rain of wood and iron. *Aground*, I thought. *Masts down*. Canvas was slatting up there. There was shouting from below.

The deck moved. It yawed and rolled, sliding. The narrow gut between the islands had fallen astern. She had bounced. Now she was sailing on, out over deep water.

Not for long.

Kids were running on the deck. I shouted, 'Lifejackets! Boat stations!'

They had been trained. There were officers on deck, now, forming them up into watches, counting heads. The man who had been helming had a wide, brown face, streaming rain into his beard. He was trying to say something. No words were coming out.

'Look after your crew,' I said.

Wilma felt sluggish, heavy. Her nose was down. She rose and fell on the small swell. Every time she rose she rose less, and every time she fell she sank deeper.

'All there?'

'All there,' said the man with the beard.

'She'll go,' I said. The man who had attacked me was lying on the deck, bleeding into the scuppers from a cut on the head.

'Take him,' I said.

The man with the beard hesitated. 'Go,' I said. There were big, ugly bubbling noises from below. Her bowsprit was dipping towards the water. '*Vixen*'ll pick you up. I'll go after the skipper.'

He said, 'You're Bill Tyrrell.'

'That's right,' I said.

He looked slightly relieved, and ran forward.

They started heaving liferafts overboard. It was oddly quiet. The thunder had stopped.

That was why the captain was not on deck.

I twisted the catch on the door to the after companionway. Air rushed past me, compressed by the water running into the ship. I slid down the steps into the state cabin.

It was a big, panelled cabin, lit by skylights. I could hear the drips falling from my oilskins on to the scrubbed teak boards of the deck.

There was a table in the middle of the cabin, big enough to seat eight on state occasions. On this occasion, there was one man sitting at the far end.

Otto Campbell.

The VHF mike was in his hand. He said, 'Thank you, Hanko Radio. Out,' and hung the mike up behind him without looking round. Then he said, 'Good afternoon, Bill.'

I did not answer. I did not move. He was wearing a red-and-black tartan shirt, the sleeves rolled up. He had put the mike back with his left hand. In his right, he held a double-barrelled shotgun, which he was pointing straight at my stomach.

'Siddown,' he said. 'End chair.'

I sat. The table was sloping down towards him. *Wilma* was holed forward, I did not know how badly. Through the bulkhead at his back I could hear water bubbling, timber creaking: the noise of a ship dying.

'Just been talking about you,' he said. 'And your floozie. She'll be on the first boat back to Estonia.'

I said, 'They're watching the ports.'

'They won't watch the freight depots,' he said, and laughed, a brisk, efficient laugh. 'Not the old *Nauvo Star*. Purely academic interest as far as you're concerned, of course.'

I said, 'Your ship's sinking.'

'Yep,' he said. 'And you with it. Nobody ever taught you how to stay alive, did they?'

'Not the way you stay alive,' I said.

'You have to be a soldier,' he said. 'It's the only way.' He fingered his long jaw; his eyes were shiny, looking at things only he could see. He was dreaming. I knew what he was dreaming about. I ran my tongue over my dry lips. 'So you're a knight errant,' I said. 'Righting wrongs. Cleaning things up for King Glazebrook of Camelot, and the knights of the Round Table. Defending the dying flames of civilization. Repel the forces of darkness by covering up for dirty old Ministers and assassinating hardened criminals like Marie Clarke.'

'Bloody clever,' he said. 'We always said, watch out for that Tyrrell, he's clever.'

'Cleverer than you,' I said.

'Really?' The eyes narrowed, fractionally. Angry, I thought. Good. 'Why do you think?'

'It happens to knights errant. You start off pure as dammit. You get a bit ambitious. And before you know what's going on, you're not at all pure, and the ambitions haven't worked out either.'

'Explain,' he said. Very angry indeed, I thought. As long as he doesn't kill you, you might get past him.

'You hitch your waggon to Neville Glazebrook. You find out that he likes to mix himself up with rent boys in nasty places. Knights errant shouldn't let people get away with that kind of thing. But you do, because Neville is helping you along with a bit of influence here and there. And when Lennart Rebane comes to see me with some photographs, you kill him off. I don't know what you told Neville about it, but you let him know he was involved. So he knew about you, but he couldn't tell anyone. So there you were. Partners in buggery and murder. The soldierly virtues, eh, Otto?'

His face was dead white. His eyes glittered like varnished pebbles. The tilt on the table was steepening. A voice from the deck shouted, 'Captain!'

'We're fine,' called Otto, calmly. 'Seeing to a couple of things. Cast off the liferafts. Tell *Vixen* to stand by.'

'So you drowned Lennart, nice and neat, while everyone was singing,' I said. 'Because Neville Glazebrook had seen him and Dean clout the photographer in the brothel and take the film. And you did your best to make people believe it was me who had done the drowning. You started the whispers, and kindly advised me to lie low until they went away. But I wouldn't. So you put Equipoise on the job. Nadia turned up. Your spooky friends told you all about her, and you had Equipoise on her as soon as she came ashore.' His face was blank as the shotgun's muzzle. 'All right so far?' I did not wait for an answer. There was no time. 'And poor old Dickie. Where does he fit into Equipoise?'

'Founder member,' he said. 'Like me.'

'But he was on the gentry side,' I said. 'The public face. After-dinner speeches and the freedom of the individual. Not filling a poor defenceless girl with dope and setting fire to her. Bloody chivalrous, Otto.' There was anger in my voice. I wanted to goad him into arguing, justifying himself. Not because I was interested in what he had to say, but because I needed time.

It did not work.

He said, 'You're not going to get out of this alive, you know that?'

There was a door behind him. It led into a passage, from which opened crew bunkrooms. It was closed. Water was spilling from underneath it. Someone at the top of the companionway yelled, 'We're abandoning!'

'Thank you,' he called, as if someone had offered him a cup of tea. Then he said, 'I asked you a question.'

I said, 'Yes, quite.'

'Bloody clever,' he said. 'You always were.' Nasty things happened to his mouth.

I said, 'So were you. Ten out of ten for intelligence. You knew my dear brother would try to pull the rug on me if things got a little embarrassing. And you worked out that I thought it was only Dickie who knew I'd be arriving in Ramsgate. But he told you, and you sent your boys looking for me. So even if they didn't get me, Dickie would still be my prime suspect. Trouble was, your man enjoyed his work too much.'

I shivered, thinking of the man with no canine. 'Accidents have to be fatal,' I said. 'He was a no-hoper. Like you.'

My mouth was dry as dust. There was nobody but us on *Wilma*. Even if there had been, he was crazy enough to fire, and take his chances.

The barrels of the shotgun were staring me in the eyes. I waited for the day to turn yellow and red, and stop for ever. It did not.

'Another thing,' I said. I wondered if he could hear the shake in my voice. 'The bit about my father. If you'd known about that sooner, you would have saved yourself a lot of trouble.'

The water was flooding under the door now, pooling up against the bulkhead behind him. 'As it was, you were having a few matinées with Ruthie. And she told you about me and my father, between the sheets. You checked with Neville, and he told you about their time in the Baltic. So you saw your chance to set up a really good accident: spy's son vanishes in Estonia. I suppose you already knew Colonel Gruskin. Old enemies, right?' I was right. 'But nowadays, it's spooks against the rest. You're on the same side, you and him. But Colonel Gruskin was a bit slow off the mark. What went through Captain Campbell's tiny mind when he heard we were back in circulation?'

The corners of his mouth were turned down. The flesh of his face was rigid as iron. He said, 'I should have dropped you over the cliff when I had the chance.' His left hand was moving across to the gun. That's it, I thought. Nothing more to say. Killing time.

Then I heard the hissing. It was a curious hiss, with an overtone of bubbles. The door behind him was made of varnished wood. The reflections in the varnish had changed. They looked distorted, with a sort of fisheye effect, as if the panels were curved.

It was what I had been waiting for.

He had both hands on the gun.

I looked past him, said, 'You're in trouble.'

'Balls,' he said.

I dropped off my chair. He fired. Something hit me very

hard in the muscle of my left shoulder. I rolled. The other barrel came down, looking for me. Beyond it I could see the door.

The door burst open. A fist of water smashed into the cabin. I heard him shout. Then it was spinning me over and over, like a rat in a washing machine.

I was wedged in a narrow place. There were rough boards under my hands, water blasting past me. I felt I was stuck inside a firehose. A hard object in the water slammed into the side of my head. My ears rang. I opened my mouth to shout. It filled with water. I thought, You bloody fool, you have come all this way, you know all the answers, he missed you with the gun. But now you are dead.

My fingers slackened on the rough board. The flow of water carried me. My chest wanted to breathe. My brain did not, because that would be the end. I tumbled through what felt like a long, dark passage.

And into the light.

The passage had been the companionway. I was on *Wilma*'s deck, rolling in the air.

I lay there for perhaps three seconds, and breathed.

As the oxygen spread round my body, so did a little sense. The deck felt bad and sluggish. I climbed to my feet.

Forward of me, *Wilma* was underwater. Her shattered masts began to roll very slowly to starboard. The deck was covered with a cat's cradle of rope. The roll was heavy, terminal. The death roll.

I began to climb uphill, struggling through the tangled wreckage, towards the port side of her.

My head was heavy as lead and my shoulder was throbbing.

Otto, I was thinking. Bloody Otto. You meet the man, get to trust him. You get to be friends. You stop being the professional newshound. You start to take it easy, accept him as part of real life, not something that whizzes like a meteorite across the front page, burns up in the oxygen of publicity. But all the time he has been watching and waiting for the moment he can use you. And when he has used you, he kills you.

The way you kill a story when it stops selling news-papers.

There was a hard, quick knocking. It was coming from a skylight forward of the companionway. The skylight looked like a miniature cold-frame, reinforced with bronze bars. Inside the skylight, behind the bars, was something pale. I stumbled closer, squinted my eyes to see.

It was a face. Otto's face, pale, horribly magnified by the water under the skylight.

The face moved. Bubbles streamed from the mouth. There were hands too. The hands had been knocking. Now they were scrabbling feebly at the glass; the toughened glass, designed to keep the sea out.

I waded up to my knees in water, feeling for the catches.

The catches were on the inside. The water would not let me break the glass. The face behind the glass had eyes. The eyes were big and white, round as saucers. The hands became still. The face sank away.

Someone was shouting. There were ropes round my feet. My arms were numb. I did not have the strength to untangle myself.

The voice said, 'Skipper!' The voice was Dean's.

I looked up. He was standing in the nose of *Vixen*'s tender. There was a coil of line in his hands. He threw it. I caught hold, fumbled it into a bowline. He took a turn round a thwart, sat down to the oars. I kicked my feet out of the ropes, clear of *Wilma*, with the corpse of Otto Campbell spinning in the currents that eddied slowly under the glass of the saloon skylight.

When I was clear, I swam to the tender.

Dean said, 'She's going.' For the first time since I had known him, he sounded respectful.

I turned in the water.

Wilma had kept her list to starboard. All of a sudden, her masts lurched, and the list steepened. She went over on her beam ends, the wooden fish-belly of her hull rising from the sea, showing the fifteen-foot trench the rock had gouged in her vitals. There was a great hiss of air. Vapour jetted from the rent, and she dived like a sounding whale into the dark water. For a moment her shape wavered under the surface, huge and pale green, spewing bubbles. Then she was gone.

'Sod that,' said Dean, polishing one of his skull rings on his jeans. Then he rowed me back to *Vixen*.

33

Two hours later, my shoulder had been bandaged, and I was in the co-pilot's seat of a Twin Otter float plane I had chartered in the name of the *Tribune*, standing on one wing above the island-strewn red dazzle of the sunset on Hanko Sound. Far to the west, anvil-topped thunderheads still towered. *Vixen* was directly below, a white knifeblade trailing a herringbone of wake into the harbour where *Xerxes* lay alongside. *Wilma* was down there, too, under a hundred and fifty feet of Baltic, marked by a single fluorescent buoy.

I pulled the VHF mike out of its clips. The pilot, a dark youth called Janni, grinned and raised his thumb. I tried a grin back. It was only partially successful.

The operator put me through to the Hotel Sibelius. Dickie started talking as soon as he heard my voice.

I had already had a quarter of an hour with Neville Glaze-brook. I pressed the talk button, blotting him out. I said, 'Neville will explain.' I did not know what Neville was going to say. Neville was going to resign. He was going to be doing a lot of talking, these next few months.

'Oh,' said Dickie, deflated.

'Any sign of Miss Vuorinen?'

'She hasn't left the country,' he said.

'Find a ship called the *Nauvo Star*. Keep it in port.'

He said, 'Just what the bloody hell is going on?'

'You talked to Christopher,' I said. 'You talked to Neville.

Now you ring your Equipoise friends. You can ask what one of their men with a black crew cut and an eyebrow moustache was doing at the Leadership Centre in North Wales, and subsequently as a gatekeeper to Varley Fitzgerald. Then resign in protest at what you're going to find out.'

'*What?*'

'You heard,' I said. 'Ask. You'll need the answers to keep you out of jail.'

Fifty minutes later, the float plane wheeled over the lights of Helsinki, touched down in the outer harbour and trailed two plumes of foam across the dirty water to the blue-white floodlights of the Commercial Docks. There was a police car and a van waiting on the shore. A man jumped out of the first. He had a snub nose, small Tartar eyes. 'Lieutenant Kaukonen,' he said. 'I am instructed to give you assistance.' He looked efficient, but sceptical. 'I believe you are interested in a ship, the *Nauvo Star*.'

'That's it.'

'We are holding this ship,' he said. 'For a customs check.'

'When did she start loading?'

'Yesterday,' he said.

'What's she carrying?'

'She is a very old ship,' he said. 'She carry everything.'

'Then we'll unload everything.'

Whatever Dickie had told him, it worked. He loaded me into his car, took me to the docks.

The *Nauvo Star* was lying under a crane at an ancient quay. There were a couple of bored-looking customs men by a mountainous pile of crates and boxes.

The driver of the van opened the back doors and pulled out an Alsatian. 'Sniffing dog,' said Kaukonen.

I sat down on a crate. It was a long time since I had eaten anything, and the handful of lead pellets in my arm were setting up a steady hammering.

Martin Carr would have wanted me to be running round with a notebook, interviewing people and capturing cute snippets of atmosphere. This was the pay-off.

But I could not make myself care about pay-offs. Nadia had gone. My father had come and gone. The face behind the

304

skylight had bubbled and choked while I watched. A Minister of the Crown was turning in his despatch box.

Terrific story, Tyrrell.

But it was not a story. It was real life.

I was not going to write any more stories, ever.

The crane-hook dipped into the *Nauvo Star*'s hold. The crates kept arching out of the black maw of the hatches into the light of the floods. Beyond the floods, it was dark. My watch said one a.m.

Kaukonen cleared his throat. He said, 'The ship must sail in the morning. I am afraid the captain is not happy. It is a shipping line with an important owner.'

I said, 'What time does the ship sail?'

'Eleven-thirty.'

I said, 'We'll keep going till five.'

The pile on the quay grew. At four o'clock, a thin, grey light began to seep up the eastern horizon.

Kaukonen yawned. 'Now we must begin to load again, I think.'

The dog started to bark.

It was standing on a crate, scratching and whining. Kaukonen stopped yawning. He started to call orders to a couple of scruffy henchmen. Then he turned to me, grinning. 'I did not believe you,' he said. 'We did not even bring a crowbar. I am sorry.'

They fetched a crowbar, and ripped the lid off. There was shouting. I levered myself to my feet.

Nadia was lashed into an armchair. She was blindfolded, and there was tape over her mouth. Her head lolled forward.

'Not dead,' said Kaukonen, cheerfully. 'Drugged. Well, well. We call ambulance.'

I went to the hospital with her. They said she had been injected with barbiturates. My shoulder was thumping with agony. I grinned at them, and passed out.

I came round in a white room. My arm was numb. There were more bandages. A doctor put his head round the door. 'Ah,' he said. 'We have taken some bullets from your arm, with local anaesthetic. Sixteen, exactly.'

I could not stand the good cheer of Finns much longer. I

rolled my legs out of bed. The room spun. I said, 'How is Miss Vuorinen?'

'She wait outside,' he said. 'She comes in.'

I struggled one-armed into my clothes. She came in. Her lips were soft as duck-down. The nurses left us alone.

She was pale. She looked as if she was making herself cheerful for my benefit. She said, 'They were waiting for me in the hotel. I was stupid.'

'Who was waiting?'

'Some bloody Estonians.' She smiled. 'The English is better, no?'

'Yes.' I held her hand. With her in the room, the aloneness was gone. But I felt cold. Something was going to happen.

She said, 'This time, you have saved my life. Now we are even.'

I did not like the direction her thoughts were taking. She smiled, as if she was interrupting herself, pushed her hair behind her ear. She said, 'It was that bastard Gruskin. He sent people.'

I said, 'You don't have to worry about that any more.'

She said, 'I have friends still in Estonia. I have talked to them on the telephone. Gruskin is from the old days. He was talking to someone from your side. What would have been your side, in the old days. Now, they are on the same side. Against us.'

'Otto Campbell,' I said.

'Otto Campbell,' she said. She was silent. So was I, because I knew what she was going to say.

She said it. 'I am going back to Estonia.'

I said, 'You're mad. They've tried to abduct you. What'll going back prove?'

She said, 'There are old people and new people. Gruskin is old people. The old people are rotting, I think. The new people will make my country a country again.'

'But they'll kill you.'

'We look after each other,' she said. 'There is no victory without danger. I have a ticket on the noon boat.'

I looked at my watch. It was eleven o'clock. I did not know what to say.

'Will you see me to the ship?' she said.

She had a small overnight bag. I hooked it over my good shoulder. The sky made a net of brilliant blue ribbons above the narrow streets as we walked down to the harbour. At the ticket control for the ferry, she kissed me. Her cheeks were wet. 'Goodbye,' she said.

'See you soon,' I said.

She smiled with her eyes. 'Maybe,' she said. She was humouring me. We were humouring each other. 'Oh,' she said. 'I meant to give you this.'

She slipped a thick brown envelope into my hands, and went through the barrier with her supple, long-legged walk. I turned away. For a moment, I did not know where I was going, and I did not care.

'Oi,' said a voice. 'Skip.'

I looked up. It was Dean.

'Just got in,' said Dean. 'Was that that Russian bird leaving?'

I walked to the edge of the quay, looked down at *Vixen*, the old brute. 'Let's go home,' I said, and went down the ladder.

'Jesus,' said Pete. 'Already?'

'Already,' I said.

They cast off. I stood at the back end of the counter, good arm round the backstay. *Vixen*'s nose swung into the harbour.

The Tall Ships were coming in. A siren sounded, long and lugubrious between the embracing headlands. A rusty, box-shaped ship was moving away from the ferry pier. On the upper deck, a tiny figure was waving. Blonde hair blew around the head.

I raised my arm. The ferry moved away south, propellors churning the sea white under its stern. The figure shrank, disappeared from view.

Vixen was on the outer edge of the harbour, now. Pete was growling at the trainees. The sails went up. I opened the envelope Nadia had given me.

There were thirty-six colour prints, and thirty-six negatives. Neville Glazebrook was there, and so was Lennart Rebane.

Both of them had passed into the shadows. In the shadows was where their dirty little secrets belonged. I crumpled the negatives in my hand. The wind caught them. They tumbled away, thin, bright, two-dimensional things, into the great solidity of sky and sea. They fluttered down the trough of a wave, caught, and vanished. I tossed the prints after them, and turned back, looking down the deck.

I said, 'Stop engine.'

A great peace fell. My right hand went up to grasp the backstay. My knees bent against the plunge and slide of the big boat's career across the low Baltic swell. *Vixen* tilted to a puff of wind, and the great grey spearhead of her deck drove hard and fast for the blue southwest.

Sam Llewellyn

Riptide

Midnight on the Bay of Biscay: a boat is sinking. A brand-new boat with brand-new fittings - except that one of them has blown off and sea-water is pouring into the hull in a force-nine gale ...

Don't miss Sam Llewellyn's next riproaring thriller RIPTIDE, coming soon from Michael Joseph in large-format paperback and hardback.

SIGNET

Published or forthcoming

TRIAL

Clifford Irving

They called it suppression of evidence and disbarred him from the 299th District Court for two long years.

Criminal Defence lawyer Warren Blackburn came back from the wilderness to pick up the crumbs – and found two cases just like the one that brought him down.

But this time he was ready to back his judgement and fight. Fight for justice and a fair trial against a legal system that would do anything as long as it got a deal...

'Riveting legal edge-of-the seater ... Has Texas and American Justice systems by the tail' – *Daily Telegraph*

SIGNET

Published or forthcoming

FADE THE HEAT

Jay Brandon

Mark Blackwell is District Attorney of San Antonio, city of favours and pay-offs. His success has cost him his marriage and family life. Now his son stands accused of rape.

During the trial that follows Mark is torn apart, caught in the judicial wheel that he has set in motion. As the pressure builds, the media and his rivals move in for the kill. Suddenly he has everything to lose and nothing to gain...

'A clever plot, a gripping novel' – Tony Hillerman, author of *Talking God*

Published or forthcoming

SIGNET

38 NORTH YANKEE

Ed Ruggero

When an unarmed convoy of American troops on a training exercise is ambushed by North Koreans near Hongch'on, the fragile peace that has existed since 1953 is shattered, and once again the US Army is in the front line of a war on foreign territory.

38 North Yankee is the blistering story of the men and machines on both sides as the powder-keg of Korea explodes into a bloody and ruthless struggle for military supremacy.